B.J. Daniels is a *New York Times* and *USA TODAY* bestselling author. She wrote her first book after a career as an award-winning newspaper journalist and author of thirty-seven published short stories. She lives in Montana with her husband, Parker, and three springer spaniels. When not writing, she quilts, boats and plays tennis. Contact her at bjdaniels.com, on Facebook or on Twitter, @bjdanielsauthor.

USA TODAY bestselling author **Rita Herron** wrote her first book when she was twelve but didn't think real people grew up to be writers. Now she writes so she doesn't have to get a real job. A former kindergarten teacher and workshop leader, she traded storytelling to kids for writing romance, and now she writes romantic comedies and romantic suspense. Rita lives in Georgia with her family. She loves to hear from readers, so please visit her website, ritaherron.com.

D0231718

Also by B.J. Daniels

Also by Rita Herron

Discover more at millsandboon.co.uk

ROGUE GUNSLINGER

B.J. DANIELS

HIDEAWAY AT HAWK'S LANDING

RITA HERRON

MILLS & BOON

First Published in Great Britain 2018
by Mills & Boon, an imprint of HarperCollins*Publishers*
1 London Bridge Street, London, SE1 9GF

Rogue Gunslinger © 2018 Barbara Heinlein
Hideaway At Hawk's Landing © 2018 Rita B. Herron

ISBN: 978-0-263-26596-5

1018

MIX
Paper from
responsible sources
FSC™ C007454

Printed and bound in Spain
by CPI, Barcelona

ROGUE
GUNSLINGER

B.J. DANIELS

This book is for Gale Simonson, part of the Simonson duo, who keeps our lives interesting in the Quilting by the Border group. You are always like a breath of fresh air. Thanks for keeping me smiling.

Chapter One

The old antique Royal typewriter clacked with each angry stroke of the keys. Shaking fingers pounded out livid words onto the old discolored paper. As the fury built, the fingers moved faster and faster until the keys all tangled together in a metal knot that lay suspended over the paper.

With a curse of frustration, the metal arms were tugged apart and the sound of the typewriter resumed in the small room. Angry words burst across the page, some letters darker than others as the keystrokes hit like a hammer. Other letters appeared lighter, some dropping down a half line as the fingers slipped from the worn keys. A bell sounded at the end of each line as the carriage was returned with a clang, until the paper was ripped from the typewriter.

Read in a cold, dark rage, the paper was folded hurriedly, the edges uneven, and stuffed into the envelope already addressed in the black typewritten letters:

Author TJ St. Clair
Whitehorse, Montana

The stamp slapped on, the envelope sealed, the fingers still shaking with expectation for when the novelist opened it. The fan rose and smiled. Wouldn't Ms. St. Clair, aka Tessa Jane Clementine, love this one.

TJ St. Clair hated conference calls. Especially this conference call.

"I know it's tough with your book coming out before Christmas," said Rachel, the marketing coordinator, the woman's voice sounding hollow on speakerphone in TJ's small New York City apartment.

"But I don't have to tell you how important it is to do as much promo as you can this week to get those sales where you want them," Sherry from Publicity and Events added.

TJ held her head and said nothing for a moment. "I'm going home for the holidays to be with my sisters, who I haven't seen in months." She started to say she knew how important promoting her book was, but in truth she often questioned if a lot of the events really made that much difference—let alone all the social media. If readers spent as much time as TJ had to on social media, she questioned how they could have time to read books.

"It's the threatening letters you've been getting, isn't it?" her agent Clara said.

She glanced toward the window, hating to admit that the letters had more than spooked her. "That is definitely part of it. They have been getting more... detailed and more threatening."

"I'm so sorry, TJ," Clara said and everyone added in words of sympathy.

"You've spoken to the police?" her editor, Dan French, asked.

"There is nothing they can do until…until the fan acts on the threats. That's another reason I want to go to Montana."

For a few beats there was silence. "All right. I can speak to Marketing," Dan said. "We'll do what we can from this end."

"I hate to request this, but is there any chance you could do a couple of book signings while you're at home before Christmas, right before the book comes out?" Rachel asked. "I wouldn't push, but TJ, we hate to see you lose the momentum you've picked up with your last book."

"That would be at least something," Dan agreed.

"If you don't make the list, it won't be the end of the world," her editor added. "But we'd hoped to see you advance up the list with this one. I love this book. I think it's the best one you've ever written."

The first week a book came out was the most important and they all knew it. If she didn't make the list—the *New York Times* list—it would mean losing the bonus she usually got for ranking in the top ten. It would also hurt her on her next contract, not to mention the publisher might back off on promotional money for her.

"We don't mean to pressure you," Dan said. "But I'm sure if the police thought this fan was really dangerous—"

"I think going to Montana is smart," her agent cut in. "You'll be safe there with your family over the holidays. We can regroup when you get back."

She rubbed her temples. "I could do one book signing in my hometown since there is only one bookstore there. Whitehorse is tiny and in the middle of nowhere. The roads can be closed off and on this time of year, so there won't be much of a turnout though."

"Isn't the *Billings Gazette* doing a story on you as well?" Trish from Marketing asked.

"Yes." She groaned inwardly, having forgotten she'd agreed to that months ago.

"That will have to do, then," her agent said, coming to her defense. "Her next book will be out in the spring. Let's plan on doing something special for that."

"We have ads coming out in six major magazines as well as a social media blitz for this one," Rachel said. "You should be fine. You have a lot of loyal fans who've been waiting patiently for this book. Your presales are good."

"Are you all right with this?" her agent asked.

She nodded and then realized she had to speak. Her throat was dry, her stomach roiling. Just the thought of any kind of public event had her terrified. But before she could answer, the call was over. Everyone wished each other a happy and safe holiday and hung up, except for her agent.

"Are you sure you're okay?"

"I will be once I get home," she told her and herself. She couldn't wait to get on the plane. She hadn't been back to Montana for years except for her grandmother's funeral.

"Keep in touch. And if you need anything…"

TJ smiled. She loved her agent. "I know. Thank you." She disconnected. Every book release she worried it wouldn't make the list or wouldn't be high enough on the list—which meant better than the last book had done. Not this time.

"You have bigger things to worry about at the moment," she said to herself as she walked to her apartment window and looked out.

I know where you live. You think you can sit in your big-city apartment and ignore me? Think again.

That ominous threat was added at the bottom of the last written attack she'd received from True Fan. What was different this time was that her fan had included a photograph taken from the outside of her New York City apartment. She'd recognized the curtains covering the window of her third-floor unit. There'd been a light behind them, which meant she'd been home when her "fan" had taken the photo from the sidewalk outside.

It was recent too. One of the wings of Mrs. Gunderson's Christmas angel was in the photograph. Her elderly neighbor had put it up only two days ago. TJ had helped her.

Just the thought of how recent the photo had been taken made her shudder. She glanced at her phone. Her flight was still hours away but she preferred sitting at the airport surrounded by security screened people to staying another minute in this apartment.

Sticking her phone into a side pocket of her purse, she grabbed the handle of her suitcase and headed for the door.

Nowadays she always checked the hallway before she left her apartment. She did this time as well. It was empty. She could hear holiday music playing in one of the apartments down the hall. The song brought tears to her eyes. She was a mess, way too emotional to spend the holidays with her sisters—especially since the three of them had been estranged for months.

She hesitated. Maybe she should change her flight. Go to some warm resort. But just the thought turned her stomach. She was going back to Whitehorse. Going home for Christmas.

She rolled her suitcase down to the elevator and pushed the button.

When it clanged its way up from what sounded like the basement, she waited for the door to open. If anyone she didn't recognize happened to be on the elevator, she would make an excuse about forgetting something she needed in her apartment and turn back until the elevator left again.

She knew it was silly, but she couldn't help it. No one was taking the threats seriously. But she had watched the tone of the letters degenerate into angry, hateful words that were more than threatening. This person wasn't done with her. Far from it. She couldn't shake the feeling that her "True Fan" was coming for her.

The elevator stopped and the door began to open. Empty. She let out the breath she'd been holding. Stepping in, she pulled her suitcase close and pushed the button for the ground floor.

The fan writing her the threatening letters could be anyone. That was what was so frightening. It could even be someone who lived in this apartment complex. Or someone she'd met at a conference. She met so many fans, she couldn't possibly remember them all. It embarrassed her when they complimented her books. She wanted to hug them all. She doubted she would ever get used to this. Writing had been her dream since she was a girl. Getting published? Well, that was like a miracle to her. She couldn't believe her good luck.

Until she'd begun getting the letters from her True Fan.

Outside the apartment building, the sidewalk was filled with people hurrying past. Shoppers laden with packages, others rushing off to work... The city was bustling more than usual. She glanced at the faces of people as they passed, not sure what she was looking for. Would she recognize her rabid fan if she saw him or her?

She couldn't help studying their faces, looking for one that might be familiar. She didn't even know if her "fan" was male or female. She also didn't know if the person was watching her right now.

After a while, everyone began to look familiar to her. If anyone made eye contact, she quickly dropped her gaze as she made her way to the curb to signal for a cab. She wrote about crazed homicidal people. Wouldn't she recognize something in True Fan's eyes that would give the person away?

With a screech of brakes, a yellow cab came to a stop on the other side of the street. The driver motioned for her to hurry. But a large delivery truck was coming too fast for her to cross before it passed.

She felt something hit her in the back. Letting out a cry, she found herself falling into the street in front of the large speeding truck.

Chapter Two

It happened so fast. One minute she was standing on the curb waiting for the large delivery truck to pass before crossing the street to the waiting taxi.

The next she was falling forward into the street and the truck bearing down on her. Her arms windmilled as she tried to catch herself, but there was nothing to grab. She could hear the deafening roar of the truck's engine, smelled diesel fuel turning the air gray and closed her eyes as she realized she was about to die.

The hand that closed over her arm was large and viselike. One minute she was falling headlong into the street in front of the truck and the next she was snatched from the crushing metal bumper as the truck roared on past.

Pulled by the hand gripping her arm, her body whipped back. She slammed into something so solid it could have been a lamppost. She turned just quickly enough that her face came in contact with the chest of a large male body as she tried to get her feet under her. He steadied her for a moment before the fingers on her arm released.

She looked up in time to see the man who'd saved her turn and walk away as if rescuing women was something he did every day. Trembling all over, she was still reeling from her near death.

"Wait!" she called after him. He'd just saved her life. But if he'd heard her, he didn't turn. All she got was a brief glimpse of granite features, collar-length dark, curly hair beneath a baseball cap above wide shoulders clad in a tan suede sheepskin coat before he disappeared into the crowd.

She turned to find her suitcase and purse had fallen to the ground at the edge of the curb. Still shaken, she reached for them. The taxi that had stopped for her was long gone. No one seemed to have noticed what had almost happened to her.

Why had the man taken off the way he had? A Good Samaritan who didn't like taking credit for his deeds? Or, she thought with a shudder, the person who'd pushed her in front of the speeding truck—and then saved her.

Was it possible the man had been her True Fan?

She remembered being hit from behind and then the viselike grip of his large hand as his fingers bit into her arm. He hadn't even taken the time to see if she was all right. A shudder rattled through her. Had this been a warning?

A cab pulled to a stop in front of her. Tears burned her eyes as she stepped toward it. After all this time of being away, she couldn't wait to go home to White-horse.

SILAS WALKER SWORE. He'd lost the man he'd been following in the crowd of Christmas shoppers. Now he leaned against the front of a building, watching the street. His leg hurt like hell. He realized he was limping badly and cursed. If it wasn't for his injury, he wouldn't have lost the man.

Or if he hadn't stopped just long enough to grab that woman who'd been jostled by the crowd and almost fallen in front of a delivery truck. He shook his head. She should have known better than to stand that close to the street, especially with the sidewalk this crowded. He hated to think what could have happened if he hadn't been right behind her.

His cell phone vibrated. He checked the screen. A text from his boss that he wanted to see him ASAP. That couldn't be good. He quickly texted back that he was on his way.

One look at the way he was limping and he knew exactly what his boss was going to say. He'd come back to work too soon. That he knew his boss was right didn't make it any easier to accept.

But after today, after messing up an easy tail, Silas had to accept that he wasn't up to the job yet. That alone would force him to lay off his leg for a while. Just over the holidays, not that he was happy about it.

A taxi pulled past. He spotted the woman in the back seat. She wore a bright red long coat with a multicolored scarf—the same woman he'd grabbed out of the way of the truck.

But that wasn't the surprising part. He recognized her. He'd studied that face on the back cover of her book more times than he wanted to admit. He couldn't believe his luck. TJ St. Clair. The thriller writer. Her photo hadn't done her justice.

As the taxi drove on past, he realized she was probably headed for the airport given that he now recalled seeing a suitcase next to her. Somewhere for the holidays?

Smiling, he told himself she might be headed home to Montana. If he was right... Well, what were the chances they might cross paths again?

TJ HAD WONDERED what it would be like seeing her sisters again. The last time they'd been together they'd argued. Well, that is, she and Chloe had argued with their younger sister Annabelle over their grandmother's house.

Grandmother Frannie Clementine had died a few months ago. In her will, she'd left everything she had—basically her house in Whitehorse—to Annabelle.

"Did you know she was going to do that?" they'd demanded.

"No, I swear I didn't," Annabelle had said on the phone since she hadn't attended the funeral or seen the will.

"Why would she do that?" Chloe had demanded.

"I have no idea," their sister had said. "Except... well, I always got the impression that she liked me the best." She'd tried to pass that off as a joke, but they'd all hung up angry.

Now as TJ stepped off the plane, she felt bad about the argument. The house had turned out to be a whole lot of work—and had held some surprises that neither TJ nor Chloe would have wanted to handle. It had been clear why Grandma Frannie had left the house to Annabelle, who they all agreed was more like Frannie than either TJ or Chloe.

The Billings, Montana, airport was small by most airport standards and sat on rimrocks overlooking the state's largest city. She hadn't gone far when she saw her sisters waving at her from the bottom of the escalator.

TJ couldn't help but grin. They were both wearing elf hats. She groaned. "This has to have been Annabelle's idea," she said under her breath. But the sight of them in those hats had definitely broken the ice.

She laughed as she reached them, hugging one and then the other. As she pulled back, she felt such a surge of love for her sisters that it brought tears to her eyes.

"We didn't want you to feel left out," Annabelle said, and whipped an elf hat from her bag and settled it on TJ's blonde head. She grinned and put her arm around them. "We look like triplets."

"Heaven forbid," Chloe said.

"I'm starving," Annabelle said, surprising no one. Since she'd quit modeling for a living, she was always hungry. "Ray J's barbecue when we get home, eat here or just get snacks like we used to for the ride home?"

"Snacks!" TJ and Chloe said together.

"Did I mention I bought your favorite bottles of wine?" Annabelle asked. "Or we can go out and party tonight."

TJ and Chloe groaned in unison and then laughed. It felt good being around them again, TJ thought, and felt her eyes burn again with tears. Coming home for the holidays had been the right choice. She realized this was the best she'd felt in a very long time.

Annabelle chattered as they walked through the terminal toward the exit. TJ half listened, thankful that the trouble between them had blown over. They were all three back in Montana just like when they were growing up. They were sisters and she couldn't have been more delighted to be with them, even though people stared.

She laughed. She'd forgotten they were all now

wearing elf hats. For a few minutes, she'd completely forgotten her near-death experience this morning in the city and True Fan's threats.

But as she and her sisters passed a group waiting in one of the departure lines, she saw a woman raise her phone and take a photo of the three of them. Glancing back, TJ saw the woman quickly begin texting someone.

Chapter Three

"Wow," Chloe cried from the front seat of the SUV as she showed TJ her phone. "It's already all over social media." There was the photograph of the three of them in their elf hats. Just as she'd feared, the woman had recognized her, tagging the photo with her pen name. "Ah the life of the rich and famous."

TJ groaned. "Now everyone will know that I've come home to Whitehorse for Christmas."

"It isn't like it was a secret, right?" Annabelle asked as she drove. "Everyone knows you're from White-horse, Montana. Not much of a leap that you would be going home for Christmas." She glanced in the rear-view mirror. "Seriously, is it a problem?"

"No," TJ lied. "It's fine. Sometimes it would be nice to be anonymous though, but I don't have to tell you about that."

Annabelle sighed. "Yep, but when now faced with being anonymous the rest of my life… Well, it's an adjustment. I have to admit, it was fun seeing my photo on the front of magazines—even if it was a doctored photo of me. Nothing is all that real with modeling."

"So you're not going back to it?" Chloe asked their

baby sister. "You're just going to marry Dawson Rogers, become a ranchwoman—"

"And live happily ever after," Annabelle said with a giggle. "Yep, that's the plan."

They began discussing people they knew in Whitehorse and how things had or hadn't changed.

TJ only half listened to their conversation. She hadn't told either sister about the threatening letters—let alone what had happened in the city only hours ago. The more she'd thought about it on the plane ride back to Montana, the more unsure she was that she'd been pushed in front of that truck. Could it have been an accident? Or had it been deliberate? Either way, if that man hadn't grabbed her...

She shivered and looked out at the snowy landscape. If that man was her True Fan, he'd been watching her apartment. When the light had gone off in her living room, he would have known she would be coming downstairs. Or he might have been a stranger passing by.

TJ shook her head, determined not to think about it. She was safe now. At least for a while.

"So we're talking wedding bells," Chloe was saying.

"Wait, I must have missed something," TJ said, sitting forward to hear. "You and Dawson? When?"

"We haven't set a date yet. I know it's quick, but I would love a Christmas wedding, something small and intimate," Annabelle said, sounding dreamy. Both Chloe and TJ groaned and then laughed.

"Love," Chloe said with a shake of her head.

"Actually," TJ said, settling back into her seat, "I always thought you and Dawson were a good match."

They talked about weddings, growing up in Whitehorse, people they knew who'd left—and those who had stayed. The time passed quickly on the drive to their hometown.

As they pulled up in front of the house they'd grown up in after their parents had died, Annabelle cut the engine. Conversation died. They all looked in the direction of Grandmother Frannie's house. Even though Frannie had left the house to Annabelle, TJ would always think of it as their grandmother's. None of them spoke. The only sound was the tick, tick, tick as the motor cooled.

"Are you two all right?" Annabelle asked.

TJ hadn't realized it when they'd met her at the airport, but Chloe had flown in only thirty minutes before she had. Which meant that like her, she hadn't been to the house where they were raised since the funeral.

"It's like it was when we were kids," Annabelle said, as if trying to reassure them.

From the back seat, TJ glanced at her sister in the rearview mirror. All three of them knew the house would never be like that again. Not after their grandmother's secrets had been unearthed, so to speak.

"If you don't want to stay here, we can go out to Dawson's ranch," Annabelle said. "We have a standing invitation."

TJ smiled at that, seeing how happy her sister was to be back together with her high school sweetheart. "I'm good with staying in the house."

"Of course you are," Chloe said. "You write murder mysteries." She sighed. "I am good with staying here too. I think it's what Grandmother would have wanted. But it's still weird. I can't believe the secrets our grandmother kept from us."

TJ chuckled. Frannie had been a tiny, sweet little woman who everyone said wouldn't hurt a fly. "Seems all those wild stories we thought she made up to entertain us had some truth in them."

"Imagine if she hadn't toned them down to PG," Annabelle said.

They all laughed and opened their car doors, the earlier tension gone. Getting the luggage out, they made their way up the shoveled path through the deep snow. *Christmas in Whitehorse*, TJ thought. The last time she'd left here, she'd been pretty sure she'd never be back. But as she breathed in the icy evening air, she knew she was exactly where she wanted to be right now.

Annabelle scooped up a handful of snow in her mitten and tossed it into the air over them before running toward the door, fearing payback. Both TJ and Chloe let out cries as ice crystals glittered in the silver evening before covering them from head to toe.

TJ shook the light snow from her long blond hair and laughed. It was good to see Annabelle like this. It had been a long time. Now, she was again that adventurous young girl who'd gotten stuck in the neighbor boy's tree house.

"I thought you'd want your old rooms," Annabelle was saying as they crossed the porch and she unlocked the door.

TJ hadn't known what to expect as the door swung open. Her grandmother had been a hoarder in her old age. The last time she'd seen this place—when she and Chloe had come up for the funeral—it had been so full of newspapers, magazines, knickknacks, old furniture and so much junk there were only paths through the house. Little had they known what was buried in there.

She stopped in the doorway, dumbstruck. The junk was gone. The walls were painted a nice pale gray, and the place looked warm and welcoming, complete with new furniture.

"Annabelle, you shouldn't have gone to so much trouble. We aren't staying that long," TJ said, shocked.

"It wasn't all me. Willie insisted on helping and I wasn't about to say no," Annabelle said. "You remember Dawson's mom. When she takes on a project… You have to see the kitchen. Dawson completely remodeled it."

TJ could only nod and follow her sister into the kitchen where their grandmother used to attempt to cook. She stopped in the doorway. This was the room where Annabelle had discovered her grandmother's biggest secret. It looked like any other kitchen in an older remodeled house.

"Remember the cookie jar where Frannie kept her grocery money?" her sister was saying. "I saved it."

Chloe had stepped in and was looking around, wide-eyed. "It's amazing." She met TJ's gaze. "Ghosts?"

"Gone," Annabelle said, and crossed her heart with her index finger. "No ghosts."

TJ thought ghosts were the least of her problems. "Did Willie help you with our rooms as well?"

"She did. Come on, I'll show you." Annabelle ran up the stairs. TJ and Chloe followed, whispering among themselves.

"She did a great job," Chloe was saying. "Remember what it was like?"

"Unfortunately, I do," TJ said. "Like a horror story."

"Or a thriller," Chloe whispered back. "Like the kind you write."

TJ didn't need the reminder.

Annabelle had stopped at Chloe's old room. They joined her. The room had been painted her favorite color, pale purple, and decorated to fit their investigative reporter sister's style.

"You do realize that this visit is temporary, right?" TJ asked. Annabelle didn't seem to hear her. Stepping down the hall, TJ stopped at a room she knew at once was hers. It was painted a pale yellow. A quilt of yellow-and-blue fabric lay on the antique white iron bed. There was a small white desk and chair to one side of the bed with a lamp and spot for her laptop. On the wall above it was a framed collage of her book covers.

"Do you like it?" Annabelle said behind her, sounding anxious.

"Oh, Annabelle." She turned to hug her sister, hoping to hide her discomfort. The last thing she wanted to see were her book covers right now. They reminded her of the threats from her True Fan, who had found fault with all of her latest plots—and even her covers.

"It's perfect."

Her sister seemed to relax. "Is this going to be all right?" she asked.

"It is, Belle," she said using a nickname for her littlest sister that she hadn't used in years. "I'm glad you kept Frannie's house."

"It was Dawson's idea. He bought it for a rental but he thought it would be nice for us to have it for when the two of you visit. After we're married, we'll build a house with guest rooms for you and Chloe when you come home. Then we'll either rent this house or sell it. But I like the idea of keeping it. At least for a while."

She loved her sister's enthusiasm, but she couldn't imagine visiting Whitehorse often. So she said nothing, just smiled and hugged her again.

Chloe came out of her room holding a framed photo of the three of them.

"Check this out," she said, wiping tears as she showed TJ a photo of the them when they were girls. "We were so cute."

"We are still cute," Annabelle said. "Let's go to Ray J's and get some barbecue. Then I'm thinking we should go to the Mint and celebrate."

"Whoa," Chloe said. "Barbecue, yes. Our old bar, no." She looked to TJ to back her up.

"How about we come back here, open the wine and make it a fairly early night," TJ said. "At least for today. It's been kind of a long day. But could we stop by the bookstore before it closes on the way to supper? I need to see if they have everything they need for my book signing."

"You're doing a book signing this close to Christmas?" Chloe said.

"Don't ask."

THE BOOKSTORE WAS actually a gift shop that carried her books because she was considered a local author. TJ stopped inside the door. It had been so long since she'd had her very first signing here. She remembered her excitement from the acceptance of her book to actually seeing her words in print. She'd been over the moon. She hadn't been able to quit staring at her book. The memory made her smile. Her dream had come true.

Her first book signing under this roof had been good. She'd known most everyone who'd waited in line to talk to her, wish her well, say they knew her when, and then get their book signed.

TJ hung on to that feeling for a moment before stepping in to look for the owner. Her sisters scattered throughout the store, oohing and aahing over this or that as she made her way to the books.

There were a dozen piled up next to an older image of her along with some articles about her on poster board. She'd been interviewed so many times and freely told stories about her life, her dreams, her process.

She couldn't help but grimace at the memory of the tongue-lashing the New York City police officer had given her when she'd taken the threatening letters in to him.

"Look, there's nothing we can do," the cop said. *"These aren't the first threats you've gotten, nor will they be the last. You writers,"* he said with a shake of his head. *"I checked out your web page, your social media. Your whole life, everything about you from what you ate for dinner last night to your favorite color, is out there for public consumption. You put your life out there to promote yourself and your books. So..."* He shrugged. *"What do you expect?"*

Not seeing the owner, TJ stepped away from the book display and the poster of her as she heard more people come into the store on a gust of cold air. She hadn't gone far when she heard a deep male voice ask if they had TJ St. Clair's latest book.

She turned and froze. The man was a good six foot five, shoulders as wide as an ax handle and arms bulging with muscle. But it was the dark curly hair at his collar, the baseball cap and the sheepskin coat that sliced into her heart like a knife.

The owner of the store was telling him about the book signing the following day and how TJ had grown up right here in Whitehorse. "Here, you'll want a bookmark. The signing is at 10 a.m. Best come early because it will fill up fast. Tessa Jane hasn't done a signing here in years so we're all very excited."

"Yes, I don't want to miss that," he said, his voice a low rumble.

TJ felt glued to the floor. This was the man who'd pulled her back from the speeding truck—and possibly pushed her to start with—early this morning in New York City and was now here in Whitehorse? Even as she told herself it couldn't possibly be the same man, she knew in her heart it was. The only way he could have gotten here this quickly was if he'd already had a flight out of the city. As if he'd already known where she was going.

Just then he turned and she saw the dark beard on his granite jaw. A pair of piercing blue eyes pinned her to the spot. What she saw, what she felt, it came in a jumble of emotions so strong and unsettling that she turned and ran.

Chapter Four

TJ stumbled blindly out the door and around the corner. She leaned against the brick wall and tried to catch her breath. Her life felt out of control. *She* felt out of control. She'd never had a reaction like that and now, shivering out in the cold, she wondered what had possessed her.

She couldn't even explain her response to the man. What had she sensed that had her running out into the cold? She shivered, hugging herself as she thought of those blue eyes and the look in them. It was as if he could see into her soul. She knew that was pure foolishness, but how else could she explain her reaction?

"What in the world!" cried her sister Annabelle as she found her leaning against the outside of the building. Chloe came running up a moment later. "What happened?"

TJ couldn't speak. She shook her head and fought tears. But it was useless. She began to cry, letting out all the frustration and fear that she'd been holding in the past six months.

Her sisters rushed to her, drawing her to them as they exchanged looks of concern. "Let's get her over to the coffee shop," she heard Annabelle say.

TJ tried to pull herself together. At the sound of a truck engine, she looked up. To her horror, she saw that it was the man she'd just seen in the gift store driving by slowly. She couldn't see those blue eyes, but she could feel them on her.

"Who is that man?" TJ asked on a ragged breath before the truck disappeared down the street.

Her sisters turned to look.

"I saw him in the gift shop." Chloe shook her head. "I have never seen him before that," she said with a shrug.

TJ had expected Annabelle to say the same thing and was surprised when her sister said, "The mountain man?"

"You know him?" TJ asked as the pickup continued down the street. The truck, she saw with surprise, had a local license plate on it. How was that possible? It was the same man she'd seen in New York City earlier today. But how could that be? She was losing her mind.

"His name is Silas Walker. He moved here about six months ago," Annabelle was saying. *He'd moved here six months ago?* That was about the time TJ started getting the letters from True Fan. "He keeps to himself. Has a place in the Little Rockies."

"You can bet he's running from something," Chloe said. "Probably has a rap sheet as long as his muscled arm."

"Do you always have to be so suspicious?" Annabelle said with a sigh.

"Seriously, he's either a criminal or an ex-cop."

"One extreme or the other?" Annabelle grumbled. "Sweetie," she said, turning back to TJ. "You're shivering. Let's get you into the coffee shop."

It wasn't until they were seated, cups of hot coffee in their hands, that her sisters asked what was going on.

She wished she knew. Fearing that she was letting her paranoia get to her, she didn't know what to say.

"TJ?" Chloe prompted.

"She's finally getting some color back into her face," Annabelle said. "Just give her a minute."

She took a sip of the hot coffee. It burned all the way down, but began to warm her ice-cold center.

"Tell us what's going on," Chloe said. "Tessa Jane, you looked like you saw a ghost back there. Do you know that man?"

Looking up at them, she knew she couldn't keep it from them any longer.

It all came pouring out about the fan that at first was so complimentary but soon became more critical, making suggestions that when she didn't take them became angry.

"Who do you think it is? Probably some aspiring writer with too many rejections who's angry at you because you got published and she didn't?" Annabelle asked.

"Or maybe another writer who's jealous of your success?" Chloe added.

TJ shook her head. "That's just it. I have no idea. It could be just a reader who doesn't like the direction my books have taken. I'm not even sure if it is a man or a woman. I'm not the first writer to run into this problem. Readers bond with an author. They have expectations when they pick up one of your books. If you don't meet those expectations…"

"What? They threaten to kill you?" Chloe cried. "Have you gone to the police?"

She told them what had happened. "The officer was right. My entire life is out there in the cloud. When I was starting out, I hadn't realized that everything I said to the press or online would be available online forever. At first I was just so excited to be published. I never dreamed…" She shook her head.

"I can't believe the police blame you," Chloe said.

Annabelle agreed. "Though I have to admit, it goes with the business. I ran into this with modeling. Once you're out there, you become public property."

"That's ridiculous," Chloe said.

"Don't tell me that you haven't run into this as a reporter," TJ said.

"People storming in angry about something I've written? Of course," Chloe said. "It's part of the job. You can't please everyone. But if you're being threatened…"

"What are you going to do?" Annabelle asked.

She shook her head. "The police officer I talked to said I should ride it out. That the fan would get tired of harassing me. But I'm worried with this new book that True Fan isn't going to like it at all. After seeing that man…"

"You think it's him, your True Fan," Chloe said. "The one who looks like a mountain man?"

TJ sighed and told them what had happened only that morning on the street in front of her apartment. "He saved me, but did he? I felt someone push me in front of that truck. If he hadn't grabbed me…" She saw her sisters exchange a doubtful look. "I know it doesn't seem likely that they are the same person, but…" She halted for a moment. "I swear it's the same man. I… feel it."

"Okay, it's a stretch," Chloe said. "But I suppose it's possible. You were in New York this morning and now you're here. Why couldn't it be the same for him?"

"He could have even been on the same flight," Annabelle said. "You flew first class, right? He probably flew coach. And since you didn't have any luggage to claim…"

"Okay, it's not that much of a coincidence if he is the same man," Chloe said. "It doesn't make him True Fan though."

"Right, it isn't like he followed you here," Annabelle said. "He's been living here for the past six months."

"Six months," TJ said in a whisper. "That's how long I've been getting the letters from True Fan."

SILAS DROVE TOWARD the Little Rockies, anxious to get to his cabin. As he drove, he contemplated what had happened back at the gift shop. It didn't make a lot of sense and he was a man who prided himself on making sense out of situations.

At least he'd been right about one thing. TJ St. Clair had been headed home for the holidays. When he'd realized that, he'd been looking forward to meeting her. But after what had happened back there…

She'd run out of the shop in tears. Because of him? Or someone else she saw in the store? Odd behavior. He considered that it might have something to do with what had happened this morning in New York. A scare like that would make anyone jumpy. He frowned to himself, wondering again about her near accident this morning.

Was she merely jostled? Had someone purposely pushed her?

He shook his head, reprimanding himself for not leaving his job behind along with the suspicions that went with it. He was in Montana now. He'd bought this place outside of Whitehorse in the Little Rockies so he could get away from his stressful, dangerous, always unpredictable job.

Here, he did so much physical labor that all of that ugliness was forgotten—at least for a while. Here, he'd put that world as far away from him as he could.

And yet you still read thrillers. Not just anyone's. You read her books.

He laughed as he drove toward the mountains. That's because she was the reason he'd moved here. After reading TJ's books, he'd been curious about Montana, curious about the wild prairie, the endless sky, the wide-open places that she talked about in her books. Once he saw the area, he was hooked. She had always mentioned the Little Rockies so of course that's where he went when he was looking for land. While he loved the prairie, he also wanted a hideaway like the lawless days when Kid Curry and Butch Cassidy and the Sundance Kid roamed this area.

He'd bought into the mystique because of TJ St. Clair and because of her books, but he'd never dreamed he'd get a chance to meet her here in her home state. Which was why he couldn't miss her book signing tomorrow. He knew even before he turned onto the snow-packed road that led up into the mountains to his cabin that nothing was going to keep him away. He realized that he'd been wanting to meet her for far too long.

TJ LISTENED TO her sisters chatting, knowing they were trying to get her mind off True Fan and her book signing tomorrow. She smiled and nodded and added a word or two when required as she tried to enjoy her barbecued pulled pork. It was delicious and she was hungry after a long day with little real food.

But she couldn't keep her mind off the man she'd seen at the gift shop. The mountain man. Her True Fan?

She thought back to the first letter. It had been so complimentary. The writer had loved the book, sounding surprised as if not a thriller reader. She tried to reconcile that first letter with the more recent bitter, hateful ones she'd been getting. She couldn't square them anymore than she could the man she'd seen first in New York and now in her local gift shop asking about her book.

The first letter had been like so many of the others that she had hardly noticed it.

"You really need to hire someone to answer these," her friend Mica had said when she'd seen the stack TJ had been working her way through on that day six months ago.

"I've thought about it, but I'd rather not answer them than have someone else do it for me. I know that sounds crazy."

"No, I get it." Mica had opened a couple of the letters and begun to read them. "Aww, these are so sweet. They love you. This one is from a woman who is almost ninety. She wants you to write faster." Her friend had laughed. "Oh and this one is long." She'd watched Mica skim it. "Good heavens, do people often tell you their entire life histories?"

TJ had nodded. "They want to share their lives with me because they feel they know me from my books.

You can see why I try to answer as many of the fan letters as I can. Unfortunately I can't answer them all. I just hope they understand."

After her friend left, TJ had answered as many of the letters as she'd had time for since she had a book deadline looming. She *always* had a deadline looming.

That part she didn't mind. She loved writing the stories. It was the other things that ate up her time that she hated. There were always art forms that needed to be filled out describing her story, her characters, suggesting scenes for the cover.

Then there were the many edits and proposals that needed to be written. Add to that the blogs and promotion requests. It was a wonder she ever had time to write the books.

She had been thinking about that when she'd picked up one more fan letter to possibly answer. The first thing she had noticed was that there was no return address on the envelope. She hadn't thought too much about it since often the readers would put their addresses inside their letters.

Slicing open the envelope, she'd pulled out the folded unlined discolored paper. She remembered holding it up to the light, wondering how old it was to have turned this color. The letter had been typed on what appeared to be a manual typewriter. TJ had an old heavy Royal she'd picked up and kept in her office only as decoration. She'd always been impressed that Ernest Hemingway had written on a manual typewriter, since she doubted she would be writing books if it weren't for the ease of computers.

Dear Ms. St. Clair

I've never written an author before. I guess there is a first time for everything.

I recently checked out your first book from the local library. It was quite pleasurable to read. You clearly have talent. I was surprised when I started reading and couldn't put it down. I definitely enjoyed your descriptions of Montana and the country around your "fictitious" small town.

I'm actually looking forward to your next book,

Your True Fan so far

TJ had laughed. The reader certainly hadn't thought he or she was going to like it. It had pleased her that her True Fan had been surprised and willing to try another one of her books. Maybe next time the person would purchase one rather than wait to get it at the library.

She had looked to see if there was a name or an address. Apparently the reader didn't require an answer. She'd tossed the letter in the trash since long ago she'd given up keeping all the fan mail. She'd thought nothing more of it.

That, she realized now, had been her first mistake. There might have been fingerprints on that first letter before things went south.

Chapter Five

"I want to read the letters you got from this so-called fan of yours," Chloe said once they were back at the house and alone. Their sister had gone to see her fiancé, Dawson Rogers, promising to come back before all the wine was gone. "Something tells me they are much more threatening than what you told Annabelle."

"I didn't bring them with me," TJ said. "I didn't even save the first few." But she remembered them and often saw them in her sleep, waking in a cold sweat, her heart pounding.

Dear Ms. St. Clair

I was so disappointed with your last book. To think a tree was killed to make the paper that book was printed on… You should be ashamed.

I expect each book to be better than the last. I don't think that's unreasonable. In my last letter, I made some suggestions as far as the plot and character development.

Clearly, you dismissed those suggestions. Maybe you think you know more about writing than I do. Since my opinion doesn't count, you won't be surprised to hear that I don't trust you as a narrator.

I'm your only honest fan. If this is the way you treat a true fan, I hate to think how you treat your other readers.

You have really let me down. We might have to do something about that, don't you think?
Your only True Fan

She'd thought that would be the last time she'd hear from that reader. She didn't remember a suggestion for a book that True Fan had claimed to have sent her. Readers often thought she should do books about various secondary characters from her novels. One even suggested getting a woman out of the criminally insane ward of a hospital so she could find her true love. What readers didn't seem to realize was that those decisions weren't always up to her—even if she was inclined to do a certain character's story.

She'd thrown True Fan's letter away—just as she had the first one—and moved on to a letter by a woman who would love a signed book sent to her sister for her birthday. Her sister loved TJ's books and was laid up after a car wreck. The sister's name was Rickey. The reader had said that the sister was a huge fan.

TJ had picked up one of her books and signed it: *Rickey, Happy Birthday. Hope you're well soon, Best, TJ St. Clair.*

She put it with the letter in the pile to be mailed, only vaguely remembering that it went to a post office box in Laramie, Wyoming.

After that, she'd gone back to writing her book and forgotten both letters.

That had been her second mistake, though she'd had no way of knowing it at the time. It wasn't until she received the next letter from True Fan:

Dear TJ St. Clair

You really aren't as bright or as talented as I first thought. Actually, I'm amazed you make any money at this. A person you don't know from Adam tells you a hard-luck story and you send them a book? You are so gullible. But "Rickey" thanks you. Tee Hee. I'm feeling so much better and I like having a book that you touched.

Unfortunately, your books are getting worse. I didn't think that was possible. I told you what to do, but you just keep ignoring me. Because you think you're so much smarter than me, more talented? You keep making this mistake and we'll see who is smarter.

Your True Fan until The End

"Believe me," TJ told her sister now. "I've read them numerous times. I can't tell if they are from a man or a woman. They could be from *anyone*. Anyone who owns an old manual typewriter."

"Well, they have you running scared, so you must believe the threats are real," her sister said.

"The last one promised that True Fan would be seeing me soon and unless I apologized for ignoring the advice the person had been giving me, I was going to die like one of the characters in my book," TJ said. "True Fan said I could pick which character and which death and kill myself because it would be less painful than if a fan had to stop me from writing by kill-ing me."

Chloe shivered. "That sounds like more than a threat. The police didn't take that seriously?"

TJ poured herself a glass of wine, her hands shak-ing. "Even if True Fan had said he or she was going to kill me, there is no return address. The postmarks have been from all over the country. Where would they begin looking for this person? We don't know if it's a man or woman. So until True Fan actually makes good on these threats…" She got to her feet. "I hate talking about this."

"This man we saw earlier, you realize it's a long shot that he's the same one from New York, but I could do some checking. Annabelle said his name is Silas Walker." She ran upstairs, returned with her laptop and began to tap on the keys.

TJ was thinking how nice it was to have an investi-gative reporter in the family when Chloe let out a sharp breath and looked up. "What?"

"He was one of New York's finest, but left a year ago after being caught in some kind of internal sting investigation."

"What kind of investigation?" TJ asked around the lump in her throat.

Chloe shook her head. "Dirty cops. He apparently was never arrested. All they said was misconduct that betrayed the public's trust. That could be anything from lying to cheating on overtime or much worse. Here's the kicker: he was rehired a month later but then quit." She looked up from her computer. "This guy could be dangerous."

"What guy could be dangerous?" Annabelle asked

as she came through the front door on a gust of winter wind. TJ and Chloe shared a look. "Are you talking about the Mountain Man?"

"He's an ex-cop who was fired at one point," Chloe said. "I was saying he could be dangerous."

"Why was he fired?" their sister asked as she shrugged out of her coat, hung it up and joined them. She poured herself a glass of wine. Her cheeks were already flushed. From the cold? Or from her visit with Dawson Rogers?

"Let's not talk about this," TJ said. "Tell us about you and Dawson."

Annabelle shook her head. "If you really think this man is dangerous then you need to cancel your book signing tomorrow."

"Bad idea," Chloe said. "She'll be perfectly safe at the gift shop with us and half the town there. This is her chance to find out if he's this True Fan who's been sending her the threatening letters."

"You really think it's him?" Annabelle asked.

"First I'm shoved from behind in front of a speeding delivery truck, he saves me, then shows up in Whitehorse and I find out that he moved here six months ago—about the same time I started getting the threatening letters. What are the chances that he's *not* True Fan?" She shuddered at the memory of those blue eyes. She'd felt strangely drawn to him at the same time she'd felt afraid.

"What does she do if he *does* show up at the book signing tomorrow?" Annabelle demanded of Chloe. "Just ask him if he's her True Fan?"

Chloe groaned. "She'll play it cool. We'll be there. If he is this crazed fan, he won't do anything at the signing, but he might say something that gives him away. Once we know for sure then we go to the sheriff."

"TJ play it cool?" her youngest sister said with a laugh. "No offense, but if today was any indication—"

"I can do it." TJ nodded with more enthusiasm than she felt. She had to. This had to end because she couldn't take anymore. If it didn't, she feared True Fan would end it the way the letters had promised. "Maybe he won't even show."

"I wouldn't hold my breath," Chloe said. "If it's him, he'll want to get as close to you as he can. He's been taunting you. Now he'll want you to know just how close he is."

As if TJ didn't already know the psychology behind a person like this. She wrote about them all the time. If this man was her True Fan, he didn't just want her to know how close he was. He wanted her to know how easy it would be for him to get to her. For the past six months, this had been leading up to the moment when she faced her killer—just like in one of her books.

Chapter Six

When TJ woke the next morning, she was shocked to see how late it was. She hurriedly showered and dressed. When she came downstairs, dressed for her signing, Annabelle handed her a cup of coffee and a donut.

She took the coffee, declined the donut and watched as Annabelle ate it.

"I love not being a model anymore," her sister said, smiling with a little sugar glaze on her lips before she licked it away.

TJ couldn't help smiling as well. Her sister looked great, not skinny and pale like she had when she'd been a top model. "I need to get to my signing."

"We're going with you," Chloe said, coming out of the kitchen. "Are you nervous?"

What did she think? She'd never been good at book signings. Probably because she'd never wanted the attention. She'd only wanted to write the stories that were in her head. Little had she known the rest that was required of a published author. TJ knew she was naive to think that she could simply lock herself away in a room somewhere and do what she loved.

When her editor had told her that she needed to

be more of a presence on social media, she'd actually thought about quitting the publishing business.

But she couldn't quit writing. When she'd take a break, the longest she could go was three days before she started writing in her sleep. The characters would start talking and she'd have to get their stories out. She loved that part.

TJ remembered how surprised she'd been when she found out that not everyone had stories going in their heads. She'd asked the person, "Well, then what do you think about when you're in the shower or driving?" The answer had been, "I've never thought about it. Something I'm sure, but not stories."

It had also surprised her when other writers had told her that their characters didn't talk to them. Well, hers certainly did. Soon the ones from her next book would be nagging at her to begin writing again.

"Come on," Chloe said, "or we're going to be late."

TJ wished they could just get into Annabelle's SUV—she'd traded her sports car for something more practical for Montana—and hit the road. She thought she could and not look back at this point in her life.

There was already a line at the gift shop when they arrived. TJ couldn't help looking for the mountain man, but with a sigh of relief, she didn't see him. Maybe after yesterday, he wouldn't show up.

"Park in the back," she'd instructed her sister.

"You aren't getting cold feet, are you?" Chloe asked.

"I always do but nothing like I have right now." They entered the back door. TJ dropped off her coat and purse in the stockroom and took a moment to compose herself. *You've done this dozens of other times. You can do this.*

But none of the other times were like this.

Stepping out of the back, she headed for the table that had been set up for her along with a chair and a huge stack of her books. The owner hustled over to see if she needed water, coffee, anything at all.

"A bottle of water would be wonderful," TJ said, her throat already dry as she felt eyes on her from the line of people waiting a few yards away. She tried to smile as she slid into the chair and picked up one of the pens the store owner had thoughtfully left for her.

"Here's your water," said a familiar voice.

TJ turned to see a dark-haired woman her age. "Joyce?" She couldn't help her surprise. She hadn't seen Joyce Mason since high school. Joyce had been voted the girl most likely to end up behind bars. It had been a play on words, since Joyce had been wild—and also a drinker who was known to make out with guys in the alley behind the Mint Bar.

"You work here now?" TJ asked, feeling the need to say something into the silence. Joyce was thinner than in high school, but wore the same shag hairdo and pretty much the same expression, one of boredom. The only thing different was that she sported a few more tattoos.

"Does it surprise you that I read?" Joyce asked.

"No." She let out a nervous laugh. "As a writer, I'm delighted."

"Yes, we all know you're a writer." Joyce put down the bottle of water and walked off.

TJ was still reeling a little from Joyce's attitude when she heard a squeal and looked up to see another familiar face. Dorothy "Dot" Crest came running up to her all smiles.

"I can't believe it!" Dot cried. "I just had to say hi. I'll get in line," she assured the waiting crowd. "I definitely want one of your books. I've read them all." She leaned closer. "They are so scary and yet I can't put them down." She laughed. "This is so exciting."

With that she rushed back toward the end of the line. As she did, she said hello to people she knew. Dot knew almost everyone it seemed.

"Ready?" the owner asked, coming up to tell her again how delighted they were to have her here.

Was she ready? She felt off-balance and the signing hadn't even begun. Normally, TJ was more organized. She'd barely remembered to grab a few bookmarks as they'd left the house. She hadn't even thought about a pen. That showed just how nervous she was.

She smiled up at the first woman in line. She looked familiar, but for a moment TJ couldn't come up with her name. That was the problem at book signings. The names of people she knew even really well would slip her mind.

"Just sign it to me," a person would say.

She often used the trick, "Would you mind spelling your name for me?"

That didn't always work. One woman who was so excited, telling everyone how long she'd known TJ, made her draw a blank. When she'd asked her to spell her name, the woman recoiled and said, "It's Pat."

TJ had been so embarrassed, but there hadn't been time to explain how often her mind went blank at these events, even with the names of her closest friends. So she never saw Pat again.

Now the older woman with the dyed-brown hair

standing in front of the desk said, "You probably don't remember me."

For a moment, TJ didn't. She looked familiar. Really familiar, but...

"I'm not surprised given how much you didn't pay attention in class."

Bingo. "Of course I remember you, Mrs. Brown. I had you for English in high school." Annabelle had told her that the woman had only recently retired after having a minor stroke. "Would you like me to sign this to you?" she asked her former teacher.

"Of course. But you probably don't know my first name. It's Ester."

She signed the book, stuck in a bookmark and handed it to the older woman.

Ester Brown hesitated. "Just the other day I told my husband I wasn't the least bit surprised when I heard you were writing books." She hugged the book to her. "You were never at a loss for words in my class." With that she turned and walked away.

TJ frowned. Hadn't Annabelle told her that Mrs. Brown's husband had died?

One after another new and old readers stepped up and TJ signed their books, visited and moved on to the next one. She was surprised how many people had turned out. But the last time she had signed a book in her hometown had been her first one years ago.

"Hi, TJ," said one of the men from the line. She'd seen him, but hadn't paid much attention. She was looking for the mountain man. But if Silas Walker was planning to attend the signing, he hadn't shown so far, and another five minutes and she would be done. The line had dwindled, she realized with relief.

Her hand hurt from signing books and smiling and trying to remember faces she hadn't seen in years.

Now as she looked at this man, his name suddenly came to her. "Tommy Harwood."

"Tom," he corrected. He seemed surprised that she remembered him. He'd been one of those on the fringe. He'd been an average student, an outsider. He'd been invisible—just like TJ. While her sisters had been popular, TJ was a dreamer who preferred to be off by herself with her head in a book.

Now Tommy was getting a little bald. From the jacket he was wearing, she saw that he worked at the local auto shop.

"Do you want it signed to you?" she asked as she opened a book and lifted her pen expectantly.

"Sure, as long as it's to Tom."

She nodded and signed *To Tom, Enjoy, TJ St. Clair.* It was the best she could do given that she didn't think she'd spoken more than a dozen words to Tommy over the years. No matter what Mrs. Brown said, she wasn't the talkative one in English class. TJ realized she must have her confused with Annabelle. Great.

"Are you in town long?" Tommy asked quietly.

"Just for the holidays." She handed him the book.

He continued to stare at her. "You're probably busy, but if you ever want to get a cup of coffee…"

"Thank you. That's sounds nice. I'll let you know."

He nodded. "I should let you get to your other fans."

She watched him walk away for a moment, trying to shake off the odd feeling he'd given her.

"I love your books," a woman said as she quickly took Tommy's place and it continued.

As the line dwindled, she began to relax. She loved

her readers and was reminded of the time before her first sale. She'd been writing short stories. That's when she'd gotten her very first fan letter. The magazine reader had said she should be writing books. She'd framed that first letter and put in on her wall. It had given her hope each time she looked at it during the writing of her first book.

She could smile at the memory. There'd been so many days when she didn't think she could finish an entire book. It had felt overwhelming. Add to that the fear that it wasn't good enough, that everyone would hate it, that it would be rejected.

And it was. Her first book was still in the bottom of her closet where it would remain, never to be published. But that first book had given her hope not only that she could finish a book, but also that she could write a better one.

And she had. A book a year for the past seven years, all of them published, each doing better than the last. She remembered the thrill of her fourth book making the *New York Times* list.

She'd heard of authors who'd treated themselves with trips to Europe or purchased new cars after making the list. She'd gone for a walk, grinning the whole way, and on impulse had treated herself to a hot fudge sundae. It was as decadent as she ever got. Restraint in everything, that was TJ St. Clair, aka Tessa Jane Clementine. Those words could have been stitched and hung on her wall.

She'd always been like that. Holding back, never letting herself go. It drove her sister Annabelle crazy.

"Don't you ever just want to let loose? Do something crazy? Take a chance?"

"I might want to, but I don't," had been her answer. The truth was she'd never been brave or daring. That huge hot fudge sundae? It had made her sick and had been a good reminder of why she used restraint in all things.

No, her heroine in her books, Constance Ryan, was the one who did crazy, brave and daring things. Constance loved defying the odds. And for so long, TJ had loved writing about her—living through her.

As she finished signing a young woman's book, TJ saw him. The mountain man, Silas Walker, had just come in the door and was headed her way.

Chapter Seven

Silas was a little concerned about what kind of reception he might get. Because of his size and the way he looked, especially during his time in Montana when he was "roughin' it," he tended to scare little children. Lately he'd been working undercover, so his beard was longer than usual. He'd let his hair grow as well.

But the woman who wrote these murder mysteries? Come on, TJ didn't scare that easily, did she?

He guessed he was about to find out as he headed for the table where she had just finished signing a book. There were still several books left, he noticed with relief. He'd run late today because of the snowstorm in the mountains last night. He'd barely been able to get his pickup out. But he wasn't about to miss purchasing a signed book from TJ St. Clair today.

When she spotted him approaching, he had to admit, she looked like a deer in headlights. It perplexed him. She couldn't possibly have thought that he was the one who pushed her into the street yesterday. He'd been the one who'd saved her.

"Hello," he said as he reached the table. "I can't tell you how excited I am that I didn't miss your signing." His gaze locked with hers and he was shocked to see that her eyes weren't blue, but a languid sea green that took his breath away for a moment. Her blond hair framed a face that he'd memorized, since he'd looked at the black-and-white photograph on the cover jacket so many times.

She'd intrigued him from the first time he'd picked up one of her books. He normally didn't read thrillers. Hell, his life was one. No, he couldn't remember what had possessed him.

He'd opened one of her books to the first page and started reading. Before he knew it, he was on page 30. By then, he was hooked and knew he wasn't walking out of that bookstore without that book.

It wasn't until he'd finished it that he saw TJ's photo. He'd actually thought the book had been written by a man. He remembered smiling. He liked surprises and this woman had surprised him and intrigued him.

Now he watched her pick up one of the hardcover books at her elbow and open it with trembling fingers. That he made her nervous surprised him even given the way she'd acted yesterday. In her books, the characters were so gutsy. He liked to believe that TJ possessed— if not all of her character Constance's gutsiness—then at least some of it. The last thing he'd expected to see in her eyes was fear.

"Who would you like me to sign it to?" she asked, her voice breaking.

He knelt down, realizing he was towering over her, although he suspected that wasn't the problem. "Silas." He spelled his name and watched her write it out in her neat penmanship. "I can't tell you what a thrill this is. From the first time I picked up one of your books, I wanted to meet the woman behind them."

He saw her pen falter on the page. Those sea green eyes came up to meet his. He smiled and saw her shiver. She quickly looked down and hurriedly signed "Enjoy" and her name. Well, not her name exactly. TJ St. Clair he'd learned was her pen name. Her legal name was Tessa Jane Clementine.

She handed him the book. "I hope you like it." Her voice was throaty, almost a whisper.

He saw that there was no one behind him since he'd caught her at the end of the signing. "I have enjoyed your books so much. I just had to tell you that." He started to rise, but stopped. "I know this is probably out of line, but is there some reason I make you so nervous?"

She parted her lips as if to speak. She had a great mouth, he noticed. She quickly closed it for a moment before she spoke. "Is there a reason you should make me nervous?"

"Not that I know of," he said. "When I saw that you were going to be signing books here, I had hoped…" He shook his head. "You probably don't accept dates from your readers. I don't blame you. It's just that reading your books…well, I feel I know you. That must sound crazy. But you're why I ended up building a cabin here." He shrugged. "I'm sorry, you're probably anxious to leave." He smiled as he rose. "Maybe we'll see each other around town. Thank you so much for this," he said, looking down at the book in his hands. "I'll treasure it." He met her gaze. "It was wonderful meeting you."

TJ SAT STUNNED as she watched Silas Walker stride over to the checkout counter and pay for his book. She kept thinking about his intense blue eyes and his disarming smile. He knew that he made him nervous. Had he been enjoying that, or was he trying to make her less nervous?

"Well," Chloe whispered as she rushed over to her. "Is it him?"

For a moment she couldn't speak. "I have no idea. Apparently, he was going to ask me out but changed his mind."

Annabelle appeared to hear the last part. She let out a laugh. *"So he just wanted a date?"*

"He gave you no indication that he might be True Fan?" Chloe demanded.

"None." And yet… She remembered the way he'd looked into her eyes. What had he been looking for? She shuddered and let out a sigh. "I am so glad this book signing is over."

"He was at your table for quite a while," Chloe said, not letting it go. "What else did he say?"

"I don't know," TJ said. "My brain was on spin cycle. He said he felt as if he knew me from my books and that was probably crazy. Oh, and that I was the reason he built a cabin here. That is, my books were."

Annabelle's eyes went wide. "That doesn't sound good, but you don't live here anymore. You live in New York City, so…"

"He didn't mention saving your life in the city yesterday morning?" Chloe asked.

"No," TJ said with a shake of her head. "I should have asked him but my suspicions all seemed so ludicrous at the time. He kept looking at me as if…" She shook her head. As if he really just wanted to ask her out? Or something else? She had no idea.

"You knew your True Fan could be charming, right?" Chloe asked. "Maybe you should have accepted the date."

"No!" Annabelle cried. "What if he is... True Fan?"

"Well, he changed his mind about asking me out, so the point is moot," she pointed out. "Tommy Harwood asked me out though." Her sisters gave her a blank look, which confirmed that Tommy had gone through high school as invisible as she had been.

When she described him, Chloe said, "I do remember him vaguely."

"Kind of getting bald guy with the little potbelly?" Annabelle asked.

"That's him. He works at the auto shop."

They both quickly lost interest in him.

"I saw Dot. She hasn't changed a bit," Chloe said.

"Joyce Mason apparently works here," TJ said, keeping her voice down. She thought Joyce might be hiding nearby listening. "She was a little strange."

Chloe put an arm around her as she got to her feet to leave. "You survived it."

She smiled. She had. But she was no closer to finding out if one of the people who'd come through the line was True Fan.

"I say we go have some lunch," Annabelle said.

"It's that or head straight to the Mint Bar," Chloe said. "Up to you, Tessa Jane."

"Didn't someone say food?" Annabelle asked innocently. "I'm starved."

Chloe looked to TJ and said, "Food. I've never seen you this thin."

"Yes, we'll get you some good Montana eats and

fatten you right up," Annabelle agreed. "How about some chicken-fried steak?"

TJ felt her stomach roil at the thought. "Yum."

Her sisters laughed as they headed out the door. It was a wonderful sound that felt like a much-needed salve. She told herself that her True Fan hadn't been in Whitehorse today, hadn't come through the line, hadn't gone home with her latest book.

And yet she couldn't help but think about each and every one of the people who'd come through the line, including the young woman who'd been right before Silas Walker. TJ had been distracted, but now that she remembered...

"I signed a book for Nellie Doll," she said as they started up the street.

Chloe stopped, coming up short. "Lanell? I didn't see her in the line."

"She sent her niece to get it for her," TJ said. "The niece had me sign it 'to Nellie, just like old times.'"

"That is kind of creepy, isn't it?" Chloe said. "You and Nellie weren't friends."

"No," TJ said. "Far from it." She tried to shake off the memory.

"You aren't thinking that Nellie..." Annabelle was walking backward in front of them, looking from TJ to Chloe and back again.

"That she's True Fan?" Chloe shook her head. "Anyway, didn't you say that the letters had been sent from all over the country? I'm betting Nellie's never been out of the county."

TJ nodded, remembering the girl Nellie had been in high school. She couldn't imagine that she'd want to drop so much money on a hardcover book, especially TJ's.

She tried not to think about True Fan. She had so many amazing readers. Why did one fan have to spoil it? What bothered her was that she really didn't know whether True Fan was a man or a woman. She'd had several women murderers in her books. In fact, in the book she'd just signed, the antagonist was a woman.

Chapter Eight

TJ woke with a headache after a night of weird dreams. She took a couple of OTC painkiller tablets after her shower. She was not looking forward to her interview with a reporter from the *Billings Gazette* later this morning.

As she dressed, she could hear her sisters already downstairs in the kitchen. Opening her bedroom door, she followed the rich, wonderful scent of coffee down the stairs.

She couldn't help smiling to herself. There was something so comforting about being back in this house with her sisters. Just the sound of them lightened her step as well as her heart. As she walked into the kitchen, she headed straight for the cupboard where she knew she would find a mug.

"Good morning!" Annabelle called from the table, where she and Chloe were already sitting with their coffee. "It's a beautiful day."

TJ blinked as she looked outside to see the sun shining on the new snow, making it glitter blindingly. "Were you always this cheerful in the morning?" she asked her as she took a seat at the table.

"Don't you hate morning people?" Chloe said, and grinned, since she was one as well.

"I thought we'd get a Christmas tree today," Annabelle said with unusual jubilance. "Willie saved some of Grandma Frannie's ornaments from the trip to the dump. We could decorate the tree later, and I need to do some Christmas shopping."

TJ could see what her sister was trying to do—get her mind off True Fan and yesterday's book signing.

"Is there a place to buy a tree in town?" Chloe asked.

"Don't be silly," Annabelle said with a laugh. "We're going to take a picnic lunch and go up into the mountains and cut one. I found an ax in the garage."

"Ax?" Chloe cried.

"The Little Rockies?" TJ said, and both sisters turned to look at her.

"Why do I detect a strange excitement in those three words?" Chloe asked. "You aren't thinking what I think you're thinking."

"Of course not," TJ said. "It's just been so long since I've been up there." Both sisters were studying her. "Come on, he isn't True Fan."

"He said you were the reason he moved here," Chloe reminded her.

"Yes, but a lot of my readers say they feel as if they're in Montana when they read one of my books and they can't wait to visit," she pointed out. "It's not that unusual."

"This one *moved* here," Chloe said.

"So you really don't think he's the one?" Annabelle asked suspiciously.

"He did nothing to indicate that he was anything more than a normal fan," TJ said truthfully. "So," she said, getting to her feet. "I'll pack the lunch. Let's go to the mountains and get a tree." She started at the knock on the door.

"I wonder who that is," Annabelle said as she went to answer.

TJ heard her laugh. "You're delivering mail door-to-door now?"

As she stepped out of the kitchen, TJ saw the woman hand her sister a letter. "You got mail," the woman said with a laugh as she looked past Annabelle to TJ. "Fan mail. Our own famous author. I tell people I know you—well, know that you used to live here—and they don't believe me."

All TJ could do was nod and smile as her heart sank. She felt all the color leave her face as Annabelle thanked the woman and closed the door.

"Carol from the post office," her sister was saying. "She said this came for you yesterday and since you don't have a post office box, she decided to drop it by. How's that for service? TJ?" Annabelle had seen that she'd gone pale.

Chloe took the envelope from Annabelle by the corner. "I'm sure there aren't any prints, but…" She held it out to TJ.

She didn't reach for it. Even from where she stood, she could see the typewritten address. Any other city and the letter would have ended up in a dead file because it had no return address and was addressed only to TJ St. Clair, Whitehorse, Montana. Another joy of living in a small Montana town.

"Aren't you going to open it?" Annabelle asked.

TJ couldn't find the words to speak.

"I'll open it," Chloe said, and walked into the

kitchen to get a sharp knife. She carefully opened the letter, using the point of the knife to unfold the discolored paper.

How had the fan known she would be here? TJ groaned inwardly. Her fan knew she was in Whitehorse. Of course her fan knew; she'd just had a book signing. Not to mention she'd been recognized at the airport. That person had put it up on social media. Everyone in the world with a smartphone knew she was in Whitehorse—especially True Fan.

"The writer mailed it to you in Whitehorse, Montana," Chloe said. "So True Fan knew you were here. Only in a small town like this would you have gotten it," she said, voicing what TJ had just been thinking.

"Remember when we first came to live with Grandma Frannie?" Annabelle asked. "Frannie said Whitehorse wasn't the end of the earth, but it was damned close. She said on a dark night you could see the fires of hell." She laughed but quickly stopped when she saw that she wasn't helping lighten the mood.

"Wait a minute," Chloe said. "This letter was mailed *before* you got here. Whoever sent it knew you were coming here. Either that or figured it would be forwarded to you."

TJ couldn't wrap her head around that. She felt as if someone was always watching her, trying to figure out what she would do next. "How bad is it?" she asked from the kitchen doorway.

Chloe turned to look at her. Annabelle was standing off to the side, hugging herself as if she didn't want to know what the letter said any more than TJ did.

"Read it to me," she said, not wanting to touch it.

Dear Tessa Jane,

I would love to see the expression on your face right now. You really think you can get away from me? I told you, I'm your True Fan until the end. Now that I have your latest book, I hope you won't disappoint me again. I'm not sure I can take any more disappointment from you. I'm not sure what I'll do.

I thought I could help you, make you a better writer. But you've continued to ignore me as if you think I have no value. That hurts me deeply. I'm not sure I can let you go on writing these books.

The only way you can save yourself is if you made up for it in this recent book. Let's both hope that you do.

Still your True Fan until The End

"What is this person talking about?" Chloe asked as she finished reading.

TJ couldn't speak for a moment. The letters had started out being addressed to Ms. St. Clair. Then TJ. Now Tessa Jane. Each growing more familiar.

"TJ, what is it this person wants you to do?" Annabelle asked, worry in her voice.

She sighed. "One of the main characters told a lie but went unpunished."

"So punish the character," Annabelle said. "It's got to be more than that."

"True Fan also wants the lead character to fall for—"

"Durango," Chloe said with a curse.

She looked at her sister. "You read my books?" This day was just filled with surprises.

"Guilty. I hate to ask since it's going to spoil your latest book for me, but Constance doesn't end up with Durango?"

TJ shook her head. "Durango dies in this book."

SILAS HAD WOOD to chop and bring into the cabin. On the way home from town he'd heard that another storm was coming in. He'd bought groceries before leaving Whitehorse since he could be snowed in for a few days with the blizzard that was reportedly coming. As long as he had plenty of firewood, he would be fine.

But when he'd reached home, the one thing he wanted to do more than anything else was start TJ's book. Her books aside, he now couldn't get the woman herself off his mind. When he'd looked into those amazing sea green eyes... He'd started to ask her out even though it was clear that he made her nervous. But just the thought of having a chance to talk to her about books, writing... Not that he hadn't noticed how attractive she was. He shook himself. He had wood to chop.

After unloading everything from town, he made short work of getting enough wood in for the next few days. The first few snowflakes drifted down as he started to carry in the last load of split logs. He stopped for a moment to look up at the heavens. Snowflakes whirled down from a white, low sky. The air was cold and crisp and smelled of the tall pines that surrounded him and his cabin.

But it was the utter silence that captivated him. He'd never known such quiet after living in the city all his life except for his stint in the army overseas. His close friends thought he was crazy for coming here.

"Why the middle of nowhere in Montana?" one friend had asked.

"It's because of that writer he likes," another friend joked. "TJ St. Clair. How'd this guy talk you into something so crazy?"

Silas had let his friends think that the books were written by a man. He'd thought so himself at first, so why not? "I liked the way the writer described the area. It's exactly like in the books."

"Just be glad he's not doing this because of some woman," his friend said.

"That's the worst," the other agreed. "We'd know for sure that he's lost his mind."

They'd all laughed, Silas the heartiest.

TJ MET THE reporter at the Great Northern. She'd suggested it because she knew they would be able to find a quiet corner in the dining room to talk. After ordering coffee, the reporter began to ask her questions.

She'd done dozens of interviews since publishing her first book. Reporters asked many of the same questions. Where do you get your ideas? Everywhere. She'd spent years being a wallflower and watching people. She was fascinated by what made each one tick. The good, the bad, the truly ugly all made for great characters.

What inspired you to write this book? She'd seen a news story on television and while her story had taken a different twist, it had been the starting point.

TJ answered one question after another, adding examples and little asides, all the time her mind on the mountain man, Silas Walker.

Finally the reporter asked her what she knew now that she wished she'd known when she started. How hard it is.

"This is the hardest work I've ever done," TJ said truthfully. "It isn't an eight-to-five job where you go home at night and forget it until the next day. There's no Thank God It's Friday. No paid vacation and sick leave. Once I start a book, those characters are with me until I finish their story. They wake me up in the middle of the night. They nag me until I finish the book."

"So one of the fallacies is that you have all this time on your hands because you don't have to punch a time clock," the reporter said.

TJ laughed and nodded. "Everyone dreams of staying home, working in their pajamas, not having a boss looking over your shoulder. It's a little more complicated than that. It's a lot of long hours at a computer."

She was glad when the interview was over and she could walk back to the house where her sisters were eagerly waiting. By then, snow had begun to fall. The flakes were huge and drifted on the breeze.

"Did you know it was supposed to snow?" Chloe asked later as Annabelle slowed the SUV to make the turn at the tiny town of Zortman stuck in the side of the Little Rockies. Zortman had a bar-café, post office, church and a small building used as a jail.

Huge flakes drifted down from the dull white sky to stick on the windshield. The SUV's wipers were having a hard time keeping up. Several inches of snow had already fallen on the road. Their tracks were the only ones so far on the road south.

TJ could see patches of dark green through the falling snow as they approached the Little Rockies. The mountains rose from the prairie in steep rock cliffs and pine-covered slopes.

Before the town of Zortman, set back against the cliffs, Annabelle turned off on a road that passed the cemetery and some summer campsites. As the road climbed deeper into the mountains, the snow seemed to fall harder.

They had gotten bundled up, determined to get rid of the pall that had fallen over them after the latest letter from True Fan. Annabelle had thrown the ax into the back of the SUV along with some rope to tie the tree on the top—once they found it.

"I'll park up here and then we can get out and walk," Annabelle announced. "I'm sure we'll find the perfect tree."

Chloe groaned as she looked out the window. "I know it's beautiful, but I don't like this. What if we get stuck?"

"It's not that far of a walk into Zortman," Annabelle said as she kept driving up the narrow, snowy road through the dense pines. "Also there are cabins up here. I'm sure we can find someone to help us."

Chloe made a skeptical sound and turned up the radio as a Christmas song came on. She began to sing along, with Annabelle joining in. TJ didn't feel like singing. She'd seen a newer mailbox back on the county road. S. Walker. Silas Walker's cabin must be up this way.

She hadn't wanted to worry her sisters, but there was something about the man. So much so that she had to know if he was True Fan. This latest letter made her even more suspicious that it had to be him. The post-mark on the letter had been Whitehorse.

"So True Fan knows someone in all these places where the letters have been mailed," Chloe had said back at the house before they'd left. "She or he gets friends to mail them, saying it's a game she/he is playing with you."

"You're saying True Fan knows someone in Whitehorse who mailed the letter?" Annabelle had said. "But wouldn't that person know TJ?"

"Not necessarily," Chloe had said, and had shot her sister a look.

"Stop trying to make me feel better," TJ had said. The owner of the gift shop had called her Tessa Jane, the name everyone in Whitehorse had known her by. And now her True Fan was also calling her by that name after meeting her at the book signing? Or had True Fan known her real name all along since it was right at the front of the book under copyright?

She knew he could have found out her name in any number of places, but that True Fan was now using it…

Annabelle pulled out in a wide spot and cut the engine and radio. The silence was as deep as the snow around them. "Ready?"

They tugged on coats, snow-pants, boots, hats and mittens and disembarked with Annabelle toting the ax. At first they walked up the road but quickly realized they would have to separate and go into the woods to find a tree.

"Remember no taller than eight feet," Annabelle warned them. "Trees always look smaller out here."

"You'd think she'd been doing this her whole life," Chloe commented to TJ before they split up. "One trip

to get a tree with Dawson and now she's an expert."
Growing up, their grandmother had had a fake tree,
one of the first ones they'd come out with.

TJ stepped off the road into the trees and then waited
until her sisters disappeared into the woods before she
dropped back down on the snow-covered dirt road.
She could see older tire tracks now filling with snow
from where someone had driven in here earlier. She
followed the tire tracks in the deep snow, determined
to find Silas Walker's cabin.

Walking through the falling snow had a dizzying
effect on her after a while. It was like being inside a
snow globe. She stopped to look back and saw how
quickly her tracks were filling in.

TJ had no idea how far she'd gone when she noticed
fresh tracks had turned up an even more narrow snowy
road that led up the mountain. There were no new tire
tracks on the road she'd been following. If Silas Walker
had driven back in to his cabin after the signing then
there was a good chance these tracks were his.

She decided to follow the tracks in the hope of coming across his cabin. Following the tire tracks, she
hadn't gone far when she caught the smell of wood
smoke on the air. She kept going through the falling
snow, losing track of time and distance.

After continuing to climb up the road deeper into
the mountains, she stopped to catch her breath and
considered turning back. But she'd gone too far to do
that. She told herself that if she didn't come across the
cabin soon, she would.

She wasn't worried, but when she looked back, she
saw that her boot tracks had filled in. All around her
was nothing but white. The snowflakes were falling

much harder now. She could barely see the road ahead through the snow. She felt a chill and realized how crazy this had been.

Just a little farther, she told herself, and was almost ready to give up when she spotted smoke rising up out of the trees in the distance. Hurrying now, she headed toward it. Annabelle had said that there were several cabins up here. She told herself that this one had be Silas Walker's. There'd only been one set of tracks this far into the mountains and most of the cabins up here only were used in the summer.

As she drew closer, she saw the truck he'd been driving parked next to the small log cabin. Wet and cold, she hesitated. She knew she should get back to her sisters. They would be worried about her.

From the side of the cabin Silas Walker stepped out carrying a huge armload of firewood, startling her. As if sensing her, he looked up. Surprise registered on his face, then another emotion.

TJ spun around and tried to run back the way she'd come. Her boots slipped on the icy road beneath the snow. She went down hard. Her left leg twisted under her as her boot heel caught on the ice. She let out a cry of pain. Struggling to get up in the deep snow, she realized her ankle was hurt badly. She dropped back to the ground, grimacing in pain, suddenly terrified because she wasn't going far on this ankle.

When she was suddenly lifted off the ground, she screamed. She struggled, but Silas had her in a bear hug and this man was way too large and strong for her to overpower him. Her scream was suddenly cut off by a large gloved hand over her mouth.

"Stop struggling, you're only going to hurt yourself

worse," he said next to her ear. "I'm going to set you down on your good leg. Okay?"

She sucked in air through her nose and stopped fighting him to nod.

The moment he set her down, she slugged him in the stomach. It was like hitting a block wall and turning, she tried to run and immediately collapsed on her bad ankle.

He was on her again, covering her mouth as she began screaming in both pain and terror. "One of us is crazy. Since it's not me," he said, "we're taking this inside the cabin where it's warm." He tossed her over one broad shoulder and turned them both toward the cabin.

She screamed and pounded his back, but it had no effect as he strode up the porch steps of the cabin, shoved open the door and stepped inside. Swinging her off his shoulder, he dropped her unceremoniously into a large overstuffed chair.

Immediately she tried to get up, letting out a cry as she put pressure on her hurt ankle. Not that she was going anywhere even if she hadn't twisted it. He dropped a hand to her shoulder and held her in place as he kicked the door shut. It was warm inside the cabin and at the smell of something cooking her stomach growled, although she hardly noticed.

"What are you doing out in a blizzard?" he demanded, towering over her. He smelled of freshly cut pine. There was a maleness about him that was intimidating and at the same time intoxicating, even if he was her demented True Fan. She thought of a mountain lion on the prowl and felt like a small rabbit wanting to run for its life.

"You have to let me go!"

He held up his hands. "Not until you tell me what's going on. What are you doing here, TJ?"

So he had recognized her, even bundled up with her hat covering half of her face.

"I was out looking for a Christmas tree. I got turned around." She started to push out of the chair but he held up his hand.

"Hold on. Looking for a Christmas tree? And you just happened to stumble onto my cabin? Tell me you didn't come up here by yourself."

"I didn't. I came with my sisters. They'll be looking for me. That's why I have to go. They'll be worried."

But even as she said it, she knew they wouldn't be able to find her. They thought she'd come up here to find a Christmas tree. They would be looking for her closer to where Annabelle had parked the SUV. By now they could have a tree and be loading it.

She imagined them calling her name, joking around until they started to get worried when she hadn't appeared. Would they try to track her? As hard as it was snowing right now, her tracks would have filled in. They'd never be able to find her.

What had she been thinking? She hadn't. She'd acted on instinct and this is where it had led her.

She tried to get up again. He didn't push her back down, but he did move to crouch down in front of her. "TJ, you're a terrible liar, no offense. What are you really doing here?"

If only she knew. It wasn't as if she'd had a plan. She'd wanted to find his cabin. She'd wanted to spy on him. She'd wanted to learn more about him because she believed he was True Fan? Or because of that exhilbarating and yet confusing mixture of strong feelings she'd had the first time she'd laid eyes on him?

What she hadn't wanted to do was get caught and end up trapped in his cabin with him. It galled her what she'd done, since there was no way she would have let the heroine in her books do something this stupid.

Past him, she could see just how small the cabin was. It was only one room with a fireplace, a very small kitchen area, the chair she was sitting in and a bed. Next to the bed was a makeshift desk. It was what she saw on it that stopped her heart.

Sitting on the desk was a large old manual typewriter.

Chapter Nine

TJ felt her eyes widen in alarm. Silas had seen her look in the direction of the typewriter. Now he was frowning at her in a way that turned her blood to slush.

She thought of all the books she'd written where the heroine escaped by hitting the villain with a makeshift weapon. Or catching him off guard and kicking him in his private parts before bolting for the door.

While there was a floor lamp next to the chair, she couldn't imagine how she could grab it, swing it and hit him hard enough to get away. That was if she could walk on her ankle—let alone run.

But given no other option—she sat up a little. He was crouched directly in front of her. She'd barely kicked out with her good leg when he grabbed it, stopping her foot before it could reach its mark.

"That only works in your books," he said, his voice deep and rough. "Most of the time, it only makes the bad guy more angry. Let's quit playing around. Tell me what's going on."

"I know who you are." She hated that she sounded near tears. "You're my True Fan."

He frowned again. "Yes, I'm a fan of your books but…"

She felt fear give away to anger. "You've been send-ing me the letters!"

"Letters?" he repeated.

"Don't deny it. I know it was you who pushed me in front of the truck in New York yesterday morning."

He rocked back on his haunches. "Whoa. Yes, I was there, luckily for you. I didn't realize that you even saw me. Only I didn't push you," he said, enunciating each word. "I was the one who *saved* you before you became roadkill."

"Right, you just *happened* to be walking past."

"No, as a matter of fact, I was following someone." He made a face as if he saw what she was thinking. "It wasn't *you*. I was on a stakeout."

"I know you're not a cop anymore because you got fired."

"Did some research on me, did you?" He grinned. "I'm flattered. But don't believe everything you read in the paper. Anyway, I work for a private investigative business now. Or I did. I just took a leave of absence. Or did you already know that as well? And, sorry, but I haven't been writing you any letters."

"You've been taunting me for months. Admit it. I just got your latest threatening letter today."

"You've got the wrong guy."

"Really? Next you're going to tell me that you just happen to have a manual typewriter like the letters have all been written on," she said, jabbing a finger in its direction. She saw his sheepish look. "That's what I thought."

"You have it all wrong," he said, getting to his feet. "If you must know, I've been trying to write a book." He shrugged, looking embarrassed. "I use a manual up here because the power goes out more than it's on this time of year. I read that you write every day so I've been trying to do that." He moved to the wood-stove. "You inspired me to at least try. Unfortunately, I don't have your talent."

She watched him throw another log into the wood-stove. Did he really think she believed him? "I need to go. My sisters will be looking for me."

He turned to look at her. "Have you checked out the weather outside?"

She hadn't, but she did so now. The wind had picked up, whirling snow in a blinding white that covered everything. Worse, the visibility was only a few yards. She'd grown up in this county. She knew how easy it was to get lost. Ranchers often tied a rope from the house to the barn so they didn't wander off track and freeze to death.

"Once the storm stops, I can try to get us out of here in my pickup," he was saying. "But the truth is, I barely made it back earlier with a load of wood I cut from that beetle kill area by the road. I shouldn't have to tell you how slick that road into the cabin is. By the way, how is your ankle?"

"It's fine." She started to get up. He didn't move to stop her. But as she put pressure on her twisted ankle, she winced in pain. Who was she kidding? She wasn't going anywhere on that leg even if she could find her way back. She dropped into the chair and dug out her cell phone.

"Good luck with that," he said as he watched her. "I've never been able to get much coverage in a storm. Sometimes a text will go through."

TJ saw that he was right. She only had two bars. She

bit her lower lip, fighting back tears as her call didn't go through. Her sisters would be frantic.

She sent a text. At Walker's cabin until storm lets up. It was the best she could do since the text appeared to have gone through.

Raising her gaze, she realized that at least Annabelle and Chloe were together. While she was the one in real trouble.

"Look, maybe we could start over," Silas said, seeing how upset she was. "We're stuck here until the storm stops. By then, your sisters will have Search and Rescue looking for you. In the meantime, I've got some beef stew and some homemade bread I baked in the woodstove yesterday. It was my first attempt so I'm not making any promises."

She swallowed and looked out at the storm before turning back to him.

"Are you all right?" he asked quietly.

"I shouldn't have come here."

No, she shouldn't have. "Hey, you thought I was this person who's been writing you threatening letters. Actually, I'm relieved. I couldn't understand your reaction to me at the gift shop or at your signing. I didn't think I was that scary." Still she said nothing. "You really think someone pushed you yesterday in New York."

"I know someone did. I was shoved in front of that truck."

She was looking at him as if she wasn't convinced it hadn't been him. He could see now where she might have gotten that idea. He should have stuck around and talked to her. But he would have lost the person he was tailing. As it was, he did anyway.

"That was pretty gutsy of you to come looking for me the way you did. Given you thought I was the person who was writing you threatening letters let alone suspecting I pushed you in front of a truck. Probably not your best plan. Good thing I'm not that person."

"Good thing," she said, a little sarcastically. "Otherwise I would be trapped here with someone who wants to hurt me."

He rubbed his whiskered jaw. "How can I prove to you that I'm not this fan you say has been taunting you?" He stepped over to the typewriter. "Truth is, I admire the devil out of you. You're why I wanted to write my own book. I thought it would be easy." He laughed, picked up a handful of typewritten pages and came back over to where she was sitting.

To his surprise, she seemed to flinch at the sight of the paper. "Don't worry, I wasn't going to ask you to read it." He realized that she was staring at the paper as if…as if what?

She snatched a sheet from his hand. "Where did you get this?" she said, holding up the paper. His expression must have conveyed his total confusion. "Copy paper is usually white or some color. This is discolored. There even appear to be watermarks on some of it as if—"

"As if it was stored in a basement for years?" he asked. "I bought it at a garage sale in town last summer."

"*Whose* garage sale?" She sounded as if she didn't believe him. But then again, she hadn't believed anything he'd said.

"How should I know whose garage sale? Remember? I'm new here." He could see that she was still expecting more of an answer. "It was some elderly woman. Her house was for sale. Apparently she'd had boxes of the stuff in her basement for a while. She was practically giving it away."

"Why would she have boxes of it in her basement?"

"I have no idea. Wait. I might have overheard someone say she used to have a business in town that sold office products. Is it really that important to you? I bought one of the boxes filled with reams of paper. You're welcome to—"

"The person who has been sending me the threatening letters typed them on a manual typewriter like the one you have on paper exactly like this." She held up the sheet, her eyes glittering with tears. "Still going to tell me that you aren't True Fan?"

SILAS HELD UP both hands. "Maybe, since we have a little time now that we're snowed in, I can convince you of my innocence. In the meantime, why don't you get out of those wet outer clothes?" he suggested. "By the way, if you have to use the facilities, there's only an outhouse in the back. It's a short walk, but if you can't make it out there with your ankle, I'll be happy to help you."

TJ wished he hadn't mentioned it because now she felt the need to go. She pushed to her feet, grimacing as she put weight on her ankle. Silas was at her side in two long strides.

"Lean on me," he suggested as he walked her to the back door off the kitchen. As he opened the door, a gust of wind showered them both with snow crystals. They stepped out into winter, Silas closing the door behind them.

He was right. It was a short walk and he'd shoveled

earlier. But the snow had filled in the path. Tucking their heads into their coats they made their way to the outhouse.

"Sorry. It's pretty primitive. No hurry," he said as he opened the door and let her limp inside. "I'll wait at the back door of the cabin. I'll come help when I see you."

She closed the door. It was freezing in the one-hole outhouse. She couldn't remember the last time she'd used one. Drawing down her pants was no easy job as bundled up as she was. As she lowered herself to the wood seat she was sure her behind would freeze to it.

No hurry, Silas had said, but she hurried, anxious to get her pants pulled back up to get heat to return to her backside. Shivering, she opened the outhouse door. Good to his word, he came charging out.

As they made their way to the back door of the cabin, TJ saw that the storm had only worsened. She thought of her sisters and felt horrible for taking off the way she had. She just hoped they were smart enough not to be out looking for her in this. Hopefully Chloe had gotten the message she'd sent.

Back inside, Silas led her to the sink and provided her with soap and warm water that he'd heated on the woodstove in a large kettle. She washed her hands, dried them on the towel he handed her and let him lead her over to the chair again. While he busied himself at the stove, she got out of her wet boots, coat and ski pants. Down to a sweater and jeans and socks, she shivered in the chair until Silas brought her over a quilt to wrap up in. She watched him take her wet things and hang them up on hooks by the door, telling herself he had to be True Fan, and yet…

As she watched him, she told herself that a man

who was this thoughtful couldn't possibly have written those vile things about her. But like her other readers, he probably thought he knew her, thought he knew what was best for her.

The man unsettled her no matter who he was. She reconciled that strange feeling she'd had at the gift shop when their gazes had met. She'd seen...darkness. Something dangerous. Something violent. She tried to shake off the memory. Where had those feelings come from? Worse, because she still felt them, why were they so strong?

She tried not to flinch as Silas pulled up a stool that had been by the fire and sat down in front of her, his expression somber. "How serious were these threats against you?"

TJ debated how much to tell him. If he was True Fan, then he already knew, so what was his game? And if he wasn't? "One of them suggested I should kill myself and do the reading world a favor. Another said I should die like one of my villains in my books. The latest one just indicated that the letter writer couldn't let me keep writing these books, that this would have to end."

He shook his head. "How did this all get started?"

"Why the interest?"

He smiled. "Believe it or not, I'm still a lawman at heart. I like catching the bad guys. But I also admire you and enjoy your books. Since we're going to be here until the storm passes... Maybe I can be of assistance."

TJ couldn't help being skeptical. It came with her personality. Maybe that was why she wrote what she did. She didn't trust what was behind a smile or kind words. Grandma Frannie used to tell her to lighten up. Like that was possible.

More to the point, she wasn't sure what to make of Silas Walker. All the evidence pointed to him being True Fan. So was this just him still taunting her?

Looking into his blue eyes, she thought she saw genuine concern. She felt confused, thrown off balance by the man. She remembered how easily he had thrown her over his shoulder and carried her into the house. If he was True Fan...

"It started like any other letter from a fan," she told him, gauging his expression as she talked. She told him about the first few letters from the person who called him or herself True Fan's being complimentary, all the time studying his face, looking for...looking for a lie in all that blue. But she saw nothing but sympathy and a growing anger at True Fan.

When she finished he got up from the stool without a word and moved to the woodstove. He seemed to be thinking as he stirred the stew.

She studied his broad back, wondering why he'd been fired from the police department. "Well?" she prodded.

He stirred the stew for a minute or two before he turned back to her. "If you really were purposely pushed into the traffic yesterday, then we would have to assume your True Fan either lived in New York or just happened to be there yesterday. But if you're right about the paper True Fan is using to write the letters on coming from the same place as I got mine, then..."

She nodded, her heart pounding. Was this where he told her it had been him all along? "True Fan had to have gone to the same garage sale you did. Someone with connections to both New York City and White-horse since True Fan also took a photograph of my apartment," she reminded him.

He raised his gaze to hers. "A fan anywhere in the country could have had a friend in New York snap a photo of your apartment. Also, your near accident yesterday could have been just that. I think your True Fan is right here in Montana."

"Right where you just happened to be. Right where you just happened to be passing by yesterday."

He mugged a face at her. "The reason it's called a coincidence is because they do exist. I had no idea the woman I grabbed to keep her from falling in front of a delivery truck yesterday was you." He crossed his heart with the index finger of his left hand.

"You're left-handed." The words were out before she could stop them.

He looked confused again for a moment before he smiled. "I forgot. Your heroine Constance Ryan always falls for left-handed men. I'm betting there were a couple of left-handed boyfriends in your past." He turned back to the stove.

He'd be wrong about that. There had been one though—Marc. He'd been left-handed and one of the mistakes she'd made when she'd first started writing was that she'd made her heroine in her ongoing series too much like herself. *Write what you know*, she'd always been told. She didn't know anyone as well as she knew herself.

But while Constance Ryan always fell for left-handed men, she was the woman TJ wished she was. Unfortunately the similarities were obvious to anyone who knew her. Constance was a blonde with aquamarine-blue eyes, five foot six, curvy. A woman who loved spicy food and drank her coffee black and by the gallon.

But that was where the similarities stopped. Constance was daring. As a private investigator, she took on cases that others had turned down. She was smart and determined. Even after almost getting killed in every book, she still came back for more.

Constance also loved men—and men loved her. She always ended up curled up in bed with some handsome man. She wasn't one to stay long with any of them. Constance Ryan lived her life the way TJ wished she could.

But TJ was too much of a prude who'd hardly dated, even at college. Also she believed in happy-ever-after—even if her alter ego didn't. She didn't want a string of men. She just wanted that one man who would make her heart pound.

Like this man was doing right now. Only was it fear? Or something just as dangerous, given the two of them were alone, snowed-in deep in the mountains?

"I CAN SEE why you thought I was writing the threatening letters to you," Silas said after dishing them both up bowls of hot beef stew with a side of his homemade bread slathered in butter.

He'd pushed his stool over against the wall and leaned against it as he ate. He was glad to see that TJ seemed to have relaxed a little. Outside, the blizzard was still raging. He'd built the cabin to withstand the winter cold so it was cozy inside, but he could hear the wind and see snow piling up at the windows. He wondered if the snow would be too deep to drive out once the storm stopped.

"I've been thinking how to go about finding this fan of yours," he said between bites. Because he'd realized he had to help her whether she wanted it or not. The only way to prove to her that he wasn't True Fan was to find the culprit. Also, finding the nasty letter writer with TJ definitely had its appeal. He'd never dreamed he would get a chance to even have a cup of coffee with her—let alone spend time in his cabin with her.

"I can't wait to hear your plan." She'd stopped, her spoon in midair, to look at him. He could see she was still suspicious. He didn't blame her. Given the evidence against him, he would have thought the same thing she did.

"It seems simple to me. It all comes down to the old discolored copy paper. Anyone can shoot a photograph of the outside of your apartment—"

"How would they know where I lived unless they had contacts...say, inside the police department?"

He smiled at that as he watched her take a bite of the stew. He could see that she liked it, which made him a lot happier than it should have. Pride cometh before the fall, his father used to say. "You like the bread?"

"You really baked this in that woodstove?" she asked skeptically.

"I did. See that iron box on the top? It's an oven. This is my first attempt. I'll get better."

"It's very good. I've never attempted bread—even in a real oven."

He smiled, warmed by her compliment more than by the stew. He took a couple more bites before he said, "As to the question of how to find out where you lived…all anyone had to do was follow you home from a book signing. How many have you done in New York and gone straight home afterward?"

She didn't answer, his point taken.

"As for the push, there were so many people rushing around with Christmas shopping. I got jostled myself just moments before that. I didn't see anyone push you but I was in a tight crowd of people who were forced to the curb. I just caught you falling out of the corner of my eye, but there were people in front of me, including a woman with a huge shopping bag who could have hit you."

He watched her lick her lips after taking a bite of the bread covered with real butter. No butter substitute in his kitchen, ever. He could tell she was considering his theory.

"So let's say True Fan knows someone in New York who could have followed me from a book signing and taken a photo of my apartment from the street."

"Or she could have even hired someone to do it," he added, thinking about the private investigative business he'd been working for since leaving the police department. It was amazing to him what people would pay to learn.

TJ nodded, no doubt thinking of Constance, the heroine in her books. "So then it would just come down to the copy paper you both purchased at a garage sale last summer in Whitehorse?"

"August. I also bought this stool there."

Her gaze darkened to deep sea green. "So it's someone who lives in Whitehorse." She shivered and for the first time, he thought she might actually be considering that it wasn't him.

"I'd suspect it's someone who knows you and has reason to be jealous of your success," he said. "Maybe an old rival? An old boyfriend? Maybe even a former friend."

Chapter Ten

"I still can't believe you really made this bread," TJ said as she accepted another piece. Her walk to find his cabin had left her famished.

He grinned, obviously pleased. "For my first time, I think I got lucky, huh."

"It's delicious and so is the stew," TJ said, feeling conflicted. Could she trust this man? Sometimes the way he looked at her with those potent blue eyes, it made her squirm uncomfortably. It was when she glimpsed a dangerous edge to him that she had her doubts. She tried not to think about the predicament she was in—trapped in a cabin in a blizzard in the mountains with a man she didn't trust.

Common sense told her he had to be True Fan.

But after seven books, she knew from experience that the villain often proved to be the person you least expected—not the obvious one. Of course, that was fiction and this felt more like any real life she'd lived so far.

There was something so charming about Silas because of his easygoing manner. And that he was a little domesticated made him even more appealing. He seemed almost shy around her. She saw none of the anger that had practically dripped from True Fan's threatening letters.

After months of running scared she wasn't sure she could trust her instincts, though. Look where they'd brought her.

As she finished her stew and bread she noticed it had gotten dark, although it was hard to tell how late it was since the thick-falling snow still made it fairly light out. She pulled out her phone, hoping for a response from one of her sisters, but there was nothing. She looked at the time and realized with a start that she would be spending the night in this cabin with this man. Her heart began to pound a little harder.

Silas rose to his feet, stepping to her to take her bowl and spoon. "Don't worry," he said as if reading her mind. "You can have the bed when you get tired. I have a sleeping bag I'll drag out. I've curled up in front of the fire on the rug more times than I can remember when I was building this place. The bed came later."

He moved to the makeshift kitchen. Earlier, he'd refilled the kettle on the stove. Now she watched him wash up their dishes in a pan in the sink. He was so self-sufficient. Handsome too in a rough, untamed way that both intrigued her and scared her.

"Don't you get lonely out here?" she asked, wondering if there was a woman in his life back in New York.

"Just the opposite," he said without turning around. "I come here for the peace and quiet. Listen." He stopped what he was doing to half turn to look at her.

She heard nothing but the pop and hiss of the fire in the woodstove.

"Not one siren to be heard. No traffic. No honking taxis. No loud music from the apartment next door."

He let out a sigh. "This is why I love this place. Sometimes I just have to get away from all the racket. Here I get up when I feel like it, I go to bed when I'm tired. I spend my days working on the cabin, cutting wood for the stove, cooking my own meals. When I'm not working, I'm reading. Or attempting to write," he said with a chuckle as he went back to his dishes.

"I had forgotten what it was like living in Montana," TJ had to admit.

"That's right, you grew up in Whitehorse."

She nodded, remembering sledding and ice-skating in the winter, tubing the river in the summer. She'd forgotten what small-town living was like, the slower pace, the unlimited space, the quiet. "I hadn't realized that I missed it."

He turned then to look at her as he dried his big hands on a dish towel. "You must enjoy the glamour and excitement of New York City though. Isn't that why you live there? You can write anywhere."

"I did enjoy the city, especially at first. It felt as if it was where I needed to be to have the career I wanted."

"But now?"

She shook her head. "I hate it. True Fan has ruined the city for me. I don't feel safe there anymore." She let out a bitter laugh. "I don't feel safe anywhere."

He put down the dish towel carefully and turned to lean back against the kitchen counter. "I'm so sorry about that. It's another reason we have to find this person and put a stop to it. I would imagine it's also been hard for you to write."

She looked away. "You have no idea. Or maybe you do."

Silas cocked his head. "I know you still don't trust

that I'm not this person. That's okay. You have to be skeptical to write the books you do—and to be safe. But I promise you I'm going to find True Fan even if you don't want to help me." He pushed off the counter. "Hot chocolate or tea?"

"Tea."

TJ watched him put a smaller kettle on the stove and prepare two cups with tea bags. "I'd like to read some of your book."

He froze for a moment before turning. "You're going to laugh, but right now I'm more terrified than when I'm facing down a junkie with a gun."

"If you don't want me to…"

"Oh, that's just it. The thought of you reading anything I've written both excites and terrifies me. Didn't you feel that way?"

She smiled, nodding. "I remember the first time I took a writing class. I just wanted the instructor to tell me I could do this."

"Did the instructor?"

"No. Looking back, the woman didn't know anything more than I did about how to have a writing career, even though she'd sold a couple of books. I don't think she wanted to get my hopes up since by then she knew how hard it was."

"Well, you don't have to worry about that with me. I enjoy writing, so I'll keep at it hoping I get better no matter what you say. But I really would appreciate your opinion."

Crossing to the typewriter, he reached beside it and picked up a few pages.

"Give me the first chapter," she said. Aspiring writers always wanted to show her their favorite chapter in the middle, not realizing an editor would never read that chapter if they couldn't get past the first one.

He brought over a dozen sheets of paper. She noticed the way he held them in those large hands, like he was carrying a bird with a broken wing.

"You don't have to read the whole chapter," he said, carefully handing her the pages.

The first thing she noticed was that the pages had been typed with a new ribbon. There were none of the light and dark letters like on True Fan's.

Silas stood over her for a moment, then quickly moved away to take his coat from the hook by the door. "I'm going to bring more wood in from the porch," he said. "I suspect the temperature is going to drop tonight. I'll have to keep the stove going." With that, he went out the door on a gust of cold, snowy wind.

For a moment, TJ watched the snowflakes that had swept in melt on the wood floor. Then she turned to the pages of his book and began to read.

SILAS STOOD OUT on the porch in the blizzard smiling like a fool. TJ St. Clair was reading his book. He felt his stomach roil. What if it stunk as badly as he feared it did? What if she told him to use it to start his next woodstove fire? Or maybe worse, he thought, what if she told him it wasn't bad? That it was good enough that he should keep at it? That he had promise?

He wasn't sure which was his greatest fear—fear of failure or of success. They scared him in ways his job never had—even when he'd recently been shot. He rubbed his thigh unconsciously, realizing that his limp had been hardly noticeable. Or maybe he'd tried harder for it not to show around TJ.

Silas felt a shudder when he thought of her True Fan. How dangerous was this person? Would they really go through with their threats if pushed too far? More than ever, he was determined to find the person and put an end to all this.

The wind whipped snow into his face and down his neck. He shivered and hurriedly grabbed an armload of split firewood to take back inside. By now, TJ would have read far enough that she'd have an opinion. Feeling as if he was about to step in front of a firing squad, he told himself he could take whatever she had to offer, and pushed open the door to the cabin.

At first he didn't see her. The chair was empty and for one heart-stopping moment, he thought she had taken off out the back door. But as his gaze shifted, he saw her standing on one foot by the woodstove. She had the small kettle handle in one hand and was pouring boiling water in each of his mismatched mugs.

He dropped the load of wood in the bin near the stove and tried to slow his pulse. "You shouldn't be on your ankle."

"I hopped over. The kettle was boiling." She studied him. "You thought I'd left."

"I thought I was going to have to try to find you out in that storm. I wasn't looking forward to it."

She nodded. "That's the only reason?"

"Maybe I like your company." He could tell that wasn't what she meant at all. She thought he'd lured her here and that he was never going to let her leave. "Here, let me finish the tea." He helped her over to the chair and she dropped into it. "Are you warm enough?"

She nodded and seemed to watch him as he went back to the stove, returning with her cup of tea.

"I'd ask if you want sugar…"

"Constance Ryan takes sugar in her coffee, not me," she said, taking the mug of tea. "We aren't our characters."

"Aren't we? I knew you took your coffee black. Wasn't sure about tea." He thought of his own protagonist in the book he'd started. It was him and it wasn't. But still there was so much of him in his words that he felt vulnerable, something he'd seldom felt even on duty as a cop.

TJ sipped her tea as he hung up his coat and walked back to the counter to pick up his mug.

"I hate to even ask," he said, seeing his chapter lying on the footstool near the chair. He couldn't tell if she'd read any of it, let alone the whole chapter.

TJ NOTICED THE way the large mug disappeared in his hands. Silas seemed so gentle and yet she'd seen the way his muscles had bulged when he'd carried in the wood. For a man his size, he moved with a grace that again reminded her of a mountain lion.

"You have talent, but I don't have to tell you that," she said as she picked up the chapter from the stool and he moved to it to sit down. "I was drawn right into your story. I wanted to read more." He was eyeing her as if he was waiting for a "but." "You've had other people read some of your book, right? I'm sure they've told you…"

He shook his head. "You're the first and only."

She couldn't help being surprised. "Then you really didn't know."

"I'm trying to decide if you're just being nice."

"I'm not. The one thing I learned a long time ago

was that people who tell you you're better than you are are of no help. You need real criticism if you're going to get better, and I believe we have to continue to strive to do so."

He seemed to let out a breath before taking a sip of his tea. "Like I said, I enjoy writing so I'll keep going, but I'm overjoyed to hear it's okay."

"It's more than okay," she said. "I won't promise you that you can have a career writing. Just being good isn't enough. It takes determination and some luck."

"I have the determination. I'm not so sure about the luck." He smiled. "But I feel lucky right now. It's nice to have company."

They drank their tea in the comfort of the cabin as the storm raged on outside. The stove popped and crackled. Silas got up to throw more wood on the fire, then turned and looked at her shyly. "You wouldn't be interested in playing some cards, would you?"

She laughed. "What did you have in mind?"

"I don't even care. Crazy eights. Old maid. Five-card stud. I love to play cards and I'm sick of solitaire."

"My sisters and I used to play all the time. Do people still play with actual cards now that they have virtual games?"

"I have no idea," he said as he brought over a deck of worn cards. From a space behind her chair, he pulled out a small folding table. "You can even beat me. That's how desperate I am," he said with a laugh.

TJ snuggled into the chair. She hadn't played cards in years. She watched Silas shuffle the deck and realized she was beginning to trust him. She hoped that wouldn't be her last mistake.

Chapter Eleven

They played cards until after midnight. Silas couldn't recall a time he'd had more fun. TJ was an excellent player no matter what game they played. She challenged him. He couldn't remember the last woman who'd done that. She'd relaxed during their games and he'd gotten to see the woman behind the best seller.

She was fun and funny, sharp-witted. He liked her, and not just because she thought he had talent.

It wasn't until the last game that she began to look nervous again. He put the cards away and went to the built-in drawers on the other side of the bed. Pulling out one of his T-shirts, he held it up.

"I think this will cover everything but your toes if you're interested in wearing it to sleep in," he said. "I'll go out and get some more wood and give you a chance to change. Or you can sleep in your clothes. Whatever you prefer." He put the T-shirt down on the bed. "You need to go out back first?"

She shook her head. They'd made several trips out to the bathroom earlier during their card games.

"Sorry, I don't have a spare toothbrush. Wasn't expecting company, but there is toothpaste and water by the sink. Let me know if there is anything else you need." He headed for his coat by the door.

Once outside, he killed time thinking about True Fan. If it hadn't been for this crazed reader, he might never have gotten this close to TJ. That was a thought he wasn't about to share. He also tried not imagining her in his T-shirt. The thought made him grin and ache at the same time.

It had been so long since he'd been truly interested in a woman. He blamed it on everything that had been going on in his life. But he knew that had only been part of it. He'd missed the companionship. Hell, he'd missed the sex. And just thinking of TJ wearing his T-shirt... He shook off the thought.

If he wanted this to go any further, he'd best take it slow. The woman was beyond skittish. She was running scared. Not just that. She still didn't trust him. He hoped to fix that.

He warned himself that she'd be gone as soon as the storm quit. That's if her sisters didn't show up with the National Guard and probably half the county's lawmen before the night was over. Otherwise, he would get her out of the mountains in the morning one way or another.

The thought that he might not see her again was almost physically painful. He'd been captivated by her since her first book. Now that he'd gotten to spend this time with her, well, he didn't want it to end.

That alone surprised him. He dated in New York, but usually he was fine only seeing a woman a time or two. He didn't feel that way about TJ—even if he hadn't been worried about her.

Loading up another armful of wood, he tapped at the

door. Hearing nothing, he stepped in. She was tucked in bed, the down comforter up to her chin. She looked so damned cute in his bed. He quickly closed the door on a blast of snow and wind and, turning his back to her, dumped the wood and took off his coat.

Seeing her in his bed made him ache. It also threw him a little off-balance. He felt both protective and attracted to this woman. Just the thought of kissing her… "Have everything you need?" he asked, his voice sounded strange to his ears.

She nodded and watched him with just her eyes as he went to the area by the bed, opened a cabinet and pulled out his sleeping bag.

Rolling it out on the rug in front of the fire, he turned out the lights and lay down on top of it. A moment later, she tossed him a pillow from the bed.

"Thanks," he said into the quiet darkness. The storm had let up a little. He felt like he did when he was a kid at a sleepover. He didn't want to sleep. He wanted to talk about all the things that interested him, from life on other planets, to Big Foot's possible existence, to what TJ's favorite Christmas gift of all time was.

"Do you remember lying in bed waiting for Santa?" she asked from the darkness.

He chuckled. "I do. I never wanted to close my eyes. I was afraid I'd miss it."

"I hated it when I found out he wasn't real."

"He's not?" The fire crackled and after a few moments, he realized that she'd gone to sleep.

TJ WOKE TO find the cabin empty. The bedroll and pillow were no longer on the floor in front of the woodstove. And while a fire was going, Silas was nowhere to be seen. Sitting up, she saw that the pillow she'd tossed him was lying next to her on the bed. His bed-roll had apparently been put away.

Had he only gone to the outhouse and would be back any minute?

She heard something outside. For a moment she thought it was his heavy tread on the porch, but soon realized it was him trying to start his pickup. She threw back the covers and got up. Her ankle was better, only tender to the touch and black and blue along one side.

Silas had been right about his T-shirt. It fell to her ankles. As she slipped it off, she sniffed it as if she thought it might contain his scent. She held it for a moment, feeling like a teenage girl again, before tossing it on the bed and quickly pulling on the clothes she'd worn. She'd moved to the chair and was putting on her socks when she heard him come up the porch stairs and into the cabin.

"Good morning!" he greeted her, brushing snow off his coat and stomping it from his boots before stepping in on the rug. "Truck's cleared off and the motor turned right over after a few tries. If I have to, I can chain up all four tires to get us out of here. I wasn't sure how much of a hurry you're in to get home."

Last night she'd been champing at the bit. This morning, she hated to leave this cabin. Hated to leave Silas. Which was why she needed to, even if she wasn't worried that her sisters would be frantic.

She glanced around the cabin. "I can go when-ever you're ready. I appreciate your taking me back to town."

"Not a problem. I've enjoyed having you here. But

I'm not much of a host if I don't offer you breakfast," he said.

She was tempted. The warmth of this cabin, the scent of homemade bread, the good-natured, handsome man standing in the doorway. At that moment, she desperately wanted Silas Walker to be anything but True Fan.

"Thank you, but I really should get back. My sisters will be worried even after the text." Actually, more worried after the text.

He nodded, not looking any more anxious to leave than she was. "I'll be in the pickup. Come out when you're ready." He turned then and disappeared back outside.

TJ stepped to the hooks by the door, pulled down her coat, tugged on her snow-pants and boots. She took one last look around the cabin, thinking she might never see it again. Out of the corner of her eye she saw the typewriter. Curiosity killed the cat and every B movie heroine who decided to see what the noise was in the basement. Still, she moved to the typewriter and shuffled through the papers. Just pages of his book. She checked the trash can next to it. No partial letters written in too much haste.

Silas Walker wasn't True Fan. But Silas wouldn't be living out here in the woods unless he was running from something. She hated that she was thinking like her sister Chloe, the investigative reporter. But something had to explain those glimpses of darkness she'd seen in his blue eyes.

Walking out of the cabin, she limped her way through the deep snow to the pickup, where he was waiting behind the wheel. He leaned over the seat, pushed open the passenger side door and held it for her to get in.

"Shoot, I forgot about your ankle," he said. "I should have offered to help you."

"It's better, but thank you. Are you always so cheerful in the morning?" she asked.

"Do I detect that you aren't?" he asked with a laugh as he shifted the pickup into low gear. "Cross your fingers."

They chugged up the hill, the back of the pickup sliding a few times before they reached the road she'd come down earlier. There was no sign that anyone had been down the road last night.

"Okay," Silas said with a sigh of relief. "That was the worst of it. At least I hope so."

The sun topped the pines, making the fresh snow sparkle so bright that it was blinding. "It's so beautiful," she breathed. "I'd forgotten days like this."

He glanced over at her, but said nothing as he quickly turned back to his driving. The pickup bucked and slid and chugged until they reached an even wider snowy dirt road and finally the plowed, though snow-packed highway.

Silas patted the dash and said, "I knew you could do it, Gertrude."

"Gertrude?" she asked with a laugh. She was relieved they'd gotten out of the mountains without any trouble. She was also relieved that the easiness between them had returned.

"Be careful," Silas joked. "Don't insult her."

"I wouldn't dream of it," TJ said.

"Old Gert here reminds me of Constance."

She lifted a brow as she looked over at him. "Your

truck reminds you of the heroine in my books?" She couldn't help feeling a little offended, since she and Constance had a lot in common. No man had ever compared her to a pickup.

"Both Gert and Connie are dependable. They're up for anything when you need them. They both have their own kind of charm."

TJ smiled. "Well, when you put it that way…"

He chuckled and drove, looking comfortable behind the wheel even though the highway was slick and the landscape so white that it was hard to tell where the two-lane began and ended.

Normally, TJ would have been nervous about going off the road and ending up in a snowbank. But there was something about Silas that was a lot like his truck.

Chapter Twelve

"I don't know how to thank you," TJ said when Silas pulled up in front of the house. "It was interesting and…fun."

He grinned. "Glad to hear it. I was delighted for the company. It was nice visiting with you. But I hope we see each other soon." He jumped out to open her door. "I meant what I said about helping find that fan of yours. If I can figure out which house I went to for that garage sale and what happened to the woman who sold me the paper, do you want to go with me to talk to her?"

She couldn't help her smile. "I do."

He nodded, his smile broadening. "Then I'll let you know."

"Thank you." She gave him a nod and a wave as she started for the house. She heard him close her door, go around and climb behind the wheel. As he pulled away behind her, she hoped she wasn't wrong about the man. His words had made her all warm inside. Not to mention what happened when she'd looked into those blue eyes.

He was the kind of man a woman could fall hard for. Which made her all the more leery. There was a reason Constance never gave away her heart in the books. Her creator had given her heart away once, only to have it broken badly. To say they were both gun-shy was to put it mildly.

She'd barely reached the porch when her sisters came rushing out, both talking at once.

As Silas drove away, a sheriff's patrol car pulled up out front. TJ and her sisters turned to see Sheriff Mc-Call Crawford climb out.

"Are you all right?" Annabelle whispered.

"I'm fine. What is the sheriff doing here?" she whispered back.

"Chloe called her."

Of course she did. TJ sighed under her breath. "Did you get a tree?"

Annabelle smiled. "Of course. We're putting it up later."

The three waited until Sheriff Crawford joined them before going inside. Chloe, who clearly had taken charge, ushered them all into the kitchen.

"I see you made it home safe and sound," the sheriff said to TJ.

"I'm sorry my sister got you over here," she said. "I'm fine."

"She was trapped in the woods in a blizzard with Silas Walker," Chloe said, as if TJ had to be reminded. "I asked the sheriff here because I want to know more about this man who had my sister, especially since he'd been fired from the police force."

McCall smiled and declined the coffee Annabelle offered her. The two were on a first name basis after what Annabelle had found in the house last month.

"I could use a cup," TJ said as they all sat down.

"Silas bought some land in the Little Rockies about six months ago," the sheriff said once they were settled in. "I believe he built a cabin." McCall looked to TJ, who nodded. "Yes, he was fired from the New York City police force as part of an internal sting operation." Chloe looked at TJ as if to say "See?"

"But Silas was innocent. He was working undercover on behalf of the department to root out the dirty cops."

"That sounds dangerous," Chloe said.

All TJ could think about was the man who'd served her homemade bread and stew he'd made himself. The man who wrote beautiful words, deep with meaning. A man with many talents.

McCall continued. "He was offered his job back, but he declined because a cop who testifies against his own isn't necessarily welcomed back with open arms. There was an attempt on his life. He was shot. He is now employed part-time by another former police officer who started his own private investigative business."

TJ realized that she hadn't been the only one limping. But Silas had been trying hard not to show it.

"Have you met him?" Chloe asked McCall, clearly still skeptical.

"I have," the sheriff said. "I found him to be quite delightful." She looked to TJ, who nodded before picking up her coffee cup. She could feel both of her sisters watching her intently.

"I hope that answers any concerns you have about the man. But your sister told me that you've been getting threatening letters from one of your fans," the sheriff said, meeting TJ's gaze.

She nodded. "I was worried Silas might be the fan."

"But you're not now?" McCall asked.

"No, I'm not." After hearing what the sheriff had to say, she realized she could trust her instincts about Silas. Her new instincts that told her he wasn't True Fan. Not that he wasn't dangerous to her. Just the thought of him made her heart beat a little faster.

"Well if you need anything, you know where my office is," McCall said as she got to her feet.

TJ said she did and was glad when Chloe walked the sheriff to the door.

"Well?" Annabelle said the moment their older sister was out of earshot. "What happened?"

"Nothing happened."

Annabelle rolled her eyes. "How did you end up at his cabin?"

Chloe had returned after seeing the sheriff out. "Yes, how did that happen?"

TJ recounted seeing the mailbox by the road and wandering back into the woods, curious about him. "I didn't realize how far I'd gone and the blizzard was getting worse. I fell and twisted my ankle. Fortunately, he helped me into this cabin. By then it was snowing too hard to drive out so he suggested I stay the night."

"Why do I suspect there is more to the story?" Annabelle asked.

"He was very nice, charming actually, and he fed me homemade stew and bread that he'd made and we played cards until it got late."

Her sisters exchanged a look. "Have you forgotten that you thought he was True Fan?" Chloe demanded.

"No," TJ said. "And at first I thought he was. But none of that matters now. You heard the sheriff. There is nothing to worry about with him." They both looked at her as if they weren't convinced. "Isn't it possible that he's just a nice man who still wants to help me?"

"What does that mean?" Chloe asked.

"He's determined to help me find True Fan," she said with a shrug.

"Seriously?" Annabelle asked, eyes widening. "He is awfully good-looking if you like that big, muscled, chisel-jaw kind of man."

"I would be very careful," Chloe said. "Even if he isn't True Fan, this man could still be dangerous."

"You mean dangerous to someone as naive as me?" TJ said, bristling because she'd figured that out all on her own—but wasn't about to admit it.

Her sister seemed to take her time answering as if taking care with her words. "You haven't dated since Marc. That's all I'm saying."

She wanted to argue that Chloe had no idea how many men she'd dated, since they didn't live in the same city. But she saved her breath. Her sister was right. She hadn't dated since Marc. He'd been her college boyfriend. Her first. Her last. Their senior year at university, he'd gotten a job with a defense contractor working in high-risk countries.

The plan had been that she would kick-start her writing career and they would get married after he had an adventure and made a lot of money. She hadn't liked the plan, but Marc had been so excited, saying he needed to live a little dangerously before he could settle down. He'd been killed in Iraq when the company office where he worked was bombed.

"I'm only saying that I don't think you want another man who lives that close to the edge," Chloe said quietly.

TJ felt tears burn her eyes. Her sister was right. Silas Walker had gone into a dangerous profession and even volunteered to go undercover to weed out dirty cops. Just as Marc had felt the need for adventure in danger zones in the world.

"Don't worry," she said, more to herself than to her sisters. "I won't make the same mistake again."

A knock at the door relieved the tension in the kitchen. "I'll get it," Annabelle said, jumping to her feet.

TJ stayed where she was. She couldn't help thinking about how gentle and caring Silas had been. And yet from the first she'd sensed that darkness, that violence, that menace. Was she doomed to be attracted to men who liked to risk their lives?

Annabelle returned on a gust of cold air. TJ had her back to the door but she saw from Chloe's expression that something was wrong.

"Who was that at the door?" Chloe asked.

"It was Carol again from the post office," Annabelle said.

TJ didn't need to turn around. She knew without seeing the letter in her sister's hand. True Fan had sent her another threat.

SILAS DROVE AROUND Whitehorse street by street, looking for the house where he'd picked up the reams of paper at the garage sale. Whitehorse was only ten blocks square so it didn't take long to find the house where he remembered stopping at the garage sale.

He pulled up out front, got out and started toward the front door. As he did, he saw a front curtain twitch.

A moment later, he knocked at the door and waited. He knocked again.

A small elderly woman opened the door a crack. "Yes?" she asked.

"Hello." He smiled, but she still looked wary. He couldn't remember the woman who had sold him the reams of papers, but he was pretty sure it wasn't this one. The house had been for sale because the owner was moving into the rest home as he recalled.

"Who is it, Mother?" said a younger voice from behind the woman.

"I don't know."

The door opened wider as another hand appeared on the edge of it.

"Can I help you?" asked a woman a good thirty years younger.

"I was looking for the woman who used to live in this house," Silas said. "She had a garage sale here last summer?"

The younger of the two nodded. "Melinda Holmes. She moved into the rest home." She pointed down the street.

"Thank you." He started to turn away.

"You bought something at her garage sale?" the woman asked, clearly curious why he would be looking for Melinda Holmes about dealing with an item from last summer's garage sale.

"Reams of paper," he said, turning back.

"Oh." She looked disappointed. Had she been hoping for a chest with a secret in it? Or something of more value that he might have wanted to return? Whatever she'd been hoping for, those hopes dashed, she closed the door.

Glancing at his cell phone, he saw that it was still early. He drove over to the house where he'd dropped off TJ earlier. Getting out, he walked to the door, wondering what kind of reception he would get not only from her, but also from her sisters.

He climbed the stairs to the porch and knocked. The young woman who opened the door was blonde and blue-eyed. There was just enough resemblance that he knew she was one of TJ's sisters.

"Hi," he said, and smiled. "I was hoping to see—" Just then another sister appeared, followed by the one he'd come for. His smile broadened as TJ came into view.

"Silas," she said, sounding a little breathless as if she'd just raced down from upstairs. There was an awkward moment where they all stood there looking at him. The sisters were definitely giving him the once-over.

"Please, come in," TJ said, shooing her sisters aside. He wiped his feet and, removing his Stetson, stepped into the house. "I don't think you've met my sisters. This is Chloe, who's an investigative reporter, and Annabelle, who is—"

"Just Annabelle now," the young woman said.

"I was going to say, just nosy," TJ finished.

All three were beautiful alone, but together they made quite a sight.

"This is Silas Walker," TJ said almost shyly.

He nodded to the other two women. "Nice to meet you."

"Can we offer you some coffee?" Annabelle asked.

"Thanks, but I'm fine. I just came by to tell your

sister..." his gaze went to TJ "...that I found that house we talked about. The owner is in the local rest home. Melinda Holmes. Do you know her?"

"She should, since you used to steal the apples out of her tree on the way home from school," Annabelle said with a laugh. "I wonder if she'll remember you."

"Isn't that the woman who beat you with the broom as you were climbing her fence?" Chloe asked.

"Ah, the memories," TJ said as she reached for her coat. "I'd love to stay and reminisce but I have to find True Fan."

"If you haven't already found him," Chloe said under her breath.

Silas merely smiled, said how nice it was to meet them and TJ closed the door behind them. He saw that she'd showered and changed into jeans, boots and a sweater under her coat. Her blond hair was brushed and now floated like a golden cloud around her shoulders.

"I apologize for my sisters," she said. "They're... protective."

He chuckled. "You should be thankful for that." Glancing over at her, he grinned. "You really did steal apples from this woman we're going to see?"

"Let's hope the reason she's in the rest home is because she has forgotten the past," TJ joked.

"Not too far into the past though," he said as he opened the passenger side of his pickup. "We need to know who all she sold paper to."

THE REST HOME sat on a hill overlooking Whitehorse and the Milk River drainage. The valley was covered in trees that seems to follow the river northward. Silas parked and started to get out, when she stopped him.

"I got another letter."

"Let's see it." He heard the fear in her voice, but when he turned to look at her, she looked deceptively calm. However, as she opened her purse and removed the envelope, he saw that her fingers were trembling.

Silas carefully opened the envelope and pulled out the letter, trying not to touch it more than necessary. He wondered if TJ had taken the same precautions or if all three of the sisters had manhandled it. Not that he thought there would be fingerprints on it. With all the crime shows on television now, only a fool would send an anonymous threatening letter and leave behind evidence of the sender.

Tessa Jane,
I had such expectations for you and your books. I am sick over what has become of you—let alone what you have dragged your characters through. I knew you would corrupt Constance. For a while, she was the best of you.

Not anymore. That she could kill Durango… That YOU could kill him. He was the good in Constance. How could you not see that? You took a beautiful thing and ruined it.

I told you I was your only True Fan until the end. Well, I'm afraid this has to end. I can't let you write another book. I'm sorry, but you've abused your talent, and for what? Fame? Fortune?

You've been playing God with your characters—and your readers.

It's time to pay the piper.

SILAS FELT FURY roiling up deep inside him. Who was this crazy person? And more important, just how dangerous was True Fan?

He looked over at TJ. She'd gone pale, as if remembering each word of the letter as he was reading it. He told himself it didn't matter how crazy this person was or if they were serious about their threats of violence; they had to be stopped. He could tell that TJ was terrified. He couldn't imagine what it must be like for her to try to write another book with this hanging over her.

"All right if I keep this for now?" he asked as he carefully put the letter back into the envelope. She nodded as if she wanted nothing to do with it. "When is your next book due?"

"Four months from now. And no, I have nothing done on it," she said. "I might have to buy back the contract—if my publisher will let me."

He swore under his breath. "Let's hope Melinda Holmes has some answers for us," he said as he opened his door.

TJ HAD FELT sick to her stomach since opening the letter from True Fan. But having Silas helping her made her feel stronger as they entered the rest home. She'd been surprised that he'd moved so quickly on this. She hadn't expected him to go in search of the garage sale house so fast.

But she was thankful that he had and that he was taking the threats seriously. Once inside the rest home they were directed to Melinda Holmes's room. Unfortunately it was empty. A passing nurse told them to try the dining room.

They found her sitting by the window staring out

at the winter day. TJ barely remembered her from the broom-swinging woman who'd pounded her backside as she scrambled over the wooden fence behind the Holmeses' house.

"Mrs. Holmes?" Silas asked. No reaction. "Mrs. Holmes?" he said a little louder.

The elderly gray-haired woman turned from the window. "I'm not deaf," she snapped, her narrowed gaze going from Silas to TJ. "I know you," she said in a hoarse voice as her gaze bored into TJ. "You're one of those wild Clementine girls. You've been in my apples again, haven't you?"

"You grow the best apples in the valley," she said as she took a seat next to her. "This is my friend Silas."

Melinda's gaze shifted to him. "You stealing my apples too?"

"No, ma'am. I wouldn't do that."

His answer seemed to satisfy her. "So what do you want, then?"

"You're the woman who used to own the store here in town that sold paper supplies, right?" Silas said.

"That was years ago."

"I bought some reams of paper from you at your garage sale last summer."

She looked from him to TJ as if to say, "So?"

"Do you remember who all you sold the paper to?" he finished.

She looked suspicious. "Why? There wasn't a thing wrong with that paper. Might have been a little discolored, that's all. Some of it got wet, but it dried out just fine."

"It was great paper. In fact," Silas continued, "I'd

like to see if I can find more of it. I thought some of the people who bought it might make me a deal."

Melinda Holmes seemed to appreciate a man who liked a good deal. "A lot of people were at that garage sale. You expect me to remember after all this time?" She huffed at that. "There was that one woman from the school. She bought a few reams. Probably all gone now since she said she was going to give it to the school district to use."

"You don't remember her name?" TJ asked.

"Never knew it," she snapped without looking at her. Her face was set in a grim line and for a moment TJ thought that was all they were going to get.

"Then there was Nellie," the elderly woman said as if there hadn't been a break in the conversation. "She bought my bowl set. It had belonged to my mother." The woman bit her lower lip for a moment looking as if she might cry, before she said, "And there was that maddening Dot." She shook her head. "That woman has always annoyed me since she was a child. And that one fella… Sulky and kind of creepy as a boy— you know who I'm talking about," she said, turning to TJ. "He used to follow you girls home every day from school. He seemed to favor you."

"Tommy Harwood." TJ had known who she was referring to right away even though she hadn't realized that he'd followed them every day from school. She'd only caught him at it a few times.

"That's all I can remember," Melinda said, clearly finished with them. She turned back to the window.

TJ and Silas rose and left. "For someone with a bad memory she did well, I'd say," he said with a laugh. "You know these people she was talking about?" She nodded as they climbed into the pickup. "Could one of them be True Fan? Maybe this creepy kid who used to follow you home?"

"Maybe. I think I heard he lives by the railroad tracks on the way out of town," she said. "But he wouldn't be home now. He works at the auto shop. But Nellie should be home. Do you want to try her?"

Lanell "Nellie" Doll answered the door, opening it only a few inches. Still TJ saw enough of the inside to see that the woman's mother, who she lived with, was much like TJ's own grandmother—a hoarder.

"What are you doing here?" Nellie asked suspiciously.

"I stopped by to make sure you got the book I signed for you," TJ said.

"I did." She looked at Silas, clearly still waiting for an explanation.

"That wasn't the only reason we stopped by," Silas said. "Last summer I bought some paper at a garage sale from Mrs. Holmes. She thought you might have bought some as well and might have some extra still."

"Paper?"

"Mrs. Holmes sold it by the ream."

"If I bought some, I can't remember," Nellie said. "I probably used it up by now."

"I'm sorry, I should have introduced my friend," TJ said. "This is Silas Walker. He's a writer. Along with inexpensive paper, he was looking for a good manual typewriter."

"And Mrs. Holmes thought I might have that as well?" Nellie asked, sounding indignant. "That old woman should mind her own business."

"If you do have either, I would be happy to buy them," Silas put in.

Nellie was shaking her head. "I don't have any paper or a typewriter to sell. I'm busy so if that's all…"

"Have you started reading my book?" TJ asked before Nellie could close the door in her face. She was odd and secretive enough that she could definitely be True Fan. Not to mention unfriendly.

Nellie rolled her eyes with an impatient sigh. "If you must know, I don't care for your books. But my niece knows that we went to school together. Yesterday was my birthday so she thought it would make a nice gift to have you sign it for me."

"I see," TJ said, trying not to laugh. This was too funny. She loved the woman's honesty. "So you didn't read at least the first one I wrote, out of curiosity?"

"I couldn't get through it. But I never was much of a reader."

TJ could hear the drone of the television in the background and recognized the sound of a daytime drama. They were keeping Nellie from her "soaps."

"We're sorry to have bothered you," TJ said and Nellie quickly closed the door.

"Well, that was fun," Silas said as they climbed into the pickup.

TJ chuckled. "Wasn't it though."

"You went to school with her?"

"We weren't friends," she said unnecessarily.

He laughed. "I would have never guessed."

"I think we can scratch her off our list,' she said.

"I don't know about that. She definitely has some hostility issues."

TJ looked out the window at the town where she'd

grown up. "Some of the people I went to school with thought I was stuck-up. Annabelle was stuck-up, but me?" She shook her head. "I was shy. Introverted. I've always had stories going in my head, which were more interesting to me than school. I remember being called on by the teacher and not having a clue what she'd been talking about. I'm sure the teacher and the other students thought I was slow if not stupid. My teachers used to tell my grandmother that I didn't apply myself."

"Me, I actually didn't apply myself." He shrugged and started the pickup. "Dot next?"

"Dorothy Crest? It seems unlikely that it would be her, but I guess that's the point. Whoever True Fan is, it's someone who is hiding behind anonymity."

"True Fan is probably capable of putting on a good front to your face. The fact that he or she doesn't sign his or her name makes me think that True Fan is a coward and probably not dangerous—at least face-to-face. But if they undermine your writing then they have to be dealt with."

She smiled over at him. "Then by all means let's go see Dot." She put in a call to Annabelle, who informed her that Dot had bought her parents' house and now lived in it with her husband, Roger. With Roger at work, TJ figured they would find her alone. She was right.

Dot came to the door in an apron, throwing it open, all smiles when she saw them. "Come in! This is such a treat. A real live famous author in my home."

TJ introduced Silas.

"You write as well? Wonderful. You'll have to tell me the title of your latest book so I can pick it up. I love to read when I have time, which isn't often keeping up this house, you know."

She led them through the living room, pointing out that she had all of TJ's books on a special shelf of their own. The house was immaculate even though Dot kept apologizing for the mess.

In the roomy farm-style kitchen, she offered them cookies straight from the oven and coffee, saying that the coffee was always on at her house.

TJ took a warm chocolate chip cookie and listened while Silas visited with Dot. He asked about the paper she'd bought at the garage sale last summer, adding, "I think that's where I saw you before." He told her he'd been using his to write a novel on.

"I gave mine to the grandchildren. They love to draw and go through so much paper."

TJ was glancing around the kitchen when Dot said, "You've never seen my house. Would you like a tour?"

"I'd love one," she said, and got to her feet. The rest of the house was just as spotless as what TJ had already seen. In what appeared to be a den, she saw a laptop, but no typewriter.

"I'm halfway through your new book. I had to quit because I wasn't going to get my work done." Dot shook her head. "But I didn't want to put it down. I'm in awe of the way you make our little town come alive."

"You do know that the books aren't about Whitehorse," TJ said.

"Of course." She gave TJ a wink.

"They're supposed to be any small town in Montana."

Dot either ignored her or didn't hear her. "I'm so

glad you stopped by with your friend. I'd seen him around but I had no idea he was a writer."

TJ found it amusing that when locals called him a mountain man they were a little leery of him. But now that they would soon know he was a writer, his mountain man appearance would be accepted as just the way writers were.

They found Silas sitting where they'd left him in the kitchen, but TJ had the feeling that he'd looked around the lower floor while they'd been gone.

They thanked Dot and left, but only at her insistence that Silas take a few cookies for later.

"It's her," he joked as they drove away. "All that cheerfulness has got to be hiding something."

TJ chuckled. "I had the same thought," she said as she settled back against the seat. The sun shone in the pickup's side window. She felt warm and content and realized she hadn't felt like this in months—except in this man's presence.

"Any other leads we should follow up, or should we have lunch?" he asked.

"You probably have other things you need to do," TJ said.

"The sooner we find this creep, the better," he said.

But as he drove down the main drag of Whitehorse, she saw him suddenly look in the direction of a man crossing the street ahead of them—and freeze for a moment.

"Silas?"

He didn't answer.

"Is everything all right?" she asked, fearing what now had him looking like a man who'd seen a ghost.

He seemed to come out of his fugue state as the

vehicle in front of them that had been waiting to turn finally moved. The man who'd crossed the street was now nowhere to be seen. He appeared to have stepped into the Mint Bar. "Sorry, I just thought I saw... Never mind. It wasn't who I thought it was."

But she caught him looking back at the bar and later watching his rearview mirror as if he thought they might have been followed. Whoever he'd thought the man was, his reaction had been powerful. Silas was still spooked and she had a feeling he didn't scare easily.

Chapter Thirteen

Silas glanced at his phone and groaned inwardly. He was still shaken. The last thing he wanted to do was cancel out on TJ. But right now he had to take care of some business—and quickly.

"I'm sorry. There's something I need to see about right away," he said to her. "Can I take a rain check on lunch? I'll call you later."

"You don't need to go see this Tom Harwood with me. I appreciate you finding the house where you got the paper. I can take it from here."

That's what worried him. "I don't like you doing this on your own. I'll take care of my business, then check with you later, if that's okay."

"Of course. But are you sure everything is all right?" she asked, looking worried. She'd seen his reaction to the man crossing the street. He felt bad enough that the man might have seen him—and TJ. He didn't want her dragged into his dirty business.

"I'm fine. We'll talk later," he said, smiling over at her. He must not have been as convincing as he'd hoped, because she still looked worried.

"I need to go Christmas shopping with my sisters,

so please, take care of whatever you need to, and don't worry about me."

He glanced over at her, his heart breaking a little with worry over her. "I can't help but be concerned. That last letter…" What he wanted to say was, "We have to find True Fan before True Fan finds you," but he held his tongue. She was already scared enough. She didn't need him sharing his instincts or experience with her.

Unfortunately, those instincts and his experience on the job told him that True Fan would be making good on those threats—and soon.

As he pulled up in front of her house, he turned to her and reached for her hand. "Do me a favor, okay?" She nodded, seeming surprised by how serious he'd become. "Don't go anywhere alone. Take one of your sisters if you insist on going out. Especially don't go chasing True Fan. Wait for me. I'm not sure how long my business is going to take me but—"

"You don't have to worry about me. I'll be fine."

How many times had he heard those words? "That's what they all say." He felt her shudder. "Just do it for me."

TJ FELT HER throat constrict. Silas was so worried about her that it gave her a chill. "I will. But promise me something," she heard herself say. "Be careful. I don't know what this business is you have to take care of, but I'm betting it's dangerous from your reaction back there."

He said nothing for a moment, just squeezed her hand. "I'll call you later."

She nodded as he let go of her hand. For a moment

she was afraid to leave him. But he reached over and opened her door and all she could do was look at him for a moment before climbing out. It felt so strange to feel this close to someone she'd met only hours before. She was making her way toward the house when she heard him drive away. There was an urgency about his leaving that made it all the more frightening.

What kind of trouble was Silas in? Something to do with his former job? Or something to do with his more recent one as a private investigator? She knew so little about him and yet she felt she knew him. Just the first chapter of his novel had made her feel closer to him. She could understand why readers thought they knew her and feared some of them did.

Her heart ached as she turned to watch his pickup disappear around a corner.

"Well?" Chloe said from the open doorway.

"Is that what you're going to say to me every time I return to the house?" TJ demanded as she stepped past her and into the warmth of the living room.

"It is if every time you leave it's with that man," her sister said.

Annabelle called from the kitchen that she'd made sloppy joes for lunch and TJ was just in time. Taking off her coat and dropping it on a chair in the living room, she followed the sweet, temping scent into the kitchen.

"I haven't had sloppy joes since I left Whitehorse," TJ said as she helped set the table. Chloe was standing in the doorway, arms crossed, looking upset. That was the problem with mystery writers and investigative reporters, TJ thought. *We see things other people miss.* Chloe knew there was more to Silas. She'd seen the darkness, the danger.

"Silas found the house where he bought reams of paper last summer at a garage sale," she said as she took a seat at the table. Annabelle brought over the dish of sloppy joes and put it on the table before taking a seat. Chloe joined them, though with some reluctance.

"The paper is the same paper True Fan uses to write me letters," TJ said. "Or at least it looks to be the same. So we asked who'd bought some of it at the garage sale last summer."

"And?" Chloe said. She hadn't touched her lunch yet.

"She gave us a few names. Dot, Nellie Doll, someone from the school and Tommy Harwood were the ones she could remember. She said Tommy used to follow us home from school all the time." She turned to Chloe. "Do you remember that?"

Her sister nodded. "He had a crush on you." She frowned. "Wasn't he at the signing?"

"He was." TJ took a bite of her lunch. "Annabelle, this is delicious. I didn't realize how hungry I was."

"So did you talk to the others?" Chloe asked.

"We didn't get a chance to talk to more than Nellie and Dot," she said, not looking up from her meal. "Silas had some business he had to take care of. He's going to call later." She lifted her gaze to meet Chloe's dark blue one. "He isn't True Fan."

"No, but he certainly has taken an interest in finding this person, hasn't he?"

TJ shrugged. "Maybe he's more interested in me."

Annabelle's eyes went wide. "So something *did* happen at the cabin. Did he…kiss you?"

TJ laughed. "No, and nothing else happened either. He was a perfect gentleman." She saw that Chloe felt that proved her point that Silas was in this just for the excitement. For the possible danger. That he was like Marc.

"So are we going Christmas shopping this afternoon?" she asked, hoping to change the subject.

"I thought we'd walk since it is such a nice day," Annabelle said. "I want to find something for Dawson. I need your opinion. I found a shirt down at Family Matters. But is a shirt too unexciting for our first Christmas together—well, first this time around?" she added with a giggle.

It was impossible not to smile at their sister's happiness. Even Chloe, whose brow had been knitted with worry, broke into a smile.

"I'll have to see this shirt," Chloe said, and finally began to eat her lunch.

TJ tried to relax. She hadn't told them about Silas's reaction earlier or her fears. She'd gotten close to this man so quickly. That alone should have been a red flag. That Silas was in some sort of trouble seemed more than likely. He'd tried to play it down, but she'd seen how scared he'd been. What did it take to scare a man like him?

She tried to put him out of her mind. It hadn't been that hard with other men she'd met and even dated. But Silas… There was something special about him. And yet, Chloe's fear that he was too much like Marc kept nagging at her. She couldn't go through that again. Her heart couldn't take it.

"YOU'RE SURE IT was him?"

Silas held the phone more tightly in his hand. "Not positive. I only got a glimpse of him."

"Okay," said his friend and employer at the PI agency Cal Barnum. "First things first, I'll see if he's still out here in New York. This town you're in, it's small, right?"

"It doesn't even have a stoplight."

"So there is little chance he just happens to be there?"

"None. If he's here, then he's come for me."

"Maybe you should make yourself scarce," Cal suggested.

Any other time, Silas would have taken that advice. "It isn't that simple right now. I'm helping a friend with a problem she has."

"A friend? A new *female* friend, I take it?"

"She's in trouble. I can't just drop it."

"Okay, so how long before DeAngelo finds you?"

Silas pulled off his Stetson and raked a hand through his hair. He'd figured out how small towns worked pretty quickly after moving here. People weren't suspicious. They were annoyingly helpful. Looking for someone? Hell, they'd draw DeAngelo a map to his cabin.

"I'm going to have to find *him*," he said.

Cal swore. "I'm sorry. You knew it was just a matter of time. From the start, you'd been suspicious of that crazy bastard Nathan DeAngelo."

Silas and Nathan had been thrown together as partners when Silas had started with the force. Nathan had been there for a while and had promised to teach him the ropes. It hadn't taken any time at all to see that his partner liked cutting corners.

"I'd hoped he'd have the sense to let it go," Cal was saying.

"That isn't his way." He put his hat back on, his mind already working. He had little choice. He'd have to run DeAngelo to ground—or wait at the cabin for the man to come gunning for him. Silas had never been good at waiting.

"Let me know if you hear anything I should know," he said to Cal.

"Keep in touch and…good luck."

It was going to take more than luck. He knew DeAngelo well. He'd helped bring the man down for his crimes. But when it came to hard time, the man had slipped the noose. Too many friends in high places. Too much dirt out there that DeAngelo was holding over even those in the judicial system.

So where to begin looking for the man? Although that wasn't the main question on his mind. *What are you going to do when you find him?*

TJ TRIED NOT to worry about Silas as she and her sisters walked uptown. Annabelle was right. It was a beautiful December day, the sun shining, the new snow so pure white and sparkling. Christmas decorations adorned all the houses they passed and each of the stores along the main drag of Whitehorse.

"We should drive down to Billings," Chloe said, not as enamored with the small Western town as her sisters.

"This is so much better than the rat race in the largest city in Montana," Annabelle said, and laughed because all three of them lived in cities that made Billings seem small.

"Okay, come see this shirt I found for Dawson," she said, dragging them into the clothing store.

TJ spotted her former high school English teacher looking at scarves and quickly stepped behind the racks of clothing to escape. By now Ester would have finished the book. TJ didn't want to discuss the theme or her mistakes in grammar. Ester was one of those teachers who couldn't help wanting to continue to teach even in retirement.

Annabelle held up the shirt she'd picked out. "What do you think?"

It was a blue checked Western shirt. "It looks just like him," TJ said.

"I'd just buy him a rope. He's going to need it, married to you," Chloe joked. TJ was glad to see that her older sister had quit worrying about her for the moment.

"What does that mean?" Annabelle demanded. "That he'll want to hang himself or that he'll have to hog-tie me to keep me on the ranch?"

"I hadn't thought of either of those, but you have a point," Chloe said. "Buy the shirt. He won't care. He adores you and anything you give him, he'll love it."

Annabelle still looked skeptical. She shifted her gaze to TJ who smiled and nodded. "What he really wants for Christmas is you."

"I need to go down to the gift shop," Chloe said after Annabelle bought the shirt and had it wrapped and they exited the store. Annabelle said she wanted to look in the gift shop as well.

TJ had no desire to go into a place that sold her

books for fear of running into someone who wanted to talk about the latest one. She knew killing off Durango was going to cause some readers to be upset. But she had to take the books where they led her.

Also, she had no desire to see Joyce Mason again. She considered her for a moment as True Fan and couldn't imagine the woman going to the trouble to write her the threatening letters. Joyce was more of an in-your-face kind of person.

"I'm going to duck into the coffee shop," TJ said. "Why don't you meet me there when you're through?" They agreed and parted. She breathed in the winter day, her thoughts instantly returning to Silas. Worrying about him, she didn't even notice a figure step out of the alley until she was grabbed.

A hoarse voice whispered, "Don't scream. It's just me, your biggest fan."

Chapter Fourteen

Silas drove down the main drag, parking next to the city park. Whitehorse had been one of those spots along the railroad that had grown into a town. Because of that the unmanned depot sat beyond the small park on the other side of the tracks.

His senses were on alert as he got out of his truck and checked the street. With all the shoppers, the small town was bustling. DeAngelo couldn't have picked a better time. The rest of the year a large, dark-haired burly man wearing city clothes would have stood out from the locals and been easier to spot.

DeAngelo always wore expensive slacks and polished black shoes. He was obsessed with shoes and many times couldn't stop himself from stopping in the middle of the sidewalk to wipe away a spot on the leather.

Silas had been expecting him to show up for over a year. He'd thought it would be outside his apartment in New York City. Or maybe even *inside* his apartment. He'd been rigging his doors all these months, so sure that it was only a matter of time before they came face-to-face.

When that happened, he'd always told himself that

he would have only a matter of seconds to make his move. In truth, he would probably not have any time at all. DeAngelo knew him too well. Also there was nothing to say that hadn't already been said in court. From the witness stand, DeAngelo had mouthed "You're a dead man" the last time he'd seen him.

But after a year had passed with DeAngelo back on the streets, Silas had thought maybe the man had wised up. Maybe even a little time behind bars had taught him that he didn't want a repeat appearance.

Silas should have known better.

And now DeAngelo had not only shown up in Montana, but also at the worst possible time. Now Silas had met TJ and promised to help her. Lately, he'd even let himself think he might have a chance at settling down, having a home, a family. He desperately wanted this chance to get to know Tessa Jane. He'd actually been thinking that he might have a future.

Now those thoughts mocked him. As long as there were DeAngelos in the world, he would never find peace, let alone chance falling for someone and starting a family.

He waited for a car to pass, then ran across the street to the last place he'd seen his former partner. Pushing open the door to the Mint Bar, he stepped into the warm beer-scented darkness.

TJ SCREAMED AND kicked as she tried to free herself from the person who'd grabbed her. The toe of her boot came in contact with bone.

"Damn, you didn't have to kick me."

She spun around to come face-to-face with Tommy

Harwood. The scream died in her throat as she saw him rubbing at his shin as if she'd nearly broken his leg.

"You can't just grab someone like that," she said, furious with him for scaring her the way he had.

"I just wanted to get your attention."

Well, he'd done that.

He quit rubbing his leg and looked embarrassed. "I thought… I thought you might want to have a cup of coffee with me."

She'd been headed for the coffee shop, she reminded herself. Also, hadn't she wanted to quiz Tommy about the ream of paper he'd bought? "I'll buy," she said. "For kicking you."

Grudgingly he agreed.

"You're not working today?" she asked after they'd ordered two black coffees and taken them to a table by the window.

"Got off early."

She realized that this could be the longest coffee date she'd ever had if the conversation was anything like this. She decided to get right to it. "I meant to ask you about some paper you bought last summer at a garage sale."

He seemed surprised by the question, but answered anyway. "At Melinda Holmes's house."

"So you remember." When he said no more and looked away, she said, "Do you own an old manual typewriter?"

He looked up then, his dark eyes boring into her. "Is that really what you want to talk about?"

"I'm looking for one to buy," she said.

"And you thought I'd have one?" He shook his head. "Why wouldn't you go out with me in high school?"

Seriously? "High school? Is that what you want to talk about?"

"Yes. You knew I had a crush on you. You weren't even famous then. You weren't even *popular*. So why not go out with me?"

He wanted to be honest? Fine. "Since apparently you followed me home every day after school you would know that I didn't date much. Also it was creepy, you always looking at me the way you did, not to mention the only time you asked me out was in the middle of Biology class. You expected me to say yes in front of everyone?"

"That wasn't my best moment, I'll admit, but you still could have said something after that."

"I wasn't interested. But I wasn't interested in anyone else either."

"You went out with Darwin."

"That was his junior prom. I double-dated with my sister Chloe. She forced me to go." TJ remembered the scratchy dress, the uncomfortable high heels, the whole awkward night right up and through Darwin's sloppy kiss. The memory made her shudder. "It was a mistake. One I wasn't about to repeat."

"So you were shy and awkward. So was I. You didn't even give me a chance."

"Tommy—"

"Tom."

"That is all history. I can't undo any of it. If I could, I would never have gone out with Darwin, all right?"

"But you might have gone out with me?"

She picked up her coffee cup. "So you don't have an old manual typewriter?"

"What if I do?" he asked challengingly.

"Then I'd like to see it."

THE BAR WAS dim enough that he had to walk halfway in to see everyone inside. He told himself that he'd recognize DeAngelo without any trouble. He was wrong. The man who turned around on his bar stool had changed. His dark hair had receded. His face was gaunt and pale, and he'd clearly lost weight. He didn't look healthy, let alone strong and dangerous.

"Took you long enough," DeAngelo said. "I see you got rid of your date," he said, looking past him. "So have a seat. You can buy," he said, patting the empty bar stool next to him. "We need to talk."

The last thing Silas wanted to do was have a drink with his former NYPD partner. From the beginning they were too different. Silas went by the book. DeAngelo never met a rule he didn't want to break. But even so, Silas had never dreamed just how crooked the man had become before it was over.

"We have something to discuss?" he asked without moving.

His former partner chuckled. "You were always as stubborn as a brick. Sit down. If I was here to…" he lowered his voice even though there was no one sitting close by "…kill you, you'd already be dead and we both know it."

That, Silas thought with a grimace, was true. He knew firsthand how dangerous this man was. A part of him was thankful that DeAngelo wanted only to talk. Silas had become complacent. Up here away from the city, he'd become too comfortable. He'd let his guard down. Given that DeAngelo was here, Silas knew he should be dead. So why hadn't his former partner made his move?

Sliding onto the bar stool, he nodded to the bartender that he'd take the same thing his "friend" was having. A few minutes later, two beers were plunked down in front of them.

"I've never seen you drink beer," Silas commented. "You always went for the hard stuff."

"Maybe I've changed."

He wouldn't bet the farm on that, but he said nothing as he took a swig of his beer from the bottle. "What are you doing here, Nathan?"

Tᴏᴍᴍʏ ʜᴀᴅ ᴡᴀɴᴛᴇᴅ her to ride in his car with him, but TJ had insisted on meeting him at his house. She let him think she had her own car. She also let him know that she had to tell her sisters where she was going since she was supposed to be shopping with them.

"Whatever," was all he said as he headed for his pickup parked across the street.

TJ waited until he drove away before she started to go down to the gift shop to tell her sisters where she was going. It was the smart thing to do. If Tommy was True Fan, she had no business being alone with him, period—let alone being with him alone and with no one knowing where she'd gone. So she was glad when the first sister she came across was Annabelle.

"I'm running over to Tommy Harwood's," she said, making it sound casual. "I'll be back soon. Shall we meet up before supper, maybe go have a steak or something?"

"Dawson's mom invited us out, remember?" Annabelle said. "You remember Willie and she wanted to see you."

"Okay. I won't be long. I have my cell." With that

she left Annabelle looking at jewelry, knowing she could be there for a while.

The walk to Tommy's house was only four blocks down the side road that followed the tracks out of town toward Glasgow. Back when the towns along this stretch of new rails were being named, whoever was in charge got tired of coming up with ideas and simply spun a globe and randomly picked. It was why there were towns with names like Malta, Zurich, Havre and Glasgow.

Tommy's car was parked in front of a small neat white house. She tapped at the front door and it opened almost as if he'd been watching out the window for her.

"You *walked*?" He sounded appalled that she'd done that after turning down a ride with him.

"I decided to leave the car for my sisters. Anyway, it's such a nice day, I wanted to walk."

He shook his head and turned back into the house. She followed. The place was as neat inside as it had been outside. She wondered if there'd been a woman in his life at some point. Hadn't Annabelle told her that he'd lived with his mother for years until her death?

"Can I get you something to drink or eat?" he asked as she closed the door behind her.

She turned and seeing how nervous he was, instantly became more nervous herself. Coming here had probably been a mistake. Knowing Annabelle she might not even remember where her sister said she was going.

"I just came to see the typewriter," she said, trying not to be rude, but not wanting him to get the wrong impression. "It's a gift for my sister Chloe."

"Yes, the typewriter," he said glumly. "It's in here."

He led the way through the house. She found herself looking for possible weapons she could use against the man if needed. Tommy wasn't large but he looked strong. Definitely stronger than she was.

He'd reached the kitchen. She saw stairs that went down into the basement but had already decided she wasn't going down there. He could bring the typewriter up if that's where he kept it. She was beginning to doubt he even owned one and was beginning to suspect this had been a ruse to get her into his house. But if that was the case, then at least he wasn't True Fan.

"There it is," he said, not going near the basement stairs.

She looked to where he was pointing and saw an old manual Royal sitting on the floor in front of a door to the screened-in back porch.

"I use it for a doorstop. It weighs a ton," he said.

She stepped over to gaze down at the machine. It had an old, worn-out ribbon in it, but from the dust on the key arms it appeared it hadn't been used in years. "This is the only one you have?"

He gave her a disbelieving look. "You didn't come here to buy a typewriter. I know. I read your book."

That stopped her cold. She held her breath, always wary when this was the way someone began a conversation with her. *I read your book.* Sometimes that was all they said. But she had a feeling Tommy had a lot more to say.

Chapter Fifteen

"Look," Nathan DeAngelo said after taking a long gulp of his beer. Silas could tell it wasn't his first. "I don't blame you for what you did. I knew the kind of guy you were from the start. A Goody Two-shoes." He held up his hand before Silas could say what he was thinking. "Don't get me wrong. You did what you thought you had to do bringing us all down. But some of the guys aren't as…forgiving."

"This isn't news," Silas said, already bored with this conversation. He took a drink of his beer, wondering what had really brought his old partner all the way to Montana. Not to tell him something he already knew.

"I've moved on," DeAngelo continued. "I've got a pretty good gig going with a security company." He shrugged. "Keeps me out of trouble. The thing is, you taught us all an important lesson. We're not going to make the same mistakes again. We're not going to get our hands caught in the cookie jar again. That's why the guys all chipped in to hire a hit man to take you out. No way to trace it back to them."

Silas looked over at him and saw that he was serious. "And you came all this way to warn me."

"Like I said, I'm more forgiving." His gaze softened. "You and I were partners. The others can't believe you'd turn in your own partner. But I knew you would. I even suspected you were coming after us."

He shook his head. "I don't get it."

DeAngelo shrugged and drained his beer before pushing to his feet. "I can't explain it myself. Maybe I'm getting soft." He did look like he was. The security job obviously wasn't keeping him in as good of shape as the police department had. Or maybe he couldn't get his hands on the kind of drugs he'd had on the streets.

"Like you said, you could have killed me yourself and been on the next plane out of here. Why hire someone?"

"A professional seemed the way to go. Also we have something on the assassin so less chance of any blowback, you know what I mean?"

He did. "When?"

His former partner laughed. "Now what would be the fun of me telling you that?" He patted Silas on the shoulder. "Thanks for the beer. Almost like old times."

"One more thing," he said. "Did you chip in for the hit man as well?"

DeAngelo laughed and raked a hand through his thinning hair. "You know I did. Don't want them gunning for me next. It's bad enough that I didn't get the amount of time a lot of them did. And before you ask, no. No one knows I came up here to warn you. I know it's crazy, but I guess it's my way of saying I'm sorry. If you hadn't been so damned straitlaced we could have been great friends."

"I wasn't straitlaced. I just wasn't a dirty cop."

DeAngelo's smile blinked out, just like the light

in his dark eyes. "See, you have to go and ruin a nice moment. Good luck." With that the man turned and walked away.

"I'M SORRY, BUT I don't have any idea what you're referring to," TJ said, just wanting to leave this house and Tommy. "You read my book and you know what?"

"Durango. I know why you killed him."

She hated to ask, but saw no way not to. "Why?"

"Because he wasn't the kind of man you wanted anymore."

"Tommy—"

"Tom."

"I'm not Constance. Durango died because he got cocky. He felt invincible. He forgot he was mortal." Also because Constance needed to move on from him. She needed another hero, maybe one not as flawed as Durango. Or maybe more flawed. She wouldn't know until she wrote the book.

"He was Marc, the guy you were engaged to in college," Tommy said.

She felt her face burn with irritation and embarrassment. That was one of the problems with a small town. People knew way too much of your business even after you left. Anger overtook her embarrassment. She didn't have to explain her actions to anyone, especially Tommy.

"I really don't want to talk to you about this," she said, and looked at her watch. Her sisters should be through shopping by now, or at least interested in eating.

"It's fine if you don't want to admit it," he said. "But if you ever quit making the same mistakes with men…"

She stared at him. True Fan told her how to write. Tommy was telling her how to run her love life? "Who are you to tell me who I should be with?" she demanded angrily.

"Just the man who's watched you make the same mistakes since you were a girl," he said, apparently unperturbed by her angry outburst.

"I can see myself out," she said, and spun on her heel, stomping out of the house. The walk back into town did her good, even though the temperature had dropped. The air smelled as if snow was imminent. She'd heard that yet another storm was coming in. Winter in Montana, she thought, and pulled her coat tighter around her.

She was almost back when a horn honked right behind her. She jumped, having not heard a vehicle approach. Turning, she told herself that if it was Tommy she would kick in one of his door panels.

But as the car pulled alongside, she saw it was her former English teacher Ester Brown. Great, she thought, as Ester whirred down her passenger side window.

"Why don't you get in," she said in a tone that made it clear it wasn't a question but an order. "It's too dangerous to walk along this road."

TJ bristled. A few too many people had been telling her what to do. She wasn't one of this woman's students anymore.

"Thanks, but no thanks. I want to walk so I'll take my chances getting run down on the road." She turned and stalked off, keeping to the edge of the road facing traffic so the elderly woman didn't mow her down on principle.

She heard Ester mumble, "Always was too stubborn for her own good," before she hit the gas and took off with the chirp of the tires.

Fortunately, town was only a short walk. She found her sisters coming out of the drugstore, both carrying an assortment of packages. They really had been Christmas shopping. She realized that she should be doing some of her own. But she couldn't get into a holiday mood—not with True Fan so close by.

"Where have you been?" Chloe asked with her usual suspicion.

"Didn't Annabelle tell you?"

Annabelle, who had been looking into one of her bags she was carrying, looked up at the sound of her name.

"You didn't tell Chloe where I'd gone?" TJ chastised. What if Tommy had been True Fan? What if she was bound and gagged in his basement?

"Oops, sorry." Annabelle turned to Chloe. "She went to Tommy Harwood's house."

"Not all that helpful now, sis," TJ said.

"Why in the world would you do that?" Chloe cried.

"I thought he might be True Fan," she said, suddenly tired. She watched Ester Brown drive by, glaring at her as she passed and turned away from the street. She was reminded of all the reasons she'd left here, threatening never to come back. "Tommy gave me a lecture on my mistakes when it comes to the men I choose."

Both of her sisters lifted brows at that.

"I'm starved," Annabelle said quickly to change the subject before they got into an argument on the street. "Let's go to the Great Northern and have some lunch."

TJ looked up the street and saw Silas coming out of

the Mint Bar. He spotted her and stopped. He'd been headed toward his pickup parked across the street when he saw her. Now he stood as if unsure what to do.

"You guys go on ahead. I'm tired and not hungry right now. I think I'm going to walk home." She headed toward Silas, ignoring Chloe's comment that for the first time Tommy Harwood might actually know what he was talking about.

JUST THE SIGHT of TJ stopped Silas in his tracks. His spirits instantly lifted and just as quickly dropped. Nathan DeAngelo was a lot of things, a liar among them. But this time, Silas believed the man. He'd found over the years that there really was often some misguided honor among thieves. He also knew how much Nathan had hoped that Silas would adopt his way of thinking when it came to following the letter of the law.

"Hi," TJ said as she approached. She was frowning.

He realized that she'd seen him come out of the bar. She'd also seen his reaction earlier when he'd spotted DeAngelo crossing the street to the bar. She was too sharp not to have put it together.

As he looked into her beautiful face, he knew he had to keep his distance from her. It was bad enough that Nathan had seen him with TJ. He couldn't have his enemies using her against him. And at the same time, he couldn't just dump her unceremoniously.

The thought surprised him since it wasn't like they were a couple. But he'd promised to help her find True Fan and the one thing he'd lived by all his life was making good on his promises. He also couldn't put her in any more danger than he had and yet, seeing her, all he wanted to do was take her somewhere, just the two of them. He felt torn. While he shouldn't be with her right now, he also couldn't explain himself on the busy street.

A snowflake drifted down, followed by another large lacy one. His breath came out frosty white as he stepped to her. "Is there somewhere we can go and talk?" he asked. "Alone?"

She nodded and let him take her arm as they crossed the street to his pickup. Once inside, he started the engine, waiting for the heater to warm up enough to chase off the frosty chill in the cab. TJ hadn't said anything since climbing into the passenger seat. Outside, snow began to fall in a blur of white.

"I could take you to one of my favorite places outside of town," she said, breaking the quiet.

He looked over at her, telling himself all the reasons this was a bad idea and yet unable to simply walk away from her. The heater began to warm, clearing off the frost on the windshield enough that he would be able to see to drive.

Shifting the pickup into gear, he pulled out and followed her directions as they left town and headed northeast. Neither of them spoke as he drove. Snow blew across the highway. He recalled someone telling him they were called snow-snakes. It had a hypnotizing effect. He had to concentrate to keep the pickup on the highway as both the snow on the ground and the now falling snowflakes whipped around the truck.

They'd gone out of town some miles before she told him to turn. He checked his rearview mirror, not for the first time. He didn't believe they'd been followed.

That was the problem with a small town. There was no reason to follow them. All the killer had to do was wait. It would be easy to find Silas's cabin. This was the kind of job even an amateur should be able to handle.

The road TJ had him turn onto went from snow-packed pavement to deeper snow-covered gravel before she told him to turn once more. He could see an expanse of flat white through the falling snow. As they neared it, he realized it was a frozen-over lake. He saw picnic tables covered with snow under the trees along the edge of the lake and pulled down into one of the campsites.

This one was somewhat sheltered by the trees. He left the engine running, knowing how quickly the cab would get cold without the heater, and watched the snow whirling around them. He liked the intimate feeling. He could almost pretend that they were the only two people on earth in the warm cocoon of the pick-up's cab.

"You're in some kind of trouble, aren't you?" TJ said after a few moments.

He glanced over at her and simply nodded. "I can't let you get dragged into it so I'm going to have to stay away from you for a while."

"What if that isn't what I want?" she asked, her voice breaking.

He met her gaze. His blue eyes shone. "It is the last thing I want. I know I promised to help you find True Fan—"

"Is that the only reason?"

"I think you know better than that." He let out a frustrated sigh and reached over to brush a lock of her hair back from her face.

TJ CLOSED HER eyes at the warm caress of his fingertips on her cheek.

"Tessa Jane." He said her name like a curse, his voice thick with emotion. "All I can think about is you. You've completely captivated me."

She opened her eyes and met his blue gaze. Without another word, he reached for her, drawing her across the bench seat of the pickup. She felt a burst of pleasure expand inside her as he wrapped her in his strong arms and kissed her. His mouth was warm and sweet on hers.

"I've been wanting to do that since the first time I saw you," he said pulling back to look into her face.

She kissed him in response, weaving her fingers through the curls at his nape, breathing in the male scent of him. Desire sparked into a blaze inside her. She didn't care what Tommy or her sisters said. Silas was all man and more enticing than any she'd ever met. She felt safe in his strong arms and desperately wanted to lose herself in him.

He kissed her again, this time slowly, expertly. He deepened the kiss as he slid out from under the steering wheel to pull her onto his lap. She pushed aside his coat and opened the buttons on his shirt until she could press her palms to his rock-solid chest. She felt him shudder, desire a blowtorch in all that blue. Heat pulsed through her to her center.

Silas unzipped her coat and found his way to her bare breast. She arched against him as he thumbed the already hard nipple to an aching point. His hand slipped into her jeans and panties. He found the spot and she knew this had been building for some time because she cried out as the release came almost immediately.

He drew her to him, holding her as she felt the waves of release ebb through her, leaving her feeling weak. She started to reach for him, but he stopped her and kissed her tenderly. "I hadn't meant for it to go this far. The first time I make love to you, I don't want it to be in the front seat of my pickup. I want to take this up sometime soon." He touched her cheek, his fingertips warm, his gaze filled with desire. He groaned and pulled back his hand. "We should get going."

She fixed her clothing, zipping her coat. Even with the heater going, the windows had fogged over. This was so not like her. She barely knew this man. This was the kind of thing that Constance would do. For some reason that made her smile to herself.

Silas slid back over under the wheel and turned up the heat. "I'm not going to be able to see you for a while." He glanced over at her.

"You're not going to tell me what kind of trouble you're in."

He shook his head as he reached over and caressed her shoulder for a moment. "I can't tell you how much I hate this. But while I'm worried about you and True Fan, being around me right now is more dangerous."

"I'm getting it narrowed down. I talked to Tommy Harwood today." She shook her head at the memory. Wouldn't Tommy love to know about this? She felt her face heat and looked out at the lake for a moment. "It's not him. I've reached a dead end."

"I thought by following the paper trail we might find this creep. I'm sorry. The paper didn't lead us anywhere."

She agreed. "Too many people could have gotten some of that paper even if they hadn't bought it at the garage sale. But I think you're right. True Fan is a coward." She turned toward Silas. "So take care of your trouble and don't worry about me."

"That won't be easy," he said as he removed his hand from her shoulder and got the truck going. She heard the worry in his voice and knew that whatever trouble he was in, it was serious.

Chapter Sixteen

Silas dropped her off at her house after another kiss. TJ could tell that he hadn't wanted to let her go any more than she had wanted to leave him. Their feelings for each other had happened so quickly, it scared her. But it also excited her. For the first time in her life, she was being adventurous. It felt good.

She thought about his kisses. It felt wonderful.

"I don't know when I'll see you again," he said, his voice rough with emotion. "But know that you won't be far from my mind."

She'd wanted to ask him how dangerous this trouble was, but in her heart she knew. She'd seen how scared he'd been when he'd recognized the man crossing the street earlier. Someone from his past? Someone he'd helped put in jail? Whoever it was, the man was dangerous.

Her heart ached. She and Silas had just found each other and now... Both of them had someone who was clearly threatening to hurt them and it had thrown them together. Earlier, at the lake, that feeling of impending doom had pushed them together faster than either of them had wanted.

But there was no denying the chemistry between

them. They'd bonded at the cabin. She thought of their card games late at night with a blizzard howling outside the cabin and hugged that memory to her, afraid she might never see Silas alive again.

"This is about those cops you put in prison, isn't it?" she asked.

He looked at her. She could see him fighting not telling her the truth. "Was that man in town to kill you?"

"No. Warn me."

Her chest felt as if an elephant had settled on it. "Can you go to the sheriff?"

He shook his head. "I have to take care of it myself."

"Oh, Silas."

He touched her cheek again. "I need you to be careful."

"You too." They locked gazes for a long moment before he reached over and opened her door. There was nothing more either of them could say.

She watched him drive away before making her way up the porch steps and into the house. Her sisters were in the living room. They'd opened a bottle of wine. Both looked up expectantly at her as she came in and hung up her coat.

"Oh no, you didn't," Chloe said.

TJ turned, feeling her face heat even as she denied it. "We kissed and made out some…"

Her sister groaned.

"Oh let her have some fun," Annabelle said.

As TJ joined them and poured herself a glass of wine, she found herself near tears with worry. "I like him."

"We can see that," Chloe said.

"You should invite him to the Christmas dance at

the old gym," Annabelle suggested. "Everyone in town will be there. Dawson and I are going." She grinned, hugging herself.

"The two of you are killing me," Chloe said.

"Isn't there someone you were interested in at the newspaper?" Annabelle asked.

Their sister shrugged. "I dated some, but no, I've never met The One."

"How do you know?" Annabelle said, turning in her chair as she warmed to the subject. "Look at Dawson and me. I left him even when he bought a ring and asked me to marry him. I thought he'd never forgive me. He said I broke his heart." Her voice cracked with emotion and tears flooded her blue eyes. "But we found our way back to each other. What about your old boyfriend, Justin Calhoun?"

Chloe shifted uncomfortably in her seat. "He wasn't my boyfriend exactly. Anyway, that ship sailed a long time ago. Didn't he marry…what was her name?"

"Nicole Kent," Annabelle said. "But he didn't marry her. They were engaged—at least according to Nici—but they broke up. She married someone else, got divorced. She lives here with a couple of her sisters and their kids."

"You've certainly gotten caught up on local gossip," TJ said, and took a sip of her wine. "Didn't Tommy live with his mother for a long time?"

Annabelle laughed. "As a matter of fact, he did. She died a few years ago and he sold her house and bought that one out by the tracks."

TJ looked over at Chloe. She seemed to be lost in thought. Justin? The two of them had seemed perfect for each other but Chloe had been on her way to college so nothing had come of it. But TJ had always wondered if Nicole Kent hadn't been the reason the two hadn't seen each other after that. She remembered the girl and felt a shiver. That one had always been trouble.

They all jumped at a knock on the door. Exchanging looks, TJ got up this time to answer it.

"You really should get a post office box," Carol said as she handed her the letter that had come for her. "You're going to get me fired."

"Thanks for bringing it by, but if anymore come—"

"Don't worry. I'll see that you get them." Carol turned on the step and, the bells she was wearing jingling, took off toward her vehicle. Carol always wore bells at work this time of year.

TJ looked down at the letter in her hand and realized her hand was shaking.

"Here, let me open that," Chloe said, taking the letter from her as TJ stepped back inside. She tore it open and pulled out the sheet, discolored like all the others.

This time True Fan didn't even bother with her name.

I told myself not to take it personally. But you have ignored everything I've told you. You seem to think you're so much smarter than me. You don't need my help. You never have.

All my attempts to make your books better have been ignored. You find me to be nothing more than a pest you can't seem to get rid of. Well, that will soon be over. I've tried to let it go. But in good conscience I can't let you go on the way you are.

I don't think of myself as a violent person.

But someone needs to stop you. This time you've gone too far. I guess I'm going to have to do it myself since you didn't take my advice. You could have done the world a favor by taking your own life, but why would you listen to me now? I'm going to have to take care of this myself. There is apparently no one else.

There was no True Fan to the end. The letter just ended.

Chloe threw it down in disgust. "This person is crazy. I think it's time to take it to the sheriff." She got to her feet. "Do you have the other letters that have come since we've been here?"

TJ nodded. There was a chilling violence to the letter, as if the person had reached some breaking point. She hugged herself as her big sister made the call.

Annabelle took the empty wine bottle and glasses into the kitchen. She'd finished washing the glasses when there was a knock at the door.

THERE'D BEEN FEW times in Silas Walker's life that he hadn't known what to do. He prided himself on making quick decisions, the kind that had saved his life more than once. But right now he felt adrift. He had no idea who had been sent to kill him—not that it would make much of a difference if he did.

He'd like to think that DeAngelo had exaggerated about just how professional this hit man was. He hoped for an amateur. Or at least someone who would give him a fighting chance by being just bumbling enough to give him a slight edge.

As he drove through the falling snow back toward

the cabin, he considered his options. He could return to New York City. Or he could take his chances at the cabin. He couldn't get TJ off his mind. Right now, the last thing he needed was his mind on anything but staying alive.

Earlier, he and TJ had come close to making love in his pickup. He'd wanted her more than he'd wanted to stay alive at that moment. To find someone like her now, now when his life was on the line, seemed too cruel a cosmic joke. It made him more determined to come out of this kickin'.

He stopped at the turnoff where he still had good cell phone coverage and called his friend and boss. "I just had a visit from my former NYPD partner. My buddies hired a hit man to take me out."

Cal swore. "How can I help?"

"I thought there might be something on the street. I'd like to know who this guy is and if he's already in Montana."

"I'll put my ear to the ground and see what I can find out. Aren't most of these old buddies still locked up?" his friend asked.

"A couple of them skated, but most of them are still behind bars, why?"

"You're talking cold-blooded murder. They knew some lowlifes on the street, but not hit men. I'd say they met someone while in the pen and contracted him. Let me see who recently got released and call you back."

Rather than hope for service at the cabin, Silas drove on into Zortman to the bar. He braved the storm and climbed out to go inside even though the last thing he wanted was alcohol. The place was packed with the approaching holiday and the weather. He found a small empty table near the door and sat down where he could see anyone who entered. When the waitress came over he ordered a beer and a burger, realizing he hadn't eaten all day.

He'd finished the burger and half of the beer when Cal called back. A boot-stompin' song was playing on the jukebox so he tossed down some money for the waitress and took the call down the hallway toward the men's restroom.

"I'm good friends with the warden at the local penitentiary," Cal said without preamble. "He says the dirty cops are in a wing by themselves fearing for their lives so they didn't have much contact with inmates. However, there was one they were seen talking to in the yard a few times. He recently got out. He's called Little Huey, a mean son of a bee who's done a lot of time for everything *but* murder. Real name's Herbert Jones. Caucasian, five foot nine, doesn't weigh a hundred and fifty pounds soaking wet, but rotten to the core."

"Might explain why he's so mean. Probably had to be at that size on the streets," Silas said. "If it's him he'll try to shoot me in the back, blindsiding me rather than come right at me."

"That would be my guess. You won't see him coming."

SHERIFF McCALL CRAWFORD read the letters twice before folding them and putting them back in their envelopes. "You say there have been others?"

TJ nodded. "A dozen or so over the past six months."

"More threatening than these?" the sheriff asked.

"Some. At first True Fan was complimentary, but

then that began to change. I didn't listen to the advice the reader was offering."

"Your fan suggested suicide?" McCall asked.

"Highly suggested it so I didn't write any more books that I would be embarrassed by," TJ said.

"And what makes you believe this individual might be in this area other than the postmark on the letter?"

TJ told her about the reams of paper that Melinda Holmes had sold after it had been stored for years in her basement. She told her about Nellie, Dot and Tommy, the people who had bought the paper that Melinda remembered. "It's a rather distinct color that would be hard to match."

The sheriff agreed. "Man or woman?"

"Sometimes I think man. Other times, woman. I have no idea."

"You had a book signing the other day. Anyone come through who made you suspicious?"

TJ laughed. "Everyone makes me suspicious. But I suspect it is someone with a connection to New York City since True Fan sent me a photo taken from the sidewalk outside my apartment. The person wanted me to know how close they were." She thought about mentioning being pushed into traffic but tended to agree with Silas that it might have been accidental.

"There are people in town with connections to New York," McCall said thoughtfully. "Others who have visited. Would be interesting to find out who might have asked one of them to take a photograph of her favorite author's apartment. Or if they did it themselves. Is that information public knowledge?"

"No, but Silas suggested that someone could have followed me from one of my book signings. I've done signings only blocks from my apartment and walked home afterward. I wasn't paying attention. Anyone could have followed me without my knowledge, waited on the street and seen me close my curtain before turning on a light on the third floor."

The sheriff nodded. "I noticed in one of your social media photos there is a pretty good view of the interior of your apartment. The curtains were open and I could see not only their design—but the building across the street. Probably wouldn't take anyone with a knowledge of the area long to find you."

TJ shivered. While she was writing about stalkers and killers and how they found their victims, there was one stalking her—and she'd probably made it easy for True Fan. She could have even given her stalker ideas on how to find her in her books.

"Mind if I take these with me?" McCall asked as she got to her feet, still holding the letters.

"Please take them," TJ said, and watched the sheriff pocket the envelopes. "You agree that it's someone here in Whitehorse?"

"It would certainly appear that way. Let me see what I can find out. If you get any more or you think of anything else, please contact me at once," the sheriff said.

"I will." TJ walked her to the door and stood on the porch hugging herself against the storm as the sheriff drove away.

As she started to turn back inside the house, she looked out at the neighborhood wondering if she was being watched at this moment by True Fan.

SILAS FINISHED HIS call and rather than walk back through the bar, decided to exit through the back. He circled around to his pickup. He'd already checked out the clientele enjoying themselves in the bar and hadn't seen anyone suspicious, let alone Little Huey. He had looked for the man who would be sitting alone. Even if Little Huey tried to blend in, he would stick out like a sore thumb in Montana.

He'd been aware of that very thing when he'd first moved here. It hadn't mattered how he'd dressed; it wasn't as if he could just put on a Stetson, jeans and boots and no one would know he wasn't from here.

That's why he knew his would-be killer would be sitting alone nursing a drink. That's if he'd already gotten this far.

Now as he walked out into the cold snow, Silas tried to think like a killer. If he was after a man like him in a state he didn't know, where would he start?

He'd fly in, rent an SUV or a pickup. A town like Whitehorse had a ten trucks to one car ratio. Then he would drive up the three hours from the airport to the western town.

Then what? If he asked a lot of questions, people would notice and say something about it. So he'd come armed with not just weapons. He'd know as much of his victim's backstory as he could get out of the men who'd hired him.

So he'd know about the cabin outside of Zortman. Silas thought of his mailbox down by the road. He couldn't have made it easier for someone to find him. Look how TJ had found him in a blizzard.

Climbing into his pickup, he started the engine and let it run. Snow had piled up on the windshield and now frozen down. His wipers were covered with ice. He let the defrost run while he thought it out.

His would-be killer would have to come prepared for the weather. That might be tougher. Unless he'd been in a Montana blizzard he would have no idea how hard it was to see—let alone get around—in the deep snow. He would have had to have purchased good boots, snow gear, a hat, goggles. Even that might not save him if he got turned around in the storm or stuck on the road.

Most people, with towns so far apart, carried food, water, blankets and matches. Silas had taken to carrying a sleeping bag behind the seat of his pickup. He never knew when he might need it. Which was also why he carried the shotgun on the rack behind his head—and the pistol under his seat.

But neither would protect him if Little Huey shot him in the back.

He saw that some of the snow had melted on the windshield, but the wipers would have to be cleaned off. He started to climb out when through the small defrosted spot on his windshield, he saw a man exit an SUV and head toward the front of the bar.

Silas felt his heart drop like a stone. His buddies hadn't sent Little Huey.

Chapter Seventeen

Kenny "Mad Dog" Harrington. Silas thought about ending this right here and now as he watched the man go into the bar. Kenny hadn't seen him with the windshield still mostly covered with snow and ice.

Silas stayed where he was for a moment and then hit his wipers. Enough snow and ice came off that he could see well enough to drive. Eventually the falling snow would cake on the wipers and he'd have a blurry mess on his windshield, but right now that was the least of his worries.

He drove out of town, watching his rearview mirror. Had Mad Dog already been out to his cabin? He would know soon enough. On the way, he tried to think. Little Huey would have been waiting in the trees to ambush him. Mad Dog was a whole other breed of violent criminal. He'd come head-on. It would take a cannon to stop the crazy bastard.

Turning on to the road into his cabin, he saw that there were two sets of tracks. Someone had gone in—and come back out. Mad Dog had been to his cabin. Which meant he would be back. Silas had no idea how much time he had to get ready for the killer.

His mind raced as he drove, all the time keeping an

eye on the rearview mirror. No Mad Dog yet. Maybe he would have a few drinks, snort some coke or take some uppers. Silas knew how hard it was to stop a junkie. A junkie with Mad Dog's size and determination would be almost impossible to stop even filled with lead shot. But Silas had no choice unless…

He was almost to the cabin when a plan began to crystallize. It would be damned risky. Crazy under other circumstances. But worth a shot, he told himself as he pulled in front of the cabin and cut the engine. He would have to move fast. He had one thing going for him: Mad Dog wasn't smart. Also it was snowing so hard, his tracks would be covered quickly.

TJ'S CONCERN FOR Silas had been growing by the hour. The thought of him alone at the cabin was driving her crazy. She kept telling herself that he was an ex-cop; he could handle himself. But she'd seen his reaction to the man.

"Can you sit still for five minutes?" her sister Chloe snapped. "This is about Silas Walker, isn't it? What has you so worked up?"

She wasn't about to tell Chloe. Her sister already thought that he was the wrong man for her. If she knew the danger he was in right now… "We left things a little…up in the air," she said truthfully.

Chloe shook her head.

"He isn't anything like Marc," TJ said in her defense.

"Nothing at all," her sister repeated sarcastically.

"What are you two arguing about?" Annabelle asked as she came into the living room with a plate of cookies. "Who wants milk?"

"Leave it for Santa," Chloe joked as she took a cookie. "We were arguing about men."

"So who's the right one for you?" Annabelle asked Chloe as she curled up in a chair and took a warm cookie.

"Justin," TJ said. "Is he still in town?" she asked Annabelle.

"Sorry, he moved away after he married some rich movie star." Annabelle almost choked on her cookie at her joke, before she said, "No, seriously, after Nici married, he was single for a long time. About five years ago, he married Margie Taylor and they moved to Bismarck, North Dakota, to farm her father's place. The marriage didn't last."

TJ raised a brow. "I'm amazed after being in town for such a short period of time how quickly you got caught up on all the local news."

Chloe groaned. "Excuse me, but we weren't talking about my lack of love life. We were talking about Silas Walker."

Her cell phone rang and she sprang to her feet. "Saved by the bell." She headed for her bedroom as she took the call from her agent.

"How are you doing?" Clara asked.

"Okay. I did the signing."

"I heard. Nice turnout?"

"Not bad."

"You made *The New York Times* Best Seller list," her agent said.

TJ knew she should be more excited about that. "That's wonderful."

"Not as high as last time, but it's early. Let's see if it stays where it is or goes even higher."

She was amazed how little any of this mattered right now.

"Have you heard from your True Fan?"

"A few letters, but I'm fine."

"Okay, but you don't sound fine. Maybe True Fan will give you a break over the holidays. When are you coming back?"

That was the question, wasn't it? "Not sure yet." She hadn't booked round-trip. Getting a flight could be difficult. But that didn't worry her either.

"Okay, I'll let you go. If you need anything…"

"I'll call. Have a wonderful holiday." She disconnected. She hadn't even asked where her book had hit on the *Times* list. Lower than last time. That was enough to know. She wasn't even tempted to check online. Normally, she watched closely the first few weeks of a release.

When she came back downstairs, Annabelle's fiancé Dawson Rogers was sitting in the living room. He got to his feet when he saw her, hugged her, wished her a Merry Christmas, then announced that he'd come to get them all for dinner out at the ranch.

"I decided to drive in for you since the visibility is poor and the roads are a little slick," he said.

She glanced out the window and realized he was downplaying how bad it was. "I hate to be a party pooper, as Grandma Frannie used to say, but I'm going to have to pass. Please give my best to your mother. I'm sure I'll see her over the holidays."

Her sisters started to put up an argument, but gave up quickly when they realized she had dug her feet in and wasn't going to change her mind. She wasn't in the mood for dinner and polite conversation. She had a terrible feeling about Silas that she couldn't shake.

As they all departed, she noticed that Annabelle had left the keys to her SUV on the hook by the door. She told herself that going out in this storm was more than risky. It might prove to be suicidal. Worse might be going to Silas's cabin when from what she could gather, there was a killer after him.

She thought about calling the sheriff. And telling her what? That Silas's former cop friends wanted to kill him? McCall couldn't do anything more than TJ could. That's when she knew that if she really wasn't going to do this, then she had not only to dress for the winter storm, but also to go armed.

"You're acting as if you think you really are Constance Ryan from one of your books," she said to herself as she went around the property getting things she thought she might need.

SILAS WORKED AS quickly as he could, given the weather. Another storm had blown in. Snow whirled around him, the cold wind biting at any exposed skin. When he'd first bought the land and begun to build on this spot, he'd thought about booby-trapping the area around it.

That was back when he'd been more worried about his former cops' plotting vengeance. He'd ditched the idea, fearful that he'd catch hikers or hunters in his traps and find himself in a lawsuit—if not worse. Also he hadn't wanted to live like that—fearing for his life every day.

Instead, he'd told himself that if they came for him, he'd deal with it then. As time went on, he'd begun to relax. Montana had that effect on him. He had liked feeling safe here, even knowing that it could change at any point.

Now as he finished loading the last booby trap, he stopped to listen. It was hard to hear anything over the wind whipping the pines and howling off the eaves of the cabin. He stared out into the storm, unable to see more than ten feet through the whirling snow.

Mad Dog would have the same problem.

Silas had worked hard since returning to the cabin. He'd known he didn't have much time. From the tracks around the cabin, he'd been able to surmise that Mad Dog had looked around, probably deciding how to come at him.

Now all he could do was wait. The question was where? Inside the cabin would make it too easy for his would-be killer. He couldn't depend on his booby traps stopping Mad Dog. All he could hope for is that one of them would delay the man long enough to give him the upper hand.

TJ STARTED THE SUV, then remembered something she'd forgotten in the house and, leaving the motor running, had run back inside.

Her heart was pounding. Common sense argued that she was doing a foolish thing. But that ache in her stomach, the feeling that Silas needed her, wouldn't let her turn back.

Inside the house, she found the flashlight she'd forgotten. It would be dark by the time she reached the cabin. She thought about texting Silas to tell him she was coming but he would just try to talk her out of it and right now she feared any reasonable argument would be all she needed to change her mind.

Back at the SUV, she was delighted to see that part of the windshield had cleared off. She used her gloved hand to take care of the rest. The snow was still falling so hard that it would cover it again if she didn't jump inside and use the wipers.

She climbed in, cranked up the heater even higher and turned on the wipers. To the steady clack, clack, clack, she shifted into Reverse and backed out.

It wasn't that far to the cabin. Once she was sure that Silas was all right… Text him, the voice in her head said. Text him. Don't make this drive in this kind of weather. Not to mention the fact that he wants you to stay away while he handles this.

She thought of Marc. She'd begged him to come home, but he was having too much fun. He loved the danger. He loved telling her about the close calls he'd had. She'd heard it in his voice. He thrived on the near misses.

Silas was different. He didn't want this. She remembered seeing both fear and dread on his face. *He knows he's mortal*, she thought. *He's strong, courageous, but only when it is demanded of him. He doesn't go looking for trouble.*

She was almost to the Zortman turnoff. She began to slow when she heard a sound in the seat behind her. Her gaze shot to the rearview mirror, her pulse taking off like a rocket as a face appeared a second before Tommy dove over the seat and dropped in beside her.

TJ screamed. The SUV swerved.

"Don't do anything stupid," he cried. "Keep driving or you're going to kill us both.

"Don't hit the brakes," he yelled as she hit the brakes.

The SUV went into another skid, but straightened as she jerked her foot from the pedal. Fortunately, there weren't any other vehicles on the road.

"What are you doing?" she demanded of him. "How long have you been back there?"

"I climbed in when you went back inside the house for your flashlight." He sounded so reasonable. "I couldn't leave things the way we did earlier."

"You were back there all this time and didn't say anything?" she demanded, furious with him.

"I wanted to see where you were going," Tommy said. "I had a pretty good idea. Nice to see that I was right."

"What do you want?"

He looked over at her in that irritatingly calm way he had about him. "Why would you drive up here in this storm? You're worried about him. You think he might have another woman in his cabin?"

"No!" She slammed her palm on the steering wheel. "I think he's in trouble. That's why you shouldn't have gotten into this vehicle. You're messing up everything."

"Wait a minute. You think this ex-cop is in trouble and you've come to save him?" Tommy reached down to look into the bag she'd brought. His gaze shifted to her at the sight of the makeshift weapons. He shook his head. "It's a good thing I came along."

"How do you figure that?" She didn't want him here, nor did she like him knowing the impulsive and no doubt foolish thing she'd done. Because seeing it through his eyes, she knew that's exactly what it had been.

The realization moved her to tears. She wiped angrily at them.

"What are you doing?" Tommy asked.

"Turning around and taking you back to town."

He stopped her with a hand on her arm. "I can help."

She looked over at him. Her skepticism must have showed.

"I have a little training for this sort of thing."

She continued to look at him.

"In the service. You do know that I was in the military, right?"

Did she know that?

"Just tell me one thing. Who wants him dead? The cops he put in prison?"

It surprised her that he knew so much about Silas. It made her wonder if his interest was before she came back to Whitehorse or if it was more about her.

"That's my guess. There's a man in town who wants him dead I'm afraid," she said.

Tommy nodded. "I wish I'd known that before we got here, but not to worry. Turn around and go into Zortman. I have a friend I can borrow a few real weapons from. Do you know how to shoot a gun?"

She shook her head as she turned around. That Tommy was taking this seriously made her feel less foolish about driving here, but just as ill-prepared.

Tommy told her where to turn once they drove into the tiny town. "Stop here." The moment she cut the engine, he grabbed the keys. "No offense," he said, and jumped out.

She waited, wondering what she'd gotten herself into. If Silas wasn't in trouble... Or even if he was, what would he think of her showing up with Tommy?

She didn't have long to consider that before he was back with two handguns and a rifle and who knew what other weapons he had under his coat. He tossed them into the SUV and then slid into the passenger side again.

"Let's go," Tommy said as he handed her the keys. "I know a back road."

She stared at him for a moment, realizing she'd never seen this Tommy, before she started the SUV.

Chapter Eighteen

Mad Dog came out of the trees and rushed the cabin like the wild man he was. He was almost to the door when he hit the first trip wire. The hatchet struck him in the thigh, falling short of the chest where it had originally been aimed.

The hit man let out a shriek of pain. The blade had left a nasty bleeding gash but did little to stop Kenny. He roared and charged the porch. The second booby trap sprung, this time working better than the first. Mad Dog was caught by his ankle and jerked off his feet.

He was hanging upside down from a tree limb five feet off the ground when Silas came around from the back of the cabin. He had only a second, not long enough to raise his rifle and shoot before Mad Dog fired.

The bullet grazed the size of his head. He rocked back, connecting with the corner of the cabin as he got off a shot. It went wild. He pumped another cartridge in and fired. Mad Dog howled with pain, swung around and let loose a barrage of bullets.

As Silas was diving behind the corner of the cabin, he caught another one; this one grazed his shoulder.

He fired another three shots, all of them hitting their mark, but Mad Dog showed no sign that any of them had done mortal damage.

Silas's head wound was losing blood fast. He could see that Mad Dog was also bleeding, but not bleeding out fast enough. Mad Dog tossed a handgun away and pulled another. Even hanging upside down, the man didn't stop.

Silas ducked back as bullets pelted the corner of the cabin. He wiped at his temple and felt the darkness wanting to close in. He felt himself getting lightheaded. He had to finish this one way or another.

Firing around the edge of the cabin, he heard his bullets hit their mark but Mad Dog's only reaction was a roar of anger. Another barrage of bullets pelted the ground and the corner of the cabin as Silas ducked back again. Even upside down, Kenny was still a damned good shot.

He heard a loud crash and the splinter of wood and knew that Mad Dog had cut the rope he'd been dangling from and had crashed down on the bottom steps of the porch. He also knew that the man would be coming for him. There was a reason Kenny had been tagged Mad Dog Harrington.

With so many bullets pumped into the man, Kenny should be down for the count. But given the drugs he'd no doubt taken, Silas was wondering if he would be able to kill him before Mad Dog killed him.

Darkness faded in and out at the side of his vision. He blinked, trying to stay on his feet but feeling the effects of his blood loss. If he didn't finish this, and soon…

TOMMY INSTRUCTED TJ to kill the engine. "This is where we get out."

She looked into the storm raging around the vehicle and could see nothing but snow and the blur of the green pines beyond it.

"You might want to stay here," he said. "I'll come back and let you know what's happening."

TJ shook her head. She'd come this far. Now she had Tom involved in this. She had begun thinking of him as Tom—not Tommy anymore. He offered her a gun. She shook her head. "I'd probably shoot myself." Instead she grabbed one of her simple-to-operate weapons, ready to brave the storm and whatever else was waiting for them.

They exited the vehicle and Tom led the way through the woods as they dropped down the mountain. He motioned for her to be as quiet as possible. She could hear nothing but the wind high in the pines and the pounding of her heart as she tried to see through the snowstorm. All her instincts were still telling her that Silas needed help. But what if she was wrong? What if it was too late?

Snow whipped in her face and down her neck. She pulled her hat lower and coat tighter around her. They hadn't gone far when she spotted part of the cabin's roof through the trees. Tom motioned for her to stay back as he moved forward toward the back of the house.

They reached the outhouse. Tom stepped around it, TJ right behind him. She saw Silas first. He lay against the side of the cabin at its corner as if he'd just decided to sit down there. She couldn't tell if he was dead or alive, but the snow was red around him. She started to run to him, but Tom held her back.

A huge man came around the corner of the cabin holding a gun. He stopped to look down at Silas. As the man raised his weapon to finish the job he'd started, Tom lifted his rifle and fired. He kept firing as he charged forward until the big man returned fire.

Tom stumbled and went down. The big man limped over to him. She could see that the man was wounded and bleeding badly, but he was still on his feet—and still about to kill both men.

As the man raised his gun, TJ did something that even her heroine Constance wouldn't have done. She charged the man.

SILAS KNEW HE must have blacked out because when he came to, he was sitting in the snow. Confused for a moment, he saw his rifle in the snow next to him and wasn't sure if it was still loaded or not. Snowflakes drifted around the corner of the cabin to melt on his face. He turned his head, not sure what he was seeing.

Mad Dog stood over someone lying in the snow a few yards from him. As the hit man raised his rifle to shoot the person, a figure came screaming out of the storm. With a jolt, Silas saw that it was TJ. She had a baseball bat in her hands.

Turning slowly as if not so steady on his feet, Mad Dog looked over at her as if he didn't believe what he was seeing. Silas felt the same way. She was so small compared to him. Mad Dog looked almost amused.

Silas tried to sit up, but felt his head swim again so he laid back. Just the act of pulling his handgun from his shoulder holster, almost made him black out again.

He finally managed to get it loose just as TJ, still charging the man, swung the bat. The sound reminded him of a pumpkin left by kids in the street being crushed by a car tire. Blood shot out of Mad Dog's mouth and flew over the snow, leaving a bright red trail. Silas fired the handgun, emptying it into the crazed man.

For too many seconds, Mad Dog didn't move. Silas could see that TJ was ready to swing the bat again if need be. As Mad Dog started to lift his weapon in her direction, Silas yelled his name and tried to get up. The darkness closed in.

TJ SAW WHAT the big man planned to do. Silas sat bleeding by the corner of the cabin. Tom was down in the snow just feet away. She looked into the big man's eyes and knew she was about to die as he raised the gun in his hand and pulled the trigger.

There was a click, then another one, followed by two more, but no gunshot. The man looked down at the gun in his hand, as confused as TJ for a moment. Her heart pounded so hard her chest ached. Her throat had gone dry. She'd looked death in the face.

She swung the bat. It caught him completely off guard. This time, his head snapped back as the bat connected with his temple. He dropped like a sack of potatoes. She stood there, the bat ready to hit him again if need be, trembling so hard she could hardly hold on to the weapon, terrified that he would get up again.

But he lay in the snow, his eyes open and blank, and after a few moments she dropped the bat and fumbled out her phone. As she did, she heard the sirens. How was that possible? She rushed to Tom. He was still breathing. Then she went to Silas. He too was breathing. He smiled up at her, then closed his eyes and dropped off into unconsciousness.

From behind her, she heard movement and swung around. Tom was on his feet. "I called the sheriff when I went in to get the guns," he said as he approached her. Then he smiled. "You really are Constance."

Chapter Nineteen

TJ had plenty of time to think about Tom's words as she waited at the hospital for word on him and Silas. She still couldn't believe what she'd done. She'd acted on instinct and it had almost gotten her killed. If the crazy big man hadn't run out of ammunition in his gun…

Her sisters spotted her and came running down the hall, only to be reprimanded by the head nurse. They pulled her into the waiting room, both talking at once. She held up her hand and realized it was still covered with blood.

Both of her sisters saw it, their eyes widening. Chloe dropped into a chair. Annabelle just stood there, mouth open for a moment.

"It's kind of a long story," TJ said. She told them what Silas had told her about the police officers sending someone to kill him and how she'd had this bad feeling that he needed her, so she'd decided to drive up to his cabin.

Chloe looked at her as if she'd lost her mind.

"I had just turned onto the road to Zortman when Tom popped up from the back of the SUV. He'd been hiding there waiting to see where I was going."

"Tom?" Chloe repeated, having noticed that she was no longer calling him Tommy.

"He told me he had experience in the military and wasn't letting me go alone after I told him why I was determined to check on Silas." Her breath caught in her throat at the memory of the crazed big man standing over Silas about to kill him when Tom starting firing at him.

"If Tom hadn't been there, Silas would be dead. You can't believe this hit man. The EMTs said when they're high on all these drugs these kind of men are nearly impossible to kill. I don't know how many times the man had been shot…" Her voice broke. "Tom was shot. He's in surgery."

"What about you?" Chloe asked as she reached over and took TJ's trembling hands in hers. "The sheriff mentioned something about a baseball bat?"

TJ nodded. Looking back it was as if it had been Constance Ryan who'd leaped out of her books to swing that bat. "He would have killed us all but he'd run out of ammunition in his gun. He pointed it right at me. The look in his eyes…" She shuddered at the memory. "I watched him pull the trigger again and again, but there was only this loud *click, click, click*."

"What did you do?" Annabelle asked, on the edge of her seat.

"I'd already hit him with the baseball bat once and it barely fazed him. But I swung it again and that time…" She shook her head. "That time he went down and he didn't get up. Tom had called the sheriff when he went into a friend's house in Zortman to get guns. I've never seen him like that."

"And Silas?" Chloe asked.

"He's going to make it. He's lost a lot of blood and has a concussion, but he's going to be fine, the doctor said. Now I'm just worried about Tom. If he hadn't come along with me…"

Her sisters got up to come over and hug her as the doctor appeared at the door to tell them that Tom Harwood had come out of surgery and was doing fine.

Silas opened his eyes. The room seemed too white. Was he dead? He blinked and brought everything into focus. A hospital room. For a moment, he couldn't remember what had happened. He touched his head. Bandaged and hurting like hell. Something shifted on his bed. He looked down to see TJ. She'd pushed her chair over so she was right next to his bed. Then she'd apparently fallen asleep with her head on the edge of her mattress.

He stared down at her, enough of last night coming back to him to make him scared for her all over again. She'd been at the cabin carrying a baseball bat? Or had he only dreamt it? He touched his bandage again and this time TJ stirred awake.

She blinked at him and brushed some stray locks from her face. "You're awake. How are you?"

"Alive. I think I have you to thank for that."

"Actually, it was more Tom Harwood. I'm sure you'll hear all about it. Right now, the doctor said you just need to rest."

"There is something about a baseball bat," he said.

"Don't concern yourself with that right now," she said, avoiding his gaze.

He wanted to throttle her. "I should turn you over my knee…"

She shifted her gaze to him and smiled. "There's time for that when you get out of here."

He laughed, even though it hurt his head. "You saved my life. I owe you."

"We can discuss that too," she said, still smiling as she took his hand and brought it to her lips.

TJ COULDN'T REMEMBER the last time she'd decorated a Christmas tree. She'd done little to her apartment during the holidays. From the back of her closet she would pull out a small fake tree that was already decorated and plug it in.

She had found herself dreaming sometimes of Christmas back in Whitehorse. Sledding and snowball fights with the boys in the neighborhood, hot chocolate back in the kitchen with their grandmother before decorating her truly ugly fake tree.

Today though, their grandmother's house smelled of pine and gingersnap cookies. Annabelle couldn't seem to quit baking. Her sisters had dragged in the tree they'd cut up in the Little Rockies and they'd stood it up. Instantly, it was like being in the woods again. Being at Silas's cabin, TJ thought.

"Is this practice for marriage?" Chloe had wanted to know when they'd found Annabelle in the kitchen early that morning baking. The house smelled of ginger and cinnamon, and TJ breathed it in as if it was her last breath. Her apartment never smelled like this, not that she baked. In the city, it was too easy to run down and pick up anything you wanted to eat.

This morning, the three of them had sat around the kitchen table reminiscing about Christmases past. They'd eaten warm cookies and milk for breakfast, laughing about some of their Grandma Frannie memories before deciding it was time to tackle the tree.

TJ had been the first one up, long before Annabelle began baking. Even before the sun was up, she'd gone to the hospital to see how Tom was doing. He was sitting up and had more color than the first time she'd seen him right after surgery.

"How are you feeling?" she'd asked.

"Not bad." He'd smiled. "You were amazing."

She'd laughed. "I could say the same about you. You saved my life and Silas's."

He'd given her an embarrassed shrug.

"Thank you, Tom."

"Tom," he'd said and grinned. "Does this mean that Tommy is behind us?"

She'd nodded.

"I'd ask if you've fallen for this ex-cop, but it's clear you have. Does this mean you'll be staying in Whitehorse? I'd like it if we could be friends. Just friends."

"Truthfully, the future is a bit blurry right now. But we can definitely be friends."

Now, she stood back for a moment to look at the beautiful tree her sisters had found and cut down all on their own in the mountains. It was a fir and smelled wonderful. The branches were thick and already naturally decorated with tiny pinecones.

"I'm so glad you saved Grandmother's ornaments," TJ said as she dug in the last of three boxes that had been full. She held up a paper angel. "Remember this one?"

The whole morning had been like that. Each ornament had a memory for one of them. That's why it was taking so long for the tree to get decorated. All those trips down memory lane had derailed them multiple times.

At the sound of someone at the door, they all turned and then shared a troubled look.

"I'll get it," TJ said and hurried to the door, expecting to see Carol from the post office standing outside. But it wasn't Carol. "Silas? I thought you weren't being released until tomorrow."

"I talked the doctor into letting me out. I had to see you."

TJ ushered him inside. He was limping badly, he had a smaller bandage on his temple, but he was alive and smiling. Her sisters said hello, asked about his health and then discreetly left them alone.

"The sheriff filled me in on everything that happened," Silas said after she'd offered him a seat. He leaned toward her. "TJ, you could have been killed!" He shook his head. "What were you thinking?"

"That you were in trouble. The feeling was so strong I couldn't ignore it."

His gaze softened. "I don't know how to thank you and at the same time, never do anything like that again."

She smiled. "I can't promise that. If I feel like you need me…"

He rose and pulled her to her feet and into his arms. "I do need you. But what am I going to do with you?"

"I bet you'll think of something," she said and he kissed her, pulling her into him as if he needed to feel her body against his as much as she did.

"Go to the Christmas dance with me?"

She laughed. "I haven't danced in years."

"Me either. But I heard there will be mistletoe." He grinned.

"Are you sure you're up to dancing? You just got out of the hospital."

His grin broadened. "Oh, I'm up for a lot more than dancing."

Just then Annabelle came careening down the stairs to race into the kitchen. Smoke billowed up from the oven. "I forgot my last batch of cookies," she cried, making them both laugh.

Silas pulled TJ to him and kissed her, backing her up against the wall. His gaze locked with hers. Then something crashed in the kitchen and they heard footfalls on the stairs and moved apart, laughing as Chloe appeared.

TJ couldn't remember being so happy. She wanted to pinch herself. When Silas looked at her like he was right now, she almost forgot about True Fan.

THE OLD GYM was rocking with the sound of loud music and the roar of voices as the Christmas dance kicked off for the season. It was a huge yearly event. Some listen to the music and watch from the bleachers as others danced. It appeared that the whole town had turned out.

The old gym had been decorated with lots of sparkly lights. It reminded TJ for a moment of the only prom she'd attended, which made her grimace. Then Silas had put his arm around her, bringing her back to the wonderful, amazing present.

Chloe hadn't wanted to come. "You both have dates."

"You're going," Annabelle had told her. "I promise you'll have fun."

Chloe had made a face but had finally agreed to come at least for a little while. TJ had seen her talking to three cowboys they had gone to school with and later dancing.

As Silas pulled her out onto the dance floor, TJ put her head on his shoulder and closed her eyes. She loved the smell of him, fresh from the shower and yet so male. He pulled her closer as they swayed with the music. She felt so safe in his arms. But it was so much more than that. That feeling of being complete, being content, being happy filled her.

She never thought she'd ever experience this. She'd been such a loner all of her life. All she'd ever wanted was to write. That had been her driving force for so long. Silas made her want more. Opening her eyes, she looked around the room and felt such a sense of community. She'd forgotten what it felt like being part of a small town.

As the song ended, she was shoved hard against Silas. She turned to see Joyce stumbling away. It appeared she'd been drinking because she turned to sneer at TJ and kept going.

"You know her?" Silas asked.

"Went to school with her."

He chuckled. "What did you do to her?"

"That's just it. Nothing that I can recall. Sometimes I think I get blamed for things I didn't do."

As they both watched Joyce weave unsteadily through the crowd and disappear out the door, TJ wondered if Joyce could be the one writing her the threatening letters. The woman seemed so angry, she could be True Fan.

"Can I get you a drink?" Silas asked as they stepped

off the dance floor. She could tell his leg was bothering him and said as much. He denied it.

"Fine," she said. "But let's sit out a few dances."

He smiled at her, cupping her cheek, his gaze locking with hers. "After this is over, I was hoping to get you alone."

Her heart hammered in her chest. Heat rushed through her, colliding at her center to make her cheeks flush. Pulse pounding at the thought of being alone with him, all she could do was nod. She watched him walk away and could tell that he was trying not to limp. She headed over to where her sisters had gathered.

"Who was that I saw you dancing with?" she asked Chloe.

"Cooper Lawson."

"Justin's best friend from high school," Annabelle said.

"Don't read anything into it, all right?"

TJ laughed. "So you didn't ask him anything about Justin?" Chloe shot her a warning look, but TJ noticed that her sister looked happier than she'd been for some time.

"Where's Dawson?" she asked Annabelle.

"Drink line."

TJ looked in that direction but she didn't see Silas. "Oh, no, there's Mrs. Brown."

Annabelle looked toward the door where Ester had just come in and now stood brushing snow from her sleeve. "I heard she had a series of ministrokes and it's changed her personality."

"Maybe she isn't as grumpy as she used to be," Chloe said, and laughed.

"Or worse," Annabelle said.

"I just remember how upset she used to get with me in her advanced English class," Chloe said. "She would go to write something on the board and actually break the chalk in her fury. She once threw the chalk at me, missed, but almost hit Kirt, who was behind me. Later I saw her in the teachers' lounge crying. I know I was terrible. But she was always singling me out, especially when she knew I hadn't been paying attention."

"No wonder she is always glaring at *me*," TJ said with a groan. "I swear she's mad at me because she has me confused with the two of you. I was the good sister." She was distracted for a moment as she noticed Joyce standing by the entrance. The woman was looking right at her before she pushed out the door. The look gave her a shiver.

SILAS INSISTED ON a last dance since it was a slow one. "I like holding you," he said as he drew her to him. "The problem is that I don't like letting you go and the holiday will be over before we know it." He drew back to look at her. "I was wondering if you'd like to come up to the cabin for a few days after Christmas. I know you'll want to be with your sisters for the holiday—"

"I would love to."

He smiled and let out a breath as if he'd been holding it. "I might even decorate the cabin."

"There's no need. The cabin is perfect just like it is."

"You really do like it," he said, sounding a little surprised.

She frowned. "Of course. I have such good memories…" Her voice trailed off. "I know it was only one night, but I felt as if—"

"As if we'd known each other a lot longer." His smile

broadened. "I felt the same way. I've never had that happen before. Dates are always so—"

"Awkward, and you promise never to go through it again," she said with a laugh.

"Exactly." His blue eyes sparkled in the twinkling Christmas lights. "But with you, it was different. With you—"

"It was nice."

He nodded and leaned down to kiss her as the song ended. They stood on the dance floor as people began to leave. He kissed her again, then stepped back as if just then realizing the dance was over. "I'll get our coats," he said, his voice sounding rough with no doubt the same desire she was feeling.

Her legs felt a little wobbly as she made her way toward the bleachers where her sisters had gathered along with Dawson and some other friends. She heard them discussing going down to one of the local bars for a nightcap or two.

She'd almost reached them when someone grabbed her arm.

"Dear, would you mind walking me out to my car," Ester Brown said as she latched on to TJ's arm with shaking bony fingers. "I think I might have overdone it."

TJ looked toward the cloakroom and the huge line. It would be a while before Silas could get their coats. Ester apparently had never taken hers off.

"It's just right outside," Ester said, as if seeing her hesitation. "It won't take you a minute." She tugged on TJ's arm and the two of them headed for the door.

TJ shot a look over her shoulder at her sisters. She

got Annabelle's attention and called, "Tell Silas I'll be right back."

"Silas," Ester said as they reached the side door. "Is he your beau now?"

Was he? She supposed so. At least until the holiday ended. "He's just a friend."

"Sure he is," the woman said under her breath. "My car's right over there." They walked through the freezing night air. Unlike Ester, who was all bundled up and in snow boots, TJ wore only a party dress and high heels.

As they stepped outside, TJ saw Joyce standing in the shadow of the building having a cigarette. She could feel her dark eyes on them as they crossed the parking lot.

"That woman doesn't like you," Ester said, following her gaze. She still had a bony-fingered grip on TJ's arm.

"I can't understand why."

Ester chuckled. "Maybe she's read one of your books."

TJ glanced over at her. Mrs. Brown had a sense of humor? She was still chuckling as they crossed the parking lot.

Fortunately, Ester didn't seem to have the breath for walking—and talking. She'd thought her former teacher might want to bend her ear about her books, but that didn't seem to be the case. While in apparently good shape other than those minor strokes she'd had, Ester appeared to be winded by the time they reached her car.

"You know, I'm not really feeling up to driving," the elderly woman said. "I hate to impose, but would you mind, dear? My house is so close by. You're welcome to bring my car back."

"I can walk. It's no problem." She was already freezing, but she couldn't say no. Ester seemed to be breathing hard. What if she was about to have another stroke? TJ definitely didn't want her driving.

"You are such a dear," Ester said as TJ helped her into the passenger side, then, taking the keys the woman handed her, climbed behind the wheel.

Ester's home was only three blocks from the old gym where the Christmas festivities had been held. Snow crystals hung in the air as she drove, the night clear and cold. All TJ could think about was getting Ester home and then returning to the old gym—and Silas. Right now, in his warm, strong arms was the only place she wanted to be.

She started to park the car in the driveway, but Mrs. Brown had already hit the garage door opener.

"I prefer to keep my car in the garage," she said as the door yawned open.

TJ pulled the car in and had barely stopped before Ester had the garage door closing behind them. She turned off the motor and started to turn to the elderly woman when she saw what Ester was holding. Her heart slammed against the walls of her ribs. "What?" The word came out on a surprised and suddenly scared breath.

"Not very succinct for a woman who makes her living writing," her former English teacher said as she waved the gun at her. Ester was still breathing hard, but she didn't look at all incapable of pulling the trigger.

"In case you're wondering, I know how to use this," the woman said. "I'm an excellent shot. Get out of the car. I don't want to shoot you in my garage, but I will if you don't do exactly as I say. It will be a first for you."

"Why are you doing this?" TJ cried.

"Because I can't let you write another one of those awful books," Ester said. "You had so much promise." She shook her head. "Parents over the years have chastised me for being too blunt." She huffed at that. "Honesty, that's what kids need. Good, old-fashioned honesty. That's what I've tried to give you. But did you listen? Of course not."

TJ stared at her as realization froze her in place. "You're True Fan."

"Not anymore," the elderly woman said. "I said I would be until the end. Well, this is the end. Now get out of the car and don't test me, Tessa Jane. If you had listened to me back when you were in my classes... Well, it's too late, isn't it. You won't be embarrassing me any further."

Ester pressed the barrel end of the gun into her back and shoved her toward the door into the house. They moved through the kitchen and into the living room. TJ's mind raced. What was Ester planning to do? She'd said that she couldn't let her write another book. Was she going to shoot her?

As they moved through the house, she looked for something she could use as a weapon. But she saw nothing that would allow her to spin around and disarm the woman before Ester shot her.

She tried to calm down, telling herself that her sisters would realize she hadn't come back. They would look for her. Silas had gone to get their coats. When he returned and they told him where she'd gone he would eventually come looking for her. If Annabelle remembered to tell him. She had to believe that he would find her—that someone would find her—as Ester jabbed her with the gun and pointed toward a door ahead.

TJ heard the word "basement" and knew that she had to do something. Surreptitiously she slipped off her bracelet. Silas had commented on it earlier. It was silver with tiny silver trees on it. She'd bought it the day before because it had reminded her of his place in the woods.

"Mrs. Brown, you can't do this," she said rather loudly to cover the sound of her dropping the bracelet next to one of the chairs in the living room. If the woman didn't find it before someone came looking for her, they might see it; they might know that she was here.

"I've already done it," Ester snapped and, reaching around her, opened the basement door.

All TJ could see was darkness. Before she could react, Ester shoved her. She fell forward, screaming as she tumbled downward.

Chapter Twenty

When Silas returned with their coats he looked around, but he didn't see TJ. Her sisters, though, were standing over by the bleachers. Most everyone had already cleared out. A few stragglers were standing around.

"We were just going uptown for an after-the-party drink," Annabelle announced when she saw him. "Do you and TJ want to come along?"

The last thing he wanted was a drink, and he was considering how to decline without hurting anyone's feelings when he asked, "Where is TJ?" He thought she might have gone to the women's room and looked in that direction.

"She just took our former English teacher out to her car," Chloe said. "It will give us a chance to talk."

He tried not to laugh as she drew him away from the others. He'd been expecting the third degree from TJ's older sister so he wasn't surprised. "I love TJ."

Chloe waved that off as if it wasn't important.

"I want to marry her. I was thinking of asking her on New Year's Eve," he said. "But I was worried that it's too early. I don't want to scare her off."

"You hardly know each other," Chloe said, sounding shocked.

"I know her. I knew her through her books before I met her."

She huffed at that. "You think she's Constance Ryan?" Chloe shook her head. "She's not. She's a prude. She's a chicken. She's—"

"She's braver than you know," he said, remembering the woman who'd saved his life. "She and Constance have a lot in common."

"She's been hurt by a dangerous man before."

He nodded. "She told me about Marc. I'm not him." He realized he was still holding their coats. He looked toward the door. "Shouldn't TJ be back by now?"

"Mrs. Brown is probably out there chastising her for some improper grammar she found in one of her books," Annabelle said, joining them. "Remember what a stickler the old bat was? All that stuff about participles and gerunds? It's a kick that Ester reads TJ's books. But then again, TJ was one of her best students. She should be proud that TJ has made a career as a writer."

Silas looked at Annabelle, hating the sudden worry that had begun roiling in his stomach. "How long have they been gone?"

"Quite a while," Chloe said, now frowning. "We'd better go save TJ from her."

Silas pulled on his coat and, taking TJ's with him, said over his shoulder, "I'll check on her. You guys go on to the bar." He headed for the door, but stopped before going out. "What kind of car does Ester drive?"

"An older model. As big as a tank," Annabelle said. "Blue, I think."

Silas told himself TJ was fine, but all his instincts told him otherwise. He thought about the boxes of old discolored paper. Mrs. Taylor had said she'd sold one of the boxes to someone from the school. A teacher? A former teacher?

Once outside he looked around. A few people were coming and going. He didn't see a big blue car. He didn't see TJ or Ester Brown. Maybe TJ had decided to drive her home. He ran back inside, asked for directions to the woman's house and then ran to his truck.

He told himself that TJ could hold her own with an elderly woman. But his fear was that she wouldn't see it coming.

TJ GASPED AS a glass of cold water was thrown in her face. She didn't know how long she'd been knocked out. After the shock of the cold water, she became aware of the pain. She hurt all over. Worse, she found herself bound with tape on the floor. In the dim overhead bulb Ester had turned on, she could see that her ankles were bound, along with her hands. Her arms and one knee were scraped and bleeding, and her head ached.

She looked up into Ester's weathered face, still feeling as if this couldn't be happening. Her former teacher had pushed her down the basement stairs. It was a wonder the fall hadn't killed her, and yet Ester didn't seem to be in the least bit concerned. *Probably because she plans to kill me anyway.*

She looked around the basement, still feeling as if her brain was fuzzy. She spotted a small desk with the old manual typewriter sitting on it. Next to it was an open ream of the discolored paper. The rest of the box sat on the floor next to the desk. She thought as her mind seemed to be clearing that this was the teacher who'd said she bought it to give to the school.

Ester had been down here secretly writing the letters? But not just those, she saw. The trash can next to the desk was filled with wadded-up paper. Even from where she was tied up TJ could see what appeared to be a stack of typed pages on the other side of the typewriter. A book Ester was working on? Why write down here and not upstairs? Why keep it a secret?

She saw that Ester was fiddling with something over by the stairs. TJ began working at the tape binding her wrists behind her. It felt a little loose. If she could get her finger under the last loop...

Ester, she realized, had been wiping TJ's blood off the basement stairs railing. The thought made her stomach drop. How long did she plan to keep her in this basement? Or was she going to kill her and maybe bury her down here? Ester knew that surely she'd never get away with this.

Unfortunately, as the woman turned toward her, TJ saw something in her eyes that told her Ester wasn't worried about getting away with it.

"Did you know that I used to do some writing myself?" Ester asked conversationally as she pulled up a chair in front of her.

TJ stared at her, wondering if she was hallucinating all of this. "I didn't know," she managed to say, since it appeared Ester was waiting for a response.

"Of course you didn't. I was talented, but I needed to make a living." At the edge of the bitterness was pain and regret. TJ had heard it before from aspiring writers. "I dreamed of writing books and being famous like you." Her voice broke.

TJ didn't know what to say. "Now that you're retired—"

Ester shook her head, the gun in her hand still pointed at TJ's heart even though she was bound to the chair. "It's too late."

She decided now wasn't the time to point out that Ester could have written in her spare time as a teacher. The woman had never married or had more to look after than a cat. Maybe she could have found time to write.

But it was clear Ester wanted to blame someone for the fact that she'd never written the books that she'd dreamed would have brought her fame and fortune.

TJ felt badly for her because there'd been a time when she'd had to work at an eight-to-five job. All she'd wanted to do was write. She remembered the frustration. She had the feeling that if she could just write full-time, she could get published. She could support herself on her writing.

It had been hard back then, but she'd gotten up early in the morning and written as much as she could before she had to go to work. Then she'd written late into the night. It hadn't been easy and what she'd written wasn't that great, but she wasn't the only writer who'd had to make a living as well as write starting out.

"That's why you're so angry with me," TJ said, realizing what this really was about. Tessa Jane had the audacity to become a writer while Ester felt she'd been kept from it by students like TJ and her sisters.

"I had talent," Ester said angrily. "I tried to share that talent as a teacher with students like you. But you never appreciated it. When I wrote you the letters, I knew you wouldn't take them seriously if they were from me. That's why I didn't sign them. I thought I could help you…" Her voice broke.

So instead of writing her own books, Ester had wanted to rewrite TJ's.

She didn't know what to say, but she knew she had to say something. Ester seemed confused, as if now that she'd taken TJ, she didn't seem to know what to do with her. Had she just wanted her to know the truth?

"Ester, I'm so glad you've finally told me that the letters were from you. I didn't realize that you were just trying to help me."

Ester stared at her. "How could you not realize it? I told you—"

"But how could I trust it not knowing who the advice was coming from?"

The older woman stared at her. "As if you would have listened even if you'd known. You were impossible in my class."

"I think that was my sister Chloe, or maybe Annabelle. Mrs. Brown—"

"You're just trying to confuse me. I need to think." Suddenly she seemed agitated. The hand holding the gun was shaking.

"You don't want to hurt me. You need to let me go. This is not the way you want to end your teaching career."

Ester huffed. "I didn't even get a gold watch. A luncheon and a pat on the head before I was replaced with a young teacher who doesn't know grammar and couldn't care less."

"I'm sorry," TJ said, not knowing what more there

was to say. Ester felt as if her life hadn't mattered. TJs heart went out to her.

"Actually, I owe you so much. I learned a lot in your class. I wouldn't have been as successful as I've been without you."

Ester cocked her head at her as if trying to judge if she was just saying this.

She rushed on, all the time still working at the tape around her wrists. "I loved the writing assignments you gave us," she said, trying to remember one of them that Ester might also recall. High school had been so long ago and yet for Ester it had been only months ago. It was no wonder the students had all run together in Ester's mind—at least TJ and her sisters.

She thought about what Annabelle had said about Ester having a series of ministrokes. That could account for some of this strange behaviour as well, especially if Ester had had them in the past six months.

"My favorite writing assignment was a character study. Do you remember that?"

"Of course I do," her former teacher snapped. "I used it in all my classes."

"I wrote mine about the hall bully. You liked it so much that you read it to all your classes. It was the first time I realized that I might actually be a writer. That I might actually succeed at it."

Ester got a faraway look in her eyes for a moment. "Rick. That was the boy's name."

TJ nodded and felt a ray of hope even though Ester was still holding the gun steady and pointed at her heart.

"I do remember that," Ester said, and looked confused again. Her gaze met TJ's. "Tessa Jane Clementine. Yes, that was one of my best." She frowned. "Your sister wrote about a character on television." She shook her head and sighed.

"You gave me hope that day. All I ever wanted to do was write."

Ester nodded, tears in her eyes. "That's all I wanted too."

"So you need to let me go. This is just a misunderstanding."

Unfortunately, the woman shook her head again. "I can't do that."

ESTER BROWN'S HOUSE was only a few blocks away. The moment Silas pulled up in front of the small white home, he saw that there were no lights on inside. Also there was no blue car parked outside. But there was a garage to one side.

Is it possible they would have gone somewhere else? He couldn't even be sure that TJ was with the older woman. But both Annabelle and Chloe had seen her leave with Ester. He told himself that TJ was so accommodating that she might have taken her by the gas station to fill up the car for her. Or even the grocery store for milk and bread.

But his gut told him that wasn't the case. Fear gripped him as he climbed out of the truck and ran up to the garage. He peered in. A big blue boat of a car filled the small space. He ran up the front steps, rang the doorbell and then hammered with his fist before trying the door. Locked.

Where the hell were they?

He tried to calm down. But he knew that something was terribly wrong.

He saw a loose brick in the planter that ran the full length of the house and jumped down to retrieve it. Back up on the porch, he threw the brick through the small window next to the door. The glass shattered. He knocked the lethal-looking shards aside and reached in to unlock the door.

AT THE SOUND of breaking glass upstairs, Ester jumped, and for a moment TJ flinched, fearing that she would accidently pull the trigger. They both froze, listening. Someone was breaking into the house.

TJ opened her mouth to scream only to have a balled-up sock stuffed down her throat. She gagged and tried to spit it out, but Ester held it in place with a strip of tape.

"Stay here," she ordered before taking the gun and starting for the stairs.

Like she was going anywhere bound like this. But she had managed to loosen the tape on her wrists. She waited until Ester's back was turned as she headed up the stairs before she worked frantically at the tape. Whoever had come to rescue her wouldn't be expecting Ester to be armed. That could be a fatal mistake.

SILAS HAD JUST gotten the door open when Ester Brown appeared. She still wore her coat as if she hadn't been home long. Her hands were in the pockets. She didn't look that surprised to see him or that upset that he'd just broken into her house.

"What do you think you're doing?" she demanded in a voice that reminded him of a teacher he'd had in middle school.

"Where's TJ?"

"TJ?" she asked, and frowned as if the name didn't ring a bell.

"Tessa Jane. She helped you out to your car, possibly drove you home?"

Ester frowned. "Well, yes, but the last I saw her was in the parking lot with Joyce Mason."

He thought of the woman who'd seemed to purposely bump into TJ at the dance. He'd seen Joyce's expression. It had been hateful. For a moment, he thought he'd broken into the wrong house. But then he saw something over by one of the chairs and recognized it at once as the bracelet TJ had been wearing at the dance tonight.

Ester had followed his gaze—and seen it as well. She stepped to the side as if to block his view, but then must have realized it was too late. Her face filled with anger.

"Ester, what have you done with TJ? TJ!" he called.

"She can't hear you."

He started to rush past her when she pulled the gun. It looked so incongruous that for a moment he thought it was a joke.

But one look in her eyes and he knew this was no joke. His heart dropped at the thought of what she could have already done.

"As I told Tessa Jane, don't try me," she said. "I know how to use it. I don't want to shoot you, but I will." Her voice was so calm he froze. He wasn't quite close enough to her to disarm her. Nor did he doubt she would shoot him. Something in her eyes.

"Where is TJ?"

"You'll see soon enough," Ester said. "Close the

door. You'll have to pay for that window you broke."
She leveled the gun at him. "Unless you're dead too."

TJ HAD HEARD Silas calling for her. Fear gripped her for
a moment as tears blurred her eyes. Ester had taken her
gun when she'd gone upstairs. The woman didn't look
like someone who would carry one—let alone use it.

And that could be Silas's fatal mistake. TJ had
certainly underestimated the woman. She wouldn't
make that mistake again, but Silas might not get a second chance. I might not either, she thought, her heart
pounding.

She heard nothing from upstairs. No gunshot. Ester
hadn't killed him. Yet. She waited a moment as if expecting to hear a gunshot and praying she wouldn't.

Then she went to work on the ropes on her wrists
again. Now she worked even more frantically, feeling
as if time was running out. As she worked, she listened.
Earlier, she'd heard someone ring the doorbell numerous times and then the loud knock; she should have
known it was Silas. Of course he would come looking
for her. The sound of breaking glass had startled her
as well as Ester.

What terrified her was that Ester seemed to know
that she would never get away with this. She didn't
seem to care. It was as if this was something she'd decided to do before she died. Ester was determined to
see this through even though it made little sense.

But TJ had seen the anger that had been apparent
in the letters. Ester was furious with herself, with the
world. And TJ had become the object of that anger.

The tape gave. She shoved it away, aware of the pain
in her shoulder. Her arms were scraped and bleeding,

her wrists aching from being taped up for so long behind her. But she barely noticed.

Tearing off the gag, she thought about calling to Silas to warn him, but realized that might put him in more jeopardy. But what if he believed Ester when she said that she wasn't here? What if he left?

Instead, she hurriedly untied her ankles and got to her feet, blood rushing into her extremities as she looked around for a weapon before she started up the stairs at a run.

SILAS COULD SEE that Ester seemed out of breath, but she still held the gun in her hand plenty steady enough to kill him. He'd complicated whatever plan she'd had and he knew it. But he could see the wheels in her head turning as she motioned for him to lead the way down the hallway.

"Where are we headed?" he asked, walking slowly. He could feel her behind him, intent on keeping that gun leveled at the middle of him.

"Don't worry about it," she snapped. "Just keep walking a little farther."

Ahead he could see a door on his left and an opening into the kitchen off to his right. The tension in the air was thick as salami. Ester was in planning mode and that was making him very nervous.

He was almost to the door on the left when he heard footfalls. It dawned on him that someone was running upstairs from the basement about the time the door was flung open. TJ came bursting through it.

Silas only had a second to decide what to do. He spun around, bringing up a foot. Ester had been distracted for only a moment, but it was long enough that she hadn't gotten a shot off. He kicked at the gun in her hand, but the woman must have had a death grip on it. All he accomplished was shoving the gun off to the side.

The report of the shot was deafening in the small hallway. Sheetrock exploded on the wall to the right, sending a cloud of chalky dust into the air. Silas rushed Ester, but not before she fired again. She was already swinging the gun back in his and TJ's direction when it went off.

He grabbed the woman's arm, heard her cry out as he wrenched it hard enough to take the gun from her bony fingers. She attacked him with her hands, flying at him. For her age, she was much stronger than he'd expected. With the gun still in his hand it was hard to wrestle her into compliance. He finally shoved her face-first into the wall and held her there as he pocketed the gun.

He realized he hadn't heard a sound out of TJ. Turning to look, at first all he saw was the open basement door. Past it was a bare foot, the high heel shoe she'd been wearing lying next to it.

"TJ?"

No answer.

He fought to move the struggling Ester along the wall so he could see TJ. Reaching the door, he slammed it closed. Sitting in the hallway staring was the woman he'd fallen in love with even before he'd met her. She had a hand over her side, blood leaking from between her fingers.

"TJ!" he cried, giving up on trying to hold Ester. He opened the basement door and put her down on the first step before closing the door and locking it. Then he dropped beside TJ and tried to call 911 at the same time as he worked to stanch the bleeding. "You're going to be all right," he kept saying, praying it would be true. "You're going to be all right."

He held her as the sound of sirens filled the air.

Chapter Twenty-One

TJ remembered little after she was shot other than being in Silas's arms and then holding his hand in the ambulance. It had all seemed like a bad dream. Or an ending to one of her books. The scream of the sirens. The blood. The feeling that it was over and yet not knowing if everyone would get out alive.

She vaguely remembered seeing her sisters as she was being wheeled down to surgery. They were both crying. Chloe telling her not to die. Annabelle saying something about Christmas. And Silas standing at the end of the hall, his face a mask of pain and worry. The rest was a blur of dreams and waking up in the middle of the night to see a nurse bending over her.

"It's all right," one nurse had said when TJ had been startled by her, making one of the machines go off. "You're safe here. It's all right."

She was in and out of consciousness so much that she hadn't known what was real and what wasn't. At one point there was a doctor standing over her. He was talking to someone. Silas. She'd felt his hand take hers and when she woke again it was still dark and she could hear Chloe arguing with the nurse outside her door.

Or maybe she'd dreamed it all. When she finally did

surface in the daylight, TJ thought all of it had been a bad dream. But she was groggy from the drugs, lying in a hospital bed, so she knew that at least getting shot had been real.

Silas sat beside her bed—just as she had sat beside his. He rose when he saw she was awake. "How are you?"

She tried to speak but her mouth was so dry. He poured her some water and helped her with the straw. The doctor came in then and told Silas he needed to check his patient.

"I'll be right outside in the hallway," Silas said, and left.

"You were lucky, young lady," the doctor said after checking her wound. "I was able to get the bullet out. No major organs were involved. It should heal nicely. Any questions?"

She shook her head because she had way too many questions. Some of her ordeal had come back, but the last part had happened so quickly...

The doctor hadn't been gone long when her sisters came in. She heard the nurse warn them that they couldn't stay long. One on each side of the bed, they looked at her with concern.

"I'm fine," she said, the words coming out in a hoarse whisper.

"That crazy old woman," Chloe said. "Who would have thought she was the one?"

"As mean as she was to me in English class?" Annabelle said. "I was scared of her."

"She was sick," TJ managed to say.

"Aren't they all," Chloe said. "She could have killed

you. Almost did. If Silas…" She seemed to catch herself. "But you're safe here and it's all behind you."

"The doctor said you might be out before Christmas," Annabelle said. "But if you aren't, we're going to hold Christmas until you are."

"She doesn't care about Christmas right now," Chloe scolded their youngest sister. "Look at her. She's drugged up and probably in pain. Are you in pain?"

TJ was, but she shook her head anyway.

"If you're in pain, you just push this button," Annabelle said. "They told you that, right?"

Maybe they had. TJ couldn't remember. She struggled to keep her eyes open.

"Okay, that's long enough," a female nurse said from the doorway, and her sisters were shooed out.

TJ closed her eyes. A few moments later she heard the door to her room open and close softly. She knew who it was before he took her hand. She kept her eyes closed, feeling herself drawn back into the darkness. With her hand in his, she slept.

THE DOCTOR FINALLY insisted Silas go home and get some sleep. He knew he needed a shower, a shave and clean clothes. He also needed sleep. He hadn't had much since the dance.

But when he closed his eyes, he kept reliving the scene at Ester Brown's house. The sound of the gunfire, seeing that one bare foot and high heel shoe lying next to it. The scene was the kind nightmares were made of.

Even when he told himself that she was going to be all right, he still couldn't sleep. He'd never been so afraid. Even Mad Dog hadn't terrified him the way Ester had because he'd looked into her eyes and he'd known that she had nothing to lose. She would have killed them both that night. As it was, she'd almost killed TJ.

"So you don't know when you're coming back to the city?" Cal had said when he'd called him.

"No. Honestly, I'm not sure I am. Things are too up in the air right now."

"Are you worried that the cops you fingered will hire someone else to come after you?" his friend had asked.

"No, Kenny 'Mad Dog' Harrington did me a favor," Silas had said with a chuckle. "He taped their conversations, including when my former NYPD partner paid him for his services. Mad Dog wasn't as stupid as they thought he was. He was worried that he'd take care of me and then they would turn on him to insure that he wouldn't rat them out some day when he got picked up for another crime. Mad Dog would have sold them out for a lesser sentence and they knew it. He was right. They would have had him killed to tie up the loose ends."

"Why haven't I heard about these tapes?" Cal asked.

"Could be because he made copies and made sure I had one. He left it for me in my cabin. I didn't see it until after he was dead. Apparently he wanted me to know who'd hired him before he killed me. So now, if they ever make a move on me, the tapes will surface."

"Tapes?"

"He made copies. Now the copies are being held in several safe places as…insurance. There's one on its way to you," Silas said. "My former…associates have been notified. They don't want any more years behind bars, or, in my ex-partner's case, he doesn't want to go straight to prison."

"So," Cal said. "This has to be about a woman."

Silas laughed. "Isn't it always? Only this woman, well, she's a keeper. That is if she'll have me."

THE NEXT TIME TJ WOKE, she found Sheriff McCall Crawford next to her bed. "The doctor said I could ask you some questions if you're up to it."

She nodded. "Ester?" The moment she saw McCall's expression she knew.

"Ester had another stroke," the sheriff said. "She didn't make it."

TJ felt a well of sadness. Yes, the woman had terrorized her and almost killed her, but she felt sorry for her too. "She felt she was never appreciated. She gave up her dream to be a teacher—at least that's the way she saw it."

The sheriff pulled out her notebook and recorder. "Why don't you tell me what happened."

She did, finishing with, "I don't remember all that much after I was shot."

McCall closed her notebook and shut off the recorder. "We found the typewriter and paper downstairs. She was definitely the person who'd been sending you the threatening letters."

TJ nodded. "There were other typewritten papers down there. Is there any chance I could have them?"

The sheriff hesitated. "It would be up to her relatives. I've been trying to find out if there are any. So far I've had no luck."

"What Ester wanted more than anything was to publish," TJ said. "I don't know if she even finished the book she was working on, but if there is any way it is publishable… I'd like to do that for her."

McCall smiled. "I'll make sure you get whatever there is."

Chapter Twenty-Two

TJ made it home for Christmas. She was still sore and had been forced to assure the doctor that she would take it easy. But Christmas Eve she was with family. Annabelle had always been like a kid in a candy store at Christmas. She'd baked and her future mother-in-law had brought over more food than they could eat in a month.

"Willie's teaching me to cook," Annabelle had said. "But we both think I have a way to go before I serve it to humans. The pigs out at the ranch love my cooking though," she added, making them laugh.

"Wait," TJ said as she remembered. "Belle, you were going to get married on Christmas!"

Her sister shook her head. "It just didn't work out. I couldn't get married without you there."

"I don't want to be the reason you didn't get married," she said. "I know how anxious you and Dawson are to tie the knot."

"It's not that big of a deal. We're thinking New Year's Day. It's just going to be a few people, nothing extravagant. Willie is insistent that it be held at the ranch and we let her take care of everything. I have the coolest mother-in-law-to-be ever." They agreed she did.

They ate, opened presents and sat around talking. TJ hated the months they'd been estranged and swore she was never going to let it happen again. "I wish Grandmother was here."

"Me too. I would love to ask her some questions," Annabelle said.

Chloe got up to adjust one of the ornaments on the tree. "It just goes to show that you never really know a person. Grandmother. Ester. Who knows what secrets everyone in this town has?"

"You're talking about how I make a living," TJ said. "If you assume everyone has a secret, well, it makes a good story."

"Have you read Ester's novel?" Chloe asked.

She nodded. "The sheriff said that no relatives have come forward. Once Ester's estate is settled, I'm going to self-publish it under her name."

"Is it any good?" Annabelle asked.

TJ hesitated, making Chloe laugh.

"You can tell us if it's awful," her sister said.

"After all, she tried to kill you," Annabelle added, and was quickly chastised by Chloe for bringing that up on Christmas Eve. "Come on, it's like the elephant in the room. If it hadn't been for Silas, TJ would be—"

"The book isn't very good, but it was Ester's first," TJ interrupted.

"And last," Chloe said.

She nodded. "I know it probably seems silly to publish it."

"No," Annabelle said. "It's sweet and more than the old bat deserves." She mugged a face at Chloe.

"So does this mean you're ready to go back to writing soon?" Chloe asked her.

"In a while."

Annabelle grinned. "She has other things on her mind."

"Speaking of Silas," Chloe said. "I hope the two of you are going to give it some time before you do anything rash."

TJ laughed. "Anything rash?"

"Leave her alone," Annabelle said. "Let her do whatever she wants to. It's her life and Silas is…"

"At the door," TJ said after there was a knock and he put his head in.

"I don't want to interrupt."

"You're not," Annabelle said, getting to her feet and motioning for Chloe to do the same. "We were just leaving." She ushered Chloe up the stairs, the two arguing all the way.

"I didn't mean to run them off," Silas said.

"It's fine. We just finished opening our presents. The two of them were starting to argue over me."

"Good thing I showed up, then," he said with a grin. "How are you?"

"Still sore, but the doctor said I am healing well."

"What about mentally? You've been through some traumatic holidays," he reminded her.

As if she needed to be reminded. "It hasn't been dull, that's for sure. But there won't be any more True Fan letters. There's no reason I can't get back to work. I have a deadline looming… What about you?"

Silas sat down across from her and took both of her hands in his. "Are you well enough that you still want to come up to the cabin with me?"

She smiled. "It's just what I need. *You're* just what I need. That and your homemade bread."

"You've got it. I'll pick you up tomorrow. Say, nine? Will your sisters be all right with it?"

"I don't need their permission."

"How about their blessing?" he asked. "I want them to like me because if I have my way…" He shrugged.

"I'll see you in the morning."

She went to the window and waved as he drove away, wondering if she would be able to sleep tonight. She was excited about returning to the cabin, but even more about spending the next few days with him up in the mountains away from everyone.

"You can come back down now," she called up the stairs to her sisters. She knew they hadn't gone far and had been listening to everything she and Silas had said. Annabelle because she was nosy. Chloe because she was worried.

They both came down the stairs, Annabelle all starry-eyed. "He wants us to like him because he's going to ask you to marry him," she said in a sing-song fashion.

"And live in that one-room cabin?" Chloe demanded.

TJ shook her head. "You're both way ahead of yourselves. Slow the roll," she said, something she hadn't said since high school. Both sisters laughed.

"Then why are your cheeks flushed?" Annabelle asked. "You're in love with him and he's crazy about you. Just make sure that you're back for my wedding on New Year's Day."

"I wouldn't miss it for anything," TJ said.

Chapter Twenty-Three

TJ almost didn't recognize Silas. He'd shaved off his beard and trimmed his hair. He no longer looked like a mountain man when he came to pick her up.

"Are you leaving?" she asked, thinking he'd done this because he had been called back to his job in New York City.

He shook his head. "I thought you might want to see what I really looked like."

She laughed, amazed that the man could be even more handsome without the full beard. She reached out and cupped his cheek, his strong jaw covered in designer stubble. "I'd take you either way."

He grinned as he stepped closer. "That's what I wanted to hear." He pulled her to him. "Ready to spend a few days at the cabin?"

TJ had never been more ready for anything. Silas drove through the snowy landscape toward the Little Rockies. It was one of those incredible winter days in Montana, not a cloud in a robin-egg blue sky, the sun making the new snow shine like fields of diamonds.

She felt herself relax. She'd come home to hide out from True Fan and make up with her sisters. Instead True Fan had been here waiting for her. The sheriff had told her that Ester used former students who'd moved away to mail the letters for her, including one now living in New York City.

"I suspect she was the one who took the photograph of your apartment," McCall had told her. "They just thought Ester was a fan."

She felt only sadness when she thought of Mrs. Brown. All those years when Ester was teaching, she had yearned to write, not realizing the only thing that had held her back was her own fear, her own misgivings about her talent.

"It is so heartbreaking," she'd said. "And yet what I told her was true. She helped me become a writer. She felt she'd wasted her life and it just wasn't true. I'm just sorry that I never thanked her for what she did do for me. Not until it was too late."

"But you got to tell her," McCall had said. "I'm thankful it ended without either of you being killed. The doctor said a lot of her behavior was due to the strokes she'd been having for some time. I don't think she realized what she was doing."

TJ looked out at the passing snowy foothills and reminded herself that it was over. She'd had a wonderful Christmas and felt closer to her sisters than she had in years. Glancing at Silas, she had to smile to herself. Annabelle was right. She was in love.

"I don't think I'm going back to New York," he said, and glanced over at her. "I don't need the job financially or emotionally or mentally. To tell you the truth I don't want to leave Montana."

She chuckled, as she'd been thinking the same thing since her return. "I love being here. And as you said, I can write anywhere. I was thinking earlier that I would let my New York apartment go. Chloe will be going back home to work and Annabelle will be getting married New Year's Day and moving in with Dawson, so the house will be empty. There's no reason I can't stay."

He grinned over at her. "I can't tell you how much I was hoping you would say that." He sounded relieved. "I want to spend as much time as I can at the cabin, but eventually either build a larger place or buy one."

"You wouldn't sell the cabin though, right?" she asked.

"No. Never. It's even more special to me since I got to share it with you."

As Silas pulled up in front of the cabin, she saw that the woodstove was going. Smoke curled up into the snow-filled pines. She couldn't wait to get inside, but he had other plans. As she started to open her pickup door, he stopped her.

"There's something I want to do first," he said, and reached into the pocket of his sheepskin coat to pull out a small jewelry box.

TJ felt her heart leap as she looked from it to his blue-eyed gaze.

"I know this is silly, but once we get into that cabin with that bed right at the center of the room, I'm going to want to make love to you. And maybe it's old-fashioned, but I want to do this right." He shifted in the seat and found a way even in the cab of the pickup to get down on one knee.

Sunlight poured through the window. Outside the fresh snow gleamed. In the warm cab of the pickup, Silas said, "Tessa Jane Clementine, will you marry me?"

She broke into a wide smile as tears filled her eyes. "Yes. Oh yes."

Silas slipped the ring on her finger. The pear-shaped diamond shone like the snow outside the windows. The ring fit perfectly.

TJ threw herself into his arms. The kiss was a promise of what was to come. Years cuddled up in that cabin. Late-night card games. Homemade baked bread. Best friends forever.

But for tonight, all TJ wanted was to spend it in this man's arms listening to the wind in the tall pines and the crackle of the fire in the woodstove. She was home.

SILAS FELT LIKE a man who'd won the lottery. He turned off the pickup engine, ran around and pulled TJ out and into his arms.

"I believe you're supposed to do this *after* we're married," she said, laughing as he carried her up the porch steps and over the threshold into the cabin.

"I feel as if our lives are starting now," he said as he put her down. He looked into her blue eyes. "Beautiful and smart and talented. How did I get so lucky?"

"You liked my books."

He laughed. "But nothing like I like their author." He kissed her, pulling her close. Outside, snow crystals danced in the air against the big sky. Inside, the woodstove crackled and popped invitingly. "How soon can we get married?"

She looked up at him in surprise. "As soon as we can find a preacher."

"I love you," he said, his gaze locked with hers. "I think I left that out earlier. Also I forgot to ask you how you feel about kids."

"I'm for them," she said. "Two, three…"

"Four, five…" He laughed, still feeling as if he needed to pinch himself. "Tell me this isn't a dream."

"If it is, I don't want to wake up," she said. "I love you, Silas Walker. I know this happened fast. But I know it's right."

"I've never been this sure of anything." He kissed her, determined to find a preacher soon and make her his wife.

* * * * *

HIDEAWAY AT
HAWK'S LANDING

RITA HERRON

To my wonderful daughter, Elizabeth, who helps real
victims of domestic violence and human trafficking
every day—you are amazing!

Love, Mom

Prologue

"Please, you have to take my baby." The young girl hid in the shadows of the awning, shivering as a dreary rain drizzled down, adding to the winter chill in the air.

Mila Manchester's heart ached for her. She knew her story. She was thirteen years old. Her name was Carina. Her mother had died in childbirth, and her father had abused her. Then he'd sold her to a man who used her as a sex slave.

Mila had helped Carina get to a shelter when she'd first escaped the monster.

Now Carina's slender pale face was shielded by a scarf, and her clothes were dark, allowing her to blend into the night.

A disguise.

She was terrified for her life.

The baby whimpered and Carina rocked her gently in her arms. "If he finds out little Isabella is his, he'll kill me and do God knows what with her."

Fear and grief laced the girl's voice. Carina was just a child herself. She should be in high school, hanging out with girlfriends, attending football games, shopping for dresses for the school dance.

Mila had wanted to report the situation to the police, but the girl had begged her not to. She'd confided about her pregnancy and claimed that the man didn't know. If he found out, he'd never let her go.

And if she went to the police, he *would* find out.

"Please, you're the only person I trust, Dr. Manchester. Promise me you'll give her a good life," the girl cried.

"Of course I will," Mila said. How could she turn her away? "But what about you? Do you want to stay with me—"

The girl shook her head, her eyes wild with panic. "No, he'll find me and kill both of us."

Mila's heart pounded. Unfortunately, she was right. "What will you do then?"

"I talked to those women at the shelter like you suggested. They know somebody who'll give me a new identity. They've even found me a place to stay so I can go to school."

So, the underground team was still operating. They'd helped so many abused women and children that she'd been afraid the police would shut them down.

Emotions clogged Mila's throat. This girl needed a chance to have a life. And so did the baby.

A noise sounded from the street, and the girl glanced over her shoulder. "They're waiting. This might be my only chance." She kissed the baby on the cheek. "I don't want you to think I'm a terrible mother—"

"I don't," Mila said. "It's obvious you love her, or you wouldn't have come here." But how could she take care of the child when she was just finishing her medical residency herself?

The girl suddenly threw herself against Mila and broke into a sob. Mila wrapped her arms around her and the infant and soothed her. "It's okay, sweetie. What happened to you isn't fair or right. You deserve to go to school and make a life for yourself."

The girl nodded against Mila, but she was crying and trembling as she turned and fled toward the waiting car.

Mila blinked back tears. She could take the child to the authorities. They'd find her a home. One with two parents.

But then she'd never know what happened to her…

And what if Carina came back one day looking for her daughter?

She looked down into the baby's sweet face. Her big eyes were watching her. Then the baby curled a tiny hand against Mila's breast.

Mila's heart melted. This baby needed her. She'd raise her as her own.

And she'd do anything to protect her.

Chapter One

Having Isabella, Izzy, had changed Dr. Mila Manchester's life forever. She would do anything for her little girl.

Time to check in.

Mila ducked into the break room at the clinic where she worked and dialed her home number. When she was working, she missed Izzy, but they FaceTimed at least three times a day. And Izzy loved her nanny, Roberta, who'd been a Godsend to them both.

Izzy smiled up at her with big brown eyes. "Mommy, Mommy, Mommy!" Izzy twirled around the kitchen, her sparkling tiara bobbing sideways on her head.

"Look, Mommy, I'm a princess today."

"You're my little princess every day," Mila said with a smile.

Izzy pointed to the sequins on the pink dress Roberta had made for her. "Look, they sparkle."

"I see. I bet when the lights are off, you'll glow in the dark." Mila's heart swelled with love.

Izzy bobbed her head up and down. "That's what Bertie says," Izzy said. She had a difficult time saying Roberta's full name and had shortened it when she'd first started talking. Roberta didn't seem to mind.

Izzy raced over to the table and picked up a silver glittery wand. "Look, Bertie made this, too, so I can do magic."

"I can't wait to get home so you can show me your magic."

"Home?" Izzy ran around in circles. "Soon?"

"Mommy will be home in a little while." Mila's heart warmed at the sight of Roberta taking a pan of cookies from the oven. "Looks like you and Bertie are making yummy treats."

Roberta smiled from the bar, where she set the hot pan, and Izzy climbed up on the stool beside her. A bowl of chocolate frosting sat on the counter, and she jammed one finger in the bowl, scooped up a glob, then licked it off.

"Yummy!" Izzy squealed.

Mila rubbed her tummy with a grin. "Save me some, sweet girl."

Suddenly the back door into the kitchen at home flew open with a bang. Roberta startled and nearly dropped the second pan of cookies as two men in black stormed in, waving guns.

Mila clutched her phone, her heart pounding. "Roberta, Izzy—"

Roberta screamed and tucked Izzy close to her to protect her as one of the men aimed the semi at her. "Please, don't hurt us!" Roberta cried.

"Izzy, run!" Mila shouted.

But it was too late. Another bear of a man snatched Izzy.

"Put me down!" Izzy kicked and pounded the man's beefy arm with her fists.

He jerked her over his shoulder, then faced Mila. "Dr. Manchester, do what they tell you or you'll never see your daughter again."

They? What was he talking about?

Mila opened her mouth to plead with them, but a loud noise in the back of the clinic made her jump. She clutched her phone with clammy fingers and spun around as the door to the break room opened.

A man wearing all black stood in the doorway, a gun in his hand. "Get rid of the other people in the clinic and do it quietly."

She glanced at her screen again to see if Izzy was okay, but the call had ended. Panic shot through her. Battling the terror gripping her, she crossed her arms and struggled for calm. "You…have my daughter? Why?"

The man in black shrugged, thick brows puckering as he approached. "Do what we tell you and she won't get hurt."

Fear choked Mila. "What do you want?"

"You're going to give our leader a new face. Then we let your family go." He jerked her by the arm and shoved her toward the door. "Now, clear the clinic. The boss wants this done quickly and quietly."

"Who is your boss?"

"No names, Doc. It's better that way."

Mila sucked in a breath. "How do I know you'll keep your word and won't hurt Izzy?"

The man's cold eyes met hers. "You'll just have to trust us."

She didn't trust them at all.

He gestured toward the door, the gun aimed at her chest.

What else could she do? They had her daughter. She had no doubt they would hurt her if she didn't cooperate.

She stepped into the hallway and spotted one of her nurses frowning from the nurses' desk. She must have heard the noise.

"Unless you want her and your other staff to die, you'd better be quiet," the man growled behind her.

Mila nodded and stepped forward to get rid of her staff and the patients in the waiting room.

BRAYDEN HAWK WAS done with women. Especially with fix-ups.

His partner at the law firm, Conrad Barker, had told him Penny Lark was gorgeous. And she had been.

But he'd failed to point out that she had a hole in her head where her brain was supposed to be. That all she cared about was her beauty regime and money and being the focal point on the society page.

Of course, Conrad didn't care. He didn't date women for their brains or because he wanted a future with them. He simply wanted sex.

Tension eased from Brayden as he drove onto Hawk's Landing, the family ranch. The wind whistled through the windows of his SUV, trees swaying slightly in the late fall breeze.

At one time he'd been like Conrad. Not that he wanted a woman for her money, but he hadn't wanted a relationship either.

The last few months with his family had changed everything.

For nearly two decades, the ranch had been a sad, lonely reminder of his missing little sister, Chrissy. And also of the fact that his father had deserted them shortly after her disappearance.

Thankfully, Chrissy's murder had finally been solved and the family had closure.

Shortly after, his oldest brother, Harrison, the sheriff of Tumbleweed, had married Honey Granger.

And a few weeks ago, the next to the oldest brother, Lucas, an FBI agent, had married Charlotte Reacher, a victim in a shooting by a human trafficking ring Lucas was investigating.

On the heels of adding two wives to the family, his mother had opened the ranch to four foster girls, Charlotte's art students, who'd needed a home after Lucas had rescued them from the trafficking ring, an operation known as Shetland.

Unfortunately, the ringleader of the operation had escaped and was in the wind.

And now Honey was pregnant, due in just a few weeks, and the house was alive again with family, with talk of babies and the next generation of Hawks.

Odd how that conversation had sparked thoughts of settling down himself.

Brayden shook off the thought, climbed from the SUV, smiling at the sound of the horses galloping on the hill. Since the girls had moved in, they'd added more livestock, and he'd hired his friend Beau Fortner as foreman of the ranch operation.

His mother swept him into a hug as he entered the foyer. "So glad you made it to dinner, Brayden."

"I wouldn't miss it, Mom." The weekly family get-togethers had meant a lot to his mother during the lean years.

Truth be told, it had meant a lot to him, too. He'd harbored guilt over his sister's disappearance and had needed his family around him.

Charlotte and Honey and the girls were laying out a spread of food that would feed half of Texas while Lucas, Harrison and brother number three, Dexter, stood by the sideboard sipping scotch. Dexter handed him a highball glass, and Brayden inhaled the rich aroma before taking a sip.

"Thanks, I needed this."

"Bad day in court?" Lucas asked.

Brayden shrugged. He would have rather been in court than on that damn date. Thank God it had only been lunch.

His mother called them to the table, and they gathered for the blessing, then the meal. Excited talk of the nursery Honey was putting together for baby Hawk floated between the women while Dexter filled them in on the new horses he'd bought.

Lucas's phone buzzed with a text, earning a chiding look from his mother. She respected all their jobs but insisted they leave their phones and business at the door.

"Sorry, Mom," Lucas murmured. "It's about the Shetland operation."

The room grew quiet. Strained.

Lucas stood and walked to the foyer away from the table. Harrison followed. Tension stretched into a pained silence as they waited to find out if the Shetland ring had struck again.

MILA SWALLOWED BACK the terror clawing at her as she approached the head nurse in the clinic.

"Rhoda, will you please tell everyone to leave? I have to get home to Izzy. She's sick."

Rhoda gave her a worried look. "Is she okay?"

Mila fought a sob, then nodded. "She will be, but she needs her mommy. Just send the patients home and we'll reschedule." She squeezed Rhoda's arm. "You go home, too. I'll close up."

Rhoda was a single mother with a ten-year-old son at home, so she didn't mind an opportunity to take off early.

Mila felt the gunman's eyes piercing her as she watched Rhoda quickly clear the waiting room, then shut down the computer at the nurses' desk.

"Anything else I can do?" Rhoda called from the front.

"No, thanks for handling that. Have a good night with Trey."

Rhoda yelled good-night, then left through the front door.

The gunman motioned for her to lock up, and Mila rushed forward, locked the doors and closed all the blinds.

Noises sounded from the back, and she walked toward the exam rooms on shaky legs.

"Why me? Why here?" Mila asked.

The gunman jabbed the gun into her back. "We know you helped some of our girls escape."

A cold chill washed over Mila. Some of their girls?

She had referred a few lost teens at the clinic to the women's shelter. And then there was Izzy's mother…

The back door burst open, and four more armed men strode in, their big bodies shielding another man in a suit who she assumed was the boss.

The guards scanned the interior, their posture braced to shoot. As they parted to search the clinic to make sure they were alone, she got her first real look at the man they called their leader.

Thick black hair framed an angular face that might be handsome if not for the scar running down the side of his cheek and the evil in his black eyes.

Eyes that looked familiar.

Pure panic robbed her breath.

She knew who he was. Arman DiSanti—the man who'd bought and used Izzy's mother as a sex slave.

Did he know that her daughter, Izzy, the little girl they'd taken hostage, was his birth child?

BRAYDEN TRIED TO keep everyone calm as they waited on Lucas to answer the phone call. When Lucas returned, he looked antsy.

"We have a lead on the ringleader of the Shetland operation. We think he's undergoing cosmetic surgery to change his identity." He pulled his keys from his pocket. "I have to go."

Harrison leaned over to give Honey a kiss. "I'm going with him."

As sheriff of Tumbleweed, Harrison had no jurisdiction outside their small town, but he'd caught the case when Charlotte had been shot during the abductions of four students from her art studio. Lucas had been called in then. At this point, the entire family and the girls were all invested in making sure the trafficking ring was shut down for good.

"Need backup?" Dexter asked.

Dex's PI skills had come in handy when they'd been tracking down the missing girls.

Lucas shook his head no. "This is an FBI operation, but thanks."

Charlotte stood and touched her husband's arm. "Where are you going?"

"A clinic outside Austin. Some plastic surgeon named Dr. Manchester is giving the bastard a new face."

Charlotte's eyes widened. "Dr. Manchester?"

Lucas nodded. "Mila Manchester. For all we know, she's on Shetland's payroll. Her volunteer work could be a cover to give her opportunities to do jobs like this."

Charlotte shook her head. "No, Lucas. Mila can't be involved."

Lucas narrowed his eyes at his wife. "You know Dr. Manchester?"

She nodded. "Her mother is the doctor who removed my port-wine birthmark when I was younger. I met Mila when I was at the clinic. And I've read about her volunteer work. She's a good person."

Lucas glanced at the table, where everyone was watching. Fear darkened the teens' faces while worry knitted his mother's brow.

"Maybe you think you know her," Lucas said. "But, Charlotte, these men could be paying her big money to help them."

Charlotte shook her head in denial again. "No, not Mila. She's kind and loving and giving just like her mother was."

Lucas looked torn but dropped a kiss on Charlotte's cheek. "I really have to go. We don't want this guy to get away."

"Be careful," Charlotte said, her voice strained. "And promise me you won't hurt Mila."

Lucas hugged her tightly. "Everything will be okay."

Brayden pushed back from the table and followed Lucas and Harrison to the door. Dexter was right behind him.

Lucas stepped outside. "I'll call you when we have him in custody."

Brayden nodded. "Just get the bastard."

Chapter Two

Mila typically took weeks to plan a facial reconstruction surgery. She had several consultations with the patient, conducted an analysis of problematic features needing correction, created computer sketches simulating what the finished product would look like and, if needed, arranged counseling with a professional. She'd also run blood work and tests to verify the patient was healthy enough for surgery.

Sometimes skin grafts were necessary. And sometimes multiple surgeries.

She had no time for any of that today.

DiSanti had shoved a photograph into her hands and told her exactly what he'd wanted. The changes would literally make him unrecognizable.

She'd been working for hours now. Her hand trembled as she finished the last of the sutures around his forehead. Perspiration trickled down the side of her face. Exhaustion bled through every cell in her body, adding to the tension thrumming through her. Her feet ached, her head throbbed and her eyes were blurring.

Twice his blood pressure had risen, and she'd thought she might lose him. That would be a blessing.

But the guards had warned her that if she made a mistake or if he died, she'd pay for it.

"How much longer?" the shortest of the guards asked.

"I'm almost finished. But he's going to need recovery time." She wanted to tell them they were fools to put him through so many alterations in one day. "I told you that I usually perform these procedures in steps."

"We don't have time for that," the bigger brute barked. "Just finish."

Images of Izzy and Roberta, terrified for their lives, taunted her with every minute she worked on the man. So far, she'd reshaped his nose, lifted his eyelids and added fillers to his cheeks and lips. His scar was history, as well.

He looked ten years younger and almost handsome.

But nothing could change the monster beneath that face.

The goons guarding the surgical room remained rigid, guns pointing at her.

Her finger slipped, and she bit her tongue as she dropped the instrument. The guard took a step forward, his glare a warning. If she lost DiSanti, she'd be dead in seconds.

She forced a breath to calm her nerves, then completed the row of stitches, dabbing away blood as she went.

Relieved to finally finish, she gestured toward her patient. "He's going to need rest, ice packs, pain medication. I'll send you with everything you need to take care of him."

A snide grin slid onto the brute's face. "We're not going to take care of him, Doc. You are."

Mila's pulse pounded. "Listen, I did everything you asked. Now let me go home to my little girl."

He shook his head. "Not happening yet. Not until he's healing and we know you didn't pull something on us."

The shorter man's phone buzzed. He stepped aside to answer, then spoke in a low hushed voice. Anger slashed his eyes as he hung up. "We have to move him now. The feds are on their way."

Mila gripped the steel counter where her instruments were spread out. If the feds were coming, maybe they'd save Izzy.

The men jumped into motion. Keeping the IV attached, they rolled the patient through the hallway and loaded him into the back of their van. The bigger guy jerked her arm. "Come on, Doc. Get whatever supplies you need to take care of him and let's go."

She dug her heels in. "Please let me go home to my daughter. I'll gather the supplies and you can take them with you."

He jammed the gun at her temple. "I said move it."

A siren wailed outside. One of the guards rushed in. "We have to go now. The damn feds are here!"

The man dragged her into the hall. She pulled back, desperate to escape. If they took her with them, they'd probably kill her and she'd never see Izzy again.

But the barrel of the gun pressed into her temple. "Fight and I'll kill you right here."

The siren wailed closer. No time to get supplies.

Mila fought a sob as the man dragged her out the back door.

Tires screeched. An SUV careened into the parking lot, a police car following. Blue lights twirled and flickered against the night sky.

Car doors opened, and a man shouted, "Stop, FBI!"

Two of the guards at the back of the van opened fire and men ducked for cover.

The man holding her arm lost his grip and fired back, then motioned for the two guards to get in the van. They jumped inside, while another one rushed into the driver's seat. The engine roared to life, then shouts and bullets flew.

The big guy shoved her toward the van, but she kicked him in the knee. He cursed and pushed her again, but she dived to the side and hit the concrete. Another round of bullets pinged around her, then the big guy jumped inside the vehicle.

Mila covered her head with her hands as the FBI fired

at the van. Through the back window the guards unleashed another round.

She screamed as a bullet pinged onto the concrete by her face.

Tires peeled rubber as the van screeched away. Footsteps and shouts followed. The officers were leaving. She raised her head to look around, but a tall, dark-haired man stood over her, his gun aimed at her.

"Dr. Manchester?"

She nodded, her body trembling.

He hauled her to her feet. "You are under arrest."

She opened her mouth to protest. But he spun her around, yanked her arms behind her and snapped handcuffs around her wrists.

KEEPING THE HAWK women calm was an impossible job.

Brayden and Dexter tried everything from encouraging the girls to talk about riding to feigning interest in the plans for Honey's nursery.

The fact that Honey didn't want to talk about the baby's room was not a good sign.

Charlotte paced in front of the fireplace in the den, where they'd gathered to have coffee and the blueberry cobbler his mother had baked. But no one was hungry and everyone wanted drinks instead of coffee. Except for Honey, of course.

"I wish they'd call," Charlotte said as she made the turn at the corner of the fireplace for the dozenth time.

"Harrison has to come back okay." Honey rubbed her growing belly. "This little boy needs his daddy."

An awkward silence followed as her comment hit too close to home. He and his brothers had needed their father, but he'd left and never contacted them again.

"I'm sorry," Honey said. "That was insensitive."

"It's the truth." Their mother patted Honey's shoulder.

"We are not keeping secrets or mincing words. Your baby needs Harrison, and he's coming back to you both."

Brayden's phone buzzed, and everyone startled.

"Is it Lucas?" Charlotte asked at the same time Honey asked if it was Harrison.

He checked the number. "Harrison." He quickly connected, then listened.

"I don't have much time. Arman DiSanti was at the clinic in Austin, but he escaped. Two FBI agents chased after him but lost him on the outskirts of Austin. We have an APB out for the van and have alerted all authorities."

The women were boring holes into him with their anxious expressions. "Are you and Lucas all right?" Brayden asked.

"Yeah," Harrison said. "Lucas arrested Dr. Manchester. We're transporting her to the field office here in Austin for questioning. Tell Honey to go home and get some rest. I'll be home later."

Brayden frowned. "I will."

As soon as he hung up, Charlotte and Honey pounced on him. "What happened? Are they okay?"

"Lucas and Harrison are safe. Unfortunately, DiSanti escaped." Brayden glanced at Honey. "Harrison said for you to go home and rest."

Honey released a sigh of relief. "I know he loves what he does, but I can't help but worry."

Charlotte put her arm around Honey. "Me, too. Every time Lucas leaves the house, I say a prayer that he'll come back in one piece."

Mrs. Hawk clapped her hands. "Well, now that we know our men are safe, how about that pie?"

Honey rubbed her stomach again. "I don't think so, but thanks."

Dexter went for it, but Charlotte declined, then cornered him by the fireplace. "What happened with Mila?"

Brayden reached for the bottle of scotch to pour another drink. He'd held off while they waited, deciding he needed to remain sober in case there was an emergency. He'd only served on the police force a year before deciding on law school, but he knew how dangerous the streets were.

"Brayden, tell me," Charlotte said, an urgency to her voice that made him step away from the bar.

"Lucas arrested her. They're taking her to the field office in Austin for questioning."

Charlotte's face crumpled. "I'm going. I have to see her."

She rushed toward the coat rack in the foyer and retrieved her purse. Brayden hurried after her.

"Wait, Charlotte, I'm sure Lucas will call you."

"He arrested her," Charlotte said. "That's not right. I know Mila wouldn't help those men."

"Apparently, she did," Brayden said. "They were at her clinic."

Charlotte shook her head vigorously. "No. There's more to the story. And she's going to need a lawyer."

Brayden threw up his hands. He didn't want to get in the middle of an argument between Charlotte and his brother.

"Please," Charlotte said. "Go with me and listen to what she has to say."

Her pleading tone sucker punched him. He didn't know Mila Manchester. But he did know Charlotte, and his brother's wife was one of the most honest, caring women he'd ever met.

He tugged his keys from his pocket. "All right, I'll drive you. But I'm not promising anything."

He explained the situation to the family and agreed to keep them posted, then escorted Charlotte to his SUV. Her shaky breathing rattled in the SUV as he drove from the ranch onto the road through town, then to the highway leading to Austin.

"Tell me about this Dr. Manchester," he said as he sped around traffic.

She retrieved a photo of the doctor on her phone. His gut pinched.

Mila Manchester was a plastic surgeon—but she could have passed for a model. Well, maybe not a model. She wasn't rail thin or gaunt-looking or covered in layers of makeup.

Instead she was naturally beautiful. Huge dark eyes stood out against ivory skin and pale pink lips. Her hair was a fiery dark color with streaks of red.

There was also a softness about her that made her look wholesome.

He jerked his eyes back to the road. He couldn't get distracted by her good looks. Sometimes the lookers were shallow beneath.

Charlotte twisted her hands together. "I was born with a port-wine birthmark," Charlotte said. "No one wanted to adopt me because of it. Dr. Manchester, Mila's mother, did volunteer work and removed it for me at no cost." She paused, her voice warbling. "I met Mila the day before the surgery. She was about my age but wasn't turned off by the way I looked. I guess she'd seen worse at her mother's practice."

"Her mother sounds like a saint."

"She was," Charlotte said. "I owe so much to her. And Mila. She visited me every day at the clinic while I healed. She told me she wanted to be like her mother."

Her story was getting to Brayden. "And you think she is?"

Charlotte nodded. "I've read about her work. She's generous and caring and volunteers with Doctors Without Borders... There's no way she'd help the Shetland operation hurt innocent girls."

Brayden hoped she was right. Lucas's wife had been

through enough without learning that her friend was a criminal.

They lapsed into silence until they reached Austin and the field office. As they parked and walked in, Charlotte grew more jittery.

Lucas was probably going to kill him for bringing her.

But her description of the doctor had piqued his curiosity.

Harrison met them at the front door.

"Lucas is about to question her," Harrison said.

"I'd like to observe," Brayden said.

Harrison frowned but glanced at Charlotte and seemed to realize Brayden was trying to appease Lucas's wife. He ushered them through security, then to a room with a viewing screen to watch the interrogation.

Brayden's gut tightened as Lucas appeared, his hand on Dr. Manchester's arm.

Damn. Even with her long dark hair tangled and escaping a haphazard ponytail, her clothes disheveled, and her face pale and exhausted-looking, she was stunning.

She heaved a weary breath and looked up at the camera in the corner as if she knew it was there. But she didn't make a move to fix her hair or put on pretenses.

Instead her big brown eyes were haunted and filled with fear.

Fear that made him want to find out the truth about what had happened today. Was she helping the Shetland operation?

Chapter Three

Mila fought tears, but they streamed down her face as Special Agent Lucas Hawk escorted her into an interrogation room.

He'd been careful to explain where they were and that she was in federal custody.

She didn't know what to do. Didn't know if Izzy and Roberta were dead or alive.

Pain mingled with panic at the thought.

If she talked, those terrible men would hurt Izzy.

Agent Hawk placed a bottle of water on the hard surface of the table in the room. She'd seen enough crime shows to know that she was being watched. That they'd record whatever she said. That they'd get her prints from the water bottle.

Sweat beaded on her upper lip and forehead, trickling into her hair.

It had been hours since she'd eaten or drunk anything. Hours since those men had broken in and threatened her. Hours since she'd started the surgeries that would enable that monster to escape.

Agent Hawk was watching her with steely eyes. Another agent named Hoover stood by the door, his arms folded, expression condescending as if he'd already tried and convicted her.

Agent Hawk's boots clicked on the hard floor as he

crossed the room. He narrowed his eyes at her as if dissecting her, then removed a key from his pocket and uncuffed her hands.

She breathed out, grateful to be free of the heavy metal on her wrists so she could reach the water. Feeling dehydrated, she turned up the bottle and drank half of it in one long gulp.

Water trickled down her chin, and she wiped at it, then glanced at her fingers. Even though she'd worn gloves during the surgery, the stench of the ugly man's blood lingered.

"Dr. Manchester," Agent Hawk began. "You know the reason you're here?"

She nodded, then looked up at him, but she couldn't stand the accusations in his eyes, so she jerked her gaze back to her hands.

He slapped a photograph of Arman DiSanti onto the table. "You performed plastic surgery on this man today at your clinic?"

She chewed her bottom lip. He knew that or he wouldn't have arrested her.

"Answer me," he said, his tone cold.

She gave a slight nod. What good would a lie do when he'd practically caught her red-handed?

"Arman DiSanti is the man we suspect to be the ringleader of a human trafficking ring called the Shetland operation," Agent Hawk said bluntly. "This group has abducted dozens of teenage girls in Texas this past year."

She willed herself not to react. But Izzy's sweet face crying as that man snatched her taunted her. Where was her little girl now?

The agent paced in front of her, then spread several pictures on the table. "These are photographs of some of the teens abducted this year. At least these are the ones we rescued." He named each girl, then pinned her with an accusatory look as if she was responsible. "No telling how many more victims he's had kidnapped."

She swallowed back bile. She knew what a horrid man he was. That was the reason she'd taken Izzy from her mother to raise her.

The agent laid another photo on the table then another and another. The first one showed a dark building with a cage in it. Blood dotted the floor.

Another photo revealed pictures of chains attached to a pole. Then another yielded a close-up of the words *Help us* crudely etched into the wall.

"He chained them to the wall and locked them in a cage like they were animals." The next picture showed two young teens dressed skimpily as they stood in front of what appeared to be a camera. Both girls were glassy-eyed, drugged.

"Then he sells them at an auction like they're cattle. That's where he got the name Shetland for his operation." He tapped DiSanti's photograph. "This is the man you helped escape the law today, Dr. Manchester." He slapped one more picture on the table, this one of a dead girl, her skeletal figure decaying.

Mila bit back a gasp.

"This is a girl named Louise Summerton. She was murdered when she tried to escape the man who bought her."

Nausea welled in Mila's stomach.

She fought it, but her stomach heaved. Panicked, she covered her mouth, her chest convulsing. The agent at the door must have realized she was going to throw up because he grabbed a trash can and shoved it in front of her.

Emotions overcame her, and tears rained down her face as she retched into the trash can.

BRAYDEN BROKE OUT in a sweat as he watched Mila Manchester purge the contents of her stomach.

"Look at her," Charlotte cried. "Something's terribly wrong, Brayden. Tell Lucas to stop this right now. I want to see Mila."

Brayden gritted his teeth. Lucas was not going to allow that, not until he was satisfied he'd gleaned all the information from Dr. Manchester that he could. He'd been trained in interrogation techniques, taught not to allow emotions to interfere when questioning a suspect.

They'd both also been taught how to read body language. And this woman's body language screamed that she was frightened.

Charlotte reached for the doorknob, but Brayden placed a hand over hers. "Let me handle it."

Tears blurred Charlotte's eyes as she looked at him. "She didn't do this, Brayden. Tell Lucas I know she's innocent."

Except she had operated on the man. Had given him a new face.

She hadn't denied that.

Charlotte lifted her chin. "Tell Lucas I hired you to represent Mila."

Oh boy. That was not going to go over well.

"I don't want to come between you and Lucas—"

"You won't," Charlotte said. "But I have to do what's right. Mila and her mother helped so many people that it's time someone helped Mila."

Maybe she was right.

He stepped into the hallway. Harrison met him, his expression concerned. "Deputy outside Austin spotted the van, but men shot at him, and he lost them. Looks like they're headed west."

"Let's pray they catch them," Charlotte said from behind him.

Harrison nodded. "Did Dr. Manchester give Lucas any information?"

Brayden shook his head. "Not yet."

"I hired Brayden to represent her," Charlotte said in a tone that brooked no argument. "Maybe she'll confide in him."

Harrison's frown was exactly the reaction Brayden expected.

"Tell Lucas I want to talk to her," he said.

"Brayden—"

"Tell him," Charlotte said. "Or I'll go in there and tell him myself."

Brayden fought a tiny smile. Lucas said the woman had spunk. He was right.

Harrison grunted, then gestured for them to follow him, and a minute later, he knocked on the interrogation room, then poked his head in. "Lucas, a word please."

Lucas joined them in the hallway, took one look at Charlotte and grimaced. "You should have stayed home."

Charlotte folded her arms. "I couldn't. I know Mila, and she's innocent."

"We have proof," Lucas said.

Brayden cleared his throat. "Let me talk to her."

"This is an interrogation, Brayden. We're trying to find the man who runs the Shetland ring." He aimed a look at Charlotte. "You do want him to be arrested, don't you? Because he will keep trafficking young girls unless we stop him."

"Of course I want him to be stopped," Charlotte said, her eyes widening in anger and surprise that Lucas would suggest she didn't.

"Maybe you should let Brayden try," Harrison said. "She might talk to him."

Lucas glared at Harrison. "If he speaks to her as her lawyer, he's bound by attorney-client privilege. What good will that do us?"

Brayden squared his shoulders. "Listen, Lucas, I'll find

out the truth. If I think she intentionally helped the Shetland group, I won't represent her." He gestured toward the closed door. "But I was watching what happened in there. She looks terrified. She couldn't fake that kind of reaction when she saw those pictures."

Lucas stood ramrod straight. "Give me another minute. If she doesn't offer anything, then you can come in."

Brayden agreed, and Lucas disappeared inside again. He and Harrison and Charlotte returned to the room to watch the interview.

Mila was wiping her face with a paper towel. She looked pale and fatigued and on the verge of a breakdown.

"Dr. Manchester," Lucas said in a quiet but firm tone. "We know you performed plastic surgery on DiSanti. We just don't know why you helped him."

Mila rubbed her forehead, a sound of anguish coming from her, but she didn't reply.

"We understand that DiSanti will need time to recover from the surgery. He's well guarded by his pit bulls. Where were they taking him?"

Mila's lower lip quivered. "I don't know."

Lucas's jaw snapped tight. "If we don't stop him, he'll kidnap more young girls." Again, Lucas tapped the photos one by one, his tone full of disgust. "More innocent girls who will be turned into sex slaves to build his empire and pad his fortune."

Mila stared at the pictures, ashen faced.

"Where were they going?" Lucas pressed.

Misery darkened Mila's expression as she looked up at Lucas. "I don't know. I honestly don't."

Lucas stared at her for a long minute, then swiped the photographs into a stack, jammed them in an envelope and stalked from the room.

Brayden rushed to meet him in the hall, Harrison and Charlotte on his heels.

"All right, see what you can do," Lucas said. "Finding DiSanti is what matters. Tell her we'll offer her a deal if she talks."

Brayden reached for the door.

"I hope to hell you're right about her," he heard Lucas tell Charlotte just before he stepped inside the room.

One look into Mila's tormented eyes, and Brayden had to remind himself to be neutral. Beautiful women lied and deceived people all the time.

He had to convince her to tell him the truth. That was all that mattered. That and putting the Shetland ring out of business.

MILA TWISTED HER hands together, fighting another wave of nausea. More than anything, she wanted to tell Agent Hawk what was happening. To beg him to send someone to her house and check on Izzy and the nanny.

But if she did and DiSanti found out, they might hurt Izzy. Her stomach knotted. What if they'd already taken her somewhere?

Panic clawed at her insides. The door opened again, and the agent appeared, but this time another man stood beside him. He was also tall, broad shouldered, muscular, with thick dark hair. They had the same dark brows.

"Dr. Manchester, this is Brayden Hawk. He's an attorney who my wife hired to represent you."

Mila stared at them in confusion. "Excuse me?"

"My wife is Charlotte Reacher," Agent Hawk said. "She's outside and insists you have counsel."

"Charlotte—is your wife?"

"Yes. We met when she was shot by DiSanti's men."

Oh God, that was right. She'd seen the news story. No wonder this man was out to get DiSanti. It was personal.

But he was allowing her an attorney...

Or was it a trap?

It struck her then—the attorney's last name was Hawk just as the agent's was. Were they related?

She scrutinized the men's features. Yes, they had to be brothers.

Agent Hawk gave his brother a dark look, then slipped from the room. Mila's head was spinning.

The lawyer cleared his throat. "Dr. Manchester, I know you've been through hell today. I'd like to hear your side of the story."

Mila's lungs squeezed for air. Was he really here to help her?

Could she trust him with the truth, or would telling him about her daughter being held hostage put Izzy in more danger?

Chapter Four

Brayden studied Mila as Lucas left the interrogation room. Some clients were desperate enough to pour out their story immediately.

Others took finessing. Especially if they were afraid.

And this woman was frightened of something…

Hoping to put her ease, he claimed the chair across from her and adopted a soothing voice. "Dr. Manchester, I agreed to talk to you because Charlotte is concerned about you." He softened his voice. "She believes in you, and Lucas and I both believe in Charlotte."

The woman's face twisted with emotions.

"Anything you tell me is confidential. But if I'm going to represent you, you need to explain your side of the story."

She rubbed her forehead, then looked down at her hands on the table.

"Please talk to me," Brayden said quietly.

Dr. Manchester sighed warily. "I already told you that I don't know where they were taking DiSanti."

Brayden let the silence stretch for a moment. "They didn't mention a city or town?"

She shook her head no. "I'm sorry. I…don't know what else to tell you."

"Stop giving me the runaround," Brayden said, his voice

firmer. "Did you know who DiSanti was when you performed plastic surgery on him?"

Fear flashed in her eyes.

"You did," he said, reading her reaction. "But you helped him anyway."

She averted her gaze, then massaged her forehead again with a shaky hand.

"We know DiSanti has amassed a fortune," he continued. "Is that the reason you did it? For the money?"

Her troubled gaze jerked to his, but she bit her lip and didn't answer.

"Charlotte insists you do good work, that you donate your time and expertise to help people, especially children, in trouble." He raised a brow. "That description doesn't fit with you giving someone like DiSanti a new identity."

Dr. Manchester pressed a fist to her mouth and breathed heavily.

"Help me out here, Doc. I'm trying to understand."

"No one can understand," Dr. Manchester said, a warble to her voice.

"I might if you talk to me." Dammit, he wanted to believe her. Wanted her to be the person Charlotte described.

"Did he donate money to the clinic in exchange for a new face?"

She shook her head, misery darkening her eyes.

Brayden's patience was wearing thin. "Did you owe him for some reason?"

She twisted her hands together.

"Come on, Dr. Manchester, I can't help you if you don't confide in me." He racked his brain for answers, then it hit him. "You're afraid. Did DiSanti and his people threaten you?"

MILA WANTED TO spill the entire story and assure him that she despised DiSanti and his men, that she'd never do anything to help them. That the entire time she'd been operating on him she'd felt sick to her stomach.

Most of all, she wanted to beg Brayden Hawk to check on her daughter.

But what if DiSanti's men were watching?

According to the news, the police suspected DiSanti had a local contact in Tumbleweed. Who knew how many he had in Austin?

Or who they were. He might have contacts right here in the FBI or at the local police department.

She didn't know whom to trust.

Brayden leaned across the table and pierced her with those blue eyes, eyes that were ice-cold. "Talk to me, Doc."

She chose her words carefully. "I wish I could tell you what you want to hear, Mr. Hawk, but I can't."

He cleared his throat. "Please call me Brayden. If you're concerned I'll tell the FBI, you don't have to be. As your attorney, I'm bound by attorney-client privilege."

Maybe she should talk to him. If he understood, he'd send someone to see if Izzy was okay. "He's your brother. How do I know this isn't a trap?"

The ice in his eyes hardened. "Because I'm a man of my word. I chose law to help people." He leaned closer. "And I think you're scared and that you need a friend right now."

Emotions swelled inside her at the compassion in his voice.

She opened her mouth to speak, but the door opened and Agent Hawk appeared again. This time another man in an expensive three-piece suit stood beside him. "Excuse me," Agent Hawk said, "but Mr. Polk, Dr. Manchester's attorney, is here."

The suited man strode into the room, his skin pale, his dark glare intimidating. "Dr. Manchester, don't say another word."

Mila bit her lip. Brayden Hawk frowned and glanced at

the man, then back at her. Suspicion took root in his expression, then a flash of anger.

She gripped the chair edge with sweaty fingers.

"Dr. Manchester, is Mr. Polk your attorney?" Brayden asked.

Mila barely stifled a scream of protest. But the attorney shot her a warning look, and she refrained.

"Is he your attorney?" Agent Hawk asked.

She blinked back tears and nodded. But she couldn't look at Brayden. She had a bad feeling that Polk worked for DiSanti and Brayden knew it.

Worse, he hadn't come to help her. He'd come to make sure she kept her mouth shut about DiSanti.

BRAYDEN STOOD, SHOULDERS RIGID, debating how to handle the situation. Dammit, he'd been making headway with Mila Manchester until this lawyer showed up. He'd seen the agony on her face when she'd looked at those pictures and was inclined to believe Charlotte.

Dr. Manchester had been coerced into performing surgery on DiSanti. That was the only explanation that fit.

And he had no doubt that Polk had been sent by DiSanti to protect DiSanti's interests.

Mila looked terrified of the man.

He didn't want to leave her alone with him, but unless she spoke up, he'd have to.

Lucas cleared his throat. "We'll let you talk."

He opened the door and gestured for Brayden to leave.

"What the hell?" Brayden said as they walked down the hall.

Lucas ushered him into a small office next to the interrogation room.

"You know that man is not her attorney," Brayden said. "DiSanti sent him to keep her from talking."

Lucas ran a hand through his hair. "Probably so. But unless she orders him to get lost or decides to answer our questions, there's not a damn thing I can do about it."

He and his brother locked stubborn gazes. "Can't you charge Polk with being an accomplice or something?"

Lucas gave him a wry look. "Not without probable cause or evidence. And we have nothing on the man."

"Then find something," Brayden said. "Because you can't leave Mila alone with him or release her in his custody. He may be the one threatening her."

Lucas narrowed his eyes. "Did she tell you that she was threatened?"

Brayden clamped his mouth closed, frustrated. She hadn't actually said so, but he'd seen the fear in her eyes.

"You know I can't divulge anything she revealed to me in private."

"Right." Their gazes locked again, both at a standstill.

Brayden pasted on his poker face. If he wanted Mila to trust him, he had to prove he was trustworthy.

And that meant honoring Mila's confidence.

If he'd only had five more minutes with her...

"What are you going to do?" Brayden asked his brother.

Lucas scowled. "Find out everything I can on Polk before tomorrow."

"What about tonight?" Brayden asked.

"She'll have to spend the night locked up," Lucas said. "Maybe some time in a cell will persuade her to talk. If not, and Polk returns tomorrow to bail her out, I'll have to release her."

"She'll face charges?"

Lucas nodded. "Yes. It may be the only leverage we have."

God, he hated to see Mila Manchester spend the night in jail. But at least she'd be safe from that bastard DiSanti.

Meanwhile, maybe Lucas could dig up some dirt on Polk, hopefully enough to arrest him and keep him away from Mila.

MILA'S STOMACH KNOTTED as Polk settled into the chair across from her. His tight lips and beady eyes made her want to scream for help from Brayden Hawk.

At least she'd thought Brayden was sincere.

She'd promised to raise Izzy and keep her safe, but she couldn't do that in prison.

"You work for him, don't you?" she asked in a low whisper.

A sinister smile crept onto his face. "What did you tell them?"

She guessed that was her answer. "Nothing."

His thick brows shot up. "Nothing? Are you sure?"

"I'm sure," she said. "I have no idea how they learned he was at my clinic."

"You didn't tip off that nurse to call them?"

"No." Anger made her voice hard. "I did exactly what I was told. Now, where is my daughter? Is she safe?"

He made a low sound in his throat. "What did you think would happen to her when you tried to escape at the clinic?"

Her stomach roiled, tears choking her. She shook her head in denial. They couldn't have hurt her little girl; she had to be all right. Izzy was her whole life.

"Where is she?" she said through gritted teeth. "Did your people hurt her? Because if you did, what's to stop me from talking to the FBI?"

"Now, now, just calm down," the man said in a condescending tone. "Your daughter is safe. At least for now."

Her breath rushed out. She hated this man and DiSanti with every fiber of her being. "She's an innocent little girl,"

Mila whispered. "Please don't harm her. She has nothing to do with this."

"But she's important to you," Polk said sharply. "So, if you want her to celebrate her next birthday, then you'll cooperate."

"I already did," Mila said. "I performed the damn surgery. DiSanti has his new face, so leave me and my daughter alone."

"You said yourself that there's a risk of infection. Your services may be needed for recovery."

He stood, and ran his hand over his diamond-chip tie clip. "I will be back tomorrow to post bond. Meanwhile, you are not to tell anyone about our conversation. And you won't discuss DiSanti."

He strode to the door and turned back to face her, his look ominous. "Remember what I said. Your daughter has lovely eyes and hair, Dr. Manchester. And a perfect face for now. Wouldn't you hate for something to happen to change that?"

Cold terror shot through Mila. She pressed her hand over her mouth to stifle a scream as he walked out and shut the door behind him.

BRAYDEN DID NOT want to leave Mila locked up in that cell tonight. For all they knew, DiSanti had someone on the inside who might try to hurt her to keep her from talking.

Unless Polk had threatened her into silence.

"Let me talk to her one more time," he said to Lucas.

"She has an attorney," Lucas said tightly. "And you seem to be forgetting that she's a criminal."

"Not if she was coerced." Brayden gritted his teeth. "For God sakes, Lucas, don't be such a hard-ass. Your own wife asked me to represent her."

"I'm doing this for my wife and those girls at Mother's

and all the other teens and women DiSanti has forced into sexual slavery."

Brayden silently counted to ten to gather his composure. On the surface, he knew Lucas was right.

But there were extenuating circumstances.

"She was on the verge of talking to me," Brayden said. "Give me one more shot."

A muscle ticked in his brother's jaw. "All right. Five minutes. But then I take her to a holding cell. Maybe a night in lockup will persuade her she needs to come clean."

Brayden agreed. What else could he do?

Lucas escorted him to the interrogation room, his expression grim. If she agreed to accept Polk's help as her attorney, his brother's hands were tied, too.

Brayden forced a neutral expression as he entered the room. The moment he saw the tears in Mila's eyes though, he nearly lost it.

Ever since he'd represented his friend, who'd been wrongly convicted, and gotten him off, he'd earned a reputation for fighting for the underdog.

Mila Manchester might be fooling him. Those tears could be due to the fact that she was upset about getting caught.

Or they were out of fear.

He crossed the room and claimed the chair across from her. "I don't think you wanted to perform plastic surgery on DiSanti, Dr. Manchester," he said quietly. "But I need you to tell me exactly what happened."

Emotions twisted her face, and she averted her gaze from his.

"If you're being coerced, I'll protect you."

She looked down at her hands, then lifted her head and her gaze met his. Emotions warred in her eyes. "Thank you, Mr. Hawk, but you can't help me. Mr. Polk is my attorney."

He studied her for a long minute, frustrated because he

sensed she wanted his help, and that she needed it. But as Lucas said, their hands were tied.

He sighed, then stood. "All right. If you change your mind, let me know."

She stared at the card he laid on the table, but didn't pick it up. He waited another minute, hoping she'd change her mind, but she dropped her gaze to her hands again and remained silent.

Those hands had given DiSanti a new face so he could escape and continue spearheading the Shetland operation.

The man was despicable and needed to be put away.

If he was wrong about Dr. Manchester, she deserved to be prosecuted, as well.

Still, his gut churned as he left the room.

Chapter Five

Frustration filled Brayden as he watched Lucas lock Mila Manchester in a holding cell.

He thought she was terrified and had been coerced. But what if her teary eyes and trembling hands were part of a well-orchestrated act?

Lessons learned in the past taunted him.

He'd been fooled once by a client's lies. A pretty young woman who'd batted innocent-looking eyes at him and cried on his shoulder. A woman who'd used him to put her boyfriend away for a crime that she'd committed. He'd gotten her off, then realized that she was a manipulative user.

Thankfully, she'd tried her scam on another guy and been caught red-handed.

But he'd walked away feeling like a fool and had vowed never to fall for another pretty face again.

Still, the sight of the doctor's forlorn expression as she sank onto that dingy narrow cot made his gut tighten.

He turned away and noticed the same frustration in Lucas's scowl.

"Charlotte's going to be angry," Lucas said between gritted teeth.

Sympathy for Lucas swelled inside him. Charlotte had gone through hell because of the Shetland ring. She'd been injured, had lost her vision for some time and had been sick with worry about her students who'd been kidnapped. She had good reason to want DiSanti locked away.

The fact that she praised the doctor's humanitarianism spoke volumes on Dr. Manchester's behalf.

"What are you going to do?" he asked Lucas.

"Check out that lawyer," Lucas said. "Maybe we can find something to charge him with and force Dr. Manchester's hand."

"I could talk to her coworkers," Brayden offered.

Lucas shrugged. "You aren't her lawyer, Brayden."

Brayden walked beside Lucas until they reached the front door of the field office. "I know. But I might find out something to explain why Dr. Manchester performed surgery on that monster. It just doesn't feel right."

Lucas nodded. "I agree. I'll get our analyst to pull up everything she can find on Polk as well as the doctor."

"There has to be something DiSanti's people used to force her to work for them," Brayden said. "Maybe an indiscretion in the past."

"Or maybe she met him when she was volunteering abroad," Lucas suggested. "Seeing the vast needs and poverty in the underprivileged areas she visited may have driven her to accept money to fund her clinic."

True. For Charlotte's sake, he hoped not.

"You want me to drive Charlotte home?" Brayden asked.

Lucas shook his head. "I need to talk to her myself."

He didn't envy that conversation between his brother and Charlotte.

Meanwhile, he'd talk to Dexter. His PI skills could be helpful in finding information on the doctor's clinic and her coworkers.

Talking to them might provide insight into what had driven Mila Manchester to break the law.

MILA DROPPED HER face into her hands, her body shaking with worry and fear. Where was Izzy now?

Was she safe? Was the nanny still with her? Or had the men taken Izzy somewhere else so the police couldn't find her in case a neighbor reported a disturbance at the house?

She rose and paced the cell, her agitation mounting. The image of that man holding a gun to Roberta and Izzy taunted her. Izzy must be terrified.

She was only three. A tiny little pip-squeak of a girl with big dark eyes and an infectious laugh and an obsession with playing dress up. She loved dolls and pretending she was a princess with a tiara and poufy skirt.

But other times she liked to dig in the earth and play with worms and kick the soccer ball in the backyard.

Izzy had started a campaign to convince Santa to bring her a puppy for Christmas and had drawn pictures and cards of how she'd take care of the animal.

She liked strawberry ice cream with sprinkles and brownies and loved mac and cheese. She enjoyed making her own pizza and PB&J sandwiches. She snacked on carrots and cheese, and apples with peanut butter and wanted b-b's, blueberries, for breakfast with her pancakes.

She hated tuna fish, turned her nose up at broccoli and stirred her green peas around on the plate to make it look like she'd eaten some when she hadn't put a single pea in her mouth.

She was stubborn and loud and messy and got up way too early on the weekends, but Mila loved her with all her heart.

Another wave of fear washed over her.

Even if she did exactly what DiSanti's men instructed her to do, how could she trust that they'd let her go and release Izzy and Roberta?

What if she did everything they demanded, but they killed her when they were finished?

What would happen to her daughter?

She heaved a breath, her lungs aching for air as panic seized her.

Would DiSanti keep her hostage or sell her into his sex slavery business when Izzy got older?

The thought made her so sick inside that she sank onto that thin mattress, then dropped her head down between her knees to keep from passing out.

BRAYDEN TRIED TO stay out of the way as Lucas explained the situation to his wife.

Charlotte burst into tears. "You can't do this, Lucas," Charlotte cried.

Lucas rubbed his wife's arms. "Brayden offered to represent her, but this other lawyer showed up, and she deferred to him."

"There has to be an explanation," Charlotte said.

"If there is, we'll get to the bottom of it." Lucas wrapped his arms around Charlotte and hugged her, the bond between them so strong it made Brayden envious. When they pulled apart, he stroked her arms. "I'll check out this lawyer tonight and see what I can find on him."

He glanced at Brayden as if he needed backup, and Brayden fought a chuckle. Nothing scared Lucas more than failing his wife.

"Hang in there, Charlotte. I'm going to look into Dr. Manchester's coworkers and see if they know what's going on," Brayden said.

She still looked worried, but she nodded and thanked him.

Brayden said good-night to them then hurried out to his SUV. As soon as he got inside, he phoned Dexter and explained the situation.

"I'll see what I can dig up on her and her staff," Dexter said.

"Let's examine her financials," Brayden said. "If DiSanti paid her, the money should show up somewhere."

"I'm on it," Dexter agreed.

"We need all the information we can gather before Dr. Manchester bonds out," Brayden said. "DiSanti has long-reaching tentacles across the world. If Polk takes her out of the country, we may never see her again."

MILA FINALLY LAY back on the cot. She doubted she could sleep, but she was so exhausted from the grueling hours of surgery and from worrying about her daughter that she practically collapsed.

She closed her eyes and said a prayer that Izzy and Roberta were all right. Roberta loved Izzy and would protect her if she could.

The fact that she might not be able to frightened her the most.

Polk said Izzy was all right. For now.

She had to do whatever they said. She'd give her life to save Izzy.

Carina's young face flashed in her mind. Izzy looked a little like Carina. She just hoped DiSanti didn't see himself in Izzy's eyes.

She hadn't heard from Carina since the night she'd fled in terror. Not that she expected to. But she couldn't help but wonder if the girl was still in school, if she'd found friends or a family where she fit in.

She'd suffered so much abuse at such a young age. That kind of trauma affected most people for life. Add to that trauma the fact that she'd given birth to a baby alone, a baby born from a rape. And then she'd given that child away.

A certain amount of guilt might plague her for that decision, although she had no reason to feel guilty. She'd made the most unselfish choice she could make—she'd put her baby's future before her own.

Had Carina been able to overcome the emotional trauma and focus on making a future for herself?

Unable to keep her eyes open any longer, she finally fell into a deep sleep, a sleep filled with nightmares that made her wrestle with the hard pillow on the cot.

She and Izzy were at the beach. The warm sunshine played off her daughter's dark hair as she raced along the edge of the water. Mila chased after her, laughing as Izzy darted back and forth to dodge the waves. She loved the water and the sand and the creatures they found on the beach.

They watched a baby crab disappear into his home underground, then used plastic sand toys to dig and create a castle complete with a moat. Izzy laughed as she spilled water from the bucket all over her feet, then squealed when Mila picked her up and swung her around.

She dropped her onto the middle of a whale-shaped float, and Izzy laughed in delight as she bounced on a wave.

The next minute, Izzy was screaming in terror. The sun and ocean had disappeared, and a big man was hauling her daughter from their house. Izzy kicked and cried, but the man clamped his hand over her mouth, then tossed her in the back of a van.

Tires squealed and the van screeched away.

A gunshot sounded and Roberta ran after the van. Then Roberta was gone, and the van lurched to a stop at a dark, rotting shed somewhere in the desert. It had to be a million degrees during the day.

And frigid at night.

Desperate to find her daughter, Mila combed the desert, walking miles and miles until she fell face-first into the scorching sand. A storm surfaced, and sand swirled and swirled around her in a blur. She couldn't see anything, not even her own hand in front of her.

Another scream. Izzy. She was lost out there in the sandstorm.

Izzy screamed again, and Mila pushed herself to her hands and knees and crawled forward.

What was that man doing to her daughter?

She had to get to her, to save her…

She was walking again, then running, her feet miring down into the sand…

Then Izzy was in front of her, her little body unmoving, the sand covering her as it raged through the air. She dug with her hands, determined to reach her, but the sand was burying her like quicksand…

Mila jerked awake, shaking and crying, her heart sinking as Izzy disappeared into the ground.

BRAYDEN LOVED THE RANCH, but he and his brothers needed privacy now they were older and busy. Still, his mother had kept rooms for them to use when they visited. Recently, Harrison and Lucas had both built houses on Hawk's Landing for them and their wives.

Brayden and Dex also had offices in Austin. Brayden had rented an apartment above his law office, and Dex found a cabin on the edge of town that he could work out of, as well.

Brayden drove to Dexter's, knowing he couldn't go home and sleep right away, not when Mila Manchester's sad eyes haunted him.

Dexter greeted him with a cold beer. His brother had a state-of-the-art computer system and was a whiz at finding information on the web. Sometimes he sensed Dex didn't follow the rules; then again, that was the reason he'd formed his own PI agency instead of studying law.

If he crossed the line, Brayden didn't want to know

about it. So far, Lucas and Harrison hadn't asked questions either. As sheriff, Harrison had called on Dex for help a few times. He was pretty sure Lucas had, too, but Lucas only shared information on a need-to-know basis.

Dex pressed a few keys and a photo of the doctor appeared along with articles on her services for the needy.

"Look at this," Dexter said. "Judging from the awards and press Mila's received, she's everything Charlotte claims. She practically runs her own clinic and offers services pro bono for families and children in need across the country. Hell, across the world."

Brayden's gaze skated over the dozens of articles featuring Mila's mother, Andrea Manchester, and had to agree.

"She's following in her mother's footsteps." Dexter accessed a photo of Mila's mother receiving an award for her Doctors Without Borders work, just a month before she died in a shooting in Syria. She'd operated on a child born with a cleft lip and cleft palate.

"I suppose it's possible Mila became overwhelmed with the vast needs for her services and the cost, and accepted money to fund her efforts," Dexter said. "But my preliminary search into her financials didn't reveal anything suspicious. No large deposits, no offshore accounts." He gestured toward another computer screen showing the doctor's personal account then her business one. "There is an account for donations that has around a hundred grand, but it'll take me time to sort through the ins and outs of the accounting to see if all the donations are legit."

Brayden scrubbed a hand through his hair. Money could be one motive. But if she'd been coerced, there had to be a more personal reason. "How about family? Does she have parents, a sister or brother, anyone DiSanti might threaten to persuade her to do his dirty work?"

"Wait, this is interesting," Dexter said.

Brayden shifted, hoping his brother had found something he could use to convince Mila to talk to him. "What?"

"Mila was adopted, although both of her adopted parents have passed," Dexter said.

Brayden's brows shot up. "Any information on her birth mother or father?"

Dexter shook his head. "Apparently she was abandoned as a baby. No father listed anywhere. Dr. Andrea Manchester was working at the hospital where Mila was brought in by paramedics. She and her husband adopted Mila."

No wonder she'd wanted to follow in her mother's footsteps. "Anything on her coworkers?" Brayden asked.

Dexter shrugged. "The head nurse is a single mother named Rhoda Zimmerman. She has a ten-year-old son and lives close to the clinic." He pressed the print button and the printer spit out a page of names and addresses. "Other employees include a receptionist, another nurse and a PA."

Brayden checked his watch. "It's too late tonight to talk to any of them. But first thing in the morning, I'll get on it."

"It'll go faster if we divide the list," Dexter said.

"Thanks. I'll take the head nurse and receptionist."

"I'll talk to the others," Dexter offered.

Brayden noticed a file on the desk, one that was labeled Hawk. His gaze shot to his brother, then he gestured to the folder. "What's that about?"

A wary look flashed across Dexter's chiseled face. "A file on Chrissy."

"You were looking for her all these years?"

Dex nodded. "Glad that's settled."

Unfortunately, she was dead and had been since the day she'd gone missing.

"Guess I can put it away now." His brother swept the folder off the desk and jammed it in the drawer.

Something about how quickly he removed it made

Brayden suspicious. He could usually read his brother like a book. But not tonight.

Was Dexter keeping something from him?

Chapter Six

Mila jerked awake from her nightmares, only to realize that she was living a real one. The dark holding cell was cold and lonely, and felt a million miles away from home and her daughter.

She scrubbed her hands over her eyes, wiping away more tears. If she lost Izzy, she didn't know what she'd do.

Desperate to keep it together until she was released so she could find her little girl, she forced her mind to her work.

Images of former patients, children in need, their parents' gratitude that she'd given their children a chance at a normal life, flashed behind her eyes.

Little Robin, who had a scar from falling through a window. Seven-year-old Jacob, who'd suffered abuse at his father's hands—she'd repaired the damage to his face, although the sweet child would never get his vision back in his left eye. Tiny Sariana, whose leg had been burned in a car accident. Baby Jane Doe, who'd been left for dead in the woods and mauled by an animal.

There were other children and families out there who needed her.

But what would they think if they discovered she'd given a new face to a human trafficker so he could escape?

Carina had borne the brunt of his vile ways and barely survived.

Mila had promised to protect her baby. But she'd failed. Now Izzy was in the hands of DiSanti's goons.

We know you helped some of our girls escape, the man who'd stormed into her clinic had said.

She massaged her temple. How had they known?

Had they been watching her? Or had they found one of the girls and forced her to talk? Maybe they'd discovered the underground ring that helped women and children and young girls escape abuse to find a better life?

Carina… Was she safe and still in hiding?

BRAYDEN WOKE TO a text from Lucas.

Bond hearing for Dr. Manchester at ten a.m.

Brayden took a quick shower, then dressed and rushed out the door. He drove to the diner near him, picked up coffee and a sausage biscuit and wolfed it down as he drove to Dr. Manchester's clinic.

It normally opened at eight. A truck and sedan sat in the parking lot while an SUV was parked in the employees' spaces. He spotted a woman in a nurse's uniform at the door with an older lady holding a baby, and a thirtyish woman with a teenage boy.

"I'm sorry, folks, the clinic is closed today," the nurse said. "Dr. Manchester won't be here."

Brayden hung back and listened to see if she offered more of an explanation, but she didn't.

"We'll reschedule as soon as I hear from her and we adjust our schedule," the nurse said.

The lady with the baby walked toward the sedan and the young woman and teenager climbed in the truck.

Brayden approached the nurse cautiously. If she conspired to help DiSanti, he'd find out.

The nurse tacked a sign saying Closed on the door, then retrieved keys from her purse.

"Excuse me, Miss Zimmerman?"

Her eyes widened as she looked up at him. "Yes?"

"The clinic is closed?"

"I'm afraid so. Did you have an appointment?"

He shook his head.

"Well, if you need one, call back and leave your number, and I'll have our receptionist get back to you."

"I'm not a patient," Brayden said, then introduced himself. "Were you aware that Dr. Manchester was operating on a wanted fugitive yesterday?"

The nurse gasped. "What? My God, that's not true."

"I'm afraid it is." He showed her a picture of DiSanti. "Do you recognize this man?"

The shock on her face looked real. "No, I've never seen him before. Why do you think he was here?"

"We know he was here," Brayden said matter-of-factly. "You didn't see him yesterday?"

She shook her head again. "No. And Dr. Manchester would never help a criminal, not if she knew who he was. She devotes her time to families, especially children in need."

That was what everyone kept saying. "Maybe so, but she performed plastic surgery on him yesterday."

A tense second passed. She shifted, then glanced through the glass door with a frown.

"What is it? You know something," Brayden said. "Were you working yesterday?"

She nodded, her eyes dark with emotions he couldn't quite define. "I did, but Dr. Manchester asked me to clear out the waiting room and sent me home early. She said her daughter was sick and she had to leave."

"Her daughter?" That was news. "I didn't realize she had a child."

The nurse's expression softened. "Her name is Izzy. Dr. Manchester loves that little girl like crazy."

"Did she seem upset? Afraid?"

Her brows furrowed. "Come to think of it, she did seem a little nervous. But I just thought she was worried about Izzy."

"Did you see anyone else here? Maybe a car in the parking lot?"

"I didn't really notice. There could have been, but I went out the front door." Worry deepened the grooves beside her eyes. "Why? What's going on?"

"That's what I'm trying to figure out," Brayden said. "Sometime after you left work yesterday, the FBI discovered that DiSanti and his crew were here and stormed the clinic. Dr. Manchester was arrested."

The nurse gasped. "My God, that's not right. Mila would never—"

"She did," Brayden said. "And I think she may have been threatened."

The woman clamped her lips together, then fumbled with her keys. "I don't know what to tell you. But I'm going to stop by her house and check on Izzy and the nanny."

Brayden put his hand over hers. "No, I'll go by and check on them."

If something was wrong with Izzy and the nanny, it might be dangerous.

He thanked her, then phoned Dexter on his way to Dr. Manchester's home address and filled him in. "She has a daughter?" Dex asked.

"According to her head nurse, yes. Her name is Izzy."

"That's odd. There's no mention of them in anything I've found about her. Dr. Manchester must keep her personal life very private."

He supposed he could understand that. But usually when people kept secrets, it meant they were hiding something.

"How about the father?" Dex asked.

"No information on him." Brayden pulled a hand down his chin. "Is there any record that she was married?"

"I didn't see one," Dexter said.

So who was the little girl's father? "I'm driving by her house to check on the child and nanny, then to the field office for the bond hearing."

"I put calls in to the other staff. I'll let you know if they add anything to what you've already learned."

Brayden thanked him, then hung up and veered toward Dr. Manchester's. She lived in a small neighborhood outside Austin, only a few miles from her clinic. He searched the area as he drove down the street. Most of the houses were renovated ranches and bungalows. Judging from the children's bikes and toys dotting the yards, the neighborhood catered to young families. The yards were well kept, complete with fall decorations and pumpkins.

Dr. Manchester lived in a Craftsman-style house at the end of the street. Her backyard jutted up to woods and land that hadn't yet been developed, offering privacy and a yard for her little girl to run and play.

Everything he'd learned indicated the plastic surgeon was the admirable selfless doctor that Charlotte, the nurse and the media claimed her to be.

But an uneasy feeling tightened his gut as he parked and walked up the drive. A dark green sedan sat in front of the garage, the only car on the premises. The nanny's? Two drives down, he noted a white van, and across the street, a black Cadillac. The neighbors'?

He scanned the front porch and windows, but the blinds were closed, and he couldn't see inside. Nothing outside looked amiss though. And he didn't hear signs that anyone was inside.

He punched the doorbell and tapped his foot as he waited. A minute later, he raised his fist and knocked.

If he didn't get an answer, he was going to check around back, see if a window was open.

Footsteps shuffled inside. A low voice. Female?

He straightened and pasted on a smile as the door opened slightly. A short dark-haired woman peered up at him.

"My name is Brayden Hawk," he said. "I'm a friend of Dr. Manchester's. I stopped by the clinic to see her, but the clinic was closed today so I thought she might be home."

"I'm afraid not. I can tell her you stopped by." She started to close the door, but Brayden caught it with his hand.

He studied her, searching for signs she was upset or being coerced somehow. "The nurse said the doctor's daughter was sick. Is she here?"

The woman's eyes darted to the side, then she nodded. "In bed. She has a fever and needs rest."

He slipped his business card into her hand. "I hope it's nothing serious," he said. "If you need anything, call me."

The woman's hand trembled as she jammed the business card in her apron pocket. "I'm sorry, mister. I need to go take care of her." She didn't wait for a response. She closed the door in his face.

MILA CLASPED HER clammy hands together as she waited on the lawyer to meet her before the bond hearing. Nerves bunched in her stomach, and her head throbbed from lack of sleep.

The door to the interrogation room creaked open, and Agent Hawk appeared with Polk. His beady eyes skated over her, threatening and unrelenting.

"You have five minutes," Agent Hawk said as he glanced between the two of them. "Then it's time to see the judge."

"It will only take two," Polk said curtly.

Fluorescent light accentuated Polk's bald head. He strode toward her, then claimed the chair across from her, his lips set in a firm line.

"Is my daughter all right?" Mila asked in a low whisper.

His thick brows furrowed together into a unibrow. "As I said last night, she will be fine as long as you do what you're told."

"Please let me go home to her," Mila said. "I promise not to tell anyone about yesterday. I've been here all night and I didn't say a word."

"*He* had a rough night," Polk said, as if he didn't intend to incriminate himself by saying DiSanti's name aloud. "Once he's on his way to recovery, you and your daughter will be reunited."

Would she?

"How do I know you're not lying, that you haven't killed her already?" Mila crossed her arms. "I want proof that she's safe, then I'll do whatever you ask."

Polk cursed, then pulled his phone from his pocket and accessed a photograph.

Tears choked Mila's throat. It was Izzy in her room. The princess clock on her nightstand read 7:00 a.m. Not long ago.

Izzy was curled in bed with her pink blanket and baby doll clutched to her. Relief made her shoulders sag.

But it was temporary.

DiSanti never left a witness behind. When he'd kidnapped Charlotte's students, his men had shot Charlotte and left her for dead. In fact, she was the only one who'd survived his men.

If they killed her when she finished nursing that monster DiSanti back to health, who would raise Izzy?

Chapter Seven

Brayden shared what he'd learned about Mila with Lucas as they entered the courtroom.

"I know you want her to be innocent and so does Charlotte," Lucas said. "And you may be right. But unless she speaks up, my hands are tied."

The court was called to order, and Lucas quieted as the judge heard two cases, then Mila's. It took no time for the judge to grant Mila's bond. Her lawyer kept a tight rein on her, his shoulder touching hers as they exited as if he needed to keep her close. Mila remained silent, her hands knotted, body tense.

Her gaze darted to him as they reached the exit, then Polk took her arm and ushered her outside.

He and Lucas followed. Brayden's instincts screamed that something was wrong. Maybe the nanny had lied to him. Maybe Izzy wasn't sick, but someone had been in that house holding a gun on her.

Or maybe his imagination was running wild. Maybe he was projecting what he wanted to be true onto Mila.

Just like he had that other woman. He'd long ago stopped using her name. It hurt too much to think what a fool he'd been.

He wouldn't repeat the same mistake.

Morning sunshine shimmered off the autumn leaves as they exited the courtroom and made their way to the steps of the courthouse. Traffic slogged by, pedestrians hurrying to breakfast and work, mingling with joggers and parents pushing baby strollers toward the park two blocks down.

Mila tucked her head down as they descended the steps. Polk kept a firm grip on Mila's arm as if he expected her to bolt any minute, then steered her to the right toward a parking deck.

"I don't like this," Brayden said.

"Neither do I." Lucas quickened his pace to keep Polk and Mila in sight, and Brayden kept up with him. Polk guided her across the busy street to the exit of the parking deck, one hand shoved in his jacket pocket.

"He's got a gun." Lucas darted across the street and Brayden sprinted after him, dodging a car that screeched to a stop barely an inch from him.

Brayden threw up a hand to apologize, but didn't have time to slow down. Mila's terrified gaze met his, making his heart skip a beat.

"Wait!" Lucas shouted as he jogged toward Polk.

A dark van pulled up beside Polk, and Polk reached for the door handle.

"Stop, Polk!" Lucas shouted again.

But the man spun around and fired at Lucas and then at Brayden. Brayden jumped to the side, and Lucas ducked behind the rear of the van for cover. People shouted and ran from the street into the parking deck, coffee shop and neighboring stores. Police officers raced from the courthouse outside to clear the streets and provide backup.

Lucas inched toward the side of the van and fired at Polk. He retaliated by opening fire and shoving Mila toward the van. She screamed, stumbling, then hit the ground on her hands and knees. A short robust beefy guy jumped out and grabbed Mila.

"Let her go!" Brayden yelled.

Lucas fired at Polk again, and this time Lucas's bullet

hit home. The man's body bounced back as the bullet penetrated his chest, then he staggered and collapsed.

Brayden lunged toward Mila, but the gunman put his weapon to her head. Brayden froze, cold terror slamming into him.

Lucas took cover at the edge of the vehicle, his gaze meeting Brayden's. Brayden understood. He needed to create a distraction.

Brayden held up his hands in surrender mode. "You don't want to do this, buddy. Just release the doctor and no one else gets hurt."

The beefy guy shook his head and pushed Mila toward the van. She cried out and slammed into the side of it.

Lucas inched up behind the bastard and jammed his gun in the man's back. "Drop it. Now."

The bastard spun around and swung the butt of his gun toward Lucas's head. Lucas knocked it away and they fought, then Lucas sent the man's gun sailing to the ground.

Mila darted away from the gunman and hit the ground a few feet away.

The brute lurched for his weapon, but Lucas fired, hitting the man in the chest. Blood spattered, and Lucas ran to him, then kicked the man's gun into the shrubs.

Brayden rushed forward and helped Mila to stand. She was shaken and in shock, her body trembling as she collapsed against him.

Shouts erupted, and several officers jogged toward them to assist. Lucas gestured for Brayden to get Mila inside. He wrapped his arm around her waist and coaxed her back into the building in case more of DiSanti's men were watching.

An officer rushed toward Brayden as they stood in the corner in the lobby of the courthouse. "Anyone hurt? Do you need medical assistance?"

Brayden tilted Mila's face up so he could examine her

for injuries, then checked her clothes for blood. "Are you hurt, Mila?"

She shook her head, but terror glazed her eyes.

He pulled her to him and rubbed her back to calm her. "Can you take us to a room where we can wait on Agent Hawk?"

"Of course." The officer led the way down a hall then into a conference room. "I'll get some water."

Brayden nodded and ushered Mila toward one of the sofas. Instead of sitting down though, she grabbed his shirt lapel. "You shouldn't have stopped him! You should have let me go!" Tears rained down her face as she pummeled him with her fists. "Why didn't you just let me handle the situation!"

"Because you were in trouble."

"I had it under control," Mila cried.

Brayden swallowed hard, then forced a calm voice. "Lucas saw Polk's gun. He thought he was going to hurt you."

"You don't know what you've done! You…you should have let me go." Sobs racked her body, and he grabbed her fists in his hands and held them to his chest.

"I know you're upset, but Polk was dangerous and so was the bastard who shot at us."

She gave up the fight and sagged against him. He held her and stroked her back to calm her, murmuring low, soothing words. "It's going to be all right, Mila. I promise."

She pushed back, anger slashing her eyes as she swiped at her tears. "No, it's not. You don't know what you're talking about."

"Then tell me what's going on," he said. "Why you helped DiSanti. Why you were willing to go with a man who had a gun on you and probably planned to kill you when he got you away from here."

A helpless look passed through her eyes, followed by fear and panic. She choked on another cry, then dropped her head into her hands. Her body shook again, more tears falling.

His mind raced with possible scenarios, all of which he didn't like. All of which involved her safety or the safety of her nanny and little girl.

He gave her a few minutes, took the water from the officer who entered with it, then slipped the bottle into her hand.

"Drink."

She twisted the cap, but her hand shook so badly that she dropped it onto the floor. She guzzled half the bottle before setting it on the coffee table in front of her.

When she looked at him, despair seemed to weigh her down.

He retrieved the bottle cap and set it on the table. "Mila, I know that you're a good person. Charlotte vouched for you. I saw your awards, and talked to your head nurse. I also know you have a daughter."

Her lower lip quivered.

"If you tell me the truth, I promise I'll help you."

Her face crumpled. "They have her," she said in a haunted whisper. "They threatened her if I didn't cooperate." Anger hardened her voice. "Do you know what that means?"

Her tormented gaze met his, his heart pounding.

"It means you and your brother may have just gotten my little girl killed."

MILA BIT HER tongue to keep from confiding the rest of the story to Brayden. But she'd sworn not to reveal the truth about Izzy's mother or father to anyone, and she had to keep that promise.

It was the only way to keep her daughter safe.

Her heart pounded. She shouldn't have told him anything.

But what choice did she have?

"Let me get Lucas. He can help—"

"No." Mila grabbed his hand. "You said whatever I told you was in confidence."

Brayden shifted, his eyes assessing her. "If you want me as your lawyer, yes, everything you tell me is private."

She released a sigh of relief. "Agent Hawk is your brother though—"

"It doesn't matter," Brayden said. "We're both professionals. He knew when he allowed me to talk to you that I was bound by attorney-client privilege."

Mila wanted to believe him. She had to trust someone. And he seemed sincere.

Brayden made a low sound in his throat. "I'm sorry, Mila. I can call you that, can't I?"

"I don't care what you call me," Mila said. "All I want is to protect my daughter."

Brayden nodded. "Yesterday when I talked to you, I suspected something was off, so I did some digging. You didn't ask to call anyone when Lucas brought you in, which was odd. When I learned about your daughter, I put two and two together. I went by this morning to check out the situation."

Mila's eyes widened. "You saw Izzy? Was she okay?"

Brayden hesitated, agitating her more. "Your nanny answered the door. She said Izzy was in bed, that she was sick."

Mila's pulse clamored. "But you didn't see her?"

He shook his head. "I'm afraid not."

Panic shot through her, and she dug her fingers into his arm. "I have to go to her, see her myself. Get her somewhere safe. Once DiSanti realizes what happened here today, he may hurt her or take her away somewhere."

Brayden nodded. "I'll tell Lucas where we're going."

"No," Mila cried. "Don't you understand? He has men at my house. They have guns. Izzy and I were FaceTiming when they burst in and took them hostage."

Brayden laid his hand over Mila's. The human contact felt comforting and made her want to spill everything to him.

But she still had secrets.

Secrets she had to keep to protect her daughter.

BRAYDEN STUDIED MILA AGAIN, grateful she'd finally come clean. Lucas wouldn't like being left in the dark, but Brayden was bound by confidentiality, and he would honor it.

Although it wouldn't take Lucas long to figure out what was going on himself.

He'd researched the lawyer. No doubt the FBI already knew about Mila's daughter.

"Please," Mila said. "I need to see Izzy."

He nodded. "You said men with guns were at the house. It's too dangerous."

Mila shot up. "I don't care. She's my little girl, and she needs me. Now either take me to her or let me go."

"We'll talk to my brother. He can send the FBI there to rescue her," Brayden said.

She shook her head no. "They will kill her if they see the feds or cops."

He touched her arm again. The simple contact sent a tingle of awareness through him that he had no business feeling for a client, much less a woman in trouble with both the law and a man liked DiSanti.

But being with her was the only way to keep her from

getting hurt and to learn the truth—if she was lying about her part in DiSanti's surgery.

"I'll drive you, but you have to do as I say and stay in the car."

Her gaze locked with his for a brief moment. Finally she gave a nod.

"I'll tell Lucas that you're upset, that I'm taking you someplace so we can talk."

Indecision warred in her eyes. "That's *all* you'll tell him."

He nodded. "Trust me, Mila."

But the odd flicker in her eyes indicated she didn't trust anyone. He wondered who'd betrayed her to the point that she felt that way.

None of your business. A little girl's life might be at stake.

He had to do his job.

Then again, she might be right not to trust. DiSanti had people everywhere. For all he knew, the man might own a judge or a cop or even a fed…

He stepped to the door to text Lucas. His brother was in the hall, so he joined him.

"How is she?" Lucas asked.

"Shaken, but physically all right."

"We need to convince her to tell us more about DiSanti."

"I'm aware of that." Brayden held up a hand. "But she's scared, Lucas."

Lucas studied him for a minute, obviously torn. "You think she was coerced, don't you?"

Brayden pasted on his poker face but gave a slight nod. "Release her into my custody, Lucas. I'll get to the bottom of this. I promise."

Lucas studied him for a long moment. "All right. But don't let her get away. She's the only lead we have to DiSanti."

He knew that. But he was more worried about her child at the moment than catching that monster.

"I'll have an officer escort you to your SUV just in case DiSanti's men are watching."

He thanked his brother, then ducked back into the room and told Mila he'd cleared her to leave with him. When they exited the room, the officer was waiting.

Brayden took Mila's arm, and the guard led them from the building to his SUV.

"I've got it from here." Brayden dismissed the guard, and the officer turned and walked back to the courthouse.

"I'm going to call my brother Dexter to meet us at the house. He's a PI."

"You promised that everything I told you was confidential," Mila said sharply.

He angled himself toward her. "It is. But I'm not a fool either, Mila. These men are dangerous. We'd be crazy to go there without backup."

"But he might call Lucas—"

Brayden shook his head. "Dex likes to bend the rules. We've kept more than one secret from Lucas and Harrison, our other brother who's sheriff of Tumbleweed." He paused, teeth gritted. "If there's anyone I trust to keep your secret, it's Dex."

A world of doubt settled in her eyes, but she must have realized that she didn't have much choice and agreed. He phoned Dexter, gave him a brief rundown and asked him to meet them at Mila's.

When he hung up, he started the engine and pulled into traffic. A strained silence stretched between him and Mila as he drove.

When he neared her house, he slowed and waited five doors down until Dex arrived. Dex climbed in the back seat and he made quick introductions, then coasted past Mila's to survey the house and property.

Everything looked quiet.

Mila leaned forward, searching, worry creating lines around her mouth and eyes.

He turned around at the end of the street, then drove two houses away and parked on the street. "Stay here, Mila. Dex and I will find Izzy."

She clenched her hands in terror, but gave a small nod. Dammit, he hated to leave her in the car. What if DiSanti's men were watching and grabbed her from his SUV?

"You can stay with her," Dex said as if he read Brayden's mind.

"No," Mila said. "I'll be fine. It'll take both of you to handle the men."

"She's right," Brayden said. "If you can stave off the goons, I'll get Izzy and the nanny outside."

He gave Mila's hand a quick squeeze, retrieved his gun from the dash, then he and Dexter slipped from the car. They ducked through the neighbor's backyard, staying low in the bushes as they approached the back deck of Mila's house.

He just prayed the nanny and Izzy were still here, and that he and Dexter could get them out alive.

Chapter Eight

Brayden gestured for Dexter to check the door while he crept up to the back window and peered inside.

The interior was dark and quiet. He didn't see movement, but the hallway offered no view of the interior of the rooms.

He mouthed to Dex that he didn't see anyone, then kept watch while his brother climbed the steps to the deck and inched to the door. His brother held his gun at the ready and checked the doorknob.

The door screeched open.

Not a good sign.

Dex gave him a questioning look, and Brayden joined him, careful not to make a sound.

Senses alert, Brayden peered inside the doorway.

No movement. Except for the low hum of the furnace, no sound came from the house.

Odd.

The hair on the back of Brayden's neck prickled. This morning the nanny had been here.

Now the place felt eerily empty.

Did DiSanti's men know about the shooting at the courthouse? Had they left with Mila's daughter?

That wouldn't be good…

Dexter headed down the hall, and Brayden followed close behind. They passed a powder room, which was empty, then two bedrooms, one on the left, the other on the right.

Brayden eased into the one on the right. Mila's. A white iron bed covered in a blue quilt, dresser on one wall, a walk-in closet and bath.

Dex checked the second room, then shook his head indicating no one was there.

Antsy now, Brayden pushed a third bedroom door open. Dex stood behind him, gun aimed in case an ambush awaited.

A white four-poster twin bed was covered in a pink comforter with dozens of dolls and stuffed animals scattered on top of it. A dollhouse occupied one corner. Blocks, puzzles and a pink baseball glove filled bookshelves in the corner. A pink sneaker lay on the floor by the dollhouse, missing its mate, and a board game looked as if someone had stepped on it. Maybe one of the goons?

The bed was unmade, closet empty. The space beneath the bed held a box of clothing and several mismatched socks.

No little girl here.

His gut tightened, and he gestured to Dexter that they should check the living room. Although at this point, it appeared no one was here.

Dex led the way with his gun still drawn. An acrid odor hit Brayden as they neared the front of the house.

The kitchen-living room was to the right, dining area on the left. A lamp had been overturned, magazines strewn on the floor, a muddy boot print left on the entrance by the door.

No sign of the nanny or Mila's little girl.

An open carton of milk sat on the kitchen counter along with boxes of crackers and snacks. The farmhouse table held a pizza box along with an empty Scotch bottle that he had a feeling didn't belong to Mila.

Dexter crossed to the table in search of something that might indicate where the men would have taken the nanny and Izzy.

The rancid odor hit Brayden again, and Brayden's stomach jolted as he spotted drops of blood spatter on the floor in the kitchen.

Nerves raw, he eased toward it, then peered around the edge of the counter, praying that Izzy wasn't there.

And that the blood didn't belong to her.

MILA WAS BARELY holding on by a thread.

She stared at the clock on the dashboard, counting the minutes and seconds as Brayden and his brother Dexter went inside her house. If they could just find Izzy and get her away from DiSanti's men, she would tell the Hawks everything.

Her mind turned to the Hawk men. Brayden looked to be in his early thirties, was tall and broad shouldered with dark, neatly trimmed hair. He was handsome and imposing in his suit like the lawyer he purported to be. But those boots hinted at a tough cowboy beneath. And so did those intense eyes.

How many Hawk men were there? Were they all in law enforcement?

What did it matter? As long as he saved her little girl. Then she could worry about the charges against her. She hoped, if she gave the police a description of DiSanti, maybe worked with a sketch artist to convey an image of his new features, they'd drop the charges. She had been forced to perform surgery at gunpoint, her family threatened.

She twisted sideways and scanned the street. She'd bought this house because it was in a safe neighborhood. Because other families and children lived and played here. Because it was close to her work, and she could run home for lunch. Sometimes Roberta strolled Izzy up to the clinic when it was sunny, and they had a picnic in the park across the street.

The streets were empty now. Kids at school. Parents at work. Except for the mother of twins in the first house on the block. She'd seen the four-year-old little boys playing on the swing set in the backyard and kicking a ball around.

Mila raked a hand through her tangled hair, well aware she needed a shower and some clean clothes. She reeked of sweat and blood from the grueling hours on her feet the day before.

When this was over, maybe she should take some time off. Stay at home with Izzy for a while.

Sometimes she missed dinner and got home too late to put Izzy to bed. Moments like giggling at the table and reading bedtime stories meant everything to her now, even more than her work, which had driven her for as long as she could remember.

Although she'd wanted to be a role model for Izzy the way her adopted mother had been for her. Her adopted parents had taken Mila in when she was just a newborn, because her birth mother had abandoned her in a junkyard. A body shop repair mechanic searching for a fender to replace the one he'd torn off when he'd crashed into a tree had found her in a beat-up old Chevy.

If he hadn't been looking for that fender that day, she might not have survived.

She'd wanted to give Izzy the same chance at life that her adopted mother had given her.

She closed her eyes, bowed her head and prayed that she got the chance.

BLOOD SPATTERED THE FLOOR, cabinets and wall of the kitchen.

Brayden cursed, although relief mixed with anger. Not Izzy, thank God. But the nanny was dead.

She lay on her back, one arm above her head, the other on her chest, fingers curled toward her palms. She'd probably thrown her hands up to protect her face.

It hadn't done any good. The bullet pierced her forehead between her eyes. Blood dotted her forehead and cheeks and pooled beneath her head.

A professional hit.

Of course it would be. DiSanti's goons had no qualms about killing a woman. Rape and trafficking, selling young girls into sex slavery, was just a business to them. Bastards.

"No one's here," Dexter called from the living room.

Brayden motioned for him to come over. "They killed the nanny," Brayden said. "Gunshot to the head."

"Damn." Dexter appeared behind him, but both held back. The last thing they wanted was to contaminate the crime scene.

"It's my fault," Brayden said. "My visit this morning probably spooked them. So they killed her and took off with Izzy."

"Don't blame yourself. They probably got word of what happened at the courthouse," Dex said.

Brayden's lungs squeezed for air. "Mila warned me that if I interfered, I'd get her daughter killed."

Dex laid a hand on Brayden's back. "Stop. Izzy may still be all right. We'll find her."

But would they find her in time?

They needed a description of DiSanti's new face. But he understood Mila's reluctance. She was terrified and had a right to be. DiSanti was ruthless.

Other than the people who worked for him, Mila was the only person in the world who would recognize him now.

Which meant he would come after her. And he'd kill her so she wouldn't identify him.

"Call Lucas and get a crime scene unit out here," Brayden said. "I'm going to check on Mila."

He hurried to the door, then jogged outside toward his SUV.

MILA STARTLED WHEN Brayden knocked on the window. His grim expression as he unlocked the door and slid into the driver's seat made her stomach knot.

"What? Oh God, not Izzy—"

"No, Izzy wasn't there."

She bit back a cry, but was afraid to ask more.

"They must have taken off with her," he said softly. "She's the only leverage they have to keep you quiet, and they know it, Mila."

Mila nodded, grasping onto hope that his logic was right.

Brayden cleared his throat. "I'm sorry to have to tell you this, Mila. But they killed your nanny."

She shook her head in denial. Roberta was gone.

Poor, sweet Roberta. Izzy loved her like a second mother. She'd met the woman at a shelter because she was homeless. Twenty years in an abusive relationship had taken its toll. Her husband, the man who'd beaten her too many times to count, had been shot by a gang member. His death meant her escape, except that she'd been destitute and determined not to fall into the trap of working for drug runners.

Mila had wanted to help her. It had been a blessing for all of them that Roberta had agreed to be a live-in nanny.

Now, because of her, Roberta was dead.

"Listen to me, Mila." Brayden gripped her arms and shook her gently to make her look at him. "I can see the wheels turning in your head. This was not your fault."

Mila fought tears, but they trickled down her cheeks

anyway. "She wouldn't have been killed if she hadn't been working for me."

"Where would she have been, Mila?"

She jerked her gaze to his.

"I don't know much about her, but you obviously cared about her," Brayden said softly. "Did she have any other family?"

She shook her head. "No, her husband died because of gang activity. She was homeless and alone…"

"And you took her in and gave her a family," Brayden said, his voice tender.

She nodded. "She loved Izzy so much, and Izzy adored her."

Brayden cupped her face between his hands. "She knew that you loved her, and she died protecting the little girl she loved."

Mila clutched his arms, her heart aching. "Izzy must be so devastated. What if she witnessed them kill Roberta? She'll be traumatized and—"

"Shh," Brayden said softly. "One step at a time, Doc. I understand you're upset about your nanny, but right now we have to focus on finding Izzy."

He was right. But once she got Izzy back, she'd give Roberta the memorial service she deserved. She'd died protecting Izzy—she was a true hero.

"Focus on the fact that Izzy is all right. And remember, for now DiSanti needs you. He won't hurt Izzy, because he needs her as leverage."

"You can't tell your brother about what happened here," Mila insisted. "It's too dangerous for Izzy."

Brayden's expression looked torn. "I'm sorry, Mila. But there was a murder at your house. We have to report it. We can't leave Roberta lying there in the house for days."

Mila struggled with right and wrong, with grief and

anger, with fear that no matter what she did, she might never see her little girl again.

"You can trust Lucas," Brayden said. "He may be a federal agent, but he's a good guy. He'll protect Izzy and you."

It was still dangerous. And there was no way she could confide the truth about Izzy's father. No one could know.

"Mila?"

She clutched his arms, her mind racing. "Then you have to make sure that DiSanti knows that I haven't talked."

"We will," Brayden said. "I'll arrange for Lucas to make a statement to the press that you aren't cooperating with the FBI. All right?"

She bit her lower lip, but agreed. "What can we do to get my daughter back?"

Brayden stroked her arms. "First a crime team will process your house for forensics. Maybe the men who killed Roberta and took Izzy left evidence behind."

"Does it matter who they are?" Mila asked. "We know they work for that monster DiSanti."

"Identifying any one member of his group might lead us to some clue about DiSanti's plans or location. Lucas's people are analyzing Polk's and the gunman's phones, contact information and correspondence for any clue as to where DiSanti is hiding."

Mila's stomach churned, but she lifted her chin defiantly. "We have to do more. Give him some way to contact me." She'd even use herself as a pawn if she had to.

Chapter Nine

Emotions warred inside Brayden. It was beyond reprehensible that DiSanti would hurt a little girl.

Then again, they knew for a fact that he had hurt countless women and young girls, some as young as age twelve. To DiSanti and his people, the female population was put on earth to exploit. He did that for money without batting an eye.

Brayden couldn't help but wonder what had made the man so cold. Maybe his upbringing?

Not that it mattered. There was no excuse or justification.

He wanted the bastard to pay now more than ever.

But first, they had to get Izzy back safely.

Mila still looked uncertain about the plan. But what else could they do?

If he didn't work with Lucas, Dexter could try to track down DiSanti. But the FBI had resources that Dexter didn't.

Brayden believed in the law. But he wasn't stupid either. He'd learned to shoot a rifle when he was a teenager. His experience on the force had taught him how to handle a weapon, about apprehending a suspect, about when to shoot and not shoot.

Most of all, it had taught him that nothing could combat a bullet except one in return. Not a pretty lesson, but being street-smart meant surviving.

He didn't intend to die at the hands of DiSanti and allow him to continue his reign of terror.

"I need my cell phone," Mila said. "DiSanti's people might contact me through it."

"Good point."

"I probably should go back to the clinic," Mila suggested. "They might show up there."

"I don't think so. They know we'll be watching it," Brayden said.

The sound of an engine made them both jerk their heads around. Lucas.

Mila twisted her hands in her lap, fear returning to her eyes. "What if I'm doing the wrong thing? What if calling your brother gets Izzy killed?"

Brayden frowned, his pulse hammering. "Mila, I think we both know that you're in over your head. There's no way DiSanti will let you live, not when you're the only person outside his people who can identify him."

Her face turned ashen, but she didn't argue.

MILA RECOGNIZED THE truth in Brayden's words. But she didn't like it, and it scared the hell out of her to involve the FBI.

If they discovered Izzy wasn't her biological child and that DiSanti was Izzy's father, she might lose Izzy to him because of legality issues.

She'd have to watch every word she said to Brayden's brother. Only tell him what was necessary to find her daughter.

Agent Hawk slowed as he approached them, then pulled over and parked behind Brayden. Brayden climbed out to talk to his brother, and she studied the two, praying she hadn't made a mistake in trusting Brayden.

But Charlotte had married Lucas, so he must be an okay guy. When she'd first seen the news story on the shooting that had rendered Charlotte temporarily blind, she'd wanted to reach out to Charlotte, but she'd held back because of Izzy. She'd hated DiSanti and hoped the feds would find him and put him away for life.

She'd never imagined that she'd be the one to help him escape.

For a moment, Lucas and Brayden appeared to be in a heated argument. Brayden gestured toward her and her house. Finally, they both walked back to the car, and Brayden opened the passenger door.

"Lucas insists on speaking to you, Mila."

Her heart pounded, but she inhaled a deep breath. She'd do anything to protect her little girl, even lie to the FBI.

She slowly climbed from the vehicle, desperately wishing she'd had a shower. Maybe once they processed her house, they'd let her inside to gather some clothes.

"Dr. Manchester, Brayden explained the situation. I'm sorry that your nanny was killed. And most of all, sorry that your daughter is missing." His gaze seemed to be scrutinizing her as he spoke.

Mila cleared her throat. "He'll kill her if he thinks I talked to you."

Lucas nodded. "I understand your fear. And I promise that I'll do everything I can to bring your daughter home."

"Then you have to let him know that I haven't told you anything." She lifted her chin. "If it means locking me back up, then do it."

BRAYDEN GLANCED AT LUCAS, ready to argue if his brother agreed to put Mila back in a cell. She didn't belong there, not after all she'd suffered in the last twenty-four hours.

But a mother's love was so strong that he realized she'd do anything for her child, just as his mother would do anything for him and his brothers. She'd been devastated when their little sister had gone missing. They all had.

He'd blamed himself. So had his brothers.

And their father had just skipped out.

"I don't think that'll be necessary," Lucas said to Mila. "In fact, if DiSanti sent Polk after you, he'll send someone else."

Mila shivered. And this time she might not survive.

"I want to place you in protective custody until we catch DiSanti." Lucas speared Brayden with a questioning look. "Agreed?"

Brayden nodded. "I could drive her back to the ranch."

Mila twisted her hands together. "How will DiSanti contact me about Izzy?"

"She needs her phone," Brayden told Lucas.

Lucas nodded. "I can arrange that. Meanwhile, I'd like for you to work with a sketch artist."

Mila clamped her teeth over her bottom lip. "If you air a picture of his new face on the news, he'll know I talked."

"We won't release it to the public," Lucas said.

Mila folded her arms across her chest. "But what if someone in the police department or the FBI is working with DiSanti?"

Silence stretched between them, fraught with tension.

"She's right," Brayden said. "DiSanti may have people in his pocket that we don't know about."

Frustration darkened Lucas's eyes. "I promise you that I'll be discreet. I'll only share with people I trust. Once you make contact, and we get your daughter back, we'll go wide and launch a full-fledged hunt for the bastard."

A white crime scene van rolled up and slowed as it passed them.

"I need to meet them at the house," Lucas said.

Mila heaved a wary breath. "Would it be possible for me to go inside and get some clothes?"

Lucas and Brayden exchanged a look. "You don't need to see your nanny like she is now," Brayden said softly. "I can collect some things from inside for you if you want."

Lucas shrugged. "That would work. Give us time to process the house first." He narrowed his eyes at Brayden. "You didn't touch anything inside, did you?"

Brayden shook his head no. "Dex and I just searched the house. We found the nanny in the kitchen."

Mila clenched her hands together as if struggling to maintain control.

"I'll let you know when you can come in," Lucas said.

Lucas got back in his car and drove two houses down to Mila's.

Despair and worry knitted Mila's brow, making Brayden want to pull her into his arms and comfort her. To assure her that everything would be all right.

But he couldn't do that. Not when he had no idea where DiSanti's men had taken Izzy.

MILA WATCHED LUCAS and the crime team park in her driveway with a sense of trepidation.

That little bungalow was her home. She'd bought it with high hopes of settling there forever and giving Izzy a happy childhood full of sweet memories.

But Roberta was dead inside. And her daughter was a victim of a kidnapping…

Worse, Izzy might have witnessed her nanny's murder. Mila hoped not. But still, the trauma of those men holding her and Roberta at gunpoint could damage Izzy for a long time.

The images from that FaceTime call haunted her and always would. She could see the men bursting through the door. The guns aimed at Roberta and Izzy. Izzy screaming as that brute snatched her.

Once she got Izzy back, could they return to the house they'd once called home?

She didn't know...

"Mila, I realize this is a terrifying situation, but try to stay positive. DiSanti wants you, not Izzy."

Her breath grew painful in her chest. If DiSanti knew Izzy was his daughter, he would want Izzy.

And he'd kill Mila for keeping Izzy from him for the past three years. But Izzy would never have a normal life if DiSanti discovered the connection between them.

He'd probably hunt down Carina like a dog, too. Mila couldn't allow that to happen.

"I promise to do whatever is necessary to help apprehend him once we save Izzy," Mila said.

A long silence stretched between them as they both watched her house. Another van passed them and pulled into her drive.

"Who is that?" Mila asked.

"The ME. They'll transport Roberta's body to the morgue for an autopsy."

Her heart squeezed. The world had been a better place with Roberta's warm smile and love of life. Even if she and Izzy survived this, they would forever have a hole in their hearts where Roberta belonged.

"A crime scene crew can clean up after the investigators are finished," Brayden said.

"That would be nice." She was accustomed to the sight of blood from performing surgeries. But seeing Roberta's spilled from being murdered was different. Personal.

Brayden turned to face her. "Mila, I have to ask you something else."

She tensed at the grave sound of his voice.

"It's personal, but the reason I'm asking is that it might have some bearing on finding your daughter."

She inhaled a deep breath. "All right."

His blue eyes softened. "Is Izzy's father in her life?"

Oh God... She forced herself to remain calm. "Why do you want to know about him?"

He shrugged. "We know DiSanti orchestrated this situation, but should we contact Izzy's father?"

"He's not in her life and never has been." At least that was true.

Another pause. "Is it possible then that he might have taken a payoff to help DiSanti get to you?"

Mila understood his question now. Oftentimes in kidnappings, a parent was involved.

That was certainly true in her case. But not for the reasons that Brayden thought.

She faced him with an earnest expression, hoping to end this line of questioning once and for all.

"That's not possible. Izzy's father is dead," Mila said.

Chapter Ten

Mila was so antsy she thought she would come out of her skin as she waited on the crime scene team to finish with her house.

All she could think about was where they'd taken Izzy. What was happening to her? Was she hurt?

Izzy didn't like scary movies or TV shows. Izzy insisted Mila and Roberta check the closets and under the beds for monsters at bedtime. She slept with a night-light on and had never had a sleepover away from home.

She had to be terrified out of her mind.

"We'll find her," Brayden said softly.

She wanted to believe him. She had to.

Needing a distraction, she asked Brayden about his family. "How many brothers do you have?"

"There's four of us," Brayden said. "Harrison is the oldest and sheriff of Tumbleweed. Lucas is second in line. Then Dex, then me." He hesitated, his eyes darkening. "We had a little sister named Chrissy, but lost her when she was ten."

Mila frowned. "What happened? Or do you not want to talk about it?"

He shrugged, but averted his gaze and looked out the window. A fall breeze stirred the trees, sending an array of colorful leaves to the ground. Yet dark clouds hovered, adding a dismal gray cast to the sky.

"I'm surprised you didn't see the news story about it. She disappeared one night when our parents were gone. For years, we had no idea what had happened. But a few months ago, we discovered the truth." He paused. "Unfortunately, she was dead and had been since the day she'd gone missing."

"I'm so sorry," Mila said. "That must have been difficult on you and your family."

"It was," Brayden admitted in a low voice. "My brothers and I all blamed ourselves because we were supposed to watch Chrissy that night. My mother went into a depression after she disappeared, but never gave up hope that we'd find her." His voice cracked. "Then my father just up and left."

"He abandoned your family?" Mila asked.

Brayden nodded. "We haven't heard from him in years."

How could a man desert his sons and wife, especially when they needed him?

"What about your family?" Brayden asked. "Any siblings?"

Mila's stomach twisted as she saw the ME and a crime worker carry Roberta out on a stretcher. Because Roberta was enclosed in a body bag, Mila couldn't see the physical damage done to her friend, but her experience filled in the blanks.

Thankfully, no neighbors were home to see what was going on, and the media hadn't shown up.

"Mila?"

She dragged her gaze from the van as the ME closed the back door.

"No. I was adopted but lost both of my adopted parents a while back."

"Charlotte mentioned a little about your past. I'm sorry about your birth mother," Brayden said.

She shook off his concern. "I was lucky to have the two

parents I had. My mother traveled to foreign countries to help children in need. I wanted to follow in her footsteps, and I did." Another reason she'd had to take Izzy from Carina—she wanted to give Izzy the same chance that her adopted parents had given her.

Lucas appeared outside her house, then drove back to them.

She tensed as he got out and approached them. Brayden opened the door and stepped out. Mila wanted to know what was going on, so she joined them.

"Are you ready to talk to that sketch artist?" Lucas asked.

Mila's stomach knotted. She still didn't trust anyone. "I was thinking that perhaps I could work with Charlotte, that way we don't have to involve anyone else."

A muscle ticked in Lucas's jaw. "I suppose we could do that."

"About my clothes?" Mila asked.

"Tell me what you'll want and I'll go in," Brayden offered.

Mila squared her shoulders. "I'll get them. I'm a doctor, I've seen blood before."

"This is different," Lucas said.

"I'll be fine," Mila said sharply. "It won't take long."

"I'll go with her," Brayden said.

Lucas nodded. "I'll stand guard outside the house."

BRAYDEN ESCORTED MILA INSIDE. "There's probably fingerprint dust all over everything. Just ignore it, and we'll have a cleanup crew in here ASAP."

Mila gripped her hands together. "She was in the kitchen?"

Brayden nodded. "Your room and Izzy's are blood free."

Unease flittered through Mila's eyes. No matter what

he'd said, she probably felt responsible for the nanny's death and would carry guilt with her for a long time.

He understood that himself. Even after they'd found Chrissy's body a few months ago, he couldn't shake the fact that if he hadn't encouraged her to sneak out with him and go to that swimming hole where Lucas and the other teens were celebrating the end of the school year, she'd still be alive.

He was eleven at the time and wanted to explore the caves at the edge of the mountain. He fell and hurt his ankle, and lost sight of Chrissy. Later he rode his bike home thinking she'd be there, but she hadn't shown up.

Instead...

He couldn't go back to the past.

Mila needed him to focus now. He hadn't been able to save his little sister. He had to save Mila's daughter.

He opened the door for her, and they walked inside. The scent of blood and death filled the air. He'd seen crime scenes before, but this one felt more personal because he knew a child had been kidnapped in the process.

Mila might be accustomed to blood and gore in the hospital and operating room, but a crime scene was different—violence at its worst. And this one involved her little girl.

She exhaled and walked quickly past the kitchen, then hurried to her bedroom. He followed but remained at the door to keep watch, offering her privacy to absorb the shock and gather her thoughts.

Her experience in crisis situations was evident as she lifted her chin and went straight to work. She pulled an overnight bag from the closet and threw in a couple of pairs of jeans, shirts and a sweater. She opened her dresser drawer, and he noticed pajamas and underwear, so he turned to face the wall.

He didn't need to see or even think about what kind of

underwear the pretty doctor wore. But his imagination took him there anyway, and he pictured her curves encased in thin black lace.

His body hardened at the image in his mind. Dammit, he could not fantasize about her. Not when finding her child took priority.

He scrubbed his hand over his eyes to clear his mind. Footsteps sounded behind him, then her voice.

"I'm ready."

He turned toward her and took the overnight bag from her. "I need my phone."

"Your phone is still being held in evidence, but we'll get you another one and set it up with the same number."

She glanced inside Izzy's room. Her composure slipped slightly at the disarray.

"She always sleeps with her stuffed monkey. She named him Brownie," Mila said. "She cries without him."

His chest clenched. "I know this is difficult," Brayden said. "But you have to stay strong, Mila. She'll need you when we bring her home."

MILA DUCKED INSIDE Izzy's room to retrieve the monkey, but she couldn't find it. Maybe she had it with her. At least the stuffed animal would give her comfort.

The sight of her daughter's empty, unmade bed tore her heart in two. Thoughts of what DiSanti did to young girls threatened, but she staunchly pushed them away. Izzy was only three. He wouldn't touch her that way.

At least not now. When she was a teenager though…

No, they'd get Izzy back.

She hung on to that thought, grabbed the pink blanket Izzy slept with, then some extra clothes and one of her dolls and stuffed them in the overnight bag.

She crossed back to the door where Brayden was waiting. They walked through the house in silence and met Lucas at the door.

"Do you want me to follow you to the ranch?" Lucas asked.

Brayden shook his head. "I'll take her from here. Just get her a phone in case DiSanti's men try to reach her."

Mila hesitated. In spite of the fact that Lucas had arrested her, the Hawk family seemed caring and determined to do the right thing. Even Lucas wasn't bad—he'd saved those teenagers and married Charlotte. He'd even arrested her to stop DiSanti once and for all. How could she fault him for that?

"Get me the phone, then take me to a hotel, Brayden," Mila said. "I don't want to put your family in danger."

The Hawk men exchanged a look, then Lucas spoke. "Let us worry about the family," Lucas said. "Harrison can arrange extra protection for the ranch."

"But what if DiSanti discovers I'm there?" Mila asked.

Brayden took her arm. "Trust me, no one will know."

There was that word again. *Trust.*

She climbed into Brayden's SUV and looked out the window as he drove. Once they left the outskirts of Austin, the city gave way to beautiful countryside. Farms and ranches and wide-open spaces.

All places Izzy would love.

Tears pricked her eyes, but she blinked them away and grappled for courage.

Once Izzy was safe, she'd see that DiSanti paid.

Exhaustion and stress wore her down, and she closed her eyes. The next time she opened them, Brayden was crossing under a sign for Hawk's Landing.

She blinked in awe at the acres and acres of beautiful land. Barns and stables dotted the hills, and horses galloped across open pastures. In the distance, she spotted a big rambling farmhouse with a huge wraparound porch, then a couple of rustic cabins nearby.

"This is where you grew up?" she asked.

Brayden smiled. "Yeah, except for losing my sister, it was pretty great."

She imagined it was. "Do you and your brothers all ride and work the ranch?"

"We all ride. As teenagers, my brothers and I worked the ranch. Dexter has a place in Austin for his PI business, but he also handles the equine operation and has added horses this last year since Charlotte's students came to live with my mom." He gestured toward a dirt road that led to acreage lush with more pastures. "My brother Harrison and his wife live up there." He pointed the opposite direction toward more land that stretched far and wide. "Lucas and Charlotte live over there. Harrison's wife, Honey, owns a renovation business. She remodeled the cabin they moved into as well as the one Lucas and Charlotte chose."

"And yours?"

He shrugged. "Maybe someday. For now, it's just me, so no need for fuss."

"The ranch is amazing," Mila said, and meant it.

The smile that lit Brayden's eyes was so sincere that it warmed her inside.

"Like Dex, I have a place in the city, too. But I keep a cabin on the ranch for when I'm home." He slowed as they neared the turnoff for the main farmhouse. "Do you want to meet my mother and the girls?"

She shook her head. "I don't want to involve them in any of this. I'd never forgive myself if one of them were hurt because of me."

"Mila," Brayden said in a husky voice. "My mother is housing four girls who were kidnapped by DiSanti. My family is as invested in seeing DiSanti brought down as anyone."

"I appreciate you saying that," Mila said. "But I spent the night in a jail cell last night. I need to clean up."

"Of course. I'm sorry. I'm not trying to pressure you." He veered down another dirt road, the SUV bouncing over ruts as he passed a pond and headed up a hill. To the right, she spotted a cowboy riding across the pasture, corralling some horses toward the barn. Instantly her nerves went on edge.

"Who is that?"

Brayden laid his hand over hers. "Relax, Mila. That's our foreman. He's the reason I went into law."

Mila narrowed her eyes. "What happened?"

"He was framed," Brayden said. "I was a cop at the time and realized the injustice, so I decided to study law to help him. I did, and now he works here."

Mila licked her suddenly dry lips. Brayden was definitely one of the good guys. A rancher at heart, a lawyer who represented the underdog.

She'd accept his help, then she'd get out of his life so she wouldn't cause him or his family any more trouble than she already had.

Then and only then would her secret about Izzy be safe.

JADE KRAMER WRAPPED the little girl Izzy in a soft blanket, then cradled her close and rocked her to sleep.

The poor little angel had cried so much her eyelids were swollen and red and she'd finally exhausted herself into sleep.

She wanted her mommy. Who could blame her?

She'd wanted her own mother when DiSanti had first brought her here, and she'd been fourteen years old.

That was over a year ago, and she still missed her family. She couldn't make herself believe that her father had sold her to DiSanti as he said.

Sure, she'd believed him at first.

But living on his compound and being bartered like cattle had taught her a lot.

DiSanti was a liar and a bastard, and he didn't care who he hurt as long as he made money.

The little girl stirred again, her tiny body trembling as she fought in her sleep.

She rocked her back and forth and stroked her hair away from her forehead, then kissed her cheek and began to sing her a lullaby. It was one her mama used to sing to help her fall asleep at night.

God, she missed her mama. Wished she could go back to being an innocent kid again. But those days were long gone.

Izzy whimpered and clawed at her arm, but Jade held her close and whispered sweet nothings in the child's ear.

She had to keep her quiet. DiSanti didn't like anyone to mess up his plans. She'd seen what he could do when he was angry.

It wouldn't matter that Izzy was just a tiny, innocent baby.

He'd give orders to get rid of her without blinking an eye.

Hot tears burned Jade's eyes. She'd long ago stopped crying for herself and for what the men had done to her. Her life no longer mattered.

But this little girl's did.

She'd do anything to keep her alive.

Chapter Eleven

Brayden considered putting Mila in one of the guest cabins, but he didn't want to leave her alone, so he took her to his place. She was so independent and frightened for her daughter that if she heard from DiSanti, she might attempt to face him by herself.

And that would be dangerous for her and Izzy. DiSanti was going to kill both of them anyway.

Unless they stopped him.

"This is nice," she said as he showed her through the kitchen/living room/dining area, then to the guest bedroom and bath. "Take your time. I'll run up to the house and see if Mother made dinner and grab us a plate."

She rolled her shoulders, obviously exhausted and worried. He waited until she ducked into the bathroom, then he locked up and drove to the farmhouse.

He spotted the teens outside with the foreman brushing down the horses, then found his mother cleaning up in the kitchen. The scent of homemade soup and corn bread lingered.

"Lucas called and explained that you have a guest." His mother's concerned gaze penetrated his. "Is there anything I can do to help?"

Brayden offered his mother a smile.

"If you have leftovers, we could use some. We haven't eaten all day."

A smile brightened his mother's face. They could always count on Ava Hawk for a good meal. "I'll pack up some soup and corn bread. And I have a fresh pumpkin pie."

His stomach growled. "Sounds wonderful."

She bustled around scooping soup into a container, then wrapped up two big chunks of corn bread, covered half a pie with foil and placed everything in an insulated bag for him to carry home.

He gave her a kiss on the cheek. "Thanks, Mom."

She hugged him tight. "Take care and be safe, son. And save that doctor's little girl."

"We're going to," he said, praying he didn't let Mila down.

His phone was buzzing with a text as he got back in his SUV. Lucas.

Charlotte and I are on our way. Bringing a phone for Mila.

He texted okay, then sped back toward his place. Hopefully, Mila's description of DiSanti's new face would enable them to track down the bastard and put him away.

MILA SHOWERED QUICKLY, grateful to finally clean the stench of DiSanti's blood from her skin. But she couldn't wash away the vile odor of what he was.

She quickly threw on a pair of sweats and towel dried her hair. By the time she emerged, she heard the door opening and Brayden calling her name.

She met him in the kitchen, where he was ladling vegetable soup into two bowls.

"My mom sent this and some corn bread and pie. I hope you like soup."

"It smells heavenly," Mila said. She couldn't remember when she'd last eaten. A breakfast bar the morning before she went to the clinic, then she'd skipped lunch while she was working on DiSanti. They'd offered her food in that cell, but she'd been too sick to her stomach to keep anything down.

They carried the bowls and corn bread to the farm table, and he returned with silverware and napkins.

"Would you like a drink? I have beer and bourbon, and I might have a bottle of wine left from Charlotte and Lucas's wedding."

"Water is good," Mila said. She had to keep her wits about her.

He poured them both glasses of ice water and sat down across from her at the table.

She was so hungry that she practically inhaled the meal. He was quiet, too, as they ate.

Then he dished them slices of pumpkin pie that made her mouth water. "Your mother is a good cook."

"She loves it. We used to grow our own vegetables when I was young, before we lost Chrissy." He shrugged. "She's talking about having a garden next summer since she'll have the girls to help."

"Giving those girls a home is admirable."

"Yeah, my mom is something else. Strong…like you."

Their gazes locked, tension simmering between them. She'd thought she was strong until she saw that gun at Izzy's head. Then she'd wanted to crumble.

"Charlotte and Lucas are on their way," Brayden said as he brewed a pot of coffee.

Fatigue knotted her shoulders, but she knew she had to face them.

If she could help find DiSanti, it would lead to Izzy.

A knock sounded on the door and Brayden rushed to get it. Lucas entered, then Charlotte.

Although Mila hadn't seen her friend in years, the connection they shared was still there. Charlotte raced over to her, and they hugged.

"God, Mila, I'm glad you're okay, but I know you're worried sick about your daughter."

Mila leaned into her friend and accepted her comfort, although the sincere worry in Charlotte's tone brought fresh tears to her eyes.

When they finally pulled apart, Charlotte cradled Mila's hands in hers. "I understand you're scared, but Lucas and the Hawk men are the best there is. They'll find your little girl."

Mila offered Charlotte a sympathetic smile. "I heard about what happened to you and your students. I'm so sorry for what you went through."

Charlotte squeezed her hands. "It was difficult, but I survived. The girls are happy now that they have a home at Hawk's Landing. Ava has given them love and emotional support." She glanced at Lucas with a smile. "I also met my husband from the ordeal. He's been amazing."

"I'm so glad you found happiness," Mila said sincerely. Charlotte had suffered ridicule as a child because of her port-wine birthmark. Mila's adopted mother had removed the birthmark, the first step in helping Charlotte recover her self-esteem.

"So," Charlotte said. "I understand that we need to sketch what that horrible DiSanti looks like now."

"Yes, we might as well get started."

Brayden offered coffee, but Charlotte declined, and so did Mila. She was already shaky. Caffeine would only make it worse.

Charlotte removed a large sketch pad and arranged her supplies on the coffee table between the two wing chairs facing the fireplace.

Lucas gave her a phone. "You have the same number as before, so if DiSanti calls, he won't realize the difference.

We placed a trace on the phone. Keep him on the line as long as possible so we can get a location."

She nodded that she understood, then joined Charlotte.

Charlotte gestured toward a photo of DiSanti. "I thought the picture would be a good starting point. Then you can tell me how you altered features and I can draw them in for a composite."

WHILE MILA AND Charlotte collaborated on the sketch of DiSanti, Brayden and Lucas convened at the kitchen table.

Lucas spread out a map, then removed three photographs of different men from a folder and laid them in a row.

"Right now we have made connections from DiSanti to each of these men, although we don't have enough evidence to make arrests."

He tapped the first picture, a dark-haired, dark-skinned man in a slick suit with a mole beside his upper lip. "This is Juan Andres. We believe he's the major connection in Colombia and is also part of the drug cartel. So far though, no one has or will speak out against him. The two people who tried are dead. Tortured and butchered and left hanging in their village to make a statement to anyone else who contemplated turning to the authorities. Another problem is corrupt law officials who turn a blind eye for money."

Disgusting.

Lucas continued, all business. "Next is a man named Lem Corley. He owns a ranch between here and Austin. Corley's operation has grown by leaps and bounds the past five years."

"Have you questioned him?"

"Not yet, I'm working on obtaining enough information for warrants. Corley also owns a second property near Juarez. We suspect he's taking payoffs for smuggling the girls through an underground tunnel across the border from the US to Mexico. From there, it's easier to send them wherever they want."

Brayden silently cursed.

"The third is a shocker because it's close to home."

Brayden's pulse jumped. "Isn't that Jameson Beck, the candidate for mayor?"

"Exactly. We've suspected he was corrupt as a councilman, but he has money and charm and has fooled people into voting for him. If he wins this bid as mayor, there's no telling how much damage he'll do."

Brayden's mind raced. Even when they found Izzy, Lucas still had his work cut out to make DiSanti's empire fall apart.

Charlotte and Mila stood and walked outside on the back deck.

Lucas poured himself more coffee and Brayden followed.

As usual, Lucas's eyes assessed him. His brother had an intimidating air, which worked well with felons and the evil dregs that he hunted down.

But he hated it when Lucas aimed those suspicious eyes toward him.

"Do you think Mila has told you everything?" Lucas asked.

Did he?

Brayden grabbed his coffee mug from the counter and blew into the steaming brew. "Yes."

Was Lucas going to remind him of the time when he fell for a client's innocent act?

"She's never married?" Lucas asked.

Irritation knifed through him. "It's not uncommon for women to have children without marriage, Lucas."

His brother sighed. "I know that. But what about the little girl's father? Did she tell you who he is?"

Brayden shook his head no. "He's dead."

A tense silence stretched between them. "And you believe her?"

"I have no reason not to. Now let's look at the facts. A dead man has nothing to do with Izzy now."

"What if she's lying?" Lucas said.

Brayden didn't want to believe that Mila would lie to him. But he'd been fooled before by another woman.

"Hell, Brayden," Lucas said. "Use your charms—do whatever it takes to find out his name. For all we know, he could be working with DiSanti."

MILA FROZE AT the sound of Lucas's question. Brayden told Lucas exactly what she'd said.

But Lucas wanted more.

He would probably keep digging away until he discovered the truth.

She couldn't let that happen.

"Mila, are you all right?" Charlotte asked.

She jerked her attention back to Charlotte and nodded. "Just thinking about Izzy. Wondering if she's hungry or if she slept last night. If she thinks I've forgotten her or knows that I'm looking."

Charlotte stroked Mila's shoulder. "Izzy knows you love her. She'll hang on to that." Charlotte glanced at the Hawk men, a tenderness in her eyes that Mila envied.

The Hawks had a close-knit, loving family here. They'd endured hard times and pulled through them together. And this ranch—it was spectacular. It offered a child a great place to grow up and a safe haven from the dangers of the world.

Not that her childhood had been bad. Her parents had helped save the world. But they'd moved and traveled so much that she'd never called a place home.

She wanted that for Izzy.

Even if she had to forgo her trips abroad, she'd give Izzy that sense of stability and home.

Charlotte took the sketch to Lucas. Both men studied it as if memorizing every detail.

"Basically, I removed his scar, then gave him cheek implants, lip fillers, a nose job and eyelid lifts," Mila said. "It'll take time for the swelling to go down and the redness to fade, but he'll be handsome and charming, and no one will know there's a monster lurking beneath that slick face."

The fact that she'd helped him achieve that made bile rise to her throat.

"Thank you for the description," Lucas said.

Mila folded her arms. "Are you going to keep your promise about airing it?"

Lucas gave a clipped nod, then flipped on the TV. "I gave an interview before I came here. It should be airing any minute."

They grew quiet as a young brunette anchorwoman spoke into the mike. "Last night the FBI and local police arrested Austin plastic surgeon Dr. Mila Manchester for allegedly helping a wanted felon Arman DiSanti escape. Authorities have been searching for DiSanti for months in relation to a sex trafficking ring called the Shetland operation." She gestured toward a screen. "I spoke with Special Agent Lucas Hawk earlier today regarding the arrest. Here's what he had to say."

The camera focused on Lucas. "While it is true, we arrested Dr. Manchester for allegedly conspiring to help DiSanti escape authorities, Dr. Manchester has refused to cooperate with us or reveal anything about DiSanti and his operation. Nor did she divulge the man's whereabouts, his plans or his new face."

Mila clenched her hands by her side. Lucas had kept his promise, at least regarding the media.

She just hoped DiSanti bought the story. And that his men took the bait and gave her a call.

Chapter Twelve

Mila had to keep her secrets safe. If Brayden and Lucas knew the truth about Izzy being DiSanti's daughter, Lucas might lock her up. They might even accuse her of kidnapping, and then she might go to prison.

Lucas approached her, his look suspicious. "Dr. Manchester—"

"Please call me Mila."

Charlotte's presence comforted her in the face of Lucas's distrust.

"All right, Mila," Lucas said. "Tell me why DiSanti came to you for help."

She chewed the inside of her cheek. "Because I'm a plastic surgeon," she said, stating the obvious.

Irritation lined Lucas's face. "But why *you*? There are other plastic surgeons who could have performed the surgery."

She shrugged. "I don't know. Maybe he, or one of his people, read about me in an article featuring my work with needy children."

Lucas arched a brow. "Had you met DiSanti before? Or done work on him prior to this?"

"No, we'd never met." That part was true.

"DiSanti is from Colombia," Lucas pointed out. "You've traveled there to perform surgeries?"

Mila couldn't lie when he could easily check her schedule. "Twice. My mother also worked at a free clinic in Colombia at one time."

Maybe that would distract him from thinking about her, and Izzy's father.

Lucas narrowed his eyes. "Did you go with her?"

She nodded. "She was the reason I chose plastic surgery and work with Doctors Without Borders."

Charlotte rubbed Mila's arm. "She was a hero to me, that's for sure."

Lucas hesitated, his gaze softening as he looked at his wife.

Then he turned back to Mila. "Was it possible that DiSanti knew your mother?"

"She never mentioned his name to me. And if she'd known what kind of man he was, she certainly wouldn't have helped him. Her work focused on children and teenagers." Although it was possible that DiSanti had heard of her mother, and that he linked her to Mila.

"Let me ask you something else," Lucas said. "When you and your mother were in Colombia, did you hear about DiSanti and what he was doing? Was there talk or rumors about sex trafficking?"

Mila strained to remember. "I suppose, but I was only twelve at the time and didn't fully comprehend the details. I do recall that guards watched the clinic, and I was warned to stay close." A shudder coursed up her spine. "A couple of times, rape victims were brought in. Those frightened me because the girls were so young and traumatized."

Lucas studied her for a long moment, then seemed to accept what she said. At least for the moment. "Let me see the sketch again," Lucas said.

Charlotte handed the drawing to him, and Lucas scrutinized the features. "Did DiSanti or his men say anything while they were in your clinic?"

"Other than threatening my daughter?" Mila asked with a hint of sarcasm to her voice.

"I know that was harrowing," Lucas said. "But think about it? Maybe you overheard them discuss where they were going to take DiSanti to recover."

"If I knew where he was, I'd tell you." Mila rubbed her temple in thought. "All I remember is being so terrified that they'd hurt Izzy that I just did what they said. I cautioned them that I usually performed extensive plastic surgery in steps, but they insisted everything had to be completed that day."

Lucas removed a manila envelope from inside his jacket, and then took out a picture. "We took this from your house. Is this one of the latest pictures of your daughter?"

Mila traced a shaky finger over Izzy's innocent face. Her heart squeezed at the picture of Izzy sitting atop that pony. She'd been so excited about her first horseback riding lesson. "That was in the summer. I took Izzy camping, and we made s'mores over the campfire, and slept under the stars." She bit her lip. "She was so happy that day."

"I'd like to issue an Amber Alert for her," Lucas said. "That is, if you agree."

Mila looked at Charlotte for advice. Yet the threat to her daughter rang in her ears. If they released a photograph, DiSanti and his men would know that she'd talked.

She shook her head. "Not yet."

Lucas sighed. "But if we don't hear from DiSanti's men by tomorrow, we should release it to the public. I probably don't have to tell you that with every hour and every day that a child is missing, the chances of recovering them grow slimmer."

Mila swallowed hard.

Charlotte tugged at Lucas's arm. "Why don't we let Mila get some sleep? Maybe she'll remember more once she's rested."

"If anything comes to mind, call me." He squeezed her arm. "Hang in there, Mila. We'll find your daughter."

His tender encouragement made emotions well in her throat.

Lucas and Charlotte left, and Mila went to look out the window. It was dark again. Nighttime.

No word about her daughter or where she was. Or even if she was safe.

She gripped the phone Lucas had left for her, walked outside onto the porch, sank into one of the porch rockers and willed it to ring.

BRAYDEN CLEANED UP the kitchen, tension lingering. Mila pushed the porch swing back and forth, her hand clutching that cell phone.

She'd spent last night in jail without Izzy. Tonight, she'd spend it alone again.

Something about his brother's conversation with Mila troubled him. He sensed she was holding something back.

But what? Everything she'd told them about her mother was inspiring. And easy to check.

DiSanti was a good fifteen years older than Mila. He could have easily met her mother when she traveled to Colombia. He could also have seen Mila and read about her in the news. It made sense.

Lucas wanted him to find out about Izzy's father.

Frustrated, he settled in front of his laptop and sent Dexter an email giving him the names of the three men the FBI suspected to be involved with DiSanti's operation.

He asked Dex to send him everything he had on all three men.

He'd crossed paths with Jameson Beck before on the job. He'd heard rumors that the man was corrupt. That he had huge financial support from an unknown source.

Beck was slick, charming and made promises left and right to the public to win their votes.

Brayden didn't know the rancher Corley personally, but he and Dex could check him out together.

Beck was all his though.

Brayden accessed his personal number from his contact list, so he called it. The phone rang four times then went to voice mail. He left a message saying it was urgent, and that he needed to speak to him right away.

He hung up, hoping Beck would return his call tonight.

The next two hours crawled by. He researched everything he could find on persons of interest in the sex trafficking trade. Two arrests caught his attention, and he texted Harrison and asked him to go to the prison and question the inmates. They might be able to offer a lead as to where DiSanti and his men were hiding out.

Or if DiSanti had another connection in the States.

Antsy that he couldn't take action tonight, he walked outside to join Mila. He was frustrated—she must be going out of her mind.

She gave him a brief glance, then returned to staring out at the ranch. Normally he'd be bragging about their operation and how far they'd come this past year in updating the ranching side of the business.

But tonight, all he could think about was Mila and the sadness and fear in her eyes.

SOMETIME IN THE wee hours of the morning, Mila finally fell into an exhausted sleep.

She dreamed about the surgery.

She was on her feet for hours. Long stressful hours when she could barely focus for worrying about what Izzy was going through.

Her head throbbed and her feet ached. Sweat poured

down the side of her face. She was so thirsty she had to pause for a quick sip of water.

"What are you doing?" one of the men barked.

"I need water," she said, then grabbed a bottle from the side table.

He kept his gun aimed at her. "Get back to it, Doc. If you try to pull anything or if the cops show up, you'll never see your kid again."

Rage heated her blood. She wanted to throw something at him, take that gun and turn it on him.

But she was a doctor, not a killer.

Although if they hurt Izzy, she might forget her oath.

She guzzled half the water bottle, then wiped her forehead with a cloth and returned to work. With every maneuver of the scalpel to alter his looks so he could walk away free, she imagined digging the blade into his cold, cold heart.

Voices echoed from the side. Concern flickered in one of the men's eyes as he answered a phone call. He motioned to the other man, and they surrounded her.

"Hurry up, we need to move."

"I need more time," Mila said. "What you're putting him through is dangerous."

"His choice," the brute said with a wave of his gun.

"I can't in good conscience finish if his blood pressure drops again."

"Just do your job. We have a place set up for his recovery."

"I can't work 24/7," Mila protested. "My hands aren't steady when I haven't slept."

"You'll have help and supplies where we're going," the man snapped.

"He's not up for travel," Mila argued.

The men conversed in Spanish for several seconds.

*Short, clipped angry words. She'd picked up a few phrases
but wasn't fluent.*

*But she thought they said something about a medical
facility close by.*

Another clinic? A hospital?

*The man with the radio jammed the gun at her chest.
"Finish and do it now. We have to go."*

Mila jerked awake, her heart racing. For a moment, she
was so disoriented she thought she was back in the clinic
operating room. But the curtain in the room was flapping,
the soft whir of the furnace rumbling.

She glanced around, clutched the bedding in her
clammy hands and blinked to focus. No, not in the clinic
or her house.

At Hawk's Landing. Brayden's cabin.

She pushed the covers aside, then padded to the door.
A dim light burned from the desk in the corner of the den.
Brayden was slumped over the desk snoring lightly.

She tiptoed into the room, which was bathed in early
morning sunlight shimmering through the French doors
leading to the porch. Dawn was just breaking the sky.

Wrapping her arms around herself, she padded over to
him and laid her hand on his shoulder.

"Brayden?" she whispered.

He startled, then jerked his head and looked up at her.
"Yeah?"

"I remembered something. They said they had a place
with medical supplies set up for DiSanti to recover. I think
it was close to the clinic."

Chapter Thirteen

Brayden sat upright and rubbed his hand over his eyes. "Did they say where it was?"

Mila ran a hand through her tangled hair. Flannel pajamas be damned. Sleepy eyed with those unruly strands draping her shoulders, she looked young and sexy.

Not a good thought, man.

"Not specifically," Mila said, her voice riddled with frustration. "They were speaking in Spanish. I'm not fluent, but I understand a few phrases and words from our trips abroad."

Needing a distraction from his earlier thoughts, he stood, walked over to the kitchen and started a pot of coffee.

"Did they mention a direction they were going? A landmark?"

Mila pinched the bridge of her nose. "It sounded like they said something about a corral."

Brayden frowned. They were in Texas, a land rich with ranches, farmland and corrals.

He poured her a cup of coffee and himself a mug, then offered cream and sugar.

"Black," she said, and thanked him.

He carried his coffee to his desk, then checked his phone for messages. Beck still hadn't returned his call. He checked his email next and had one from Dexter list-

ing a property that Jameson Beck owned that he thought
they should search.

He sent his brother a text asking him to look for locations that might involve a medical setting, old doctor's
office, abandoned hospital or lab, using the word *corral*.

Dex sent him a quick response that he was on it.

"Hopefully, Dex will get back to us about the corral.
I'm going to talk to Jameson Beck."

Mila sipped her coffee. "What does he have to do with
this?"

"He may be involved with DiSanti's operation," Brayden
said.

Mila looked perplexed. "Jameson Beck is supposed to
be helping citizens, not exploiting them."

"If we prove he's involved," Brayden said, "everyone
will know exactly what he's done. Not only will his politi-
cal career be over, but he'll serve time."

"I'm going with you," Mila said.

Brayden hesitated. "I'm not sure that's a good idea. I
haven't told Lucas—"

"I don't care," Mila said. "DiSanti's people still haven't
contacted me. If Beck is involved and knows what's happening with my daughter, then he should have to face me."

She had a point. It might be easier for Beck to blow him
off, but not so easy when Mila made the situation personal.

"All right," Brayden said. "But let me do the talking."

Mila agreed, although determination flared in her eyes.
"I'll get dressed."

He rushed to shower himself. Jameson Beck could be an
imposing man. He wanted to present himself as an equal.

But if he had anything to do with Mila's daughter being
taken, those kid gloves would come off.

Mila studied Jameson Beck with a skeptical eye. She'd always considered him a slick, cunning politician. He was

impeccably dressed, hair groomed, teeth postcard white. He said the correct things and smoothed ruffled feathers with locals over unemployment, issues facing the ranchers and taxes.

He pretended to be an advocate for the lower income although he sported an expensive foreign car and the cost of his Italian loafers would go a long way toward feeding the impoverished.

Nerves pricked Mila's spine. Beck shook both their hands, invited them into his office and offered coffee. But her stomach was twisted so tightly she could barely swallow water.

She certainly didn't intend to swallow his lies if he dodged their questions.

And what if he was conspiring with DiSanti and tipped him off that she was cooperating with the police?

"I received your message late last night," Beck commented. "You said it was urgent."

"It is. I'm assuming you saw the news story about Dr. Manchester's arrest," Brayden said. "I'm representing her."

Beck's gray eyes showed no reaction. "I'm afraid I didn't see the story," Beck said. "I was out of pocket all day yesterday and didn't get in until late last night."

Mila didn't believe him. In his position, he had people who kept him informed of what was happening in his city. With the upcoming election, he could pounce on anything juicy or topical and bend it to impress his constituents.

"Dr. Manchester was forced at gunpoint to perform surgery on DiSanti, a man suspected of spearheading the Shetland operation. You are familiar with that, aren't you?"

Brayden's biting tone seemed to raise Beck's hackles, but he quickly masked a reaction.

Beck rolled an expensive pen between his fingers. "Of course. I believe your brother made some arrests a few months ago and recovered four missing girls who'd been abducted by that group."

"That's correct." Brayden used a calm voice. "We need your help. If you know anything about DiSanti and his whereabouts, it's important that you tell us."

Beck leaned back in his desk chair, a picture of calm. "I wish I could help you, but I'm afraid I can't."

"Can't or won't?" Brayden asked, his voice challenging.

Beck clicked the pen. "I represent the people, Mr. Hawk. I would never associate with someone involved in illegal activities."

Brayden stood and leaned his hands on Beck's desk. "We both know that's a lie. Now, listen to me. I'm not after you. All I want is information about DiSanti and where he's hiding."

Anger slashed Beck's eyes. "I told you that I'm not involved with him."

"Maybe not," Brayden barked. "But if you're connected with someone who is, then tell me what you do know."

Beck buttoned his suit jacket. "I've asked and answered your question. Now it's time for you to leave."

Mila couldn't stand it any longer. She lurched up from her chair. "Mr. Beck, this man not only abducts and sells young women as sex slaves, but his people kidnapped my three-year-old little girl." Her voice broke. She snatched a picture from her wallet, a candid of Izzy at Christmas holding her baby doll. "Her name is Izzy," Mila said. "She's three, and she's afraid of the dark, and she likes macaroni and cheese and rainbows and ice cream."

A vein throbbed in his neck.

Mila gave him an imploring look. "If you know where he's holding her, please tell me."

His gaze met hers. His was full of steel, although a twinge of something akin to worry flickered in his eyes. Worry for himself or for her daughter?

He exhaled. "I'm sorry, Dr. Manchester. I hope you find her."

The calmness in his tone infuriated her even more. He was lying. She sensed it and refused to let him off the hook.

She snatched him by the collar and jerked his face toward hers. She expected Brayden to yank her away, but he didn't.

"If he hurts her, and I find out you knew where she was and didn't help me," she said through gritted teeth, "worrying about winning the election won't be an issue."

His gaze shot to Brayden. "You need to calm your client, Mr. Hawk."

Mila shook him. "This is calm, Mr. Beck." Venom laced her tone. "I promise you that if I don't get my daughter back safe and sound, jail will be the least of your problems."

"You heard her threaten me," Beck said to Brayden.

Brayden shrugged. "I didn't hear anything of the sort."

Mila straightened and reluctantly released Beck.

Beck cleared his throat, his nostrils flaring. "The next time you want to talk to me, go through my attorney."

Brayden shot him a cynical smile. "Fine. I'm sure the residents of Austin will be interested in knowing that instead of helping us find a known sex trafficker and a missing child, that you lawyered up to protect your own ass."

Brayden didn't wait for a response. He took Mila's arm and they left the room.

Her heart hammered in her chest. Brayden Hawk was a formidable man and lawyer.

He was also one of the good guys, not like Beck, who was all show with a selfish, greedy side lurking beneath.

BRAYDEN'S PHONE BUZZED as he and Mila climbed back into his SUV. Dex.

He quickly connected. "I'm just leaving Beck's office. That bastard knows something, but he sure as hell isn't talking."

"I'll keep digging," Dex said. "I did find something though—at least I think I did. You said Mila mentioned something about a corral?"

"Like I said, they were speaking in Spanish, so she wasn't sure of the translation."

"I found an abandoned hospital in a small hole-in-the-wall town called O'Kade Corral," Dex said.

Brayden's pulse jumped. "Where is it?"

"Sending the address to your phone now," Dex said. "The town was built around some old mines, which was the reason for the hospital. But the mines yielded nothing, so the workers moved on and the town crumbled."

But it would provide a hiding spot for DiSanti during his recuperation.

Dex agreed to meet him there, and Brayden hung up, then glanced at the address Dex had sent. Mila was checking her own phone, willing it to ring again, he guessed.

Disappointment lined her face as she laid it back in her lap. "What's going on?"

Brayden explained about Dex's call. "The town isn't far from here."

Mila fastened her seat belt. "Let's go."

Brayden fastened his own seat belt, started the engine and veered into traffic. He wove through the downtown streets of Austin, then onto the highway leading out of the city.

Mila twisted her phone between her hands, constantly checking it as he raced down the highway. He considered calling Lucas, but he didn't want to waste Lucas's time if this was a wild-goose chase.

The city landscape gave way to farmland and ranches, then he veered onto a narrow road that wove through miles and miles of nothing. The road was bumpy and filled with potholes, another sign that the area was deserted.

He maneuvered a turn, then spotted several small buildings in the distance. The town looked like a ghost town—a small building that had once been a mercantile, a bank, a diner and honky-tonk. All deserted, the buildings weathered, paint fading.

He scanned the streets and surrounding land for cars or signs indicating someone was here. A few pieces of rusted mining equipment had been left near the overgrown trails leading to the mines.

"It looks vacant," Mila said, disappointment tingeing her voice.

In the distance sat a larger building that could be the old hospital. A white van and an ambulance were parked near the building, half hidden by weeds and patchy shrubs.

Mila clutched his arm. "They were driving a van the night they brought DiSanti to the clinic."

Brayden pulled over between a clump of trees to wait on Dexter. The last thing he wanted was to alert DiSanti's men they were here before backup arrived.

If he got himself and Mila killed, he couldn't save Izzy.

He texted Dex to tell him to approach with caution and pull off where he'd parked. The air in the car felt charged with tension as they waited, Mila's anxiety palpable.

Five minutes passed, then Dex coasted up in his black pickup. He slowed and veered into the space beside Brayden and parked. Brayden removed his handgun from the locked dash and checked the magazine.

Both he and his brother eased their doors open and slid out, carefully closing them so they didn't make noise. Mila joined them, but Dexter and he exchanged understanding looks.

"Stay here while we take a look around," Brayden said.

"But if Izzy's there, she'll be scared and need me," Mila whispered.

Brayden gently touched her arm. "It's too dangerous, Mila. Once we scout out the hospital, we'll let you know if it appears anyone is there. If DiSanti's here, we'll call Lucas for backup."

"But if Izzy's in there—"

"Rushing inside without a plan could work against us," Brayden said. "We have to play it smart. The most important thing is to get Izzy out safely."

Mila sighed and gripped the edge of the SUV. "Please find her, Brayden."

His heart stuttered. Dex's face twisted with emotions, as well.

"We'll do our best," Brayden said. "But I need you to stay in the SUV, lock the doors and keep down. If DiSanti has men watching or riding the property, we don't want them to see you."

Mila agreed, and he waited until she was locked inside the vehicle, then he and Dexter headed through the woods toward the building.

Dex pulled binoculars from his pocket and focused on the van and ambulance first, then across the property.

He shook his head, indicating he didn't see movement.

Brayden gripped his gun at the ready, and they crossed behind some trees, taking cover as they moved toward the building.

Dex motioned that he'd check the side windows, while Brayden veered around the right to the back window near the parked ambulance.

Just as he grew close, something caught his eye.

A small stuffed monkey. It looked well-worn and loved, its ears frayed.

His throat closed. If it belonged to Izzy, she might be here.

Chapter Fourteen

Brayden stooped down, picked up the stuffed monkey, his heart clenching at the tattered ears. Izzy, or some child, had loved this little toy. It had probably given comfort.

He stuffed it inside his pocket and inched forward until he reached the back door, a metal one with a window covered to offer privacy to patients it had once served—or to hide whoever was inside.

Dex gave a low whistle from the side of the building and gestured that he couldn't see inside.

In fact, all the windows were covered.

Suspicious.

Brayden crept forward and gently turned the doorknob. Locked.

Dex appeared a second later. Brayden ignored the fact that his brother carried a lock-picking tool and that they had no warrant. If he had to, he'd say they thought they heard a child crying inside.

Dex picked the lock and turned the knob, pushing it open an inch at a time. Brayden peered through the opening. The interior was dark. Quiet.

His heart hammered.

Dex motioned for them to go inside, and Brayden slipped into the doorway. Dex kept his gun at the ready and went right, and they both paused to listen. A rattling sound. Wind whistling through the cracks in the windows.

No voices. No lights.

Still, they moved with caution in case DiSanti's men had been here and left a lookout guy to ambush them. He followed his brother down the hall, each checking rooms on the side of the hall. Exam rooms, a surgical wing, a pharmacy with glass cabinets that had once held drugs, a recovery room, then several patient rooms, two of which still housed hospital beds.

All empty.

Dex motioned to another room at the end, and he inched along behind Dex, both treading quietly until they reached the room. Brayden peered through the window of the door. Empty.

But it looked as if someone had been there recently.

He pushed open the door and stepped inside, waving Dexter to join him. The lights were off, so he pulled his flashlight from his pocket and shone it around the room.

Alcohol, blood stoppers and medical supplies filled a metal side table. Bloody clothes were stuffed into a bin next to a hospital bed that appeared to have recently been slept in. A sheet and blanket stained with blood were rumpled on top of the mattress, and a used syringe lay on another steel table.

"They're gone," Dexter said. "Do you think they knew we were coming?"

"I don't know how they could," Brayden said. "You only discovered this place today."

"Maybe one of them figured out that Mila overheard their conversation."

"I guess that's possible." Brayden's hand rubbed the stuffed monkey in his pocket, and he showed it to his brother. "Let's search the cabinets and closets in case Izzy was here."

Dex traded a worried look with him. If she was, and

they thought Mila had ratted them out, they might have ditched her.

He prayed that wasn't the case, but DiSanti was the most ruthless man he'd ever encountered.

WHAT WAS TAKING so long?

Mila remained hidden, but the minutes dragged by, intensifying her anxiety. Had the Hawk men found something inside?

She turned and scanned the property for vehicles, but the place appeared deserted. Fresh tire marks marred the dirt leading up to the hospital, another set leading past the hospital to the opposite side.

Someone had been here recently, and they were gone. But where? What lay to the south?

She reached for the doorknob to go and look in that van herself, then remembered Brayden's warning.

Still jittery, she checked her phone. No text or phone call.

She logged in to her work email and checked messages at the clinic. Not that DiSanti would send her a message there. It would be too easy for the police to check.

Why hadn't they called? Lucas had announced that she wasn't cooperating.

Maybe she should ask Brayden and Lucas to set up a TV interview where she could make a public plea for her daughter's return. By now, DiSanti and his men could be hundreds of miles away.

If they had Izzy with them, she might never see her little girl again.

Panic robbed her breath. She reached for the door handle once more, but saw movement ahead.

Brayden and his brother Dexter exiting the building.

Disappointment swelled inside her. Izzy wasn't with

them. They were no closer to getting her back than they had been before.

Lucas's statement taunted her. She'd read the statistics, too. Every minute, every hour, every day that they didn't find Mila's daughter diminished her chances of finding her alive.

Brayden halted by the van, opened the door and climbed inside while his brother searched the back of the ambulance. She held her breath as she waited, her patience waning when they finished and walked toward her.

She slipped from the SUV. "Did you find anything inside?"

Brayden's dark expression made her stomach knot. "They were here," he said. "There were bloody cloths and medical supplies spread out, but they're gone."

Mila gestured toward the tire tracks. "It looks like a vehicle left that way," she said.

Dex shone his light on the tracks to examine them.

Mila rocked back on the balls of her feet. "Brayden, was there any sign of Izzy?"

Brayden removed something from his jacket pocket and handed it toward her. "Is this hers?"

Mila nodded, then took the tiny monkey and pressed it to her chest.

BRAYDEN'S PHONE BUZZED. LUCAS.

"Was there any clue where?" Mila asked.

"I'm afraid not," Brayden said. "But DiSanti's men could have taken her to another location, maybe where they're holding other victims."

They'd kept Charlotte's students at an abandoned ranch off the grid. If Izzy was with other girls, she wouldn't be quite so terrified. Except they usually kept those girls drugged and incoherent.

There hadn't been reports of any abductions near Tumbleweed or Austin in the past few weeks, but DiSanti's people might be moving victims from other states through. Or they could be playing it more low-key, taking one victim at a time, choosing from runaways or girls without families who no one would report missing.

His phone buzzed again. "It's Lucas. I need to get this."

Mila leaned against the car while he walked a few feet away for privacy.

"Where are you?" Lucas asked.

Brayden braced himself for one of Lucas's big-brother lectures. But if they wanted to find DiSanti and Izzy, they had to work together, so he explained.

"Dammit, Brayden, why didn't you call me?" Lucas asked.

Because he didn't want to get his brother in trouble in case Dex and he straddled the law. "There wasn't time," Brayden said. "Besides, I didn't know if it would lead to anything. I want you working your end."

"I am," Lucas said. "But I can't do that if I have to worry about you going off on your own."

"I'm not alone," Brayden said.

Lucas exploded with a string of expletives. "Dex is with you?"

"Yes, but we haven't broken any laws, Lucas. Dex and I just checked out an abandoned hospital. DiSanti was here, but he's gone."

Lucas hissed between his teeth. "Any sign where they went from there?"

"No, but I found a stuffed toy indicating Mila's daughter was here."

"Dammit." Lucas paused, breath wheezing out. "I heard that you paid Jameson Beck a visit."

Brayden clenched his jaw. "Yeah, but he's not talking."

"I didn't expect him to. But our analyst traced one of

his phone calls to an old inn in a small town about thirty miles south of Austin."

The tire tracks leading away from the hospital were headed south.

"Send me the address."

"Brayden, let me do this."

"Let's meet, Lucas. If Izzy's there, she'll need Mila." He lowered his voice so she couldn't hear. "And if Izzy's hurt or if there are other hostages, they might need medical attention."

A strained heartbeat passed. "I don't like it, but you're right."

He ended the call then went to tell Dexter and Mila the plan.

MILA TWISTED THE monkey in her hands as Brayden drove toward Cactus Grove, a small town south of Austin that drew tourists for its desertlike garden, variety of cacti and sagebrush. A local museum showcased the history of the wagon trains that used to travel through the town to Austin, and the town still boasted a working train station.

"Is Dexter coming?" Mila asked.

Brayden shook his head. "He's going to check with one of his CIs. Maybe he'll have information that can help."

"Does Lucas think DiSanti's in this town?" Mila asked.

Brayden shrugged. "It's possible. He traced a call from Beck to Cactus Grove. If DiSanti's operation is using the town as a holding place for trafficking and we can connect it to Beck, then we can use it as leverage to force Beck to talk."

Mila fidgeted with her phone. "Why haven't they called me, Brayden?"

Brayden clenched his jaw. "Maybe they're just regrouping." Or maybe they'd left the country and taken Izzy with them. The countryside flew past as Brayden sped down the road to Cactus Grove. The wind stirred the pines and sage-brush, flinging dust across the road in a brown fog.

As they approached the small town, traffic built slightly, although compared to Austin they were in the wilderness. They passed the train station and museum, then a newer inn in town that was decked out for Thanksgiving. At the end of the square, an old-fashioned diner and a Western saloon invited customers to enjoy a taste of days gone by. Brayden parked in front of the town stage.

"What are you doing?" Mila asked.

"Waiting on Lucas."

Mila studied the wooden platform in front of them. "What is this place?"

"Every year the town performs a reenactment of a historical gunfight that occurred in the town a hundred years ago."

She tapped her foot, impatient as they waited on Lucas to arrive. A black sedan crawled by and slowed as if looking at them, then a dark gray Cadillac.

Lucas pulled up and motioned for them to join him in his sedan. When they climbed in, Lucas gave them both stern looks.

"I'm in charge here, so you two need to do as I say."

"Yes, sir," Brayden said with a tinge of irritation.

"I mean it, Brayden. I know you have experience, but I don't want either of you getting hurt."

"I don't give a damn about getting hurt," Mila said. "All I want is my daughter back."

"That's exactly what worries me," Lucas said with a frown.

Brayden raked a hand through his hair. "He's right, Mila. When we get there, you have to stay inside the car and remain hidden. If we find something, we'll come and get you. I promise."

Mila bit down on her lower lip and nodded. She'd been held at gunpoint by DiSanti's men. She knew what it was like to be powerless. The last thing she wanted was to get her daughter hurt or to die and leave Izzy without a mother.

Lucas started the engine, then turned onto a narrow road leading toward more farmland.

"There's an inn out here?" Mila asked.

Brayden nodded. "It was the original one and catered not only to tourists, but miners who still thought they might find gold in the mines. They abandoned the inn a couple of years ago when they built the new one by the train station. Made it easier for people to walk the town."

They passed several abandoned small cabins and a building that had probably once been used to store mining supplies, then she spotted the inn, an antebellum house with a big porch that looked homey and quaint.

Those abandoned buildings could be used to hold trafficking victims.

A black van was parked in back of the inn, an old pickup near the warehouse.

"We'll check the inn first, then those buildings," Lucas said.

Brayden gave Mila a pointed look. "I meant what I said. Stay put."

"I will," she said, her hand stroking the monkey's ears.

"If you see something, text me," Brayden said. He shocked her by slipping a small .22 into her hand.

She looked at the gun, not sure if she could use it. But an image of Izzy being held by that monster taunted her, and she knew she could shoot if it meant saving her daughter's life.

Lucas took the lead as the men climbed from the car and inched toward the inn.

She held her breath, praying for their safety and that they found Izzy before it was too late.

Time seemed to stand still. The tension thrumming through her made her feel sick inside.

Suddenly her phone buzzed. She startled, then glanced down at it. Brayden?

No.

A text. She opened it and gasped. A picture of her little girl huddled in a dark corner, teary eyed and terrified.

Then a message.

If you want to see your daughter again, ditch the cops. Will contact again with instructions.

Chapter Fifteen

Brayden approached the inn, his senses alert. Lucas motioned to let him take the lead, and Brayden did. Entering an unknown situation that could be an ambush was never his favorite part of police work.

He'd gotten spoiled by dealing with trouble and crime in the courtroom instead of on the front line. Although the law could be frustrating at times, too.

Seeing a guilty criminal released without being punished was infuriating and happened too often, while watching an innocent person go to prison was intolerable.

Lucas paused to listen at the door, his brows furrowed. When he looked back at Brayden, his brother gestured that he heard something.

Maybe someone was inside?

He eased open the door, gun at the ready, and inched inside. Brayden peeked past him. The interior was dark and appeared deserted. At one time, this place housed tourists and travelers driving from Austin toward Mexico. It had drawn miners but also catered to cattle ranchers and horse lovers.

Paintings of wild mustangs hung in the entryway, where the wallpaper was fading, the curtains a dull pale gray.

Lucas swung left and Brayden went right. He scanned the dining room while his brother ducked into a formal living room/parlor that had probably once hosted after-noon tea for guests.

The room was empty, but led to a large kitchen with a giant oak table. A case of bottled water sat on a grimy counter. Loaves of bread, canned beans and cans of soup filled a box indicating a recent shopping trip.

Someone had been here.

A noise sounded from upstairs, and he froze. Maybe someone was still here.

Lucas's footsteps echoed from the front. He must be going up the staircase. A back stairwell caught Brayden's eye, and he headed toward it. He forced his footfalls to remain light, although the old wooden floors squeaked as he climbed them.

He stopped on the landing and noted a large room to the right. The hall led to other rooms that had once been rented to guests.

Lucas appeared at the opposite end, then ducked into one of the bedrooms. Brayden veered into the larger room, which must have been used as a suite. The front area held a love seat, chair and coffee table. He crept toward the inner door and thought he heard a noise coming from behind it.

He hesitated, listening for voices, determined not to walk into a trap. No male voices. Maybe someone crying?

His pulse jumped. Was it Izzy?

Body coiled with tension, he eased open the door, keeping his gun braced in case one of DiSanti's men lay waiting on the other side. Another sound. A moan.

Crying. Definitely crying.

Anger forced him forward, his temper rising even more when he spotted three cots in the room. Cots where three young girls lay.

In one quick glance, he realized they'd been drugged. Two of them were either asleep or unconscious while the third, a scrawny brunette who was probably about thirteen, lay huddled with her knees up, sobbing into her hands.

He took a deep breath, then slowly approached her. His foot made the floor creak, and she startled and jerked her head up, her eyes wide with terror.

"Shh, it's okay," he murmured. "I'm here to help you."

She scooted as far as possible against the wall, body trembling, eyes red and swollen from crying. He took a step closer, wanting to check the other girls' pulses, but she shrieked and shook her head wildly, causing him to stop.

He held up his hand in a sign that he wouldn't hurt them. "You're okay now. I'm going to get help."

She stared at him wide-eyed, and he backed toward the door. He ran into Lucas in the hall.

"There are three girls in there," he told his brother.

"Two more in the other room," Lucas said gruffly. "Both drugged and unconscious." He removed his phone from his pocket. "I'll call an ambulance."

Brayden nodded. "I'll get Mila."

"Good idea." Lucas walked to the door to peek in on the three girls Brayden had found, his expression grim.

They still needed to check the outbuildings, but he'd get Mila first.

MILA CHECKED HER phone a dozen times, hoping for another message, but nothing yet.

She had to do whatever DiSanti's men said. But separating herself from Brayden and Lucas would be difficult. And how would she rescue Izzy on her own?

If she went with them, they still might kill her and Izzy…

A movement on the hill startled her. Brayden exited the inn. His face looked stony as he scanned the property and exterior of the outbuildings. Then he hurried toward the woods where they'd parked.

She'd hoped he'd find Izzy, but that text had killed her hopes. If there was nothing here, maybe Brayden was ready to go. She'd have him drive her back to her place or the clinic, somewhere she'd have access to a car.

He tapped on the window, and she unlocked the door and opened it with a shaky hand.

"We found some girls inside," Brayden said. "They've been drugged. We need you."

Her medical training kicked in, and she scrambled out of the car.

"I don't have a medical bag with me," she said, frustrated. She always carried one in her car. She might need one when she found her daughter.

"It's okay. Lucas called an ambulance so help should be here soon. One girl is conscious and terrified of me. Maybe you can calm her until the medics arrive."

"Of course." Mila raced beside him as they climbed the hill. "Any sign of DiSanti or his men?"

"Just some cans of food and water, but no evidence of DiSanti or medical supplies." His breath heaved out as they made it to the door. "No telling how long the girls have been here. This is probably a holding spot until they can move or sell them."

Lucas met them at the bottom of the stairs. "Two in the room on the end. Both have pulses, but they're weak. I was afraid to get too close to the others and spook the one who's conscious. Ambulance should be here in ten."

"No sign of Izzy?" Mila asked.

Lucas shook his head. "Perhaps the girl who's conscious can tell us something about where they were going."

Mila latched onto that hope as she followed Brayden up the stairs. The dust, cobwebs, fading wallpaper and scratched floors were a sign that the inn hadn't been used in at least a decade.

DiSanti had taken advantage of that just like he took advantage of everything else.

"Brace yourself," Brayden said in a low voice. "It's not pretty."

"I've seen a lot of bad things in my field," Mila said, although the inhumane treatment people inflicted on others never ceased to amaze—and disgust—her.

Brayden opened the door, but she motioned for him to let her enter first. The lighting was dim, the smell of sweat and urine strong. Someone had also been sick.

She breathed out, emotions welling inside her at the sight of the two unconscious girls on the cots. Both wore dresses way too short for them, which had ridden up their legs as they lay sprawled on the beds.

The third girl was shaking and crying, her arms wrapped around her knees, her fear a palpable force in the room.

"Hi," she said in a soft tone as she slowly walked toward the teens. "My name is Dr. Mila Manchester." She offered the frightened girl a warm smile. "My friend Brayden works with the police. We're here to rescue you." The crying girl sniffed and clenched her legs tighter.

"I promise, we won't hurt you. We know some bad men brought you here, and we're going to take you to the hospital for treatment, then make sure you're safe."

The girl's face crumpled, and a wail escaped her. Mila was afraid she'd said the wrong thing, but she didn't have time to second-guess herself. No telling what DiSanti's cronies had done to the young girl.

She approached the cots where the two unconscious girls lay, hair spilled on the pillows, bodies limp. At first glance, they didn't appear to be breathing. She stooped between the two cots and gently pressed her hand to the first girl's cheek, a sandy-blonde girl with pale skin and freckles. Her skin felt cold and clammy, and she didn't respond. Mila checked for a pulse and was relieved to find one, although, as Lucas reported on the other two teens, it was weak.

She gave Brayden a quick nod to indicate the girl was alive, then turned to the other, an auburn-haired girl. Bruises darkened the pale skin beneath her eyes and covered her legs. One arm dangled from the side of the bed, while the other hand clutched the sheet to her as if she was fighting to cover herself and preserve her dignity.

Mila checked for a pulse, then breathed a sigh of relief that she had one. Gently, she stroked the girl's cold cheek with the back of her hand. "Hang in there, sweetheart. You're going to be okay."

Anger churned in her belly at what these girls had endured. They had to survive.

All the more reason to save Izzy. If not, and DiSanti killed her and kept Izzy alive, she might end up like these teenagers. That was not going to happen to her daughter, no matter what she had to do.

Satisfied the girls were breathing, she turned her attention to the brunette staring at her with terror-glazed eyes.

"Hey, sweetie, I told you my name is Dr. Manchester, but you can call me Mila."

The girl clamped her teeth over her lower lip and simply stared at her with distrust.

Who could blame her? She had reason not to trust.

Mila offered her a sympathetic smile. "Your friends, the other girls here, they're alive, and I'm going to make sure they receive medical treatment." And psychiatric help if needed.

"I understand that you're scared," Mila said, inching closer. "But everything's going to be all right. You're never going to have to see those bad men again."

The girl's breath hitched.

Mila offered her another smile. "What's your name, sweetie?"

The girl gave a wary nod, then whispered, "Keenan."

"Hi, Keenan, it's nice to meet you. Like I said, my name is Mila. I'm a doctor. Can you tell me how you ended up here?"

The girl whimpered. "They took me…from the shelter," she said in a raw whisper.

"I'm so sorry, honey." She patted the girl's thin hand. "Do you have some family I can call? A mother? Father? Grandparent?"

Keenan shook her head no. "My grandma took me to the shelter when we got evicted, but she was sick…and she didn't make it."

"Do you remember the name of the shelter?"

The girl rubbed her forehead, then shook her head. "No, it was late, and I was so upset over Granny that I didn't pay attention."

"Shh, it's all right now. I promise I'll take care of you." She reached out and patted Keenan's thin shoulder, relieved when the young girl didn't jerk away. "I think you were drugged. Am I right?"

Another nod.

"Do you have any idea what they gave you?"

Keenan shook her head no.

"Was it in your food? Or did they inject you?"

The girl held out her arm. Mila gritted her teeth at the sight of the needle marks. Fury mushroomed inside her.

The sound of a siren wailed from outside, and Brayden stepped back into the room and motioned that the ambulance had arrived.

"The paramedics are going to transport you and the other girls to the hospital," Mila said.

Fear flashed in Keenan's eyes, and she clutched Mila's hand, her ragged nails digging into Mila's palms.

Mila's heart ached for her. "I'll go with you," Mila promised. "And I'll stay with you every step of the way."

The girl nodded vigorously, tears trickling down her cheek. Fear streaked her face as she glanced at the door. "They're coming back for us," she said on a sob.

Mila glanced at Brayden, then squeezed the girl's hand. "They won't find you, I promise. Brayden's brother is with the FBI."

Brayden murmured that it would be okay, too. "We'll post someone here and catch them when they return," Brayden assured her.

Mila inhaled a deep breath. "Keenan, the men who brought you here and drugged you work for another man named DiSanti. Does that name sound familiar?"

Keenan gave a small shrug. "Maybe."

Mila patted her arm. "I need to ask you one more question." She removed her phone and showed her a picture of Izzy. "I think those same men kidnapped my little girl. She's only three and her name is Izzy."

The girl's eyes widened, and she gasped for a breath, as if she was having a panic attack.

Panic clawed at Mila. "Did you see Izzy? Was she here?"

Chapter Sixteen

Mila felt as if her heart stopped beating. "Keenan, have you seen this little girl?"

The young girl wiped at her tears with the back of a bruised hand and gave a little nod.

Mila's pulse jumped. "Was she here?"

The girl nodded again.

Mila swallowed back a sob. "Was she okay? Was she hurt?"

Keenan's look softened. "She was scared, but Jade took care of her."

"Jade?"

"She was one of us," Keenan said. "She kept the little girl close to her, and told the men to leave them alone."

Relief lightened Mila's fear for a millisecond. At least they hadn't hurt Izzy. Not yet.

But Lucas was searching the outbuildings now.

She held Keenan's hand again, warming it between her own. "When did they leave you here?"

"This morning."

Damn. If they'd only gotten here sooner…

She straightened. She had to focus. "Was Jade with Izzy when they left?"

Keenan nodded. "The little girl was clinging to her."

Emotions throbbed inside Mila's chest. "Did the men say where they were going?"

The young girl rubbed her forehead again, her eyes crinkling. "No…at least I didn't hear them."

Footsteps sounded in the hall, then Brayden appeared with two medics.

Mila patted Keenan's hand and stood. "It's going to be okay now. Hang in there, sweetie."

Mila hurried to meet the medics and watched as they began taking vitals.

"Let's get them to the hospital stat," Mila said. "I want a full blood panel to identify the drugs they were given, also rape kits and full body workups."

The next few minutes were hectic as the medics carried the teens to the ambulance. Keenan was weak, but seemed to be stronger now that she realized she could trust Mila, and insisted she could walk. Mila helped her down the steps and outside.

Lucas and Brayden met them at the ambulance.

"Nothing in the outbuildings," Lucas said.

Brayden touched her elbow. "Did the girl tell you anything?"

Mila whispered to Keenan to climb in the ambulance and assured her she'd ride with her. But first she had to talk to Brayden. "Keenan said Izzy was here. A girl named Jade was taking care of her, protecting her from DiSanti's men."

"Any idea where they went?" Brayden asked.

"I'm afraid not. But they just left this morning so maybe they haven't gotten too far," Mila said.

Brayden stepped to the back of the ambulance. "Keenan, did you see what kind of vehicle the men were driving when they left?"

The girl shook her head. "They put us in a white van."

They'd used white vans before. So generic, dammit. "I'll ask Lucas to have their analyst check traffic cams on the highways near here."

Mila checked her phone again.

Still nothing.

Frustration knotted her stomach, but she climbed in the back of the ambulance.

She'd help Keenan and the others while Lucas searched for the van.

LUCAS CALLED A crime scene team to process the house and property, then Brayden and his brother followed the ambulances to the hospital.

The staff rushed the girls to the ER, and Lucas spoke with the doctor on call to request rape kits for the victims, although the doctor reported that Mila had already requested the exams be done. Keenan became upset at the idea, but Mila soothed her and promised to stay with her every step of the way.

The next hour dragged by as they waited on tests and for the girls to regain consciousness. Lucas checked in constantly with his people, hoping for word on the van or DiSanti.

Brayden phoned Dexter to relay the latest events.

"I've been digging into locals who might be involved in this trafficking unit. Lem Corley is on Lucas's short list," Dexter said. "Word is that he's retired and hired a cowboy out of El Paso to run the cattle ranching business. He's also bought up property near the Mexican border in Juarez."

"We know that. Do you have anything new?" Brayden asked. "What about his financials?"

"Corley has a hefty savings, but he could argue that he's built that from the cattle operation." Dexter paused. "I found an offshore account with a couple million in it. There's no indication that his business pulled in that kind of money."

Brayden chewed the inside of his cheek. "That is suspicious."

"Could be drugs," Dexter said.

"Or he could be shuffling young women across the border for DiSanti." Brayden glanced at Lucas, who was talking to one of the nurses. "Send me the address for the ranch near Austin. We'll talk to Corley once we finish here."

"Copy that. I'll keep digging and see if I can find out more on that property in Juarez."

Brayden thanked him, then hung up and joined Lucas.

"The girls are traumatized," the doctor said. "Two of them regained consciousness, but they're terrified and not talking. I've requested a psych exam and counselor."

"Let me call my wife, Charlotte," Lucas said. "You may remember her from a few months ago when her art therapy studio was invaded and four of her students were abducted."

The doctor nodded. "Yes, I was glad to hear that they were all found alive and safe."

"We think the man who orchestrated their abduction spearheaded the Shetland operation," Lucas said. "We also believe he's behind the trafficking ring that was holding the five victims here hostage. It's imperative I speak with them when they regain consciousness. They might be able to give us a lead as to where the ringleader went."

"I understand, but as I said before, these patients are severely traumatized. They need rest, medical treatment and therapy."

"My wife, Charlotte, can help," Lucas insisted. "She's an art therapist and has experience with DiSanti's victims. These girls might feel comfortable with her and open up."

"Excellent," the doctor said. "The other girls are stable, but were heavily medicated, so it may be hours before they become lucid."

"When they do, I want Charlotte to talk to them," Lucas

said. "A little girl is missing and is in the hands of the leader of the trafficking ring."

The doctor wiped perspiration from his brow. "Of course."

Lucas thanked him, then stepped aside to call Charlotte. Mila appeared at the entry to the waiting room, looking worried and exhausted.

Brayden rushed toward her. He wanted to hold her, to promise her everything would be all right.

"Keenan is finally calmer and sleeping," Mila said.

"Was she able to tell you anything else?" Brayden asked.

Mila shook her head. "I'm afraid not. Unfortunately she was pretty incoherent when the men were around."

Brayden's heart went out to the girl and to Mila. She was a gutsy, strong woman. Even though she was terrified for her daughter, she had compassion for these victims.

"The doctor said two of the girls have regained consciousness. Maybe they can help."

Mila's eyes darkened with concern. "I hope so."

Brayden couldn't resist. He pulled her up against him and wrapped his arms around her. "It's going to be okay, Mila. We'll find her."

Her heavy breathing punctuated the air. He thought she might pull away, but she laid her head against his chest and seemed to give in to her own needs for a moment. He rubbed her back, rocking her gently in his arms. When she lifted her head and looked into his eyes, the agony in hers nearly sent him to his knees.

"Keenan is so lost," Mila said. "I don't know if she'll ever truly recover. Or the others."

He offered a smile of encouragement. "It may seem like that now, but I've seen the progress Charlotte's students have made these last few months. It's amazing. With her help and my mother's love, they feel secure now and are moving on, even looking forward to the future. They have a family, even if it's not the one they were born to."

Mila bit down on her lip, then pulled away.

"Did I say something wrong? You don't think that my mother could love them like they're her own?"

Mila stiffened. "Of course I believe that. I was adopted myself." She thumbed a strand of hair away from her cheek. "You said two of the girls are awake now. I'd like to talk to them."

"I know. So would I, but the doctor asked us to wait. Lucas is calling Charlotte to come and counsel the girls. Maybe you and Charlotte can talk with them together."

Mila nodded. "Yes, I'm sure they need a counselor after what they've been through. And I promise not to push them too hard. I want what's best for the girls, too."

She was the most unselfish woman Brayden had ever met. He was falling for her.

That thought should have shaken him up.

But for some reason, in the midst of the ugliness surrounding him, it felt right.

"Charlotte is on her way." Lucas's commanding voice forced Brayden to put his personal thoughts on hold. He jerked his mind back to the case.

"Dexter sent me GPS coordinates for Lem Corley's ranch. He checked Corley's financials and found an offshore account with a hefty amount in it. He's also looking into his property in Juarez."

"It's near the border," Lucas said. "We have an agent investigating it."

"He could be helping DiSanti move victims across the border into Mexico."

A muscle ticked in Lucas's jaw. "I'm going to talk to him now."

Brayden cleared his throat. "I'll go with you." He glanced at Mila. "That is, if you'll be okay here for a while."

Mila clasped her hands together. "I'll be fine. I want to stay with the girls until they're out of the woods."

MILA MEANT WHAT she'd told Brayden. But even as she'd assured Keenan she was safe, all she could think about was Izzy and what was happening to her.

If DiSanti could possibly have figured out that she was his child.

She prayed not, that her secret was safe.

She'd die before she'd let that bastard know he had a precious little girl. Izzy belonged to her.

She went to the vending machines, bought a cup of coffee and carried it back to the waiting room. Charlotte was just coming in the door when she arrived. She made a beeline toward Mila, then embraced her.

They were both a little teary when they pulled away.

"Lucas said that one of the girls saw Izzy. That's good news, Mila."

Mila forced a smile, although her heart wasn't in it. "That's been hours though." It had been hours since that text message too and still no word of what she should do.

DiSanti wanted her to lose the feds. Did that mean he was watching her to see if she complied?

She glanced around the hospital, suddenly suspicious that one of the staff or maybe one of the people in the waiting room—there was a big guy in a hoodie—might be on DiSanti's payroll. He could have planted someone to follow her.

The doctor on call, a man named Dr. Hembry, approached her. "Dr. Manchester, I came to give you an update. The two girls who regained consciousness are physically going to be fine. But they're scared to death."

Mila gestured toward Charlotte. "This is Charlotte Reacher Hawk, the wife of the federal agent you were talking to. He told you she could help."

"That's right, you're the therapist." He shook Charlotte's hand. "At this point, having a kind face, especially a woman's, will go a long way."

"Then I can see them?" Charlotte asked.

Dr. Hembry nodded. "We thought it might help if we put the girls in the same room," Dr. Hembry said.

He led the two of them to an ER room, and they slipped inside.

Miia took one look at the two young girls, and hated DiSanti more than ever. The battered teens looked lost and terrified and small in the hospital beds.

She and Charlotte approached slowly, and Mila explained that she was with the federal agent who'd rescued them.

Charlotte introduced herself, then Mila did the same.

She offered them a sympathetic smile. "I understand you've both been through a frightening ordeal, and we want to help you."

Charlotte scooted a chair between the beds, so she could face both girls. "I'm here for whatever you need," she said softly. "I know some other girls who were abducted by the same man who took you. We rescued them last year, and they're safe now. So are you."

The girls traded wary looks, both limp from the drugs and their ordeal.

"You can start by telling us your names," Charlotte said. "Also, tell us if you have family or a friend that you want us to call."

Unfortunately, the girls had no one to call just as Keenan hadn't. Perfect targets for DiSanti's people.

She and Charlotte spent the next hour soothing the girls and coaxing them to open up. Anita Robinson was fourteen, from El Paso and had run away from home after her mother died. Left with a stepfather who abused her, she took to the streets. She had no idea how long she'd been held hostage and had no family to call. But she'd ended up at a group home called Happy Trails.

Frannie Fenter was thirteen. She was kidnapped outside the group home where she was living. The same group home, Happy Trails, a ranch that supposedly helped orphans as the Hawks were doing.

Was the home legit or part of the Shetland operation?

Izzy CURLED UP with the raggedy blanket the big girl had given her. She was cold, hungry and scared. She wanted her mommy bad.

Tears ran down her face, but she pressed her fist to her mouth so she wouldn't cry out loud.

Jade, the girl who'd let her sleep with her the night before, rubbed her arm and shushed her.

She tried not to cry. But she couldn't help it. She wanted her mommy. She missed her and Roberta and Brownie and her pretty bed with the pink quilt. She wanted to run and play in her backyard and dig up worms and climb on her jungle gym. There were bird's eggs in a nest, too. Had the babies hatched already?

"I wanna go home," she whimpered. "I want Mama."

Jade wrapped the blanket around her tighter and pulled her up against her. "I know, sweetie. I know."

Jade looked sad, too. She said she hadn't seen her mother in years.

That made Izzy even more scared that she'd never see her mama again.

Chapter Seventeen

Mila stewed over what the girls had revealed so far. None of them had families, making them easy targets for DiSanti's men. Without family to report them missing, it might take months before anyone realized they were gone.

Except the head of the group home would have known.

Mila wanted to know more, but first, she had to ask them about her daughter. She showed them Izzy's photo. "This is my little girl. She's only three. Keenan said that she was at the house where you were. Do either of you recall seeing her?"

Frannie nodded, but Anita shook her head.

"I'm sorry. I don't remember much," Anita said.

"Did the men say anything about where they were going when they left?" Mila asked.

Frannie's lower lip quivered. "I heard one of them say they had to move us again, but they needed to take care of something first."

"Do you know what that something was?" Mila asked.

She shook her head. "It seemed important though. He shouted at the other man."

Charlotte stroked Frannie's arm. "You're doing great, sweetie. Did he mention a name? Or a place?"

Frannie's face paled. "I'm sorry. I wish I could help, but…he saw me watching, and gave me more drugs."

"Did they mention where they were taking Izzy?" Mila asked. "A town or another state? Or out of the country?"

"I…don't know…" Frannie grew agitated, and Anita wiped at more tears. Mila knew she was pushing hard, but her daughter's life was at stake.

"Tell us about the group home where you were living," Mila said gently.

"It was called Happy Trails," Frannie said. "We were supposed to work with the horses and learn to ride. But it didn't turn out that way at all."

"What happened?" Charlotte asked.

She cast her eyes downward, fear flashing across her face.

"Listen to me," Charlotte said in a tender but firm voice. "You're not in trouble, and you haven't done anything wrong."

"She's right," Mila said softly.

Charlotte cleared her throat. "You can tell us anything, no matter how bad you think it might sound, and we promise not to judge. We're here to help, and will do whatever necessary to make sure you're safe."

Frannie and Anita exchanged looks, then Frannie cleared her throat. "It wasn't a horse ranch at all. At first, they made us do chores and work outside on the farm. But then…"

Mila's stomach knotted. "Then what?"

"They brought men in," Anita cried. "They made us dress up in skimpy party dresses, then took pictures of us. I think they put them on the internet."

Mila forced herself not to react, but she was seething inside. DiSanti's men would use the photos as advertisements to sell the girls to the highest bidder.

"You told Harrison where we're going?" Brayden asked Lucas as they drove to Corley's ranch.

"Yeah. I would have asked him to meet us, but Corley's ranch is out of his jurisdiction. Harrison assigned a couple of deputies to watch Hawk's Landing in case DiSanti's men traced Mila there."

"Good. We want Mom and the other girls safe." Brayden paused. "And Honey, too. That baby means everything to Harrison."

"He is excited about being a daddy," Lucas said with a twitch to his mouth.

"How about you and Charlotte? Any talk of kids?"

Lucas cut his eyes sideways. "She went through a lot this last year. We're taking our time, but maybe soon."

Envy stirred inside Brayden.

"Has Mila said anything else about Izzy's father?" Lucas asked.

Brayden clenched his jaw. He hadn't exactly pushed her for information the way Lucas had suggested. "I told you he's dead, so I don't see how he'd have anything to do with this."

Lucas veered down the long drive to the Corley ranch, which consisted of acres and acres of pastures for his cattle. The barns and stables looked weathered as if they were in disrepair. Odd since his financials indicated that he had money to invest back into the place.

Late-afternoon shadows darkened the tree-lined drive. A couple of pickup trucks were parked by one of the outbuildings.

Lucas barreled over the ruts in the road and came to a stop at a farmhouse that looked as if it had been built a hundred years ago.

"He sure as hell hasn't put his money into fixing up his place," Brayden commented.

"I spoke to the deputy director earlier. He sent two agents to investigate Corley's property near Juarez."

Brayden's stomach tightened. "We can't let DiSanti's men take Izzy across the border."

"I've alerted the border patrol along with the airports and train stations to be on the lookout for Izzy," Lucas said.

Brayden had mixed feelings about that. He wanted a damn Amber Alert issued across the country. But doing so might spook DiSanti into carrying out his threats.

He couldn't live with that.

"I requested a warrant for Corley's computers, finances and electronic transmissions," Lucas said as he parked. "But the judge denied it. Said we didn't have probable cause."

Brayden silently cursed, Sometimes the law worked for them and sometimes against them. The reason Dexter did things his way.

"A missing child sounds like probable cause to me."

"I'm still working on it. Our analyst is looking for connections." Lucas checked his gun, then opened his car door and slid out. Brayden followed, his gaze scanning the property for signs of trouble. No gunmen in sight.

That didn't mean they weren't hiding in the shadows though.

He and Lucas walked up the graveled drive to the sagging porch and climbed the steps. A beagle lay snoring near a rusted porch swing.

Lucas knocked, and a minute later, a short robust woman wearing an apron answered the door. Lucas flashed his ID and introduced them, then asked her name.

"Harriet," she said.

"Have you worked here long?" Lucas asked.

"A few months," Harriet said. "I do the cooking and cleaning for the hands."

"We need to speak to Lem Corley," Lucas said. "Is he here?"

She gestured for them to come in. "In the back. He was just about to head back out. I'll go get him."

"Wait," Lucas said. "Can we ask you something first?"

A wary look crossed her face, and she wiped her hands on her apron. "I suppose. What's going on?"

Lucas showed her a picture of Izzy. "We're looking for this little girl. She's missing."

She narrowed her eyes as she studied the picture. "Haven't seen a child around this place, not since I've been here." She looked back up at Lucas. "What makes you think she'd be here?"

Lucas removed another photo from his pocket. DiSanti. "This man is wanted for human trafficking. We believe he and his men kidnapped the little girl. Have you seen him before?"

"I don't believe so. It's pretty quiet around here. Mostly the ranch hands. Occasionally Mr. Corley has one of his friends from the Cattleman's club out to talk business, but they hole up in his study so I don't really know any of them." She folded her arms across her ample stomach. "Why would you think Mr. Corley knows this man?"

Lucas maintained a poker face. "We're talking to anyone who owns large plots of land where DiSanti's men could hide the girls they abduct before trafficking them to buyers. Corley has property here and near Juarez, so his name cropped up."

She looked relieved. "I see. Well, I've never been to his Juarez place, but I can tell you that I haven't seen or heard of any girls being brought here."

Dammit. The property was large enough for the men to hide away from the house. But he and Lucas needed a warrant to search the land.

"What in the hell are you telling my cook?" a man's deep voice bellowed.

Harriet startled and pressed one hand over her mouth as Corley stomped toward her.

"Harriet?"

"I'm sorry, Mr. Corley," Harriet said. "These men are looking for a missing child, and were just asking some questions."

Corley pushed past her and confronted them, eyes blazing with anger. "I don't know why in the hell you'd think I'd know anything about a missing kid. I run cattle here."

"We're aware of that," Lucas said. "But you have a big spread, and it's possible that the men who abducted her could be hiding out on your property without your knowledge."

Corley scrubbed a hand over his balding head. He looked confused by Lucas's statement. Brayden admired his brother's tactic.

"The men who kidnapped her are extremely dangerous, Mr. Corley," Lucas said. "You wouldn't want to endanger your hands or Harriet, would you?"

"Uh…of course not," Corley stammered.

"Then you won't mind showing us around your property," Lucas said, his voice calm, nonjudgmental.

Corley shifted. "Do you have a warrant?"

Lucas's brow lifted in a challenge. "If you don't have anything to hide, then why would I need one?"

Corley inched backward as if to argue, but then seemed to think better of it. "All right. I'll show you around, then you can get off my property and leave me alone."

"Thanks for your cooperation," Lucas said.

Brayden followed them outside to Corley's truck.

Lucas gestured toward the vehicle. "It's a tight fit. Why don't you wait here, Brayden?"

Brayden jammed his hands in the pockets of his jacket and watched Corley and Lucas drive away.

Lucas had just given him a chance to dig around. He'd talk to Harriet again, then slip out to the stables and barn and talk to Corley's hands without Corley breathing down his neck.

MILA PATTED FRANNIE'S HAND. "Can you tell us how to get to Happy Trails?"

The girl shrugged. "Not really. The social worker from the shelter drove us there."

"From the shelter?" Mila asked.

Frannie nodded. "That's where I met Keenan."

Keenan had mentioned a shelter where her grandmother had taken her.

"What was the name of this social worker?" Charlotte asked.

Anita piped up. "Valeria. She was nice until she took us to that ranch. When I told her I didn't want to stay, she got mad and said I had no place to go, that I had to earn my keep."

"She told me the same thing," Frannie said.

Mila gritted her teeth. "Do you remember Valeria's last name?"

Both girls shook their heads.

"How about an agency she worked with?"

Again, neither knew the answer to that question. Which meant she might not have worked with an agency at all.

"Maybe Lucas can find out her name," Charlotte said.

"We need to locate this place, Happy Trails," Mila said. "Izzy might be there."

Charlotte clenched her hand. "We'll let Lucas and Brayden know. If she's there, they'll get her back."

Charlotte's trust and confidence in the Hawk men was rubbing off on Mila. She couldn't give up.

Her daughter needed her.

Charlotte retrieved her sketch pad. "Girls, let's see if you can describe the social worker who dropped you at Happy Trails."

"We'll try," Frannie said.

Anita spoke up. "She was tall, thin and had dark hair pulled back in a tight bun."

Charlotte quickly drew the image.

"Her features were sharp," Frannie said. "She had high cheekbones. Plump lips. And thick eyebrows."

Charlotte finished detailing the features.

"Was there anyone else with you at the ranch?" Mila asked.

Anita glanced down at her bruised knuckles. "Another lady. She was older, and she seemed afraid of the men."

"What was her name?" Mila asked.

"They called her Shanika," Frannie said.

Charlotte settled her sketch pad on her lap and removed her pencils.

Mila gripped her phone in her hand. "I'm going to call Brayden and tell him what we learned."

Charlotte nodded, and Mila left the room.

Her pulse hammered as she checked her phone for messages. Still no word about what DiSanti wanted her to do.

BRAYDEN GAVE HARRIET his business card. "This little girl's life is in danger. If you hear something that can help, please call me." He touched her arm gently. "I'm a lawyer. I can protect you."

She gave him a wary look, but nodded that she would. Brayden walked out to the barn and approached one of the hands, a tall dark-haired Hispanic cowboy. He was cleaning one of the stalls.

The cowboy jerked his head up at the sight of Brayden, then started to run. Brayden jogged after him and snatched him before he could exit the barn. He jerked the man around to face him and pushed him against the stall.

"You know the reason I'm here?" Brayden asked.

The man frowned. "I...heard you with Mr. Corley."

"What's your name?"

The man's gaze darted sideways.

"I'm not playing around here," Brayden said in a low growl. "What is your name?"

"Jorge."

Brayden clenched Jorge by the collar. "Is Corley working with DiSanti, helping traffic women and girls?"

The man shrugged. "I don't know anything about it. I'm just supposed to clean stalls and repair fences."

"Tell me what you do know," Brayden said.

"I told you I don't know anything." Fear vibrated in Jorge's voice.

Brayden arched his brows. "Then why run?"

Jorge lowered his gaze toward the ground, and the truth hit Brayden. "Because you're in the country illegally, aren't you?"

Shame and fear darted into the man's eyes as he glanced up at Brayden. "He said he knew somebody. That I could earn my freedom."

Anger radiated through Brayden. So Corley, or DiSanti, or both, had used Jorge's status as an immigrant to coerce him into doing their dirty work.

His gaze met Jorge's. "Just what did you have to do to earn it?"

Chapter Eighteen

Indecision played across the ranch hand's face. Jorge was definitely scared. Of being deported? Or maybe his family had been threatened as Mila's had?

The sound of an engine roaring closer made panic streak Jorge's face. Corley and Lucas returning. Dammit.

"I told you I know nothing," the cowboy said. "I just do my job."

"Does that job entail holding innocent girls hostage?"

A muscle ticked in the young man's jaw as he looked down at his shovel.

"We think that's what Corley is into," Brayden said. "Do you really want to live off money made that way? Is your freedom worth the life of a little three-year-old girl?"

Jorge winced.

"Think about it," Brayden said as Corley approached. "Do you have a sister or friend with a sister? Would you want her sold as a sex slave?"

The man looked up at him as if he was going to say something, but Corley's truck roared to a stop in front of them, gravel spewing, and Jorge clammed up.

Brayden slipped a business card from his pocket and pushed it into Jorge's hand. "Call me if you can help. If they take this little girl out of the country, her mother may never see her again."

The truck door slammed, and Corley climbed out, looking pissed. Lucas followed, his expression indicating he hadn't found anything helpful.

Brayden's cell phone buzzed. Mila.

He quickly connected. "Yeah?"

"Did you find her?" Mila asked, her voice quivering.

God, he hated to tell her no. "Not at Corley's. Hopefully one of the ranch hands or the cook will talk. We'll see."

A tense heartbeat passed. "Charlotte and I have been talking to the girls who regained consciousness. They're frightened, but they said that they were taken from a group home called Happy Trails. It was supposed to be a ranch for girls, but men were brought there for them to entertain. They were also dressed up and photographed."

"For potential clients," Brayden guessed.

"I think so."

"Where is this place?" Brayden asked.

"Neither girl knew the location. I was hoping you could find out."

"I'll talk to Lucas. Anything else?"

"A social worker named Valeria took them to the home. She might be in on the Shetland operation."

Hard to believe another woman would be involved, but it happened.

"A woman named Shanika was also at the ranch," Mila said. "Izzy could be there, Brayden."

"Lucas and I will get right on it. Hang in there."

"I could go with you," Mila said.

Brayden hesitated. If Happy Trails was a holding ground for the Shetland operation, it would be dangerous.

"I think you're better off there," Brayden said. "You and Charlotte did good today. See what else you can learn from the victims."

Silence stretched between them for a long moment.

"Mila?"

"I'm here," she said. "Just find her, Brayden. I can't let her end up like these girls."

He wouldn't let that happen either. "I promise, we'll bring her back to you."

Damn, even as he made the promise, he knew he shouldn't, that he might not be able to deliver on it.

Then Mila would hate him.

That bothered him more than he wanted to admit.

He wanted to be her hero. Save her daughter.

Be the man she could turn to and trust.

Disappointing her would crush him.

THE AFTERNOON DRAGGED into evening as Mila and Charlotte sat with the girls. They moved Keenan in with Frannie and Anita and encouraged them to rest.

Mila checked her phone a dozen times, but still no word. She paced the waiting room while Charlotte went to check on the other two girls.

Why had DiSanti's men sent her that message and not followed through?

Her anxiety rose with every passing second. Did they know she'd turned to the Hawks for help? Had they discovered that Lucas and Brayden had rescued these girls?

Would they punish her daughter because they'd foiled DiSanti's plans?

Charlotte appeared with coffee in hand. "Unfortunately, the other girls couldn't offer anything more. Except that one of them confirmed that a girl named Jade was with Izzy and that she was taking care of her."

That was a small relief, but Mila latched onto it as they walked back to say good-night to the girls.

Lucas had arranged for guards to watch the girls' rooms, and the doctor agreed to keep her updated. Charlotte planned to coordinate with the Department of Family and Protective Services regarding the teens.

Charlotte hugged each of them and promised to visit the next day.

"What's going to happen to us?" Keenan asked.

Charlotte stroked Keenan's hand. "We'll find you a safe place to live, someone who'll care for you and help you get back on your feet, and back in school. Everything's going to be all right."

Mila hugged her, as well. "She's right, Keenan. Charlotte and I are on your side. You're not alone now."

Keenan didn't look completely convinced, but her eyes were closing, fatigue weighing on her, and she drifted to sleep.

"Come on," Charlotte said. "Ava has dinner waiting for us."

"Ava?"

"Lucas's mother," Charlotte said. "She's amazing. Honey and Harrison will be there, too."

Mila hesitated, willing a message to appear on her phone. But she checked it. Nothing.

"I don't want to endanger the Hawks," Mila said.

Charlotte grabbed her hand. "We all have a vested interest in seeing that DiSanti is stopped once and for all. You'll understand when you meet the girls the Hawks took in." A twinkle flickered in Charlotte's eye. "Besides, we have to talk to Ava and see if she has room in her heart for a few more young women in need."

IT TOOK A while to locate Happy Trails. Brayden would have thought it would have been well-known, at least on the internet, but it wasn't.

A sign of what it had been used for and by whom. DiSanti's group had wanted to keep it under the radar.

Damn him.

Charlotte had faxed sketches of Valeria and Shanika to Lucas to forward to the FBI field office in Austin. Their analyst forwarded them to law enforcement agencies and alerted airports, train and bus stations, and the border patrol to be on the lookout for the women, especially if they were traveling with a little girl.

Izzy had been gone too damn long for comfort. For all they knew, DiSanti's people could have carried her halfway across the world by now.

Or killed her and dumped her little body someplace where they might never find her.

No. He couldn't let himself think about the worst case. And he certainly couldn't divulge those concerns to Mila.

He and his family understood how painful it was to live year after year with no word of where your loved one was, or if they were dead or alive.

First his little sister, Chrissy. Then his father.

Lucas's phone buzzed, and he hit Connect. "Yeah. Okay. See you there."

"That was Charlotte," he said when he hung up. "She's driving Mila to the ranch. Mom has dinner. I told her we'd meet them there."

Brayden nodded. His mother would love Mila.

He liked her. A lot. Maybe more than like. He wanted to be with her and rescue her daughter more than he'd ever wanted anything in his life.

Lucas steered the vehicle down the road leading to Happy Trails. Brayden spotted smoke in the distance.

"Look," he said, pointing toward the east. "There's a fire."

Lucas hit the gas and sped up. "That's the ranch," he said through gritted teeth.

Brayden gripped the seat edge as Lucas raced toward the smoke. Gravel spewed from their tires, gears grinding as he maneuvered a pothole and flew over a small hill. The smoke was growing thicker, curling up into the sky.

As soon as they dipped downhill, Brayden spotted

flames. They engulfed the main house and two buildings to the side.

"Call the fire department," Lucas said as he took the curve on two wheels.

Brayden punched 9-1-1 and gripped the seat edge as Lucas swung the vehicle near a cluster of live oaks and careened to a stop. Flames shot into the sky, lighting up the darkness. Suddenly a black pickup darted from behind the burning building and roared past them.

Brayden threw the car door open and jumped out. "Go after him! I'll see if anyone's inside!"

Lucas hesitated for a second, but Brayden waved at him to go. If the person in the car knew where Izzy was, he was getting away.

Lucas sped after the vehicle, and Brayden ran toward the burning farmhouse. Flames shot from the roof and back of the house, and smoke billowed upward in a thick fog.

Brayden yanked a bandanna from inside his jacket and tied it around his mouth, then darted through the front door. Smoke seeped through the entry, but the blaze hadn't yet reached the doorway.

He conducted a quick survey of the house. All one floor. Rooms to the right, a hall to the left that probably led to bedrooms.

"Is anyone here?" he shouted as he glanced down the hall.

Wood crackled and popped in the blaze, but he didn't hear voices. Still, he shouted again and again as he raced down the hall to the bedrooms. He jumped over wood that had splintered down from the ceiling, dodging flames as the fire crawled along the doorways eating the rotting wood.

Two rooms held a series of single beds that resembled a dorm. He counted a dozen, although fire was spreading quickly. He dodged flames as he checked the closets to make sure no one was hiding or had been left inside.

Flames rippled up the wall, catching the curtains on fire and crawling toward the beds. He raced to the next room, dodging falling debris, and wove between patches of burning embers to check those beds and the closet. Clothes inside the closet were aflame, but no one was inside.

Relieved, he headed back to the front then into the hall toward the kitchen. Already fire blazed a trail along the back wall. He coughed, but had to check the storage closet.

Smoke created a thick fog, but he dived through it, calling out as he went. Surely DiSanti's goonies wouldn't have left anyone inside, especially Izzy.

He reached out to touch the doorknob of the pantry, but it was hot, so he searched the kitchen for some cloths, grabbed one, wrapped it around his hand and opened the door.

His gut tightened at the sight of a woman inside the closet. Dammit. Too late. She was dead. A gunshot wound to the front of her head.

He stooped to check for a pulse anyway, but knew she was gone. Judging from the sketch Charlotte had sent, this was Shanika, the woman from Happy Trails.

THE HOMEY SCENTS of apple pie and beef stew wafted through the Hawks' main house, stirring memories of Mila's own family when she was little. Granted, they hadn't stayed in one place long, but they had shared meals as often as possible.

Mrs. Hawk took her hands and pulled her into the kitchen. "I'm so sorry for what you're going through, dear, but my boys will find your daughter. I have faith."

She wanted to have faith, too, but she was struggling. "Thank you for having me here tonight, Mrs. Hawk."

"Please call me Ava," the woman said. "We're all family."

Four teenagers were chatting and laughing as they set the table. Charlotte pulled her toward the doorway. "Mila, this is Mae Lynn, Evie, Adrian and Agnes."

The girls piped up with hellos and how much they loved the ranch.

Mila's adopted mother would have loved Ava. She'd opened her home to four teenagers in need and treated them like her own children.

The girls helped carry platters of food to the table, then the door opened and Ava greeted her oldest son, Harrison. Amazing how much the men resembled one another, but each was distinct.

"I'm Honey," a perky, very pregnant blonde said as she gave Ava a hug.

Mila exchanged greetings with the couple, her heart squeezing at the sight of Honey's blossoming belly. She hadn't gotten to carry Izzy herself, but she loved that child as if she had.

"My grandson will be here soon," Ava said with a beaming smile for Honey. "It'll be pure joy to have a baby around the house again."

Izzy's little face taunted Mila. Her arms felt empty, and she ached to hug her daughter. Never again would she take it for granted when she sang Izzy a lullaby or tucked her in bed or read her a good-night story, even if she read the same story a dozen times.

She barely managed to keep her emotions at bay during the meal. Thankfully the girls filled the silence with talk of Christmas shopping and the gifts they were making for the children's hospital. Ava was teaching them to piece quilts, and they were making blankets for the kids to snuggle with and take home when they were released.

After dessert, the teenagers retreated to the arts and craft room Ava had set up for them to work on the Christmas projects.

Harrison cleared his throat and stood. "Mom, thanks for dinner. I'm going to get Honey home. The baby's been keeping her up at night."

"It's only the beginning," Ava said with a laugh.

Mila watched as Harrison helped Honey stand. He was sweet and protective and loving just as Lucas was to Charlotte.

"I hope everything goes well during delivery," Mila said.

Honey gave Mila a sympathetic smile. "Thanks. I can't imagine what you're going through. I'll say a prayer that Lucas and Brayden find your daughter soon."

Mila thanked her, then they said good-night. "You have a beautiful family, Ava," Mila told Brayden's mother.

"I'm blessed, for sure," Ava said. "My boys, and now their wives, and now Mae Lynn and Evie and Adrian and Agnes." She pressed her hand over her chest. "My heart is bursting with love."

"I'm so proud of those girls," Charlotte said. "You've made such a difference in their lives, Ava. They're blossoming under your care."

A broad smile curved Ava Hawk's face. "They've given me just as much as I've given them." She clasped Charlotte's hand. "Tell me about the ones you rescued today."

Mila listened quietly while Charlotte filled her in. But worry and fatigue weighed on her, and finally she stood. "If it's all right, I'm going to the cabin to get some rest." Maybe if she was alone for a while, DiSanti would finally get back in touch.

Concern darkened Charlotte's eyes. "I'll drive you over."

She didn't have time to respond. Footsteps sounded from the front. Then Lucas's and Brayden's voices.

Mila hurried to meet them, hoping they had good

news. But the moment she saw their grim expressions and smelled the smoke on Brayden, her hopes died.

Charlotte and Ava joined them, and Ava gasped when she saw Brayden's soot-streaked face. "Son, what happened? Are you all right?"

"I'm fine," Brayden said. "When we reached the house at Happy Trails, it was on fire. I ran in to make sure no one was inside."

Lucas relayed how he'd chased the man who'd set the fire. "I tried to catch him, but he crashed into a ravine and died instantly."

Brayden gave Mila's arm a soft squeeze. "Izzy wasn't in the house or outbuildings, Mila. I searched every nook and corner." He sighed. "Unfortunately, we found that woman Shanika."

"Did she tell you anything?" Mila asked.

Brayden's eyes darkened. "I'm afraid not. She was dead."

Fear clogged Mila's throat, despair threatening. DiSanti's men killed the woman who'd helped them at Happy Trails.

What did that mean for Izzy?

Chapter Nineteen

Brayden sensed despair in Mila's body language.

She had been taking care of DiSanti's victims, he reminded himself. That alone would weigh on anyone with a heart. And Mila had plenty of heart.

"Would you like to go back to the cabin?" he asked.

Mila nodded and looked down at the floor. "You're probably hungry though. Your mother made a delicious dinner."

"I'll pack him a plate to go," Ava said.

"Thanks, Mom, but Lucas and I grabbed something earlier."

Hugs went all the way around as Lucas gathered Charlotte, and he escorted Mila out to his SUV.

"Did you really eat?" Mila asked as Brayden drove her back to his cabin.

"We grabbed a burger while we were waiting on the location of Happy Trails."

He parked in front of the cabin and they went inside. "Do you mind if I take a shower?" Mila asked.

A shower was nothing. He wished he could offer her more. "Of course not. It's been a long day."

"The longest," she said in a weary voice.

He swallowed hard as he watched her duck into his guest bedroom, then the shower kicked on, and he decided to clean up himself. He smelled like smoke and soot and sweat.

The hot water felt heavenly, although thoughts of Mila in his other bathroom naked and wet ignited a different kind of tension, one that made his body harden with desire.

Dammit, Brayden. The last thing Mila needs is you coming on to her.

He toweled off, shrugged on clean jeans and a T-shirt and strode into the den. But the sound of Mila crying echoed from the bedroom and tied him in knots.

He moved to the door, his heart aching as he listened to her sob. He wanted to go to her, pull her into his arms, comfort her, assuage the agony she was feeling.

He ordered himself to walk away instead.

But her crying grew louder, and he lost his restraint.

He pushed open the door and slipped inside. She stood at the window, her hair damp, her body trembling.

He closed his arms around her and pulled her against him, then held her tight.

MILA SANK AGAINST BRAYDEN, soaking in his warmth and strength. His arms felt like a safe haven, one she desperately needed at the moment.

Images of Izzy, terrified and crying for her, bombarded her, making her feel weak and helpless, chiseling away at her hope.

Brayden murmured soft, comforting words, his calm, gruff voice full of understanding.

She purged her emotions until she was exhausted with the tears. God, she'd never been a crier, had always been tough and took charge of things like her mother.

Struggling for control, she wiped at the moisture on her cheek, then lifted her head and looked into Brayden's eyes. She expected pity, but saw compassion.

She ordered herself to pull away. But she wanted so much more.

Selfish as it was, for just a brief moment, she wanted to feel his lips against hers. Anything to drive away the pain and worry.

His eyes flickered with something dark. Sexy.

A passion that lay beneath.

His chest rose and fell against hers, and she stroked her hand over it, absorbing the solid strength in his embrace. He thumbed a strand of hair from her cheek, then heaved a breath and started to pull away.

She caught his arm and drew him back to her. Their gazes locked, heat flaring between them. He'd run into a flaming building tonight to search for her daughter, had risked his life.

Brayden Hawk was honorable and caring and a damn good man, just like his brothers. The Hawks were the most loving family she'd ever known.

Hunger blossomed inside her, and she lifted her hand and placed it against Brayden's cheek. He sucked in a harsh breath.

"Mila, you should go to bed," he said in a gruff voice.

The need in that voice and in his eyes mirrored her own. She couldn't resist. She rose on her tiptoes and pressed her lips to his, melding their mouths in a sensual kiss.

Sex appeal oozed in his touch. He was a cowboy—rugged, tough, a fighter. A man who loved the land.

He ran his hands up her back and tangled them in her hair, moving his lips across hers. First gently. Then desire spiraled, and he deepened the kiss.

She welcomed his tongue and teased him with her own.

Passion spiked inside her, and she moaned, then pushed at his T-shirt, desperate to feel his hot, bare skin against hers.

Suddenly he wrenched away. His breathing was erratic,

his eyes hot with passion. "Mila, we can't." He rubbed her arms. "I don't want to take advantage of you."

He spun away from her, then walked outside onto his deck.

Tears of humiliation burned the backs of her eyelids, then she realized what he'd said. Not that he didn't want her.

He didn't want to take advantage of her.

Even in the face of her throwing herself at him, Brayden Hawk was doing the honorable thing.

His honorable intentions made her want him even more.

She inhaled a deep breath, then joined him on the deck. "It's not taking advantage of me if I want it."

BRAYDEN'S HEART POUNDED. More than anything he wanted to turn around, drag Mila into his arms, carry her to bed and make love to her.

But he forced himself to remain still. If he looked out at the ranch long enough maybe he'd forget the desire he'd seen in her eyes.

He'd tried to do the right thing. He cared too much about Mila to hurt her or take advantage of the moment.

But it was damn hard to deny that he wanted her.

"You're vulnerable now," he said, forcing out the words. "What kind of man would I be to ignore that?"

Her footsteps sounded behind him, then she eased around to face him. Anger flared in her expressive eyes. "Either you're trying to be chivalrous, which isn't necessary since I'm a grown woman and can make decisions for myself, or you really just don't want me."

He released a pent-up breath. Then he made the mistake of looking into her eyes. Raw need darkened the depths, triggering his own hunger to override his reservations.

She parted her lips, then traced her finger over his lips, and resistance fled.

"You're sure?" he growled as he yanked her to him.

A seductive smile tilted her mouth, and he kissed her again, this time with all the need he'd tried so hard to squash earlier.

She slid her arms around his neck, and teased him with her tongue again, driving him mad with hunger. Taking her cue, he traced her lips with his own tongue, then delved inside.

She tasted like sweetness and desire and raw need all at the same time. Her hands pushed at his T-shirt, and cool air brushed his belly. Realizing they were still outside, he broke the kiss long enough to coax her inside, then swept her into another embrace.

Their hands grew frantic, pushing and tearing at each other's clothes. Lips and tongues melded and danced in a sensual rhythm that ignited a burning fire in his belly. He wanted her naked, her skin sliding against his.

He wanted her in his bed.

She shoved his T-shirt over his head and tossed it onto the couch, and he grabbed her hand and tugged her to his bedroom. She pulled at his belt, and he ripped it off, then slowed her by slipping a finger beneath the hem of her shirt.

She made a soft sound in her throat, then removed her shirt and threw it to the floor. Heat darkened her expression as he gazed at her beautiful breasts spilling over tiny scraps of black lace.

Black lace—just as he'd fantasized.

Her lustrous hair dangled over bare shoulders, inviting his touch, and he threaded his fingers through the silky strands and yanked her to him once more. She moaned as he kissed her again, then raked his tongue and teeth along her ear and down her throat.

He backed her to the bed, and they fell on it in a tangle of arms and legs and frenzied passion. Her jeans came next, then his. He groaned at the sight of that thin strip of lace covering her femininity.

Another deep kiss, then he trailed his mouth down her throat again to her breasts. He tugged the lace aside with his teeth, then closed his mouth over one turgid nipple. She moaned and moved against him, drawing him into the V of her thighs. His sex hardened, his body pulsing with sensations as he stroked her heat with his erection.

He teased one breast, then the other, suckling her until her body quivered against him, then he dipped lower to lick and kiss her belly. His fingers toyed with the edge of her panties, his mouth watering for a taste.

She threw her head back in abandon, offering herself, and he tugged her panties off, parted her legs and dived into her honeyed sweetness with his tongue.

Passion overcame him as she fisted her hands into his hair, and he teased and tormented her with his tongue until she cried out in pleasure with her orgasm.

A SHIVER RIPPLED through Mila as erotic sensations engulfed her. Her body tingled all over, the connection so intense that she clawed at his back to keep him from leaving her.

She wanted more.

She wanted Brayden.

He started to move off her, but she grabbed his arms and flipped him to his back. Surprise lit his eyes, and he traced a line down her throat to her breasts. Her nipples hardened to buds, begging for his mouth.

But it was time to give him pleasure.

She kissed him again, then lowered her body on top of him and stroked his thick length against her warm center. She wanted him inside her.

He kissed her deeply, then gently pushed her away.

"Brayden?"

He held up a finger, then reached into his nightstand and snagged a condom. Relieved he wasn't ending their lovemaking, she snatched the foil packet, ripped it open and rolled it over his rigid length. He grew harder, thicker, and a low growl escaped him as she finished.

"You're torturing me," he said in a husky whisper.

She climbed on top of him, angled her head for another kiss, then impaled herself. Inch by inch, he filled her, stirring her arousal again. He traced a finger over her nipples, then ran his hands over her hips and yanked her harder on top of him.

Passion flared, and a frenzy of need overwhelmed her as they increased the tempo. Skin against skin, lips against lips, bodies dancing in rhythm together... Titillating sensations built within her until they erupted in a firestorm of colors.

Brayden groaned her name, then rolled her to her back and plunged inside her, over and over until he called her name as his own release overcame him.

Mindless with pleasure, they rocked back and forth until the sensations ebbed and slowly subsided. Even then, he wrapped his arms around her and held her so close she could feel his heart beating.

When their breathing steadied, he slipped into the bathroom. A minute later, when he returned he dragged her into his arms again. She curled next to him, taking solace in his strength.

Thoughts of DiSanti threatened, and she kissed him once more, then crawled down his body to take his length into her mouth. Brayden groaned and protested, but she brought him to arousal again, then he rolled her to the side and made love to her.

This time when she came, emotions and exhaustion mingled, and she collapsed against him.

As long as she closed her eyes and felt him next to

her, she could convince herself that everything would be all right.

Eventually, she fell asleep, a deep sleep where she dreamed that Izzy was home and that Brayden was in their lives and they were a family.

BRAYDEN LISTENED TO Mila's labored breathing for a long time. She had to be exhausted from the emotional strain of the last couple of days. Making love to her had been mind-blowing.

He cradled her closer, willing her to rest. And for tomorrow to bring them good news about her daughter.

God knows he'd wished this same thing for years where Chrissy was concerned. He prayed for a better outcome with Izzy.

Then what? Mila would return to her life with her daughter. And he would go back to his life. Alone.

Except the thought of that disturbed him.

He liked Mila. He wanted her to have her daughter. But he wanted to be in their lives, as well.

Would she have room for him once Izzy was returned?

And what if he couldn't deliver on his promise to bring Izzy home safely?

He had to…

For hours, he lay in bed contemplating what he should be doing differently on the case. How he could find DiSanti.

Hours later, he drifted to sleep, but a loud knock jerked him awake. He blinked, confused for a moment, then saw Mila asleep in his bed, and memories of the night before returned. Sweet, blissful, erotic memories of lovemaking that he wanted to repeat.

The pounding sounded again.

Mila stirred, but he pulled the covers over her, and crawled from bed. He yanked on jeans and a T-shirt, then padded into the den. Another knock and he swung open the door.

Lucas.

He looked angry.

"What's going on?" Brayden asked as Lucas stormed past him.

Lucas spun around, arms folded, dark intimidating eyes filled with suspicion. "You tell me."

Brayden scratched his head. His eyes were blurry from lack of sleep.

"Mila has been lying to us," Lucas said through gritted teeth.

Brayden glanced at the closed bedroom door, where Mila was still warming his bed. "What are you talking about?"

"The analyst at the Bureau can't find any record of Izzy's birth or of Mila having a child," Lucas said with a dark scowl.

"What? There has to be a mistake," Brayden said.

"Yeah. The mistake is in believing Mila. She's been playing you, Brayden," Lucas said grimly. "Mila isn't just afraid of DiSanti because he threatened her. I think the bastard is Izzy's father."

Chapter Twenty

Brayden stared at his bedroom door, his stomach knotting as Lucas's statement echoed in his head. "What makes you think he's the father?"

"When I saw Izzy's picture," Lucas said, "the similarities struck me. I can't believe you didn't notice."

Because he'd been blinded by Mila.

"So I had my analyst start digging for information. Mila was actually volunteering in Colombia at the same time DiSanti was there four years ago."

Brayden's mind raced, putting the pieces together. If DiSanti was Izzy's father, then Mila had had a relationship with the man.

Had slept with him.

The idea of that monster's hands touching her made him want to punch a wall.

Had she crawled in bed with *him* last night as a distraction to keep him from discovering the truth?

She'd said Izzy's father was dead—which had obviously been a lie. No wonder she'd been secretive and uncooperative when Lucas had arrested her.

Had DiSanti known all along that Izzy was his daughter and taken her because she belonged to him?

Had Mila lied about being coerced to perform the surgery, too? Had she helped DiSanti escape because they had a child together?

A sense of betrayal cut thought Brayden like a sharp knife. He was a fool. Had done the very thing he knew not to do—he'd fallen for a client and been used again.

Brayden made the mistake of glancing at his closed bedroom door, and Lucas paced in front of the fireplace. "Good God, don't tell me you slept with her. What the hell were you thinking, Brayden?"

That I wanted her and admired her and thought we might have something special.

Idiot.

The door to his bedroom squeaked open, and Mila appeared, her hair tousled. She had dressed in jeans and a flannel shirt, and dammit, she looked beautiful.

But her wary gaze met his. Had she heard their conversation?

"Dr. Manchester," Lucas said, eyebrows arched in question. "Maybe you should join us."

Mila gave a little nod and entered the room, her expression wary. "Did you find Izzy?"

Lucas shook his head no. "But I did learn some interesting information about your daughter's father."

Brayden held his breath, hoping Lucas was wrong. That there was another explanation other than Mila being with DiSanti.

But she heaved a breath and averted her gaze for a brief second, and he had his answer.

"You…and DiSanti," Brayden said, the harsh words erupting. "You lied to me, used me."

Mila shook her head and walked toward him, but he threw up a hand, warning her to stop. She halted, then lifted her chin. "It's not what you think."

"What I think is that you had a relationship with that bastard, then helped him escape to protect your little girl's father." Disappointment mushroomed inside him. "How did you meet and get involved? Did you know who he was and what he was doing when you were together?"

Mila glared at him and then Lucas, then folded her arms. "You have it all wrong. I wasn't involved with DiSanti."

Brayden simply waited. "But you—"

"I told you it's not what you think," Mila said flatly.

He and Lucas exchanged confused looks. Then a sickening thought occurred to Brayden. "Mila…he didn't… force you, did he?"

Mila's face turned ashen, and she walked to the French doors and looked out at the back deck. Brayden's heart hammered. Lucas stood still, his body tense as they waited.

Brayden crossed the room to Mila, took a deep breath and gently turned her to face him. He braced himself for the gory details. "Tell me the truth. What happened?"

"It wasn't me," Mila said in a low voice.

He narrowed his eyes. "What do you mean, it wasn't you?"

"DiSanti didn't rape *me*," she said, emphasizing the word *me*.

"I don't understand," Brayden said.

"Just tell us the truth this time," Lucas interjected. "We've wasted enough time on your lies."

Mila swayed backward as if she'd been punched. Brayden was angry, too, but he gave his brother a warning look. Mila might have lied to them, but the terror in her expression was real. "Please, Mila, I told you that you could trust me, and you can."

Indecision warred in her eyes. "It's complicated."

"Is DiSanti Izzy's father?" he asked through gritted teeth.

Mila closed her eyes as if pained, then opened them and gave a wary nod. "Yes, but I'm not her birth mother."

Shock slammed into Brayden. That was the last thing he'd expected to hear.

And it complicated everything. If Mila wasn't Izzy's mother, then who was? Worse, DiSanti had kidnapped his own child, meaning they had no legal recourse to take her from the man.

MILA'S HEART ACHED at the look of betrayal on Brayden's face. She'd never wanted to lie to him, but she had to protect her daughter at all costs.

But now her secret was out.

What would Lucas and Brayden do with it?

Brayden suddenly swung away from her, disappointment and anger radiating from him. "I need caffeine."

Lucas remained pensive as Brayden started a pot of coffee, making her even more antsy. She had no idea what was going on in that head of his.

Brayden poured coffee in mugs, then brought Lucas and her one. She sank onto the sofa and cradled the cup between her hands to warm herself as she struggled to find a way to begin.

Brayden returned for a mug for himself, then joined them, the tension thick.

"Tell us what happened," Lucas said. "You took DiSanti's baby?"

Mila sipped her coffee, then decided to tell him everything. She might be in trouble, but the most important thing was saving Izzy from that horrible man. "You asked if I was raped and I told you no. But Izzy's birth mother was one of DiSanti's victims."

Brayden hissed between his teeth at the image she painted.

"Go on," Lucas said.

The memory of Carina coming to her that rainy night flashed back, stirring pain and fear. "The girl's name was

Carina," Mila said. "I met her at the clinic after she escaped DiSanti. She was pregnant and alone and terrified. She had no place to go, so I arranged for her to stay in a shelter."

"She could have come to us," Lucas said. "If she'd testified, we could have protected her."

Mila swallowed back disgust. "You don't understand how terrified and traumatized she was. She was a little girl herself. She'd been drugged and forced to entertain men. Then DiSanti decided he wanted her for himself." She sipped her coffee again, the chill inside her growing more intense at the memory. "He locked her in his private lair and raped her repeatedly."

Silence, thick and filled with the horror of her words, stretched between them for several seconds.

Lucas cleared his throat. "How did she get away from DiSanti?"

Mila traced a finger around the rim of her mug. "She said the minute she realized she was pregnant, that she decided she had to leave. She didn't want him to know about the baby." She paused, thinking about how frightened Carina must have been. And how brave.

"DiSanti traveled a lot," she continued. "One night when he was gone, she sneaked out the window. She said she ran for miles and miles. His men came after her, but she hid in a drainpipe, then an abandoned mine for days with no food. She drank water from a nearby creek at night when she thought no one was looking for her."

Emotions twisted Brayden's face, but he didn't comment.

"Then what?" Lucas asked.

"One night she hitched a ride to Austin. By then, she was feverish and dehydrated. A woman picked her up and brought her to my clinic. She was terrified and so alone, but eventually she told me her story."

"You knew who DiSanti was?" Lucas asked.

Mila nodded. "I'd heard his name floating around in relation to human trafficking." Mila released a pent-up breath. "When she was feeling better, I helped Carina move into a shelter. In the past three years, two more girls escaped DiSanti and showed up at the clinic. I helped them find a safe place, as well."

Brayden finally spoke. "Good God, Mila, does DiSanti know all this?"

"When he showed up at my clinic for the surgery, he said I'd taken girls away from him and that I owed him."

"That's the reason he chose you for the cosmetic surgery," Brayden said, as if it made sense now.

"Did DiSanti know about Izzy?" Lucas asked.

She shook her head. "I don't think so. At least, he didn't mention her or her mother."

"No doubt he would have if he'd known," Lucas said.

Mila nodded. "He would probably have killed me right after I finished the surgery."

A strained silence fell between them, mired in the truth of her statement.

Brayden shifted. "So how did you come to have Izzy?"

Mila rubbed her temple where a headache was staring to pulse. "One rainy night shortly after Izzy was born, Carina showed up at my door. She said the people at the shelter found a home where she could live and attend school. She knew she was too young to raise a child on her own and wanted to make a future for herself. Then she begged me to take Izzy and raise her." Her voice cracked. "What was I supposed to do?" she said in a raw whisper. "I couldn't turn her away or let that little baby go into the system. And I sure as hell couldn't let DiSanti have her."

Only now he did.

"Do you know where DiSanti is or where he was going?" Brayden asked.

Mila gaped at him. "Of course not. If I did, I would have told you."

"Did Carina sign Izzy over to you? Did you file adoption papers?" Brayden asked.

Mila chewed the inside of her cheek. There was no use lying. He would find out that there was no official adoption. "No, she was scared and in a hurry when she left. I was afraid if I filed for adoption, that DiSanti would discover the truth and come after Izzy."

Brayden cursed, then stood and walked to the French doors. She wanted to join him, to ask him to forgive her for keeping secrets.

But he obviously didn't want to hear it.

Lucas cleared his throat. "Have you been in touch with him since we left the FBI field office?"

Mila glanced down at her hands again. She wanted to trust them, to tell them about the text.

But DiSanti had her little girl. And she couldn't do anything to jeopardize Izzy's life.

So she shook her head no.

BRAYDEN NEEDED TIME to assimilate everything Mila had confessed.

Faced with the fact that she'd lied to him, he didn't know whether to trust her now. She'd bent the truth to help Izzy and her young mother, or at least that's what she wanted them to believe.

The Mila he thought he knew would have done that.

But for some reason, he sensed she was still holding back.

Not to mention she'd broken the law. Technically DiSanti had legal rights to his daughter whereas Mila could be charged with kidnapping.

He believed in upholding the law, but this time there

were grays. Mila's daughter was an innocent, trusting little girl.

How could he put her back in the hands of the monster who sold and traded young girls and women?

Lucas's phone buzzed, and he stepped aside to answer it.

"I'm sorry, Brayden," Mila said. "I wanted to tell you everything that day at the FBI office, but I was afraid."

"Afraid you'd go to jail for kidnapping?" Brayden asked, his voice harsher than he'd intended.

Hurt flashed across Mila's face. "No, afraid DiSanti would learn about Izzy. If you'd seen this thirteen-year-old girl, beaten and bruised and terrified of DiSanti, you'd understand."

He had seen Evie, Mae Lynn, Adrian and Agnes. "You should have trusted me to understand."

Mila shrugged. "All I wanted to do was help Carina recover and have a future. That's what she wanted for her baby, too." She touched his arm. "What else could I have done?"

A muscle ticked in Brayden's jaw. Before he could respond, Lucas stepped back inside. "I have to go. Charlotte is on her way to pick you up, Mila. One of the girls at the hospital wants to talk to you."

"Does she have information?" Brayden asked.

"I don't know," Lucas said, "but they opened up to Charlotte and Mila yesterday. Maybe one of them remembered something helpful." He gestured to his phone. "Meanwhile, forensics identified a print from Dr. Manchester's house. Belongs to a man associated with Jameson Beck. I'm going to question him."

Brayden couldn't just sit around. He wanted to do something.

And he needed space from Mila. Although he understood her reasons for keeping secrets, it hurt that she hadn't trusted him.

Especially after the night before.

A knock sounded, and Brayden let Charlotte in. She took one look across the room and must have felt the tension. "Should I come back?"

Mila shook her head no. "Let me freshen up. I'll be right back." She ducked into the guest room and the shower water kicked on.

"What's going on?" Charlotte asked.

Lucas explained the situation while Brayden cleaned up in his bathroom. Ten minutes later, he was ready. Mila emerged about the same time. She'd pulled her hair back into a low ponytail, and looked young and vulnerable, and so damn sad that he wanted to draw her in his arms again and make love to her until they both forgot the obstacles between them.

But he was done playing the fool.

As soon as they got Izzy back, figured out what to do with her and captured DiSanti, she'd be out of his life.

Chapter Twenty-One

Mila's nerves were on edge as Charlotte drove toward the hospital. Her friend turned into the parking lot of a small diner before they arrived and cut the engine.

"Come on, we're stopping for a hot breakfast," Charlotte said. "You look like you need it."

Mila swallowed the lump in her throat. She needed her daughter back. "I'm really not hungry."

Charlotte touched her arm and offered her a stern look. "You may not be, but you need to eat and keep up your strength."

Tears blurred Mila's eyes. "I can't believe you're being so nice to me. Aren't you angry like Lucas and Brayden?"

Charlotte's heartfelt sigh mirrored the tender understanding in her eyes. "How can I be mad at you for protecting your child?"

Mila bit her lip. "Didn't Lucas tell you the rest?"

Charlotte squeezed Mila's hand between her own. "What? That DiSanti is her father?"

Mila nodded miserably. "Her mother—"

"Was a terrified young girl who was raped," Charlotte said. "For that alone, DiSanti needs to go to prison. And then there's all his other crimes. When I think of what he did to Evie and Mae Lynn and Adrian and Agnes, I get riled up all over again."

"She was so scared when she came to me," Mila said softly.

"And brave," Charlotte said. "She escaped him, and she did the most unselfish thing anyone can do. She must have loved the baby to give her up."

"She wanted her to have a better life," Mila said. "And I wanted that for both of them."

"I know you did," Charlotte said softly. "And I promise that we'll find Izzy, and she'll have a future with you."

"But Brayden looked so hurt, and they're both furious that I didn't tell them the truth sooner." Mila gulped. "And technically Izzy isn't mine. What if I get her back and they take her away from me?"

Charlotte hissed between her teeth. "Don't worry about that. The Hawk men may be miffed now, but they're the most protective bunch of males I've ever met. They won't let DiSanti keep Izzy. And they'd never let anyone take a baby out of her mama's arms."

She released her hand. "Except legally I'm not her mama."

"You are in every way that counts," Charlotte assured her. "The rest is paperwork. And Brayden is excellent at cutting through red tape." She opened her car door and motioned for Mila to follow. "Now, let's grab some breakfast before we visit the girls. It's going to be another long day."

Mila checked her phone as she got out and said a prayer that she'd hear something today.

She didn't know how much more waiting she could take.

BRAYDEN'S EMOTIONS BOOMERANGED all over the place. Dammit, he still wanted to help Mila. And he sure as hell wanted to save Izzy from DiSanti.

"I know you're upset, brother," Lucas said. "I didn't realize you and the doctor had gotten...chummy."

Brayden silently cursed. "It just happened. She was upset, worried. I wanted to comfort her."

Lucas pulled down a side street. "You sleep with all your clients to comfort them?"

Anger flared inside Brayden. "That's not fair, man. You slept with Charlotte."

Lucas grimaced. "For the record, I'm not proud of the fact that I was on the job." A smile tugged at his mouth. "That said, I'm not sorry it happened though. She's the best thing that ever happened to me."

That was true.

For a second last night, Brayden had entertained the idea that Mila was his Charlotte.

Fool.

Brayden scanned the parking lot of the feed store where this guy Theo was supposed to be working. "Once we catch DiSanti and rescue Izzy, what's going to happen to Izzy?"

Lucas shifted the vehicle into Park and cut the engine. "Let's just get him and save Izzy. Then we'll discuss where to go from there."

What more could Brayden ask for?

For Lucas not to arrest Mila for kidnapping? Technically she hadn't... In her situation, he would have done the same thing. And no way would Lucas have let that baby be carted off by DiSanti.

Lucas climbed out, and Brayden followed him up to the door of the feed store. The store looked empty, a truck parked to the side by a loading dock. Brayden took a few steps and noticed more trucks in the back at the loading dock. Voices echoed from the dock, and cigarette smoke curled into the air near the rear door.

He motioned to Lucas that he was heading that way while his brother strode inside the store. He dug his hands into the pockets of his jacket and adjusted his Stetson, glad he'd worn jeans and a T-shirt and cowboy boots. Sometimes the suit was intimidating.

Two men looked up and went still, their conversation quieting.

A big burly guy in a jean jacket and battered boots sauntered toward him, his posture defensive. Brayden wasn't a small guy, but this man probably outweighed him by fifty pounds and carried himself like a street fighter. "What can we do for you, mister?"

Brayden tilted his hat to the side. "Looking for Theo Reeves? Is that you?"

The guy's brows pinched together. "Who's asking?"

It was Reeves. Damn. Brayden had to stall. He might need backup. He moved forward, lifting his chin. "I'm looking for a missing kid. A three-year-old little girl named Izzy Manchester. I think you know where she is."

Panic flashed across the brawny man's face. "Don't know what the hell you're talking about."

"Really?" Lucas appeared from the back door. "Because your print showed up at her house. The very house where she was abducted at gunpoint."

The man's gaze shot from Lucas to him, then he growled and broke into a run. Lucas raised his gun and shouted for the man to stop, but Reeves dived into the driver's side of a feed truck.

Brayden was closer and jogged after him, then yanked at the door as the man started the engine. The engine fired up, and Theo started to back away.

Lucas fired a shot at the tires. Brayden yanked at the car door and pulled it open. Theo punched him in the face, and Brayden's head jerked backward. Dammit, he didn't intend to let this bastard get the best of him.

Mila and Izzy needed him.

He clutched the door and grabbed Theo's beefy arm. But

Theo lifted his free hand and raised a gun with it, pointing it straight at Brayden.

Brayden cursed and reached for his own, but the man pushed the gun at Brayden's temple, and he froze.

A second later, a bullet whizzed by his head. Theo's body bounced backward, and blood spurted from his forehead where Lucas's bullet had hit its mark.

MILA HADN'T THOUGHT she could eat, but she felt marginally better after a hearty breakfast and coffee. Still, the uncertainty of where Izzy was and what Brayden and Lucas planned needled her.

When they arrived at the hospital, she checked on Keenan and Anita and Frannie while Charlotte went to visit the two other victims.

Keenan was sitting up and looked more rested and focused, as if the last of the drugs had been flushed from her system.

"Did you find Izzy?" Keenan asked.

Mila shook her head. "Not yet."

Keenan twisted the sheets between her fingers. "I remembered something else. I don't know if it's important or not."

Mila stroked the girl's shoulder. "Even the smallest detail might help, sweetie."

"I heard them talking about a plane."

"You mean a flight they were going to catch?"

Keenan shook her head. "I think it was a small plane. A private one."

Mila sucked in a sharp breath. Of course, DiSanti had the money for a private jet. It also made it easier for him to escape.

"Did they mention where they were flying?"

Keenan shook her head. "They said they had to wait until he was feeling better."

"He?"

"They didn't use his name. But I knew who they were talking about."

Mila's phone vibrated in her pocket. She grabbed it and checked the screen.

You aren't listening, Dr. Manchester. I thought you wanted to see your daughter again.

Fear caught in her throat. She told Keenan she'd be right back. She walked down the hall to the vending machine then sent a return text to DiSanti, but the text immediately bounced back.

She made a pained sound, barely stifling a scream. A footstep sounded behind her. She started to spin around to see who was there, but something sharp jabbed her in the back.

Then a man's low growl in her ear, "If you scream or try to alert someone, the kid is dead."

Mila went perfectly still. "I'll do whatever you say, just don't hurt my daughter."

"Then walk."

Mila forced a breath in and out, then did as he ordered. She passed two nurses she recognized from the night before, then ducked into the elevator. The man holding the gun on her remained close behind her, the barrel of his gun digging into her back.

Her heart pounded when a janitor and a young couple with a baby entered the elevator. The baby in the pink blanket reminded her of her daughter.

The janitor narrowed his eyes at her as if he recognized her, maybe from the night before, but she simply smiled at him, then pretended interest in her phone.

The doors whooshed open on the second floor, and the janitor exited. The couple followed, and she was left alone with the man and his gun. He ordered her toward an exit, and she walked on unsteady legs to the door.

Outside, the skies had turned a dark gray, and the wind had picked up as if a storm was brewing. Mila stumbled as he pushed her forward, then caught herself and walked on.

A white van pulled up in front of the emergency room door, and the man shoved her toward it. A second later, the side door opened and he pushed her inside. As soon as she fell onto the floor, someone dragged a bag over her head.

Then she felt a hard whack to the back of her skull, and the world went black.

LUCAS STAYED WITH Reeves's body until the ME arrived while Brayden checked in with Dexter. Nothing new. Dammit.

Lucas's cell phone buzzed. "Charlotte," he said, then connected the call.

Maybe one of the girls at the hospital had offered some new information.

Lucas scowled, then cursed. "All right. I'll see if we can trace her phone."

A bad feeling shot through Brayden.

"Call me if you hear anything." Lucas hung up, his expression grave.

"What's going on?" Brayden asked.

"Mila's gone."

Brayden's lungs tightened. "What do you mean *gone*?"

"She and Charlotte had breakfast on the way to the hospital, then split up to talk to the girls," Lucas said. "When Charlotte went to find Mila, she saw her at the end of the hall leaving with a man."

Fear robbed Brayden's response.

"Charlotte called security, but by the time they showed up, Mila was outside. The guard saw a man push Mila into the back of a van."

Brayden released a string of expletives. "Did security get the license plate?"

Lucas shook his head. "Apparently there wasn't one."

Brayden pinched the bridge of his nose. This couldn't be happening. He'd promised Mila he'd protect her and bring Izzy back to her, but now DiSanti's men had them both.

"What now?" Brayden said. "We've exhausted our leads."

Lucas gave him a big brother look. "Don't give up. I'll call our analyst and see if she can trace Mila's phone. Charlotte said Keenan mentioned hearing the men talk about a private airplane. I'll get our people looking into that."

"Don't you think it's time to go wide with the media on this?" Brayden said. "We kept quiet because of Mila. But we need any lead we can get."

"That would help," Lucas said. "Or it could spook DiSanti into killing Mila."

Emotions crowded Brayden's chest. "We both know he's probably going to kill Mila anyway. If DiSanti knows Izzy is his child, he's probably furious and out for blood."

Lucas nodded. "You're right. I'll issue an Amber Alert for Izzy and send her picture and Mila's out to the media and all the authorities."

Desperation made sweat break out on Brayden's neck. They had to find Mila and Izzy before it was too late.

MILA'S HEAD THROBBED as she roused from unconsciousness. She rolled to her side and realized she was still in the back of the van, the hood over her head.

The van bounced over potholes and tossed her against the side of the vehicle. The floor was cold, hard.

She forced herself to listen for sounds that might indicate where they were taking her. A bus? Train? Traffic? Planes?

Nothing but dead quiet and the chug of the engine.

Fear mingled with relief that she would at least get to see Izzy again. But what would happen then?

Her phone vibrated in her pocket, but her hands were bound, and she couldn't get to it. Had Charlotte realized she was gone by now? Was Brayden looking for her?

The van rolled to a stop, brakes squealing, then the door screeched open. Cold hard hands grabbed her and she fought, but he dug in her pocket, grabbed her phone, then slammed the door again.

Tears pricked her eyes. Brayden and Lucas could have traced her with the phone, but the brute had probably tossed it.

The engine started up again and roared away, throwing her across the back of the van. They rode for what seemed like forever before tires ground on the graveled road, and the van bounced to a stop.

She waited on it to start up again, but it didn't. Instead, the van door screeched open, and the brute yanked her from the back of the vehicle. She stumbled, willing him to remove the hood, but he dragged her forward, keeping her in the dark.

Thunder rumbled, then another male voice echoed in the distance.

She struggled to remain upright, her feet slipping and clawing at the rough gravel as they climbed a hill. A minute later, she heard another door open, then the man pushed her forward. The ground turned to a wooden floor, and they were walking. A hall?

Another male voice echoed in the distance, but her abductor yanked her arm again. Her feet grappled for control as she struggled to keep up with him.

A door creaked open, then he pushed her again, this time so hard that she stumbled. With her hands tied and face covered, she lost her balance and completely collapsed onto the floor.

The door slammed shut.

She cried out in frustration, but a low whisper rose from the corner. She went still.

Then shuffling and someone was lifting the hood from her head. She blinked into the darkness, disoriented, heaving a breath.

The person who'd removed her hood slowly slipped into focus.

"Dr. Manchester," the girl whispered.

Shock hit her like a fist in the gut. "Carina?"

Tears trickled from the young girl's terrified eyes. She was bruised and battered, but she was here.

"How? Why?"

"He found me," she said on a ragged whisper. "He knows everything."

Chapter Twenty-Two

Mila tried not to react, but then she saw Izzy curled in the corner, trembling, curled in a fetal position, and her composure crumbled.

"Untie me," Mila cried. "I have to get to Izzy."

Carina moved behind Mila and worked the knots in the rope.

"Are you hurt?" Mila asked. "Did they hurt Izzy?"

"We're both okay," Carina said softly. "They didn't hurt her. She's just scared and misses you."

The tenderness in the girl's eyes made Mila's heart ache. Carina had probably earned those bruises protecting Izzy.

"She's beautiful," Carina said as she finished untying Mila.

Mila shook the feeling back into her fingers and hugged Carina. "Yes, she is. Now we have to get her away from DiSanti and his men."

How she was going to do that she didn't know.

She crawled toward her daughter, her heart racing. "Izzy, it's Mommy," she whispered. "I'm here."

She gently stroked Izzy's soft hair away from her face, and Izzy lifted her head. When she saw Mila, her eyes widened, and she threw her arms around Mila, her little body shaking.

Mila cradled her daughter against her, then rocked her while she cried. Her own tears blended with Izzy's, then Carina was beside them, and she pulled the young mother up against them.

"WE HAVE AN ADDRESS," Lucas said as he and Brayden sped down the road. "Mila must have left her phone on so we could trace it."

Thank God she was smart. He just hoped she was still alive.

He said prayer after prayer as Lucas careened around a corner and sped onto a graveled road.

Brayden's phone buzzed. He checked it, hoping for a miracle. Not Mila though. A number he didn't recognize.

He pressed Connect. "Brayden Hawk."

Silence. Breathing.

"Hello? Who is this?"

"Mr. Hawk?"

Brayden stilled. The voice sounded familiar. "Yes."

"It's Jorge."

The ranch hand that worked for Corley. "I'm really busy, Jorge, so unless you called to help—"

"I did," Jorge said in a muffled voice as if he didn't want anyone to hear him. "Did you mean what you said about helping my family?"

Lucas glanced over at him with a raised brow, then slowed as they neared an abandoned stretch of land. Boulders created a natural landmark where the road forked.

"Yes, I meant it. I'll do whatever I can to make sure your family is safe and you're with them," Brayden said.

"I saw the news. Is it true that this man DiSanti kidnapped Dr. Manchester?"

"It's true. She and her daughter are both in danger. Now, tell me what you know."

Jorge cleared his throat. "I heard Mr. Corley talking on the phone. He said they needed to move the merchandise, to get the contacts in Juarez ready."

So Corley was involved. "Did he say where the merchandise is being held?"

"No. But Mr. Corley told him to take care of his problem before he flew out."

Keenan had mentioned a private plane. "Anything else?"

"He said he didn't want the feds breathing down his neck." Jorge paused again, static on the line as if he was muffling his voice. "He's back. I have to go."

"Thanks, Jorge. I'll be in touch about your family."

The phone clicked silent.

Lucas screeched to a stop at the group of boulders, then climbed out.

"What are we doing?" Brayden asked as he joined his brother.

Lucas's dark scowl tracked the area as if searching for something. "This is where the trace ended."

Brayden's heart clamored. Either Mila's phone had been tossed here... Or her body had.

MILA WIPED AWAY Izzy's tears. "I'm here now, honey. I've been looking for you, and I'm going to find a way to take us home."

Carina was watching Izzy with a mixture of love and sadness in her eyes.

"All of us," Mila said, knowing she couldn't abandon the girl who'd given birth to Izzy.

The door suddenly opened, and a big barrel of a man with black hair and black eyes strode into the room. He was heavily armed.

Without a word, he jerked Mila to a standing position. "DiSanti needs you, Dr. Manchester."

Mila fought a cry of terror. Was he going to kill her now? If so, what would happen to Izzy?

She and Carina traded an understanding look—they would both protect Izzy with their lives.

She held up a finger to the man. "Just one second." She jerked away, then stooped and gave Izzy another hug and a kiss. "I love you, sweetie. You and Carina hang tight while I take care of my patient." She squeezed Carina's hand, déjà vu taking her back to the night Carina brought Izzy to her door.

If she died, Lucas and Brayden would keep looking for Izzy. Maybe they could help Carina, too.

The man grunted, then motioned it was time for her to go. She grappled for courage, then stood and followed him out the door on wobbly legs.

Without the bag over her head, she took inventory of her surroundings as they walked down the hall. The house was an older ranch, wood floors, rooms on both sides of a kitchen in the center. Through the windows, she spotted acres and acres of farmland.

They were in the middle of nowhere.

How would Lucas and Brayden ever find them?

A noise sounded, and she hesitated, then realized it was the sound of a small airplane. DiSanti's private jet.

The brute with the gun gestured for her to walk down the hall, and she entered a large room with a king-size bed. The double window offered a view of a landing strip.

Against the wall stood a steel table with medical supplies and bandages. A woman dressed in a nurse's uniform was jotting notes on a clipboard. She must have been caring for DiSanti. But the bed was empty.

Then Mila saw DiSanti. He was sitting in a chair in the corner, hidden in the shadows. His face still looked puffy and slightly red, but she had to admit that he was some of her best work. If she didn't know who he was, she wouldn't have recognized him.

DiSanti looked up at her with cold, rage-filled eyes, then stood and walked toward her, his shoulders rigid. "You stole my daughter," he said. "Now you know what that feels like."

Mila inhaled a fortifying breath. "Her mother wanted her to have a future, to be raised in a normal, safe environment."

The man raised his hand and slapped her across the face. She stumbled backward.

"She's mine and she belongs with me," he growled.

"Why?" Mila asked sharply. "So you can sell her or turn her into a sex slave for a monster like yourself?"

Another blow, this one so sharp and hard that her face stung, and she tasted blood. Then another one and another until Mila fell to her knees, the world spinning.

BRAYDEN RELAYED HIS conversation with Jorge to Lucas, and Lucas phoned his analyst at the FBI to search for a location that might house a private runway. While he spoke with her, Brayden began to search the area for Mila's phone, praying she was still alive.

The land was parched, although gray skies above threatened a downpour. He had to hurry before the clouds unloaded.

Tumbleweed blew across the terrain, miles and miles of desolate land stretching before them. He checked around the boulders, but didn't find a phone or any signs of Mila. No footprints either, meaning the men hadn't gotten out of the vehicle.

Of course, they could have simply slowed and pushed her body out of the van, but why would they do it in an open area? Granted, this property was off the grid, but DiSanti's men would most likely have found a ravine or wooded area, someplace not easily detectable.

God... He had to stop thinking like that. Mila was not dead. She couldn't be.

He loved her too much to lose her.

Love?

He kicked gravel from his boot. He had no time to think about love when Mila's and Izzy's lives hung in the balance.

He walked along the edge of the road, searching the

bushes and weeds and the ditch, then crossed the road to the opposite side. About six feet down, something shiny glinted against the dirt.

He jogged toward it, then knelt and dug the phone from the foliage. A quick examination confirmed it was Mila's.

He brushed it off and yelled to Lucas that he'd found the phone as he headed back toward his brother.

Lucas nodded. "I don't think Mila's here. They probably just dumped her phone to throw us off." His phone buzzed and Lucas skimmed a text, then motioned for Brayden to get in the car. "Let's go. I have the location of an abandoned ranch equipped with its own runway. It's not far from here."

Brayden's pulse hammered as he buckled up, and Lucas sped away. Gravel spewed behind them as Lucas careened down the road. The scenery whisked by in a blur.

Minutes dragged into half an hour, making Brayden's nerves more frazzled. He thought they'd never get there, but finally the property appeared in the distance. The ranch was enormous, with acres and acres of unused land. Wild mustangs galloped on a hill in the distance, the land beginning to roll into hills as it stretched for miles.

Lucas slowed as he turned down the drive, he and Brayden alert in case DiSanti's men were watching.

A mile onto the property, and someone shot at the car. Lucas swerved to the right, and Brayden rolled down his window and fired. One shot, two. He hit the bastard who was perched on the back of a flatbed truck.

Anger coiled inside him, and Lucas was stone-faced, his hands clenching the steering wheel in a white-knuckled grip. Another mile and Brayden spotted the farmhouse, a giant rambling structure that had seen better days.

Set back here in the middle of nowhere, it was the perfect place to hide. Another reason DiSanti had chosen

Texas. Its vastness alone offered a multitude of remote locations, undeveloped properties and abandoned farms.

Lucas parked a half mile from the house, and the two of them got out, both armed and alert.

A gunshot blasted the air, and Brayden ducked. Lucas spun to the left and fired, nailing the shooter, who'd been hiding in a thicket of trees.

They crept closer, weaving between the bushes bordering the drive, then slipped up to the house.

More gunshots. Two men firing from the barn by the house. Lucas fired back and had to roll in the dirt to dodge a bullet.

An engine sounded from the back of the house. The plane.

Dammit.

Lucas shook his head, warning Brayden to stay put, but Brayden ignored him and raced around the side of the house. Lucas was right on his tail, and they made it to the back just as three big gunmen emerged, guarding DiSanti.

Brayden wanted to shoot him then, but they had to find Mila.

The back door opened, and two men hurried out, dragging someone with them.

Dear God. Mila. She was beaten and limp, her hair tangled around her bloody face.

Behind them another man hauled a too-thin teenage girl beside him. She looked frail and frightened but clutched a little girl—Izzy, it had to be—in her arms. Izzy had her head buried against the teen, obviously terrified.

If DiSanti had hurt Izzy, Brayden would kill him with his bare hands.

Lucas motioned for Brayden to follow his lead, then Lucas identified himself and ordered the men to halt or he'd shoot.

They didn't listen. They opened fire, and all hell broke

loose. Lucas took cover behind a bush and fired at the men while Brayden aimed his gun at the man holding the teenage girl and Izzy.

He didn't take time to analyze what he was doing. He was going to save that kid.

He fired at the bastard and nailed him in the head. The big man's body bounced back with a grunt, then he dropped to the ground like a rock.

Brayden motioned for the girl and Izzy to run. Just as they did, Lucas fired at the men holding Mila, but the men dodged the bullet and dragged Mila toward the plane.

Two more shooters fired from behind barrels stacked next to the hangar, forcing Brayden and Lucas to duck to avoid being hit.

Another shot from the right, and Brayden swung around and fired, hitting the shooter and taking him out.

Lucas caught the big guy in the shoulder, and Mila suddenly shoved the other man to the ground and ran toward her daughter and the teen.

The bastard rolled on the ground and lifted his weapon again. Brayden fired, but the man managed to get off a round first.

At the same time, Izzy started running toward Mila. Panic seared Brayden. No... Izzy was in the line of fire.

The teen suddenly threw herself in front of Izzy. The bullet hit her in the back, and she collapsed to the ground, shielding Izzy with her body. Brayden nailed him, but the damage was done.

Mila screamed and dived for Izzy and the girl while Lucas raced toward the plane.

The door to the plane closed, the engine roared and the plane sped down the runway.

Lucas chased the plane, shooting at it, but the plane soared into the sky. Brayden ran to Mila. She was sobbing and lifting the limp teenager away from Izzy.

Brayden knelt and helped her roll the girl off Izzy, and Mila pulled Izzy into her arms, frantically checking her for injuries.

Izzy was wide-eyed in shock, still clinging to the young teen. Mila dragged the girl into her lap so she could hold both her and Izzy.

Then the girl's eyes fluttered open and she looked up at Mila.

"Take care of our little girl," Carina whispered.

Mila sobbed the girl's name and promised that she would.

Chapter Twenty-Three

Brayden held Mila and Izzy while they waited for an ambulance. Mila was devastated over Carina's death. What a senseless loss.

Even after all she'd suffered, Carina had loved that child.

And he had overheard Carina ask Mila to take care of her daughter. He'd use that in court as leverage to file adoption papers. Although getting DiSanti to release his rights would be difficult—maybe impossible.

He would figure out the details later. For now, he was grateful Mila and Izzy had survived.

Although seeing Mila battered and beaten tore him in knots. Lucas called reinforcements to take care of the bodies and his people were working on tracking DiSanti's plane.

But he might be long gone.

Mila and Izzy wouldn't be safe until he was locked away—or dead.

Brayden would prefer the latter. In fact, he'd like to be the one to put a bullet in DiSanti's head.

When the ambulance arrived, Brayden stepped aside while they examined Izzy and Mila. True to her nature, Mila was more worried about her daughter than herself.

Lucas approached him, expression stony. "I'll stay here

and tie things up at this place if you want to go with Mila and the little girl to the hospital."

Brayden murmured agreement. His emotions were wreaking havoc with his nerves.

"Who was the teenager?" Lucas asked. "One of DiSanti's victims?"

He nodded. "Izzy's birth mother." That touching exchange had cemented his drive to make sure Mila kept Izzy. "Just before she died, she asked Mila to take care of their little girl."

Lucas raised a brow. "So Mila was telling the truth about the girl giving her Izzy?"

Brayden nodded. "It won't be easy, but I have to figure out a way to make sure Mila is granted legal custody."

A tense silence stretched between them as the medics helped Mila and Izzy into the ambulance and the crime workers arrived to process the scene.

"You know he'll come back for them, Brayden? They won't be safe until we find him."

"I know." Brayden raked a hand through his hair. "We have to protect them, Lucas."

"We will," Lucas assured him.

But Brayden's heart was heavy as he went to join Mila and Izzy.

MILA WAS AN emotional basket case. Carina had died protecting her baby girl.

It wasn't fair.

At the hospital, she assured the staff that she was okay. Bruises would heal. She was far more concerned about the emotional and psychological trauma to Izzy.

At least physically, Izzy was unharmed. Mila cradled her close in the back seat as Brayden drove them to Hawk's Landing. Fearing the house where she'd been abducted might trigger traumatic memories for her daughter, Mila agreed to stay at Brayden's with Izzy, at least for the night.

DiSanti had escaped. Again.

She squeezed Izzy tighter. She couldn't think about that right now. Izzy needed to be comforted and to feel safe.

Carina's face flashed in her mind, and a wave of grief washed over her. One day, she'd tell Izzy the truth about her birth mother, about the selfless, brave love Carina had for her.

Not tonight though.

Brayden steered the SUV down the drive to the ranch, and Izzy clutched Mila's arm. "Where are we going, Mama?"

Mila soothed her with a kiss and stroked her hair. "Brayden is a nice man, honey. He helped me find you. And he's going to let us stay at his ranch for a few days so we can rest."

Fear flickered in Izzy's eyes. "Are the bad men coming back?"

Mila hugged Izzy tighter. "Not tonight, sweetie. We'll be safe at Brayden's ranch."

Izzy stared at her wide-eyed for a moment, then bobbed her head up and down.

"Do they gots horses at the ranch?" Izzy asked.

Mila smiled, grateful that children were resilient. "Yes, they do. Tomorrow we'll ask Brayden if we can see them." She stroked Izzy's hair again. "But tonight we're going to soak in a warm bubble bath and get a good night's sleep." Izzy probably hadn't really slept since she'd been abducted. At least, the doctor confirmed that she hadn't been drugged or molested.

Izzy spied a horse galloping in the pasture nearest the road and squealed in delight.

Mila took it as a good sign that her daughter would be all right, but she would watch for nightmares and signs of anxiety. Brayden had been quiet the entire ride, leaving her wondering what he was thinking.

He'd risked his life to save her and Izzy. His face was bruised, although she had no idea how he'd earned it. She looked worse, but she didn't care.

Tonight Izzy would sleep beside her safe and sound. That was all that mattered.

BRAYDEN COULD BARELY control his rage over the bruises on Mila's face and arms. He wanted to make DiSanti suffer for hurting her.

But she and Izzy had seen enough violence. He inhaled a deep breath as he parked to rein in his temper.

Still, he'd make it his mission to find the bastard and keep him from abusing another girl, woman or child.

He opened the back door for Mila and helped her out of the car, his jaw clenching at the dried blood on her lower lip.

"Do you want me to carry Izzy?" he asked gruffly.

She shook her head no. "Thanks, but I think she needs some alone time with me right now."

That was probably true. But he felt like Mila was shutting him out.

He closed the door after her and hurried to steady her as she climbed the steps with Izzy in her arms.

Izzy looked up at him with wary, big dark eyes as he unlocked the door.

"I heard you like horses," he said with a smile.

Her eyes crinkled with childlike excitement as she bobbed her head up and down.

"Tomorrow I'll take you and your mom around the ranch. You can even pick out one to ride."

"Really?" she asked in such a sweet, innocent voice that she instantly snagged a piece of his heart.

"Really." Mila gave him a grateful smile as they entered.

"Let me know what you need," he said as she carried Izzy toward the bedroom.

"We're going to soak in a nice bath." She looked at her daughter. "Do you want something to eat, sweetie?"

Izzy gave a little nod.

"I don't have much," Brayden said, "except for some frozen mac and cheese."

"I love mac and cheese," Izzy squealed.

"Then mac and cheese it is," he said with a wink.

Mila laughed, and Brayden thought what a beautiful sound. A sound he wanted to hear more often.

Every day.

Deciding Izzy had probably seen enough blood and bruises in her lifetime, he washed up in his bathroom, then took the box of mac and cheese from the freezer and followed the directions to heat it. He also had a frozen pizza so he stuck it in the oven.

Not a gourmet meal, but he had a feeling food wasn't as important tonight as mother and daughter simply being together.

That was what family was about.

Damn. He wanted that family for himself.

Shaken, he stepped onto the back deck for some air.

It was a good half hour before Mila and Izzy emerged from the guest room. Izzy was cocooned in a pair of pink flannel pj's with kitty cats on them, and Mila had dragged on a pair of sweatpants and a long-sleeved T-shirt. Her hair lay in damp strands over her shoulders. She'd dabbed on a little powder to help camouflage the bruises on her face, most likely an effort to spare Izzy.

He lit a fire in the fireplace and made coffee, then set out his brown whiskey and the wine he'd offered Mila before.

They gathered at the farmhouse table by the fire to eat.

Izzy looked brighter and surprised him by wolfing down the mac and cheese and a slice of pizza.

Mila laughed as the little girl inhaled a glass of milk on top of it. He had some chocolate chip cookies his mother and the girls at the house had made, and she snatched two of them with a giggle.

Mila sipped a glass of wine after eating, the love in her eyes for her daughter so intense it humbled Brayden and made him forget his anger over the information she'd withheld from him.

But hurt still needled him that she hadn't trusted him.

Izzy yawned, and Mila started to clean up, but he caught her hand and took the plate from her. "I'll handle this. Just enjoy your time with Izzy tonight."

She gave him another grateful look, then scooped Izzy into her arms and carried her to the bedroom. When the door closed behind them, Brayden had a feeling he wouldn't see either one of them until morning.

He cleaned the table and plates, then checked outside to make certain it was quiet. Satisfied DiSanti and his men hadn't had time to track Mila and Izzy to Hawk's Landing, he poured himself a shot of whiskey and carried it to the recliner by the fire.

He stared into the burning embers, his mind contemplating the last few days and all that had happened.

Last night he and Mila had shared the hottest, most mind-boggling sex he'd ever experienced. But it was more than just sex.

He was in love with her.

He had no idea what he was going to do about it though.

Chapter Twenty-Four

Mila savored the next three days at Hawk's Landing. She made arrangements for Roberta and Carina to have proper memorial services and for another doctor to assume her responsibilities at the clinic for a while. She wanted to focus all her energy on being with Izzy.

Her little girl blossomed at the ranch. True to his word, Brayden gave them a ranch tour and helped Izzy choose the tamest riding horse they had for lessons.

Izzy had asked about Roberta and Carina, and about some girl named Jade, who stayed with her when she was abducted.

Brayden and Lucas added Jade to their list of missing girls. Mrs. Hawk also found room for the girls at the hospital to move onto the ranch temporarily. One of her friends had agreed to open her home to them but needed renovations done to make room. Honey volunteered to oversee the project.

The Hawks were amazing people. She understood now why Charlotte had fallen fast and hard for Lucas. And why she loved his family so much.

She watched as Brayden rode Izzy around the riding pen. He was patient and kind and funny. Izzy adored him.

And she was in love with him.

Lucas approached her, his look solemn. Her stomach

knotted. She'd hoped every day that he'd find DiSanti so she and Izzy could live free of fear.

He anticipated her question and shook his head no.

She tamped down her sigh of frustration. He was doing everything possible to find the bastard.

But with every passing day, the chances of DiSanti's men finding her at Hawk's Landing increased.

"I appreciate all you and your family have done for me and Izzy," Mila said. "But Izzy and I can't stay here forever."

"You don't like the ranch?" Lucas asked.

Mila sighed. "I love it here, and so does Izzy, but we're imposing on your family." And Brayden. The longer she stayed, the more she didn't want to leave. It was starting to feel like a home, the one she'd always wanted.

"I know you're anxious," Lucas said. "But it's not safe for you to go home yet or back to work."

"As much as I don't like it, I agree." Mila leaned on the rail, soaking in the sight of Izzy with Brayden. The little girl's father was a terrible man and didn't deserve to have a child.

On the other hand, Brayden would make a wonderful father.

She glanced back at the farmhouse and saw Honey in the porch swing chatting with Ava. Evie, Mae Lynn, Adrian and Agnes were showing the new girls their favorite places on the ranch.

Hawk's Landing had become a safe haven for the lost.

But she couldn't stay here forever.

"I have to leave," Mila said. "It's too dangerous for your family for me to stay here."

Indecision and regret played across Lucas's face. Charlotte was walking toward them with Mae Lynn, her cheeks rosy with the cold.

The day before Charlotte confided to Mila that she was

pregnant. After all she'd been through, she deserved to have her baby and a life with Lucas in peace.

"We don't want you to go," Lucas said.

Mila's heart squeezed. "I appreciate that, Lucas. Your family is the most generous, loving one I've ever known. But that's the reason I *have* to go. DiSanti will use anyone I care about to get to me and Izzy. I won't do that, not to you and Charlotte, or Brayden, or Honey and Harrison or your mother and the girls who escaped him."

Lucas's gaze met hers for a tension-filled moment. Izzy squealed as Brayden swung her down from the palomino he'd chosen for her. Izzy loved that horse and had already started calling the animal hers.

She couldn't allow her daughter to become more attached to this place and these people, then yank her away from this family.

"Will you arrange for us to go into WITSEC?" Mila asked.

Lucas nodded. "I can do that. But you know if you join WITSEC, none of us, including Brayden, can know where you and Izzy are. You'll have to sever all contact with him, and you and Izzy will change your names and go wherever the US Marshals place you. And Mila—" he hesitated "—you won't be able to practice medicine or do any related kind of work. DiSanti and his men could use that to find you."

Pain washed through Mila, but she murmured that she understood. She'd do whatever necessary to protect Izzy and this family that she'd grown to love.

Even if it meant she couldn't be with them.

Three days later

"Mila, don't go," Brayden said as Mila stood by the car that Lucas had arranged to take her and Izzy away. "I'll do whatever I can to protect you and Izzy."

Mila pressed a hand to Brayden's cheek. "I know you will. That's one reason we have to leave. I won't endanger you and your family."

Emotions darkened Brayden's eyes. "But I love you," he said, his heart pounding with fear. He was losing her, had been arguing with her about this ever since she'd told him her plan.

He had a bone to pick with Lucas, too. His brother had made arrangements with WITSEC without including him in the decision-making process.

"I could go with you," Brayden said. "Then you and Izzy won't be alone."

Mila shook her head. "No. I have to do this by myself, Brayden. Izzy is my family, not yours."

Dammit. Her dig hit home.

He'd professed his love, but she hadn't reciprocated. Because she didn't love him.

That hurt the most.

After all she'd been through, he couldn't force himself on her and her daughter. They needed to be free, even if it meant they needed freedom from him.

He was the fool for falling in love with her.

Emotions clogged his throat. "Will you let me know if you're all right?"

"You know I can't do that," Mila said. "When we leave, it's a clean slate for all of us."

As much as he didn't like it, she was right. Talking to him would only put her in danger. By now, DiSanti and his men might have discovered that he and his family had helped her and given Izzy a home.

He had to let her go to keep her safe.

He opened the car door, where Izzy sat in her car seat, clutching her stuffed animals and pink blanket to her chest. Tears pooled in her big dark eyes.

"I'm going to miss you, sweet pea," he said, then gave her a hug.

She wrapped her arms around him and held him tight, a sob escaping her little body. The precious little girl had definitely stolen his heart.

"I love you," she choked out. "I don't want to leave Blondie." The palomino.

"I love you, too," he murmured, then he pressed a kiss to her hair. "And Blondie will be waiting when you and your mommy can come back."

Mila gave him a warning look as he pulled away.

He didn't know how Mila had survived when Izzy had been in that monster's hands. His heart felt like it was literally breaking into pieces.

Mila gave him a quick kiss on the cheek, then ducked into the car, and the driver sped off.

He watched to see if she looked back at him. But Mila didn't look at him once.

THREE WEEKS LATER, Mila was still crying into her pillow at night.

She didn't dare show her feelings to Izzy, who talked about Brayden and Blondie and the ranch and the Hawk family every single day.

The apartment the US Marshals had put them in was in the middle of this small town in Colorado, far away from Hawk's Landing and the people she loved.

Brayden's face haunted her. She wanted to see him, talk to him, be with him. Every day she relived the sound of his voice telling her that he loved her.

She hadn't said it back. If she'd admitted her feelings out loud, she wouldn't have been able to leave him.

And how could she have asked him to abandon the job and ranch and family that he loved for her? Not when being with her might get him or his mother or family members killed. Ava had lost one child. Mila refused to take away another.

Izzy finished drawing another sketch of Hawk's Landing and the horse she'd ridden. "I miss Blondie, Mommy."

Mila nodded, vying for patience. It wasn't Izzy's fault they were in this mess.

"Do you think Santa will find us here?" Izzy asked in a tiny voice.

Mila pulled Izzy into her lap. "Of course he will, sweetie."

"Will he bring me a puppy?"

Mila hesitated. She hated for Izzy to get attached to anything else, and then possibly lose it, but she'd be damned if her child would have to sacrifice owning a pet. They couldn't have a horse here, but maybe a puppy...

"Santa knows you're the best girl in the world and he'll remember you on Christmas Eve."

Izzy laid her head back against Mila. "I asked him for something else, too."

Mila closed her eyes and rocked Izzy in her arms. "What was that, sweetie?"

Izzy shrugged. "If I tell you, it won't come true."

Mila kissed her forehead and ran her fingers through her daughter's hair in a loving, soothing gesture. In time, they'd both adjust and accept their new life.

She just wished Brayden was in it.

THANKSGIVING CAME AND WENT. Now it was five days until Christmas. Brayden was miserable.

His family had gathered for their weekly dinner. Lights and decorations adorned the tree. The scent of cinnamon apples and pine filled the air.

Harrison and Honey were cuddled on the couch laughing as they discussed baby names.

Charlotte and Lucas were almost as obnoxious. With

Charlotte's announcement about her pregnancy, Lucas would barely let her out of his sight.

Dexter piled another log on the fire to keep it going, while the girls who'd taken refuge at Hawk's Landing decorated cookies in the kitchen.

But someone was missing.

Two people—Mila and Izzy.

His mother pushed a coffee in his hands. "I know it's difficult, son. You love her, don't you?"

Apparently his poker face only worked in the courtroom. He was as transparent as glass around his family.

"It doesn't matter. She doesn't love me."

His mother made a low sound in her throat. "Don't tell me you believe that."

He shrugged. "I told her how I felt and she said nothing. No, wait, she did. She left."

"She left to protect her little girl."

"I know that, and I love Izzy, too. I could have protected them both."

"Men." His mother rolled her eyes. "Mila left *because* she loves you."

"What?" That made no sense.

"Mila is loving and kind and donates her time to help kids and families. Do you think she would have stayed if being here endangered our family or you?"

Brayden rubbed a hand over his eyes. "No, but—"

"Go after her," his mother said. "She wanted to protect you and us. I heard her talking to Charlotte before she left."

Emotions welled in his throat. Was she right? Did Mila love him?

"But, Mom, I can't leave my job and you. I know how hard it was when you lost Chrissy and then Dad—"

His mother gripped his hands and turned him to look at her. "We all had a difficult time. But one thing I learned from all of it is that when you love someone, you have to show them. You have to treasure every moment you have with them." She kissed his cheek. "You and your brothers are awesome men, Brayden. I'm so proud of you I could burst. That means I want you to be happy."

Brayden swallowed hard.

"Mila and Izzy need you." She gestured toward the kitchen, where the girls had burst into Christmas carols. "I'll be fine. And one day when the danger is over, you'll all come back to us."

Brayden sucked in a breath. "I love you, Mom." He kissed her on the cheek, then gave her a heartfelt hug.

He headed toward Lucas to tell him to arrange for him to join Mila and Izzy.

He just hoped his mother was right and that Mila wanted him.

He motioned to Lucas that they needed to talk. Dexter and Harrison followed them onto the deck with tumblers of whiskey.

Then Brayden explained his decision.

Lucas shook his head. "We can't let you do that," Lucas said.

"Do you know where she is?" Brayden asked.

"No." Lucas sighed.

"Then find out," Brayden said. "You never should have talked her into this without consulting with me."

"It was Mila's choice," Lucas said. "She came to me, Brayden."

"Because she wanted to protect us," Brayden said. "But she's dealing with all this alone, and that's not right."

Lucas offered him an understanding smile, then held up a warning hand. "Listen. We have a lead on DiSanti. I got a call last night. I'm heading out to track him down."

"I'm going with you," Brayden said.

Harrison squared his shoulders. "He messed with my town. I'm in, too."

Dexter shrugged. "Might as well make it four."

Lucas hesitated, then nodded.

Brayden's heart raced. The Hawk men always stuck together. If anyone could stop DiSanti, once and for all, it was them.

Chapter Twenty-Five

Brayden was anxious to get DiSanti.

Harrison met with Jorge to offer protection and arrange for him to be reunited with his family. With Lucas's connections, they'd already struck a deal to help the man get citizenship.

Brayden and Lucas traveled to the property Corley owned in Juarez. Internet chatter revealed that a large merchandise shipment was about to be transported across the border, confirming the information Jorge had supplied. Dexter was headed to a second location they suspected was used to house more victims.

Lucas called for backup when they arrived in Juarez, and they met two teams of agents on the outskirts of the compound.

"I wish you'd stay back," Lucas told Brayden. "Let us handle this, brother."

Normally, Brayden would do exactly that. But this time, he had a personal stake in the case. And he wanted to have his brother's back. After all, Lucas was going to be a father.

And he wanted to see DiSanti locked up, or dead, himself. It was the only way to free Mila and Izzy so they could come out of hiding and have a normal life.

If they failed today though, he would join her in WIT-SEC. He hadn't slept a single night for wondering where she was, if she and Izzy were okay, if DiSanti might have found them. The only way he'd know she was safe was to be with her. They'd face the danger and uncertainty together.

Lucas parked a mile from the compound, a large ranch fenced with barbed wire and only a couple of miles from the border. Armed and ready, they hiked on foot until they reached the property. He and Lucas went one direction while Harrison and Dexter joined another team. They split up to approach from different angles.

Gunshots came out of nowhere, and Lucas and Brayden returned fire, taking two guards out. They slipped past the dead guards, snatching their semiautomatic weapons to use if they ran out of ammunition.

The next half hour all hell broke loose. Brayden and Lucas and the teams charged the compound. A helicopter dropped in reinforcements, and they stormed the property.

A bullet clipped his arm as he inched down a long corridor inside the main structure, but he shook off the sting and ducked into a room. Empty.

Lucas's voice echoed from the mike. "Team A located the merchandise. A storage container on the property. Ten girls. Jade was one of them. They were about to be forced through an underground tunnel that crosses into Mexico."

"Any sign of DiSanti?"

Static echoed back. Then gunfire.

Brayden's heart pounded. "Lucas?"

Silence.

Dammit, had Lucas been shot?

"Talk to me, man."

More gunfire. Shouts. Then a low grunt.

Brayden took off running. He couldn't lose his brother.

MILA SMILED AS Izzy added sprinkles to the cookies they'd just baked. A dollop of icing dotted her cheek, and she reached up and wiped it away with one finger.

"I think you have as much on you as you have on the cookies," she said with a laugh.

Izzy licked a gob of sprinkles and icing from her hand. "Yummy!"

Mila laughed and set the second tray in front of her daughter. They had enough cookies for a party.

But it was just the two of them.

"Can we get a tree, Mommy?" Izzy asked.

Mila glanced at the tiny house they'd rented. It was satisfactory, but nothing about it spelled home. They hadn't brought anything with them except clothes and a few of Izzy's toys.

A Christmas tree would at least make the house feel festive. "Of course we'll get a tree. I saw a tree farm in town. We'll go pick out one later and buy some decorations."

"Yippee!" Izzy bounced up and down, and Mila hugged her.

Izzy deserved a happy holiday with Christmas cookies and decorations and Santa Claus.

"Mommy?"

"What, sweetie?"

"Is Santa going to bring me that puppy?"

"We'll see." Maybe they'd visit a rescue shelter later, too, and Izzy could pick out a dog. A pet would be good company for both of them.

Mila looked out the window again at the fresh falling snow. It was beautiful, but she missed Texas and her work.

Most of all, she missed Brayden.

BRAYDEN RACED THROUGH the compound, dodging bullets from two more goons. He found Lucas outside at the back of the compound near a hangar, where he spotted DiSanti's private plane.

Lucas stood, hands raised in surrender as two men pointed guns at him. One of them was DiSanti.

"I'll find her," DiSanti said. "And I'll get my child back."

"Why?" Lucas barked. "So you can sell her like you do other people's children?"

DiSanti motioned to one of his goons, the one with the gun on Lucas. "Kill him, and let's get out of here."

Brayden went cold inside. He refused to lose his brother to this monster. DiSanti had already destroyed too many lives.

He moved slightly so Lucas could see him, then held up three fingers, counting down.

When he reached zero, he aimed a shot at DiSanti's head. Lucas whipped around and punched the goon with the gun, and they fought.

Brayden's bullet hit its mark, the center of DiSanti's forehead. Blood and brains splattered as the bastard collapsed to the ground.

A gunshot blasted the air, and he jerked his head back to Lucas and the man on the ground. His heart raced. Lucas?

His brother rolled off the shooter, checked the man's pulse, then looked over his shoulder at Brayden.

Thank God. Lucas wasn't hit.

Lucas shoved the man's gun aside, then stood and walked over to DiSanti.

Brayden breathed a sigh of relief when Lucas gave him a smile of approval.

DiSanti was finally dead.

He could go after Mila and bring her home.

MILA DRAGGED IN the Christmas tree, shaking snow from her boots. Colorado was beautiful but cold.

Izzy's teeth chattered.

"I'll make us some hot chocolate," Mila said. Although first she wanted to make certain they hadn't been followed. All day she'd had the strangest feeling that someone was watching her. She'd especially sensed it at the Christmas tree lot.

Izzy ran in, yanking off her gloves, hat and coat, then raced toward the bag of decorations they'd picked up at the thrift store.

Mila hurried back to the door to close it. A dark SUV pulled into the drive, sending fear through her.

Had DiSanti found her?

She started to scream at Izzy to run and hide, but the driver's door opened, and a man emerged. Not DiSanti.

A tall dark-haired cowboy in a Stetson, boots and jeans and a long Western duster coat.

Her heart flip-flopped in her chest.

Brayden.

But fear followed. Was he here to tell her that she and Izzy had to move again?

She opened the door, soaking in the sight of him as he climbed the steps.

A slow smile curved his mouth as his gaze met hers.

"Brayden?"

"He's dead."

Relief nearly knocked her off her feet. "When? What happened?" Heart racing, she stepped onto the porch. "Never mind. I don't care. I'm just glad you're here." She couldn't help herself. She'd missed him so much, she threw her arms around him.

He swept her into a hug and growled in her ear. "I love you, Mila. I want you and Izzy to come home with me."

Love swelled inside her, and she lifted her head to look into his eyes. "I love you, too, Brayden."

"You do?"

Her pulse hammered. "I do."

"Then you'll marry me?" The tentative look in his eyes warmed her heart even more. Did he really expect her to say no?

She slid her arms under his and wrapped them around him. "Yes, I would love to marry you," she whispered.

They both laughed, then their lips fused for a tender, passionate kiss. Seconds later, Izzy squealed and joined them. She wiggled in between them, and they all hugged, then Brayden scooped her up.

"Izzy, I want to marry your mommy, is that okay?"

She bobbed her head up and down, her eyes bright with laughter.

"That means that you'll live with me," Brayden said. "I'd like to be your daddy, too."

"Yes, yes, I want you as my daddy!" She giggled and wrapped her little arms around his neck. When she finally pulled away, she looked over at Mila.

"Santa came early, Mommy."

Mila rubbed her daughter's back. "What do you mean?"

"I tolded you I asked Santa for something else."

Mila smiled. "Yes?"

"I asked him to bring me a daddy of my own!" Izzy squealed. "And he did!"

Tears pricked the back of Mila's eyelids. Izzy and she would have a family now with Brayden at Hawk's Landing.

Santa would also make all of Izzy's wishes come true. Not only would she get a puppy, but she'd get a pony. Blondie would be hers forever.

* * * * *

COMING SOON!

We really hope you enjoyed reading this book. If you're looking for more romance, be sure to head to the shops when new books are available on

Thursday
18th October

LET'S TALK

Romance

For exclusive extracts, competitions
and special offers, find us online:

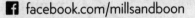

[f] facebook.com/millsandboon

[◎] @millsandboonuk

[𝕏] @millsandboon

Or get in touch on 0844 844 1351*

For all the latest titles coming soon, visit
millsandboon.co.uk/nextmonth

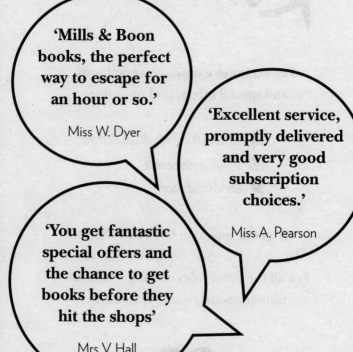